# Last
# GENTLEMAN
# Standing

# JANE
# ASHFORD

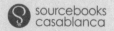

sourcebooks
casablanca

Originally published as *Bluestocking* in 1980 by Warner Books, Inc.,
New York.

Published by Sourcebooks Casablanca, an imprint of Sourcebooks,
Inc.
P.O. Box 4410, Naperville, Illinois 60567-4410
(630) 961-3900
Fax: (630) 961-2168
sourcebooks.com

Printed and bound in Canada.
MBP 10 9 8 7 6 5 4 3 2 1

# One

MR. JULIUS TILLING, A VERY SOBER AND CORRECT middle-aged gentleman conservatively attired in black worsted, had only just been admitted to Elham House in Berkeley Square when he perceived a teacup hurtling through the air immediately in front of him. He stepped back hastily, jostling the young footman who had opened the door to his knock and causing him to so far forget himself as to say, "'Ere now, hold hard."

Ignoring this suggestion, Tilling watched the cup shatter on the drab wallpaper of the entrance hall. He looked less surprised than vexed at this unusual occurrence. "I take it that Mr. Elham has the gout?" he said to the footman.

"Yes, sir," replied that harried-looking servitor, "took bad, he is."

Through the open door of the library, whence the teacup had also come, a voice high and shrill with age could be heard crying, "Swill! A dying man, and I am given swill. Take it away, take it away. And send that damned fool Ames to me at once." There was a rattling of crockery, and amid mutterings of "I shall teach him to send me gruel," and "let a man but get old and the servants begin to bully him," a frightened young maid hurried out of the room carrying a tray. Mr. Tilling surveyed her with raised eyebrows as he handed his hat to the anxious footman.

"Very bad it is today, sir," added that servitor unnecessarily. "The doctor has been twice."

The voice from the library continued irascibly. Apparently, Mr. Elham was talking to himself. "Where is that dratted solicitor? Graceless young jackanapes. Firm's all to pieces since his father died. Can't think why I keep 'em on. For what I pay, he might come when I summon him." This gradually sank into a confused mumbling, accompanied by sounds of coughing and of a chair being hitched along the floor.

Mr. Tilling sighed, straightened his shoulders, and walked into the library, wishing yet again that his most difficult client did not always insist upon seeing him when he was laid up with the gout. "Good morning, Mr. Elham," he said in a pleasant tone as he crossed the large room toward the fireplace. "I understand you're feeling poorly today. I am sorry."

Mr. Elham snorted. He was sitting in a large easy chair before the fire. One leg was swathed in bandages and propped on a hassock in front of him, and he was so bundled in blankets and shawls that his dressing gown of bottle-green brocade was scarcely visible. His head was completely bald, and this, combined with a hook nose and a high color, made him resemble an old vulture. He looked at his guest with a mixture of suspicion and contempt. "Ha!" he said. "No good trying to turn me up sweet, Tilling. I'm old and I'm ill, but I'm not senile quite yet." He grimaced. "No, and not about to stick my spoon in the wall. You don't like me, and I don't like you, so let us get down to business and cut the gabble-mongering. Have you done what I asked?"

Mr. Tilling's countenance was wooden and his accents cold. "Yes, sir." He took some papers from his coat pocket. "I have located all three young people and ascertained their circumstances."

Mr. Elham ignored the sheaf of documents being offered him and squinted up at the younger man. "What should I do with those blasted things?" he asked, blinking his watery blue eyes. "Put 'em there." He waved impatiently toward the desk in the corner of the room. "And tell me about 'em. My heirs," he cackled. His scratchy laugh turned quickly to a cough, and it was some time before he could control it.

Looking annoyed, Mr. Tilling walked slowly to the desk, put the papers on its littered surface, and returned to the fireplace. Elham, who was just regaining his breath, signaled peremptorily for him to speak. "Yes, sir," responded Tilling, "your potential heirs." He took a small note card from an inner pocket and referred to it. "Both your brother and your sister—"

"Don't mention 'em," screeched Mr. Elham, malevolently. "Sneaking, whining rascals; I swore twenty years ago I'd never hear them named again."

The solicitor pressed his lips together in annoyance. "Pardon me," he answered. "I should have said, your only remaining family consists of two nieces and a nephew." He ticked them off on his fingers. "Miss

Elham, the daughter of...ahem, Miss Brinmore, and her brother."

"Yes, yes, I know that," complained the old man. "Tell me about 'em. That's what I asked you. Daresay they're as addle-brained as their parents. Brinmore's brats had the cheek to ask me for money about a year ago."

Mr. Tilling nodded shortly. He had not been asked to sit down, and he was not used to such cavalier treatment from his clients, who unfailingly received the current head of the distinguished old firm of Tilling & Bates with marked politeness. In truth, he did not like Mr. Elham and kept up his connection with him only out of respect for his deceased father's memory and Mr. Elham's extremely large fortune. "That would be when their parents were killed," he replied coldly. "In an accident on the Channel while returning from France, leaving the two children penniless."

"Eh," was the old man's only response to this information. "Well, I told Sylvia when she married that she'd likely never have two coins to rub together. Ay, and be saddled with a pack of puling parson's get as well. She knew she could expect no aid from me. A country churchman!" He expressed his disgust by an unpleasant hawking, pressing a handkerchief to his lips.

Tilling averted his eyes. "Mr. and Miss Brinmore are currently residing with the family of their paternal uncle," he continued, in a voice kept carefully expressionless. "The senior Mr. Brinmore has a small estate in Bedfordshire and offered them a home there."

"The more fool he," sniffed Elham. "Is he plump in the pocket then?"

"His means are moderate. He has five children of his own."

"He must be crack-brained." The old man seemed to lose interest in Brinmore. "What about the other one, Eliot's girl. She must be, what, twenty, by this time? What the devil is her name?"

"Miss Elisabeth Elham is four and twenty years of age," answered Tilling repressively. "She is presently a teacher at Miss Creedy's Select Seminary for Young Ladies at Bath, where she was a pupil until her fath— that is, until she was orphaned. As you may be aware, Miss Elham's mother died when she was very young."

Old Elham nodded. "Never knew her," he said shortly. "So Eliot left nothing when he went off?"

The solicitor shook his head.

His auditor appeared pleased with this news. "As I always said," he murmured. "At least she had the sense not to apply to me. Doing well for herself, is she?"

Tilling's expression showed his doubt, but he said only, "She appears successful and well-liked at the school. In response to our discreet inquiries, Miss Creedy evinced complete satisfaction with her character and her work." There was a pause. Elham was nodding to himself. "Mr. Anthony Brinmore is presently seventeen years of age," added the solicitor without being asked, "and Miss Belinda Brinmore is eighteen."

The old man seemed much struck. "Belinda!" he exclaimed, in strong accents of distaste. "Good God!"

Something almost like a smile animated Tilling's features for a moment. "Her mother was reportedly fond of Mr. Pope's poetry."

"Very likely. A more hen-witted female I never met.

But she must have been touched in her upper works to name the girl Belinda." He grinned maliciously. "I suppose she called the boy after me in hopes of getting my money. Well, it won't do." The disapproving lines in Tilling's face became even more pronounced. Looking up at him, Elham chuckled. "Yes, yes, I know you find my lack of family feeling quite shocking, Tilling. But then you never knew my family, did you? A ramshackle set of heedless wastrels, all of 'em. Eliot was a care-for-nobody from the time he was out of short coats. Never had a groat and did nothing but laugh in my face when I tried to advise him. And m'sister! An air dreamer and a watering pot, sir. Full of silly romantic fantasies and continually indulging in fits of the vapors. Pah!" He pulled his shawls closer with clawlike hands and shook his head. "In any case, I don't care a straw what you think. I called you here because I am ready to make my will."

Mr. Tilling exhibited astonishment. "Beg pardon, sir?" he said.

"My will, I said," snapped the old man. "Are you deaf? Bring out your papers and all the other damned foolishness before I change my mind."

Swallowing his surprise, the solicitor prepared to draw up a will. Mr. Elham gave instructions for more than an hour, taking no advice and listening to no suggestions. He had very clear ideas about the disposition of his substantial property, and he did not wish to have them modified or criticized. When he finished speaking, he looked quite knocked up; his face was a sickly white, his breathing harsh, and his hands trembling even more than usual. This did nothing to improve his temper, and he dismissed Tilling venomously, commanding him to produce the finished document for signing the following day. The solicitor left the house shaking his head, less at Elham's rudeness, which it must be conceded he was accustomed to and expected, than at the amazing fact that he had disposed of his property at last. Old Elham had been refusing to make a will for nearly twenty years. Why he had chosen to do so now, Mr. Tilling couldn't say, but he wondered at it very much indeed.

When the solicitor had gone, Elham rang the bell in the library, summoning his butler to the room. "Ames," he said, when that worthy servitor appeared, "I want a brandy and soda. A large one, mind."

Ames had served in Mr. Elham's household for most of his life, a feat that demonstrated both his great skill at his tasks and his immense reserves of tact and patience. Hearing this order, he looked at once pained and resigned. "It's only half past eleven, sir," he ventured, "and the doctor did say…"

"Hang the doctor!" snapped the old man, as Ames had expected he would. "And blast you, Ames. Does the doctor pay your wages? I want a drink." He smiled grotesquely. "I've made my will, Ames. I want to toast my heirs." His pale eyes sparkled with an unholy glee. "I daresay they'd all given up hope, but I've done it at last. I'll show 'em." He looked sharply up, his eyes narrowing. "You think I don't know society has set me down as short of a sheet and likely to leave my fortune in Chancery?" His amusement returned, and he cackled. "Well, I shan't. There have been Elhams at Willowmere for five hundred years.

By God, we refused a title twice. Most of 'em were as buffleheaded as my brother and sister, I expect, but no one shall accuse me of breaking the line. Now, bring me a drink!" He subsided into coughing as Ames left the room and had only just managed to stop when the butler returned with a tray upon which sat several bottles and a large brandy and soda. He took the latter gratefully and swallowed a major portion of it. It appeared to do him good, for he fell back in his chair with a sigh, but his temper remained uncertain. "Weak," he told Ames, glaring at him from under lowered eyelids. "You always make 'em weak nowadays." He held out the glass commandingly.

His look of resignation deepening, Ames took one of the bottles from the tray and added more brandy to the beverage. "You know, sir," he said, "that I have only your health at heart."

Elham snorted. "Indeed. That puts me in mind of something. Was it you ordered gruel for my breakfast?"

Ames nodded stiffly. "The doctor said, sir…"

"For God's sake, leave off telling me what the doctor said or didn't say. It'll be you and that damned quack send me to my grave, not a touch of the bottle now and then." He held out his now empty glass, and the butler refilled it reluctantly. Elham drank and sighed again. "That's the dandy. Just give me what I've always had and liked. A man might as well cut his stick as eat gruel and such messes. D'you hear me?"

"Yes, sir," replied Ames stolidly.

The old man looked at his rigid figure and cackled. "Well, what are you hanging about for?" he added. "Get out, get out."

When he was alone again, Mr. Elham looked into the fire with narrowed eyes and sipped his drink. Occasionally, he laughed softly. Whatever he was thinking seemed to afford him some amusement, and as he was a man who had received most pleasure in his life from thwarting and annoying his fellow human beings, this sight was ominous.

The next day, the will was duly signed and witnessed. The impressive appearance of the document seemed to delight Mr. Elham, who ran his fingers over the seals and ribbons. When all was complete and Tilling was preparing to go, the old man looked up suddenly and said, "Mind, I don't want word of this to get out."

"Of course not," replied the solicitor, offended at this doubt of his integrity.

"I don't even want it known I've made a will," Elham went on. "Let 'em wonder." Tilling said nothing, but continued to gather up his papers. "Put it in one of your metal boxes," commanded the old man. "I fancy you won't need it for years yet. Just keep it safe and keep it secret."

"Of course," answered Tilling.

Mr. Elham was rubbing his hands together gleefully. "How they'll talk," he cackled. "I shall miss that, but it can't be helped. They've forgotten Anthony Elham now, but I'll show 'em they were dead wrong about him."

"Yes, sir," said Tilling expressionlessly. "And now if you'll excuse me?"

"What? Go on, go on, I'm done with you. Just ring the bell as you leave."

When Ames entered the room in response to this summons, the old man ordered a bottle of his special claret to celebrate the occasion. In spite of Ames's protests and reminders of the previous day's indulgences, he got it and drank not only that bottle but part of another. The next day he felt out of curl, in a week he was dangerously ill, and before a month had passed, he was dead.

# Two

As a result of these events, Miss Elisabeth Elham found herself riding in a post chaise from Bath to London at the height of the summer heat. She was alone, though Miss Creedy had begged to be allowed to accompany her on her journey, and she stared out the window of the oppressively stuffy vehicle with an ironic smile. It was a characteristic expression. Miss Elham had inherited from her father a very unconventional attitude toward the world. His response to the succession of mishaps that had plagued his life had been laughing resignation, and his daughter to some extent emulated him. This was no substitute for the worldly goods she had not inherited, but it had stood her in good stead through several trying years when she'd been forced to make her own way and earn her own living.

She'd been employed at Miss Creedy's for five years now, and if she was not precisely happy there, neither was she miserable. Thus, her receipt of a letter from Mr. Tilling informing her that she was her unknown uncle's sole heir and requesting that she come up to London had made her laugh. Even the hundred-pound cheque he enclosed did not arouse her awe. She was very glad to have it, for she did not see how she could have gone to London else, but she was by no means overcome.

Miss Elham was a rather tall girl and not, most observers would agree, a beauty in the accepted mode. But her figure was slender and elegant and her carriage assured. And if her nose was a trifle too aquiline and her mouth a bit wide, her hair and eyes more than made up for these deficiencies. Her hair was of a color between brown and blond, which gave it a kind of glow that had reminded one appreciative gentleman of honey in the comb. Her eyes were a curious dark blue, almost violet, and very expressive, sparkling with amusement or anger and smoky in thought. Indeed, they were generally held to be her best feature. For the rest, she had an air of calm assurance out of keeping with her twenty-four years and perhaps due to her experience as a teacher of young girls for five of them. Her clothing was plain and a little worn, and at the present moment, she looked very hot.

She arrived in town about eleven and proceeded directly to Brown's Hotel, which Miss Creedy had recommended as a very genteel hostelry, suitable for a young woman traveling alone. She was greeted politely by the proprietor. Though it was obvious that her clothing and equipage did not impress him, the quiet assurance of her manner soon did, and she was accorded every courtesy. There was some bustle as the postilions were paid off and her meager luggage carried in. By the time all was settled, Elisabeth found she was tired out and very glad to go straight up to her room, declining the cold supper offered her.

She woke early, dressed and breakfasted with dispatch, and set out by nine for the offices of Tilling & Bates near Temple Bar.

The clerk who opened the door to her bowed deferentially when she gave her name and ushered her in immediately. "Yes, indeed, Miss Elham," he said. "Mr. Tilling is expecting you." He held the door a moment longer, leaned forward to peer into the street, then shut it, looking embarrassed and puzzled.

A smile escaped Elisabeth. "I fear I have come quite alone," she said.

The clerk blinked. "Yes, miss. Quite, quite right. If you'll, ah, just be seated for a moment, I'll fetch Mr. Tilling." He turned and disappeared into a closed staircase at the back of the room.

Elisabeth sat down, still smiling, but she had not long to wait, for Tilling came down at once. He bowed as she stood up and took the hand she held out to him. "Good morning, Miss Elham," he said cordially. "I hope you had no difficulty finding our offices. I wish you had allowed me to call at your hotel."

Elisabeth shook her head with an easy smile. "No, indeed. How selfish you must think me. I'm persuaded that you have a great many things to occupy you, while I am not at all busy. Quite the contrary. This trip is my first holiday in years. Only imagine, I did not leave my bed until eight o'clock this morning."

The rallying tone of this statement drew a smile from the solicitor. "A pleasant circumstance that may now be repeated as often as you like," he told her. "If you will come upstairs, I shall explain to you exactly how that comes about." He indicated the stairway with a slight gesture. "Your maid can wait here. Annsley will fetch some tea." He looked about the room, then glanced inquiringly at his clerk, who shrugged deprecatingly.

Elisabeth's eyes twinkled. "I fear I have no maid," she replied. "I have not employed one in five years."

Shocked, Mr. Tilling spoke before he thought. "You have never traveled up to London alone? I beg your pardon; I didn't think. I should have sent someone to accompany you."

The amusement in Elisabeth's eyes deepened. "I assure you it was completely unnecessary. Miss Creedy wished to come with me, but I refused her company. I am not a schoolgirl, you know, Mr. Tilling, to be in need of a chaperone. Indeed, I have myself acted as a duenna for a number of years."

The solicitor looked doubtful, but he had by this time recovered from his surprise, and he uttered no more criticisms. "Of course," he said. "I'm glad you had a safe journey. Now, if you will step this way." And he ushered her upstairs to his private office.

Mr. Tilling went over the terms of Mr. Elham's will slowly and carefully, accustomed as he was to laymen's misunderstanding of legal terminology. But Miss Elham seemed to grasp everything immediately, and he soon found there was no need to repeat things several times, as he did for some of his clients. When he finished, however, she was frowning.

"My uncle left me everything, then?" she asked. "The townhouse, Willowmere, and all of his money?"

Tilling nodded. "Yes. Without restriction. Excepting only the small legacies and pensions I have enumerated to you. I must tell you that the country place is in very poor repair, however. From what I can discover, nothing has been done there for years."

"Yes, but why?" replied Elisabeth.

"Well, your uncle preferred to live in town. And in recent years, he was not really able to travel. I expect he had not set eyes on the place for ten or fifteen years at least."

"No, no. I mean why the whole, Mr. Tilling? Why did my uncle, whom I do not believe I ever saw in my life, leave me all his property? I know that he and my father were at outs from the time they were very young."

The solicitor shrugged. "That I do not know. Mr. Elham was not one to explain his reasons for doing as he pleased."

Elisabeth laughed. "From what Father occasionally let drop, I imagine he was a horrid old tyrant."

Tilling looked down. "I say nothing on that head, but if pressed to explain Mr. Elham's will, I might venture…"

"Yes?"

He frowned. "I received the impression, though this is purely conjecture, mind, that your uncle was most impressed with the way you fended for yourself when your father died. Particularly since you did not apply to him for assistance as did your cousins in a similar situation."

"How should I, indeed," answered Elisabeth indignantly, "when my father always told me that his brother was the most disagreeable old clutchfist in nature and unlikely to part with a groat to save his own mother from starvation? Oh, no, I was not about to risk a humiliating setdown from him. And you see how right I was from the way he responded to my cousins' really desperate plight."

Tilling was looking at her with a bemused expression. "You really are an odd family, you know," he said.

Elisabeth met his eyes. "No, are we? I have had no intimate experience with any other, of course." She paused, frowning. "I admit that my pupils at Miss Creedy's seemed to have quite a different attitude toward their relations than my father instilled in me. However, I daresay their families are much nicer, you know."

Mr. Tilling was betrayed into laughter. "I daresay."

Elisabeth smiled. "Well, did *you* like my uncle, Mr. Tilling?"

Sobering, the solicitor replied, "I…I cannot say that precisely, but…"

"Of course you cannot. Because he was shockingly unpleasant, was he not? I knew it. Let us talk of my other relations. What of my cousins? Why leave nothing to them? Surely they are as deserving as I?"

Tilling frowned. "I do not know. He was informed of their situation. Perhaps, finding that they had a home with their paternal uncle, he thought them provided for."

"Oh, but it is a sad strain on Mr. Brinmore's purse to have them. Belinda has written me of it."

He shrugged. "I cannot explain his motives, Miss Elham. I am sorry."

"Well," said Elisabeth decisively, "I shall invite them to live with me. There can be no objection to that, I suppose?"

"None at all. You are in complete control of your fortune, though advised to heed the counsel of your banker and me."

Elisabeth smiled at him quizzically. "And do you advise me not to have my cousins?"

"No, indeed," replied Tilling quickly. "I think it a laudable scheme." He caught her ironic glance and relaxed somewhat. "And they will be company for you, as well. You have no acquaintances in London, I think?"

She shook her head. "I daresay some people remain who knew my father. But I'm not at all certain they would be proper friends for me." She smiled. "And in any case, I'd be at a loss to find them now." She shrugged. "Several of my former pupils have made their debuts in the last two or three years, but whether they'd be pleased to meet me I cannot say. I will be glad of my cousins' company."

Tilling nodded. "And you will want some older female companion as well."

"Shall I?" responded Elisabeth.

The solicitor looked at her. He was beginning to get her measure pretty clearly and to feel the strength of her personality. "Perhaps *you* will not. But I assure you that if you set up in London alone without some older woman to act as chaperone, it will create a scandal. You would be considered fast and more than likely would not be received in polite society."

Elisabeth grimaced. "A terrible fate."

"Your cousins might find it so," continued Tilling carefully. "They might have some wish to enter *ton* circles. And I am convinced that you, too, will wish to take up the position to which your birth and fortune entitle you, when you have had time to consider the matter."

The girl sighed, then smiled at him. "I perceive you are a very cunning advisor, Mr. Tilling. I shall have to take care with you. But I suppose you're right." She frowned. "I cannot think where I shall find a proper chaperone, however. I have no older female relatives. Can one hire a respectable companion? Oh, I wouldn't like that," she added.

"Understandable," agreed the man. "I hope we may not come to that, though one can, of course, hire perfectly satisfactory persons, if one knows how to go about it. I've looked into your father's family pretty exhaustively, and it's true there are no suitable candidates there. What of your mother's connections? She was an Ottley, was she not? A fine old family."

"Fine enough to cast her off when she insisted upon marrying my father," replied Elisabeth. "I daresay they wouldn't care to hear of me now. But that is beside the point; I never met any of my mother's family. She died when I was very young, you know. I can scarcely remember her." She sighed, then her eyebrows drew together. "Wait a moment," she exclaimed. "There was a visitor to the house once or twice when my mother was in her last illness." She concentrated as Tilling maintained an obedient silence. At last, she looked up triumphantly. "Cousin Lavinia," she declared. "It was Cousin Lavinia. I remember her as a very pleasant woman, in fact, a fascinating creature. Her pockets were always full of candies." She smiled. "I believe she was a cousin of my mother's."

Mr. Tilling nodded encouragingly. "And what was her surname?"

Elisabeth grimaced. "Oh, dear, I haven't any notion. I don't believe I was ever told it. Can it have been Ottley?"

"Possibly," he answered drily. "You have no recollection?" Elisabeth shook her head, and he sighed. "I shall make inquiries."

"Thank you. I am giving you a great deal of trouble."

He denied this stoutly. "You will wish to go over your properties as soon as may be, I expect," he continued. "I should be happy to escort you to Elham House this afternoon, if you like. Will you go down to Willowmere?"

"I suppose I must. It's in Hertfordshire?"

"Yes, near Hempstead."

"Ah, perhaps I can fetch my cousins at the same time then. I must write to them immediately."

They agreed that Mr. Tilling would call for her at Brown's at two, and Elisabeth departed, bearing with her a sheaf of documents she'd been advised to "look over." Back in her room, she sat down to compose a letter to her young cousins, but this proved more difficult than she'd expected. To explain all that had happened required a long missive, and she had neither the time nor the patience for that at present.

After a good deal of thought, she managed to produce a creditable short letter telling of her uncle's action and the plan she had formed for their future. As she sealed it, she was astonished to find that it was one o'clock. She had only just time to partake of a light luncheon before Mr. Tilling arrived.

At Elham House, Elisabeth met Ames and the other servants and looked through the rooms. She was appalled by the size of the house and the dilapidated state of its furnishings. Everything seemed worn, faded, and outmoded, even to one who was not familiar with the latest London fashions. When she mentioned this, Mr. Tilling agreed. "It will require complete refurbishing," he said. "And we must find you some kitchen help and someone to take charge of the stables."

They'd retired to the library by this time, the only really habitable room on the ground floor, and Elisabeth had sunk into her uncle's easy chair. "It's a herculean task," she said ruefully. "I hardly know where to begin. And I'm certain it will cost a great deal of money."

Mr. Tilling smiled. "Fortunately," he answered, "you have a great deal of money, more than you could possibly spend furnishing twenty houses."

"Am I so plump in the pocket? I hadn't really taken it in." Elisabeth's eyes lit suddenly. "Good God, I suppose I'm an heiress."

Mr. Tilling laughed aloud, then quickly begged her pardon.

"Quite all right. This is excessively diverting; it struck me all at once. There were several heiresses at Miss Creedy's, you see, and I was recalling the care we were forced to take, wrapping them in cotton wool as if they had been made of spun glass." Her expression was momentarily disapproving, then amusement lit her eyes once more. "I'll have to be on the lookout for 'gazetted fortune hunters,' won't I?"

Smiling, the solicitor agreed.

"But that is a future worry, and in any case, I don't regard it. Now, I must deal with this house." She thought for a moment. "What do you say to this plan? I shall go over all the rooms again on my own, perhaps tomorrow, and mark the things I wish to keep. There are some good pieces of furniture here. Then, I shall chose colors, hangings, carpets, and so on in the city. I daresay I shall make several London merchants very happy. Then, as soon as I have finished, I shall leave directly for the country. This cunning scheme allows me to escape all the trouble of hiring workmen and seeing to the servants during repairs and put all my cares upon you." She laughed up at him.

Mr. Tilling, who was well on his way to being captivated by his new client, readily agreed. "I can also oversee the completion of your staff if you will trust me to interview candidates from the agency. I suppose Ames will lend me his aid."

Elisabeth clasped her hands. "But can I be such a wretch as to leave you with this bumble-broth? I was only funning when I suggested it. I never meant to desert you in the midst of paperhangers and carpenters."

"Nonsense," replied Tilling. "I'm happy to be of service."

"Splendid man! Why have I never before had a solicitor? I hope I pay you very well indeed."

This settled, they returned to the hotel, and Mr. Tilling took his leave. Elisabeth packed her things and prepared to move into her new house, for she had decided that however out of repair it might be, it was the best place for accomplishing the great amount of work she had set herself in the next few days.

It was an intensely busy period. Elisabeth made notes on each room in the house, then spent several afternoons in the modish showrooms of London merchants, choosing furniture and other necessities. She had an interview with her new banker, a very distinguished gray-haired gentleman in the City, and found time to engage a personal maid from among the candidates Mr. Tilling sent over. And though she was ruefully in awe of this very formidable lady, she felt, by the time a week had passed, that much progress had been made. However, she was exhausted with running about London, and it was with a profound sense of gratitude that she left Mr. Tilling in charge of the work on the house and climbed into a chaise to travel into the country.

## *Three*

As she rode, Elisabeth looked at the letter she'd received from her cousins just before her departure. Though it was signed by both of them, it had apparently been composed by Belinda, who expressed such enthusiasm for her proposed plan that Elisabeth had decided to go directly to Mr. Brinmore's house in Bedfordshire, stopping at Willowmere on the way back to London.

Miss Belinda Brinmore's epistolary style scandalized a former teacher of composition and penmanship; her letter was full of misspellings and odd phrasing, and Anthony's signature at the end was much blotted. But the sentiments were warm and their gratitude patent; Elisabeth felt that she would like her rediscovered cousins very well. Their uncle had also enclosed a note, welcoming her to visit his house for as long as she liked.

She arrived at Mr. Brinmore's estate late in the afternoon. The house was small but set invitingly on a knoll amid gardens. As her chaise swept up the drive, Elisabeth admired the neat lawns and banks of flowers. It was a peaceful scene. But just as the driver was negotiating the curve leading to the front door, a very large and shaggy dog shot out from behind the far corner of the house and ran directly into the carriage's path. Elisabeth started up, crying, "Oh, look out!" The driver pulled the horses up sharply, stopping the coach but causing the animals to rear and plunge sideways. Elisabeth was thrown to the floor, wrecking her new bonnet and sadly mussing her buff traveling dress. By the time they stood still , she was a trifle breathless, and she could hear the driver cursing.

"Careless young fool," he said. "You might have killed the lady, letting that rubbishing mongrel run loose. Of all the hey-go-mad, mutton-headed, cockle-brained... Aye, you'd best hold him. For if I get my fingers near that beast's throat, there's no saying what might happen."

"He is not a mongrel!" a young voice answered hotly. "He is a very rare and seldom-seen breed of dog. I daresay there are not three in all of England."

The driver snorted, "Now that is a cawker, and well you know it, young sir. I know a commoner when I see one, and that dog ain't no more a rare breed than I'm a royal duke. Which I hain't," he added unnecessarily.

There was no answer to this remark, but in a moment, a young man's face appeared in the carriage window, peering anxiously at Elisabeth. "Are you all right?" he asked. "I am terribly sorry. I was teaching Growser to fetch a stick, and his...his spirits got the better of him for a moment. He didn't mean any harm."

Elisabeth had righted herself by this time and was

trying to adjust her crushed bonnet. "I'm sure he did not," she replied. "And no harm was done, after all. Except perhaps to my headgear," she added ruefully. "I'm very glad we did not hit him."

"Oh, yes." The young man, only an overgrown boy really, looked at her doubtfully. "Are you my cousin Elisabeth?"

"If you are, as I suspect, Anthony Brinmore, then I am. Now, why do I get the sinking feeling that that large animal belongs to you? Do you mean to take him to London?"

Anthony grinned. "Well, he does. But Growser is very gentle, I promise you. He'll be no trouble to you at all, and he's a capital watchdog besides." Seeing her wry smile, he flushed. "That is, I should say, he would be no trouble if you allow me to take him to London. If you don't want him, I daresay he can remain here. I do not wish to…"

Growser chose this moment to jump up against the chaise. His front paws reached the sill of Elisabeth's window, and after eyeing her measuringly, he thrust his head through it to favor her with a moist lick, further imperiling her bonnet.

Appalled, Anthony pulled the dog back. "Down, Growser, you looby. What are you doing?"

The driver nodded wisely, murmuring, "Mongrel. I said so. Mauling a lady about."

But Elisabeth merely laughed and fended him off. "Oh, dear," she said, "I can see he's formed a lasting attachment for me already. I shan't have the heart to leave him behind. He would probably fall into a decline."

Anthony's face lighted. "You are a brick, cousin Elisabeth. I guarantee he will not be a trouble to you. I shall manage him, never fear."

Seeing an older man and woman coming down the steps of the house, Elisabeth's hands went automatically to her bonnet once more. "Yes, yes," she said. "But now will you please remove him from the door. If I'm not mistaken, that is your aunt and uncle, and Growser has so jostled me that I don't know what they will think."

"No need to worry over that," replied the young man, "they're a pair of right 'uns." But he pulled the dog off and held his collar.

Elisabeth stepped down from the chaise and held out her hand to the advancing couple. "How do you do," she said. "I am Elisabeth Elham. A little the worse for wear at the moment, I fear."

Both of them smiled as they shook her hand and introduced themselves. "That dog," said Mr. Brinmore, shaking his head. "He's been nothing but trouble since Tony brought him home." He made a helpless gesture. "His former owners wished to be rid of him, understandably enough, and Tony took him to save him from being shot."

Elisabeth looked down at the shaggy face and lolling tongue of the animal. Growser clearly could boast a sheepdog somewhere in his ancestry, but his color was nearer brown than white, and his ears stood up in pointed alertness. "I'm not precisely certain," said Elisabeth, "what rare breed is he?"

As his uncle gave a shout of laughter, Anthony stammered that he had not ascertained as yet the exact breed, but he assured Elisabeth that Growser's ancestors included any number of superior canines. Elisabeth smiled, pulling her skirts out of reach of this aristocratic animal just as he was showing some inclination to chew on them.

"Shall we go in?" asked Mrs. Brinmore then. "I'm sure you're tired after your journey and would be glad of a chance to rest. Belinda is upstairs changing her dress, but she will be down directly when she hears you've arrived."

"Thank you," answered Elisabeth. "I should like to set myself to rights. Belinda will think me demented if she meets me in such disarray."

Anthony snorted derisively, and the whole party, with the exception of Growser, Elisabeth saw gratefully, went into the house.

Half an hour later, after tidying her hair and changing out of her traveling dress to a faded blue muslin, Elisabeth started down to the drawing room. She hadn't had time to acquire a new wardrobe in London, and she suspected that Belinda would think her a shocking quiz, especially if she was the sort of young lady who changed her dress for a visitor's arrival.

Elisabeth paused a moment outside the drawing room door, hearing voices within. Her cousin Anthony was talking to someone. "No need to get into a pucker," he said. "Cousin Elisabeth is bang up to the knocker. She says I may take Growser to London."

"Oh, no," replied a soft female voice. "You've never let her see that dreadful dog. What must she think? Anthony, you promised me you'd be on your best behavior with our cousin."

"Well, I was," answered the young gentleman indignantly. "But I tell you there's no need to put it on. She's not starched-up."

Belinda's response, for Elisabeth had concluded that this must be Belinda, sounded a little petulant. "You cannot know that. I daresay she was being polite to you. You mustn't spoil this for us, Anthony. You know how important it is. And you promised me…"

"Take a damper, Belinda," said the boy with annoyance. "I'll not spoil anything. Have a care for yourself. You may think our cousin won't see through your cajolery, but I believe she's a downy one, up to all the rigs. You'd best watch yourself with her."

A silence fell, as Belinda did not deign to reply to this warning. Elisabeth moved into the doorway and got her first real sight of Belinda and a closer look at her brother. Anthony was standing at the front of the room, leaning against a window frame and gazing out at the garden. Belinda sat sedately on the sofa across the room, her hands folded rather tightly and her mouth pursed in an expression of annoyance. Elisabeth blinked a little as she watched her, for her memories of the two were completely outdated. Belinda was quite the young lady, and dazzlingly pretty, with very pale blond curls and a perfect complexion., Large limpid blue eyes, an enchanting nose, and a perfect mouth completed a picture calculated to throw any gentleman into raptures. Anthony, who had begun restlessly pleating together the fringes on the drawing room curtains, did not much resemble his sister. His hair was a much darker blond, almost the color of Elisabeth's own, and his features were less regular. His figure was tall and rangy, and he held himself in a way that showed his total disregard for his looks. Elisabeth had already noticed that his eyes were a sparkling hazel, and now, when he looked up to see her in the doorway, they filled with vitality and mischief.

He strode forward to greet her. "Welcome again, cousin Elisabeth. I hope you are perfectly recovered." He punctuated this with a very creditable bow.

"Yes, indeed," replied Elisabeth, smiling. "But I admit I'm pleased to see that Growser is not present."

"Oh, he isn't allowed in the drawing room, or in any of the upstairs apartments. You needn't fear to meet him." He met her amused glance with appreciative understanding.

"That dreadful dog," added Belinda, who had risen and was approaching them slowly. "He's utterly without manners."

"He's only a little high-spirited, I fancy," answered Elisabeth, forestalling the hot protest she saw on Anthony's lips. "You are Belinda, I know. I am your cousin Elisabeth."

"Oh, yes," said the girl in a very soft and tentative voice, quite unlike the one Elisabeth had heard from the hall. "I'm so pleased to meet you." Belinda dropped a tiny curtsy. When she raised her eyes again, Elisabeth found that she was being subjected to a very thorough, if subtle, examination. She was made extremely conscious of her outmoded dress and her governess-like appearance. Though Belinda naturally said nothing, and made no overt sign of her opinion, Elisabeth felt that she'd been weighed and found wanting and that Belinda was disappointed in her newly met cousin.

"Let us sit down," suggested Elisabeth. "We have a great deal to discuss, and ought to become better acquainted, too. I was very glad to hear that you agree to my plan of living in London. I shall be grateful for your company."

"It's we who are grateful," said Anthony seriously. "Your offer is most generous and…and…magnor—"

"Magnanimous?" offered Elisabeth, smiling.

"Yes, that's it." Anthony grinned. "I should tell you at the outset that I'm not at all bookish."

"Are you not? Well, you needn't worry. I've been a teacher for years, you know, and we shall soon have you set to rights." Anthony's eyes bulged, and both the young people looked dismayed. Elisabeth laughed. "I'm bamming you, of course. No need to look so hunted."

Anthony grinned again, but Belinda looked uneasy. "I read sometimes," she insisted softly. "Indeed, I like it very much."

"Trashy novels," jeered her brother. "I'd as lief do my Latin. You've never seen anything half so silly, cousin Elisabeth, full of ghosts and fainting and all manner of idiocy."

"You've read them, then?" she asked him with twinkling eyes.

"Lord, no." He caught her gaze and shrugged deprecatingly. "Only looked over a few pages, you know, just to see if there was anything in them."

"Of course," said Elisabeth, suppressing a smile.

"They are very affecting," protested Belinda. "They make me feel," she paused, putting one slender white hand to the side of her throat, "I don't know, sad and happy all at once."

This piece of affection left Elisabeth silent, but Anthony was much disgusted. "You are a silly wet-goose, Belinda," he told her. "Cousin Elisabeth will think you a complete ninnyhammer."

Seeing with trepidation that tears were threatening to form in Belinda's eyes, Elisabeth said hastily, "Not at all. But we must talk of our plans. When will you be ready to leave for London?"

"Oh, as soon as you like," answered Anthony. "We have determined to do everything just as you wish and be no trouble at all to you."

Elisabeth did not think this very likely, but she smiled. "Most reassuring. You will turn me into a positive tyrant with all this docility." Anthony grinned, but Belinda appeared to be at a loss. "I thought we might set out next week," continued the older woman. "We must stop at Willowmere on the way to look over the property."

"Willowmere!" exclaimed Belinda. "Oh, Mama used to talk of it so affectingly. I have always longed to see it."

Noting the curl of Anthony's lip, Elisabeth said hastily, "Have you been taught anything of estate management, Anthony? I am sorely in need of good advice on that score."

He shook his head, looking regretful. "I might have learned from my uncle during this year, but I never thought to have an estate, you know. I shan't be much help. I should be very glad to learn, however. Perhaps your bailiff could instruct me."

"Perhaps. The place has a steward, I'm told. But it appears that our uncle Elham neglected it shockingly, and there is probably more to be done than both of us could manage." She smiled. "We shall go next week and see." She sat back on the sofa. "Why don't you tell me something of yourselves? For cousins, we know amazingly little of one another."

Anthony responded to this request eagerly and launched into a summary of their history and catalogue of his interests. His pictures of their early childhood were idyllic. It seemed, indeed, that until his parents had been killed, nothing had marred his happiness. But after that, everything had changed. The living which had been their entire source of income had been bestowed elsewhere, and he and Belinda were left with nothing but their family's personal possessions. In the midst of their grief, they had to try to plan for the future. By this point in his story, Anthony was very serious. "That is when my uncle came forward and offered us his home," he continued. "He was out of reason kind to us. He has all he can do to provide for his own family, you know, but he paid no heed to that. So, we've lived here for more than a year. And we've been very happy." Elisabeth noticed that he looked at Belinda a bit defiantly as he said this. "But we were excessively glad when your letter came, because we feel so uncomfortable, you know, taking my uncle's money. And we were at a loss as to what we should do with ourselves in a few years, when we are grown up."

"I'm grown up now," put in Belinda. "You're always talking as if we were still children."

"What are your chief interests, Belinda?" asked Elisabeth. "Anthony likes riding and—"

"Everyone calls me Tony, you know," interrupted the young man.

"Very well. Tony likes riding and outdoor pursuits. What are your favorite pastimes? Do you ride also?"

Belinda shook her head. "No. That is, if I have a very *gentle* horse, I sometimes do so, but I do not care for hunting."

Her brother made a derisive noise, and Elisabeth hurried on. "Ah. So, you're fond of novels. What else?"

"I…I like embroidery and fancywork," replied the girl uneasily. "I've learned about household management from my aunt," she added quickly.

Elisabeth nodded encouragingly, but Belinda had apparently finished. Though she tried for some time to draw her out further, it wasn't until she'd given up and was talking of what they would do in London that the younger girl showed any animation. "We'll all require some new clothes, of course," Elisabeth said, looking ruefully down at her drab gown.

Belinda brightened. "Shall we?" she asked. "I haven't had a new dress in…oh, an age."

Elisabeth smiled at her. "You will need a great many dresses now, for I think you will wish to make your come-out this season, will you not?"

Belinda's lovely cheeks flushed, and she gave her cousin a beatific smile. "A London season," she breathed. "Shall we go to balls and to Almack's and… and everything?"

"Yes, indeed," laughed Elisabeth, "particularly everything. Though I cannot make promises about Almack's. I understand that one must procure vouchers to enter there. We must hope to meet one of the Patronesses."

"Oh, I'm sure we shall." With this, Belinda lapsed into blissful silence.

"What nonsense," said Tony. "I don't care for that. But I own there are a deal of things I should like to see in London. And I shouldn't object to having one or two new coats." He grinned and extended his arms, showing his cousin that the sleeves of his present garment ended well above his wrists. "I keep growing out of the cursed things."

"We shall order you any number of new ones, then, possibly in different sizes so we may be ready."

Tony laughed, bouncing a little in his chair. "I shall get—what is the name, Weston—to make them for me." He looked at Elisabeth. "He's the best; I've seen his name in the *Gentleman's Monthly Magazine*. I wonder if I can get into any clubs?"

"I am afraid I know almost nothing about how a young man should go on in London. Perhaps your uncle could help you?"

Tony looked doubtful. "Perhaps," he said. "But I don't believe he's been to town above once or twice in his life."

"Well, we shall do the best we can," said Elisabeth. "I daresay you'll make some friends who can advise you."

"Of course," replied the young man staunchly. "I don't mean to be the least trouble, Cousin Elisabeth. You may count on that."

Elisabeth spent a lively week at the Brinmores'. Three of their five children were away at school, but the two youngest remained at home, and they provided Belinda and Tony with spirited companions for games of span-counters and lottery tickets in the evenings. In the afternoon, Elisabeth sometimes went riding in the countryside or for long walks with her new charges. She often thought wryly that she'd merely exchanged one sort of teaching for another, as they bombarded her with eager questions about London, most of which she couldn't answer. Tony wished to know whether he could have a curricle like the outrageously expensive racing vehicle pictured in the *Gentleman's Monthly Magazine*, and Belinda filled her room with models from the *Fashion Gazette*.

Elisabeth found that Belinda had excellent taste and was an accomplished needlewoman. She'd nearly dismissed the younger girl as a pretty peagoose, but in this area, she was expert. The dresses she had made for herself up to now were much more stylish than Elisabeth's, and the ones she planned to create when given her head in London were very modish and elegant indeed, without being in the least unsuitable for a girl just out. And when Elisabeth told her that she might have some gowns made up by the Bond Street modistes, Belinda only looked skeptical and shrugged.

The day set for their departure came very quickly. Anthony and Belinda bade their aunt and uncle goodbye at great length; and at last, the three cousins climbed into the post chaise. To Elisabeth's vast relief, they'd been able to arrange with the carter who was to transport the trunks for the conveyance of Growser as well, and thus he did not join them in the carriage but capered about the lawn excitedly. However, when the vehicle started down the drive, he took such exception to Tony's departure without him, that the young gentleman was forced to get down again and coax him into a shed, locking him up until they were safely gone. He did this with a great deal of reluctance, and even asked once again if Growser might not come in the chaise, but Elisabeth's firm denial and Belinda's horrified protest discouraged him, and he left Growser behind with many promises to see him very soon.

The chaise started out once more and, with much waving by all the Brinmores, turned onto the lane in front of the house and went on its way. The cousins were on the road to London.

# Four

WILLOWMERE WAS NEARLY ON THE WAY TO LONDON, and they arrived in the neighborhood late in the afternoon. Tony had kept up a constant flow of talk throughout the drive, and Elisabeth had to admit to herself, a bit guiltily, that she would be very glad to sit alone in her bedchamber for a while before dinner. The unbroken company of such a lively young man was somewhat wearing.

They were directed to the house by an innkeeper and had no difficulty finding the signpost that marked its turn-off. But as they drove down the lane, they saw no signs of a dwelling. Finally, the chaise slowed before a set of stone gateposts wildly overgrown with weeds. The avenue between them was hardly more than a double line of ruts with a bit of gravel here and there. "Can this be Willowmere?" asked Elisabeth apprehensively. "It looks as if no one has driven down that in years."

"This should be the right place, according to the inn-keeper's directions," replied Tony. "Let us go and see."

"It's just like the beginning of a novel," added Belinda. "Do you think Willowmere is haunted now?"

"No, I do not," said Elisabeth sharply, not wishing to encourage the development of nervous fancies. "I suppose we must try it." She gave this order, and the carriage started slowly up the avenue, the driver watching carefully for potholes and soft spots.

Almost immediately, they passed between two rows of huge oak trees that had been allowed to grow across the path. For about a mile, the sides of the chaise were brushed by great branches, and the coachman had to steer it from side to side to avoid being obstructed. They could hear him muttering his disapproval. When Elisabeth was just about to suggest that they turn back, they emerged from the trees into a wide circular clearing, and they were able to move more rapidly up to the house at the other end.

Willowmere was not a large house, but it was very ancient. Elisabeth knew that the oldest section had been built in Tudor times, and the stones from a medieval manor on the site had been used in its construction. It had been added to in a rather haphazard way, Elisabeth thought as she looked it over, and now seemed to be an unorganized jumble of bow windows, wings, and turrets. Save for a small area around the front door, the grounds were a mass of weeds and brush. Belinda, however, was in raptures. "It must be haunted," she cried. "It looks just as I always imagined the houses in novels to look."

As they sat in the carriage debating what to do, the front door of the house opened suddenly, and two people came out. They seemed upset; the woman was wringing her hands nervously, and the man shaking his head, hands on hips. Elisabeth got down and went to meet them. "Are you Mr. and Mrs. Lewis?" she asked. "Mr. Tilling told me that you were caring for the house. I am Elisabeth Elham."

The woman's hand-wringing intensified. "Oh miss," she said. "Mr. Tilling wrote to say you were coming down, but I don't know what we're to do. The house isn't fit to live in, and there's no food to speak of. I only got the letter today." She seemed on the verge of tears.

"Yes, I think we must go to an inn," replied Elisabeth in calming accents. "Mr. Tilling didn't tell me that the house was uninhabitable. But I expect you couldn't keep it up alone."

Mr. Lewis was truculent. "That's the trouble, miss," he said gruffly. "We work day and night, but the two of us can't do all the work around a place this size. Not but what we haven't tried."

"Of course you cannot. And I'm sorry we've descended upon you with so little warning. I thought Mr. Tilling's letter would reach you much sooner. I want to look over the house, you know, so that I might see what work needs doing and get it started as soon as may be." She smiled at them.

The man softened considerably at these words. "Will you be making repairs then, miss?" he asked. "It's gone sadly against me to see it fall to pieces this way."

"Yes, indeed. I hope to restore it completely."

"Praise be," said Mrs. Lewis.

Turning to her, Elisabeth said, "And we must get you some help in the house. I daresay a place this large could employ three or four maidservants?"

Mrs. Lewis appeared too overcome to speak, but her

husband answered, "It could for certain, Miss Elham, and as many men in both the gardens and the stables. Your uncle never cared much for Willowmere; we've been alone here nigh on twenty years."

"Well, that will change very soon," she replied. "But I hope you will stay on even when it becomes crowded again." With this remark, she elicited the first smile from Mr. Lewis.

Belinda and Anthony had climbed down by this time, very eager to explore the house, and accordingly, they all went inside. Elisabeth was agreeably surprised as they looked over the rooms, for though most of them were shut up and the furniture under covers, the house itself was sound and some of the furnishings quite usable. All in all, it was not so bad as she'd feared, and her mood had lifted by the time they returned to the drive in front of the house.

"Let's go all round the gardens," urged Tony. "We must see the stables and the grounds."

"I want to look in the gallery," said Belinda. "Can you believe it? A great hall with a gallery! I never thought to really see one."

"Go on then," Tony replied. "Cousin Elisabeth and I will poke around outside."

"Oh, I couldn't go there alone," said Belinda with a shiver.

Elisabeth laughed. "For my part, I'm tired and dusty," she said. "And I have no desire to look at anything more today. We'll return tomorrow, and you may explore as much as you please, but now I think we should find rooms for the night."

Mr. Lewis directed them to The Pony, about four

miles away, and they set off once more. The inn was small and off the main highway, but their rooms appeared comfortable and clean. They were the only guests, and the landlady bustled about cheerfully providing them with hot water and towels and taking their orders for dinner.

Elisabeth did manage to spend a few quiet moments alone, but very soon, she was called down to dinner and rejoined her eagerly chattering cousins in the parlor set aside for them. She was becoming more and more conscious of the fact that watching over her two young relatives would be an arduous task.

Throughout dinner, they discussed the house. Anthony was of the opinion that everything should be swept away and replaced with modern furnishings, while Belinda argued with some spirit that all should be kept as it was, only a little cleaner. Elisabeth mediated their disputes, agreeing now with one, now with the other, for her own view was somewhere between the two. They would apparently have carried on the dispute for hours, but Elisabeth convinced them that an early night was in order if they were to return to Willowmere in good time tomorrow, and sent them off to bed. Fatigue caught her as she undressed, and she too was soon in bed and asleep, dreaming endlessly of dust and hangings which fell to pieces in her hands.

The next morning dawned clear and sunny, and Elisabeth woke early. She lay for a while in her bed, watching the branches of the chestnut tree outside her window sway in the light breeze, then rose and dressed, going downstairs in expectation of finding Tony and Belinda before her. But when she reached the parlor, she found that she was the first down, so she strolled out into the early sunshine. In spite of the promise of great heat later on, the day was glorious, and Elisabeth decided to take a short walk before breakfast. She found a footpath leading off toward a little copse behind the inn and took it, delighting in the scents of the fields and the freshness of the air. In her enjoyment of the peaceful scene, she went farther than she had intended. The inn was out of sight by the time she turned back, and the sun was well above the horizon.

She had recrossed a stile and was traversing an open field when she heard hoofbeats behind her. Turning, she was just in time to see the rider urge his magnificent chestnut up and over the fence she had just climbed. The form of both was flawless, and she forgot herself in her admiration of the jump, watching unself-consciously, as the horseman approached her.

The chestnut had white feet and was one of the most beautiful and spirited animals she'd ever seen. He moved with the ease and power of a true thoroughbred and might have made almost any rider appear insignificant, but the man on his back matched his quality. He looked to be tall, and his figure was well-molded and athletic. His buckskin breeches fitted him to perfection, and his coat fairly cried out its fashionable origin in the workrooms of a Weston or a Stultz. Elisabeth had seen a few gentlemen of the *haut ton* in Bath, and she knew enough to recognize that the deceptive simplicity of the folds of his cravat and the carefully casual arrangement of his hair were the signs of a veritable tulip, a top-of-the-trees Corinthian. At that moment, she met his slightly mocking gaze and looked down in confusion, recalling herself with annoyance. She had been gaping like a schoolgirl, she thought.

The rider pulled up before her. "I almost feel I've been in a competition," he said. His voice was deep and resonant. "I hope you gave me full points for that jump."

Elisabeth looked up. His eyes were pale blue, she noted, in spite of his black hair and rather dark complexion. "I was staring quite rudely, I know," she replied. "I beg your pardon. But I was transfixed by the way your horse took that fence."

The man patted the chestnut's neck, "He's wonderful, is Tristram."

"Tristram?" repeated Elisabeth, smiling. "That's an uncommon name for a horse. Do you take it from *Tristram Shandy*?"

The rider looked at her with much more interest than he'd first shown. "Yes, I'm fond of Sterne."

"Oh, it is my favorite of all books. I thought hardly anyone read it now."

He smiled back at her somewhat quizzically. "And I should hardly have thought it fit reading for young ladies." He surveyed her. He was the despair of his mother and several aunts, who had all at one time or another introduced to him dazzling debutantes calculated to urge him into marriage. But though he'd treated them politely, he'd been extremely bored in their company and really had very little notion of what to say to conventional young women. Seeing that Elisabeth was a bit uncomfortable under his gaze, he continued, "But then I rarely find young ladies wandering about my land unattended. So I can't quite make you out. Are you someone's governess, perhaps? Do you teach your pupils from Sterne?" His amused smile faded as he went on before she could answer. "No, that doesn't seem right."

Looking down at her drab garments, Elisabeth laughed. "I'm sure I don't know why you say so. I do look very like a governess. In fact, until a few weeks ago, I was a teacher at a seminary for young ladies. Now that my uncle has obligingly left me his fortune, I shall have to change my style of dress."

"Uncle?" he asked. His eyes narrowed. "You can't mean old Anthony Elham? I heard of his death."

"Yes. I am Elisabeth Elham. Though it is not at all the thing to go about introducing oneself to strange men," she told herself reflectively.

The rider laughed. "I hope I'm not strange. But I beg pardon. I should have made myself known to you immediately. I am your neighbor, Derek Wincannon. Do you mean to say that old Elham has left you Willowmere?"

Elisabeth shrugged. "It is part of the estate. And a very ramshackle part, I must say. I have never seen so neglected a house."

"It's the scandal of the neighborhood," said Mr. Wincannon. "Your uncle was a shocking landlord and a worse neighbor."

"From what I heard of him," answered Elisabeth, "he was uniformly shocking. I'm rather sorry I never met him." The man laughed again. "But in any case, you may inform the neighborhood that I shall be putting the place to rights as soon as I may."

"That's good news. Will you be settling there?"

"No. At least, not immediately. I shall live in London for a time, at Elham House."

"For the season, I assume."

"Yes, I'll be bringing out my cousin."

"*You* are bringing out someone? I'd have thought it would be the other way about."

"Oh, no," Elisabeth smiled. "I'm beyond that sort of thing. Quite on the shelf, in fact," she added lightly.

"I see it now," he responded dryly, "a veritable antique. How can I have mistaken you for girl in her twenties?"

She laughed. "Well, I daresay I shall attend a few parties also, if I'm asked."

He smiled. "There can be little doubt of that, I should think. You'll wish to sample the gaieties of the season and attend the assemblies at Almack's."

"Almack's? Oh, no, I shouldn't think so."

He raised his eyebrows.

"My father used to tell me stories about London, and he was most severe on Almack's. He called it the Marriage Mart and painted such a vivid picture of the trials young girls undergo as they are catalogued and labeled according to their faces and fortunes that he gave me quite a horror of the place. I don't at all wish to go there *now*."

Mr. Wincannon's interest was definitely caught. "Now?"

"Well, of course I might have done so some years ago had I been offered the opportunity," Elisabeth explained obligingly. "When one is thrown penniless upon the world at the age of nineteen, one is willing to try any shift to come about again. I was very willing *then* to marry to make my fortune. But I wasn't given the chance, and how fortunate that was, really. For now, you see, there is no need."

Derek Wincannon laughed. "You are a most unusual girl," he said.

"Because I prefer to order my own life now that I have the means to do so?" asked Elisabeth. "I'm persuaded you can't really think so. Would you give up your independence without need? No indeed. When I was desperate and might have married, no one dared offer for me. I certainly won't encourage anyone to do so now that I have an income."

"Much good that will do you, I should say."

Elisabeth looked puzzled. "Oh, I collect you mean that I'll receive offers now that I am wealthy?"

"Scores of them."

"Well, if that isn't the way of things. When you want or need something, it's beyond your touch, but the moment you don't, it's thrust upon you. Utterly nonsensical, and despicable besides, is it not?"

"Utterly," he agreed, smiling.

"I'll simply ignore the whole matter," she finished decisively.

"Will you?" he asked. "How?"

"Why I shall avoid Almack's and all such places, and I'll refuse anyone who has the lamentable bad taste to make me an offer. That should answer admirably."

Wincannon made no reply but simply watched her with twinkling eyes from his horse's back. After a moment, Elisabeth became conscious of his regard. She smiled, but flushed a bit as well. "My tongue has been running like a fiddlestick, and I've been talking a lot of nonsense, I don't doubt. You must forgive me. I quite miss having a sensible older person to talk to, you see. At the school where I taught, I had the headmistress and my fellow teachers. Now I have only my cousins."

"And they are not sensible?" inquired Derek.

"Oh, well, they're young yet, I did not mean to say…of course, Tony is…ah, my wretched tongue. I believe I should cut my losses, as my father used to say, and retreat. I've stayed out much longer than I meant to, and I'm keeping you from your ride besides."

"Not at all," he answered politely. But as she made unmistakable signs of departing, he bowed slightly in the saddle. "I shan't try to keep you, but I hope we may meet in London. My mother is bringing my younger sister out this season. If you will allow them to call on you, I'm sure she can help with your cousin." His eyes twinkled. "I promise she won't force you to go to Almack's."

"Oh, I…you are very kind, but…"

"Good, I'll tell her." He pulled up his horse's head. "And now I shall take my leave and not keep you standing when you wish to go." With that, he moved away and was soon galloping off across the fields the way he'd come.

Elisabeth returned to the inn a little bemused. Her unconventional conversation with Mr. Wincannon had left her breathless, and she was a little angry with herself for allowing it to happen. Whatever had led her to run on in such a foolish way, she wondered. As she walked, she went over the scene in her mind, and she flushed deeply as she recalled what she'd said. "What a wet-goose!" She put her hands to her hot cheeks and shook her head.

It was very helpful to stride through the fields, venting some excess energy. By the time she reached the innyard once more, Elisabeth had regained her customary spirits, and she was much inclined to dismiss the incident with a laugh. It was highly unlikely, she thought, that she would see Mr. Wincannon again. And if she did, he would doubtless have forgotten meeting her walking on his land. His suggestion about his mother she put down as mere politeness. She vowed to forget the incident and was reasonably successful, though the image of the handsome Mr. Wincannon lingered.

The cousins returned to Willowmere at midmorning, and the whole of that day and the next were spent examining the house and making notes of necessary repairs and additions. Anthony had perfected, or so he thought, a scheme for placing a series of fountains in the gardens at Willowmere, and he kept the ladies laughing with his preposterous designs for piping water to them. Mr. Lewis assured Elisabeth that he knew of several reliable workmen in the neighborhood and engaged to hire them. And Mrs. Lewis said she would have no trouble finding new servants. The couple promised that she would not know the place when she visited again.

At the end of the week, the three cousins set out for London and reached Elham House easily in one day. The main rooms were painted and refurnished, and Tony and Belinda settled happily into the rooms provided for them, while Elisabeth collapsed in her own. The innumerable tasks before her would simply have to wait, she thought, as she lay on her bed before dinner.

When the formidable Ketchem, who had arrived in their absence, came in to help Elisabeth change for dinner, she had to wake her. And she had a good deal to say about foolish persons who travel in the summer heat and wear themselves down. Elisabeth endured the scold meekly, but when she went downstairs to dinner, she felt something akin to despair. Why had she taken on this household of strangers, she wondered, and would she last a fortnight among them?

# Five

ELISABETH LEFT ORDERS THAT SHE BE ALLOWED TO sleep late the next morning. Thus, when she was awakened at seven by an uproar downstairs, she was annoyed. But as the volume of the noise grew progressively higher, she became alarmed and got out of bed, pulled on her dress, and went down.

In the entry, she found chaos. The hall table had been overturned, and a vase of flowers shattered, leaving broken crockery, water, and bedraggled blossoms littering the marble floor.

But this alarmed Elisabeth less than the piercing shrieks issuing from the library. She heard Anthony's voice shouting, "Down, down, sir. Where are your manners?" And she had a sinking feeling that she knew the origin of the trouble.

Her fears were confirmed when she entered the room. Growser had arrived. But the plump little lady standing on an armchair and swiping at him with her umbrella was a stranger. Anthony, on his knees, had seized the dog about the neck, but Growser continued to bark and try to jump up on the chair.

Obviously, he thought this great sport. Elisabeth hurried forward.

"He's only trying to be friendly," said Tony to the lady on the chair, who'd stopped shrieking now that the dog was being held. "He thought you were playing. He's not at all vicious, I promise you."

"Tony, who let that dreadful animal into the house?" asked Elisabeth. "I am sorry, ma'am. I hope he hasn't hurt you." She put out her hand to help the lady down.

Eying Growser, she climbed off the chair. She made some attempt to straighten her hat, which had been knocked askew in the excitement. "Oh, dear, no," she replied. "I was just a bit decomposed, and only for a moment, you know, out of surprise. He is an excessively energetic animal; I feared he would injure himself. I am sorry to arrive so early. I expect that is what put him out, for no one cares to have guests arrive before breakfast, of course. Though you mustn't consider me a guest, of course, or indeed treat me as one, for you know I wish to help in any way I can. I stupidly took the first stage and reached London at six. Can you conceive of it! Who would wish to get to town at such an hour? And what to do with oneself? Excessively discountenancing. With my bag and all. I couldn't stay in the street, and the tea shops were all closed, except one, indeed, which I passed, but it didn't look at all the thing, you know. So I was forced to come along here; I must have seemed quite fictive to your watchdog when I was let in so early. Such a splendid idea, a watchdog. My father always wished for one, but the first he had chewed his carpet slippers to shreds, and the other attacked the parlormaid, so there was nothing for it but to…" She became aware of the blank expressions of the two young people. "You are Elisabeth, I know," she continued equably. "I should recognize you anywhere. Such a sweet child you were. I'm your cousin Lavinia, you know."

"Oh," replied Elisabeth. "I did not know…I wasn't sure…" The abrupt appearance of this talkative little lady had left her speechless, and she surveyed her new chaperone with some misgivings. Cousin Lavinia was small, scarcely reaching Elisabeth's shoulder. But she was very plump, and her rotundity was accentuated by the dressing of her gray hair, which radiated in curls all around her head. Her face was also round, and merry.

She suffered Elisabeth's gaze with equanimity. "Second cousin, I should say," she continued. "For, of course, it was our parents who were cousins. Our grandfathers were brothers; mine was the oldest of the family and yours the youngest, which accounts for the difference in our ages, you see." She began to look a bit anxious as Elisabeth continued to stare.

"Lavinia Ottley, you know," she said helpfully. "You *did* receive my letter?"

"So it was Ottley," murmured Elisabeth vaguely.

The lady peered at her. "Ottley, yes. I came as soon as I got Mr. Tilling's letter. Such a polite gentleman, everything that was proper. He said he would send a cheque for traveling expenses, but I saw no need to wait for that."

Elisabeth noticed now that Lavinia's gown was quite shabby and worn and her expression worried.

"You must pardon our welcome; I'm not quite awake yet, I fear. Tony, take Growser to the kitchen at once. And tell Cook to send up some breakfast for me and Cousin Lavinia."

"Oh, my goodness," said Lavinia. "Please don't go to any trouble on my account, though I admit I am rather hungry. I set out so early, you see. But you mustn't…of course you'll be having your breakfast now in any case, I suppose, so that…"

"I will indeed," interrupted Elisabeth firmly. "Come into the breakfast room and have a cup of tea. It will do you good after your fright. Run along, Tony, and tell Cook we require a pot of tea immediately."

"I would, Cousin Elisabeth, gladly," answered Tony. "The thing is, the cook won't have Growser in the kitchen. It seems to upset her no end, though all he did was sniff at the joint left out in plain sight on the table. Any dog would do the same."

Feeling harried, Elisabeth put a hand to her forehead. "Well, put him somewhere else, then. In the back garden."

Grumbling a little, Tony went out, pulling Growser with him. Elisabeth led the way to the breakfast room. When they were seated and a pot of tea had been brought, Elisabeth smiled at her companion. "Now we shall be more comfortable," she said. "I'm sorry your welcome was so unorthodox. I returned to town only yesterday, you see, and I've had no time to see Mr. Tilling or look over my letters."

"Oh, dear," answered Lavinia, "then you had no notion I was coming. I should have waited for a reply. I precognated it somehow, but I was so eager to come," Tears started in her eyes, and she began to rummage in her reticule for a handkerchief.

"Oh, pray, do not…" began Elisabeth.

"Ninny!" interrupted her cousin, with seeming rudeness. "Oh, what a complete ninny! How could I be so bird-witted?"

"What's the matter?"

With a tragic expression, Cousin Lavinia pulled a crumpled envelope from her reticule and held it up between them. "My letter to you," she explained. "I never posted it. What a shatter-brained creature I am." She shook her head sadly.

Unable to resist, Elisabeth burst into laughter. Her cousin didn't seem offended, but smiled vaguely and encouragingly, then joined her. When Ames brought in the breakfast tray, he found the two ladies very merry, and he beamed at them approvingly. "Good morning, miss," he said. "We have some sausages today."

As they began to eat, Elisabeth asked where her cousin had been living, hoping that her request for a chaperone had not overset her arrangements.

"Oh, dear, no," replied Lavinia. "I haven't a *sou*, you know, and I was living as cheaply as possible at a reverential hotel on the seacoast. Not one of the *fashionable* resorts, you understand. I did a bit of sewing and took in some pupils to earn my living. My father always insisted that I receive the very finest instruction in evolution and deportation, so I was able to give some of the local young ladies a hint as to how to go on."

Elisabeth maintained a look of polite interest with difficulty.

"But I only just managed, I don't mind telling you. So few girls wish to be properly educated these days. I think it scandalous. So, I was very glad to receive Mr. Tilling's letter." She looked up from her plate. "Not that I mean to force myself upon you, my dear. If you decide we do not suit, you need only say so."

"Oh, I'm sure we shall," answered Elisabeth quickly. Though she did indeed have some doubts on this score, she hadn't the heart to squash her cousin's obvious happiness. "You must tell me something about my mother's family, Cousin Lavinia. I know almost nothing about them." And the older lady launched eagerly into the history of the Ottleys, a subject in which she apparently had a passionate interest.

Lavinia and her brother William were the sole representatives of the current generation, it seemed to Elisabeth at first. Her cousin's narrative was none too clear. She realized her mistake when Lavinia continued, "I am the last of the Ottleys now, of course. If only William had not been killed at Salamanca, the family name might have been preserved." She sighed.

"He was in the army, I collect?" asked Elisabeth.

Her cousin nodded. "A colonel, my dear. And he died a hero's death. But that is really not any compensation, is it?"

Elisabeth was about to agree when Belinda appeared. Anthony soon joined them, after having been forced to tie Growser in the mews behind the house. He'd already breakfasted, but he was easily persuaded to eat something more. Both of the young people seemed to like Cousin Lavinia, though they obviously found her rather odd, and some of Elisabeth's doubts were quieted.

"Cousin Elisabeth," said Belinda, "are we to go shopping today?" The girl looked at her hopefully.

"Oh, yes," answered Elisabeth. "I daresay we shall shop for several days together before we even begin to purchase all the necessaries. I'm worried about Tony, however. I don't know where to direct you," she said to him. "I haven't the addresses of any tailors."

"Oh, I shall manage that," replied the boy airily. "I shall stroll nonchalantly down Savile Row until I see the place I want." He grinned.

Elisabeth gave him a satirical glance. "We must also call at the agency to find a maid for Belinda and a valet for Tony. You will require a maid as well, will you not, Cousin Lavinia?"

As Lavinia began to deny all desire for such an extravagance, Anthony whooped. "Shall I have my own valet?" he cried.

Elisabeth looked at him with amused perplexity. "Is that not the usual thing?" she asked. "My father had one. I thought it was customary."

Anthony hastened to assure her that it was so; Belinda asked when they might go out; and Lavinia continued to beg her not even to consider hiring her a maid. Elisabeth sat quietly amid the rising babble, unsure whether she wed to laugh or fall into despair. How had she become the head of such a clamorous household, she wondered to herself?

An hour later, she had regained control. Tony had set off on his own in search of a tailor, while the three ladies were preparing to go to Bond Street. Elisabeth had convinced Lavinia that she must accept some new gowns, but only by promising not to procure her a maid.

The shopkeepers and modistes of Bond Street were overjoyed to receive such free-spending customers at this slack time of year. Elisabeth tried to keep track of the dress lengths, gowns, and accessories they purchased, but finally she gave it up in despair and left all to Belinda. The latter entered into this expedition with a knowledge and gusto far beyond that of her older companions, and the decisions she made were always correct. In every shop, she soon earned the respect of the most starched-up clerks, for she never hesitated to express her opinion, and she knew exactly what she wanted. Thus, she chose several subdued, but elegant, outfits for Lavinia, staying chiefly with lavender and other quiet colors. For Elisabeth, she picked a number of dresses in cambric and sprig muslin for daytime and found a dress length in blue to match her eyes. And when Elisabeth saw the evening dress Belinda had chosen for her, a pale yellow satin with an overdress of figured lace, all objections died on her lips, and she followed meekly as Belinda led them on.

The girl ordered few dresses for herself, but purchased a number of dress lengths. She maintained, when pressed, that her own designs were superior to those she'd been shown, and Elisabeth could not argue with this. Belinda's skill was quite amazing. The ladies arrived home laden with packages, even though most of their purchases had been sent, to find Tony reclining on the sofa in the drawing room impatient for his tea.

Elisabeth was too tired to do more than hope his taste equaled his sister's. She vowed that she would seek out Mr. Tilling and try to delegate some of the work ahead to him.

When she set out for Mr. Tilling's office early the following morning, Elisabeth was accompanied by her new maid. This tall austere lady was about forty years of age, as nearly as Elisabeth could tell, with iron gray hair and a manner that made her new mistress quake. As they walked along together, Elisabeth glanced at her nervously.

Ketchem caught her change of expression and raised her eyebrows almost imperceptibly. "It's good to step out of the house, isn't it, miss?" she said. "One never knows when that beast will be about with his nasty threatening ways."

"I collect you mean Growser," replied Elisabeth. "I'm sorry you've taken such a dislike to him."

Ketchem lifted her chin. "I wouldn't stoop to have any feeling about a mongrel such as that," she answered somewhat haughtily. "But I will say that it's not the sort of animal belongs in a townhouse." She sniffed. "Or indeed any respectable person's house. What people will think, I cannot imagine."

At this, Elisabeth's own eyebrows went up. "They may think what they please," she replied rather coldly.

"Yes, miss," continued Ketchem, "as I'm sure they will."

Elisabeth was glad to reach Mr. Tilling's office. The solicitor acknowledged Ketchem's presence with an approving look, which Elisabeth answered with a laughing grimace. While Ketchem was being settled downstairs and offered tea by the respectful and nervous young clerk, Elisabeth followed Mr. Tilling up to his office. Once seated, she immediately began, "Mr. Tilling, you must come to my rescue. I am about to fall into a decline."

Mr. Tilling smiled but made no pretense of believing this obvious bounder. "What is the trouble?" he asked.

"There is simply too much to do," replied Elisabeth. "Horses to buy, valets to hire, a huge reconstruction project to oversee in the country. And Mr. Tilling, have you met my cousin Lavinia?"

Her expression was so comically woebegone that the solicitor laughed. "I have not yet had that pleasure. Indeed, I had no notion she'd arrived in London. Is something amiss with her?"

"Oh, no, I believe not. She's only a little, eccentric. I take it she has been living alone for some time?"

He nodded. "Since her father died about ten years ago, I understand."

"That may account for it."

"What is the problem? Is she not respectable? I was assured…"

"Not that," put in Elisabeth hurriedly. "It's rather difficult to explain."

Mr. Tilling frowned. "You need not have her, you know. We can as easily find someone else."

Elisabeth smiled wryly. "I couldn't turn her out after offering her a home so much superior to the one she comes from. I don't object to having her, but I'm uneasy about taking her into society with us when Belinda comes out. People might find her, ah, strange."

"From what I've heard," laughed Tilling, "that might be said for many members of the *ton*. However, perhaps you will find other chaperones for Belinda once you make some acquaintances in London."

"Perhaps," answered Elisabeth. "In any case, I mustn't burden you with problems you can do nothing about." She grinned. "Particularly when I came here to hand you a number of others."

He bowed his head. "I am at your service."

Leaving the solicitor's chambers almost an hour later, Elisabeth was quite pleased with herself. She'd arranged that Mr. Tilling would watch over the reconstruction of Willowmere, or send an agent to do so, send round some prospective maids and valets for her cousins to interview, and investigate carriage builders, so that she might call on the best and order a vehicle. This left only the question of horses, and Elisabeth had a notion that Tony might be of help in that area.

She arrived home meaning to ask him about it, but when she walked into the hall, she heard shouting upstairs.

"He's at it again, miss," said Ketchem righteously, "just as I foretold. We won't have one quiet minute in this house until that animal goes."

Elisabeth turned to Ames, who was just shutting the front door after them, with a pained question in her eyes.

"Yes, Miss Elisabeth," said Ames. "Miss Belinda is rather upset with Mr. Tony, being as Mr. Tony's dog has chewed up her pink muslin."

"Now it's muslin," put in Ketchem. "And the dear knows what he'll be into next. None of us is safe."

Elisabeth sighed and rubbed a hand across her forehead. "How did it happen, Ames? Do you know?"

"Not precisely, miss. Cook is of the opinion that the animal devoured the rope Mr. Tony tied him with so as to break into the house."

Ketchem shook her head. "Just as I said," she repeated.

The corners of Elisabeth's mouth began to twitch. "Growser's teeth must be uncommonly strong," she said.

Ames agreed blandly. "I believe he demonstrated their efficacy on a large beefsteak the kitchen maid left out last evening."

"Good money wasted, and the cook nearly had a fit of the vapors then and there," added Ketchem.

"Wretched animal," laughed Elisabeth.

"I venture to suggest a chain, miss," said Ames, "always supposing you don't wish to send him to the country."

Elisabeth sighed. "Tony would rebel." Ames signified his agreement by his silence. "Well, I suppose I must go up to them." The sounds of the quarrel had not abated during this time. Indeed, they'd increased.

As Elisabeth started up the stairs, Ketchem was heard to murmur, "Boys," in accents of loathing.

When she entered the drawing room, Elisabeth found a red-faced Tony facing Belinda belligerently. "The horrid creature should be shot," Belinda was saying. "He's a menace to everyone in the house."

"Much you know," replied her brother inelegantly. "Cousin Lavinia said that it is a very good idea to have a watchdog."

"A watchdog? That animal is no more a watchdog than I am. He's too stupid."

"Stupid! He's not as stupid as a scatterbrained female who…"

"Enough," said Elisabeth. "Stop this quarreling immediately."

"Cousin Elisabeth," said Belinda eagerly, "do you know what that horrid dog of Tony's has done now?"

"He's chewed up one of your dress lengths. Where was it?"

"Why, I was just cutting the pattern in my room, and I went downstairs for a moment to fetch more pins and…"

"Did you leave the door open?" asked Elisabeth.

Belinda looked petulant. "I suppose I did. I had no notion I must lock my bedroom door in my own house."

"I hope there's no need of that, indeed," said Elisabeth dryly. "But one should not go about leaving doors open, either." She turned to Tony, who had begun to grin. "However," she continued repressively, "I left strict instructions that Growser was to be limited to the kitchen and the yard. What was he doing upstairs?"

"Well, I'm not precisely certain," said the boy. "I tied him securely this morning. I expect he was lonely down there and came in search of me."

"And not finding you, he took out his natural disappointment on Belinda's muslin, I suppose," offered Elisabeth. "Ames tells me he chewed through the rope you used."

"Did he indeed?" said Anthony appreciatively. "He is a very resourceful dog."

"I daresay he is. But if he is not kept in the kitchen in future, Tony, we shall have to send him down to

Willowmere. We cannot have him wandering about the house eating good muslin and frightening Cousin Lavinia out of her wits."

"Cousin Lavinia has made friends with him," said Tony defensively. "She likes him quite well now."

"That is beside the point, and you know it." Elisabeth looked at him sharply. "I meant what I said, Tony. And if you were sincere when you promised you would do everything as I wished, you will see to Growser."

Tony looked contrite. "Of course," he answered.

"Good. Belinda, we will find you another piece of muslin tomorrow. Perhaps you should start with one of the other lengths." Looking dissatisfied, Belinda flounced out of the room.

"I'm truly sorry, Cousin Elisabeth," said Tony when she had gone. "It is just that Belinda put me in such a flame with her silly muslin. How bird-witted to care for such things."

"Belinda does not think it bird-witted. And I am sure that you wish to show consideration for your sister's feelings."

"Huh," said Tony, but as Elisabeth gazed at him, he lowered his head. "Yes, I suppose so," he admitted finally.

"Good. Let us say no more about it." She smiled. "Do you know anything about buying horses?"

Tony's mulish expression yielded to an eager confidence. "I should say I do. I used to pass on all my father's choices before he shelled out the ready. Bought them, I mean," he added sheepishly.

Elisabeth smiled. "Should you like to find some suitable horses for us?" she asked.

His eyes glowed. "Above anything. I know just where to go, too. Tattersall's. That's where the best animals are to be found in London."

"Very well. I shall trust your judgment. We require some carriage horses; you may come with me to choose the vehicle as well, if you wish. And I'd like a mount for riding in the park. I imagine you want one as well."

Tony nodded vigorously. "What sort of horse do you like, cousin? I'll wager you're a bruising rider."

She laughed. "Not bruising precisely, but I like a spirited mount. Will Belinda wish to ride, do you think?"

Tony shook his head contemptuously. "She's never cared for it."

"Well, that should suffice at first, then. I put the whole matter in your hands."

"Thank you. This is...is simply splendid of you, Cousin Elisabeth. And I promise you will get only sweet-goers."

In the next few weeks, everything was somehow accomplished. Tony did his part with enthusiasm, procuring a team of neat bays, a black gelding for himself, and a beautiful little brown mare for Elisabeth. He also persuaded her to get him a curricle and bought a pair of high-stepping grays to draw it. Elisabeth was a bit uneasy about this purchase, as she doubted his promise to drive carefully. However, in spite of his boyish starts, Tony was nearly of an age to be on the town, and as he had vehemently denied any wish for further education, Elisabeth supposed he must be allowed some latitude. She felt very unsure when trying to guide him, but she knew enough to realize that responsibility was good for him and that too much restriction would cause him to rebel.

Their clothes were made up and delivered, the new servants hired, and Elisabeth received favorable reports from Willowmere. Altogether, things had gone more smoothly than she had dreamed they could. By the time society was beginning to trickle back into town, they were prepared to join the gaieties of the season. As Elisabeth sat alone in the drawing room one afternoon, having sent all her cousins off to see some of the sights of London, she pondered her only remaining concern. How were they to enter society when none of them knew a soul in London except Mr. Tilling?

# *Six*

ELISABETH SAT IN HER REFURBISHED LIBRARY, TRYING
to remember the names of friends of her father with
whom she might claim acquaintance. But it had been
years since he was in London, and she could recall
none. The same was true for Belinda and Tony, and
she hesitated to ask Cousin Lavinia. Ames entered the
library and announced that she had two callers. She
looked up sharply. "Callers? Why, who can they be
Ames? We know no one who might be calling."

Ames handed her a visiting card. "It is the Viscountess
Larenby and her daughter, miss," he replied with a
clear consciousness of the sensation he was creating.

Elisabeth was astonished. "The Viscountess Larenby?
I've never heard of her. What can she want?"

"I don't know, miss. Perhaps you'd care to ask
her yourself? I've shown the ladies into the drawing
room."

"Yes, I suppose I must." She puzzled over the card.
"Tell them I'll be there directly." She ran quickly up
the stairs to her bedroom and surveyed herself in the
mirror. She was wearing one of her new gowns, a

sprig muslin with long sleeves and a high collar, and Ketchem had recently cut her hair and dressed it in a knot on top of her head with curls falling over her ears. It was quite becoming.

As she was going back downstairs, she stopped to tap on Belinda's door. The younger girl jumped up excitedly when she heard they had visitors.

Elisabeth entered her drawing room feeling a little nervous, and the sight of the ladies who rose to greet her did nothing to put her at ease. Both were tall and brunette; the elder possessed an impressive dignity and elegance of both dress and air, and the younger was strikingly handsome. They looked much alike— slender with chiseled features and large pale blue eyes startlingly attractive with their dark coloring. Elisabeth felt they surveyed her appraisingly. "How do you do," she said. "I am Elisabeth Elham. Please sit down; it's very kind of you to call."

Her tone and manner seemed to soften the older woman a bit. "Thank you. We've taken the first opportunity to do so. We arrived from the country only recently, you see."

"Oh," said Elisabeth. "It's very good of you to come."

The three women sat down, and a short silence fell. Elisabeth cast about desperately for something to say.

"Your drawing room is lovely," said the viscountess, looking around at the pale blue walls and darker blue carpet and hangings.

"Thank you," replied Elisabeth. "I've had a great deal to do in the house since I came to London. My uncle left it in a sad state."

The viscountess smiled slightly. "Yes, his treatment of Willowmere would lead one to expect that."

"Indeed," said Elisabeth, eagerly grasping this conversational gambit. "I've begun repairs there as well. I think the estate could be quite beautiful if properly cared for. Do you know it?" Here at last seemed to be a clue to her callers' identity. "You are from that neighborhood?"

Lady Larenby looked surprised. "Yes. Our country place, Charendon, is on the adjoining land."

"Ah. I am so pleased to make the acquaintance of my neighbors. But you are in London for the season?"

The viscountess nodded. "I am bringing Amelia out this year." The younger of Elisabeth's visitors smiled a bit self-consciously.

Elisabeth returned her smile. "My cousin, who will be down in a moment, is also to make her debut." Amelia murmured some polite nothing. Elisabeth turned back to her mother. "It's really very kind of you to think of calling on a new neighbor. I know very few people in London as yet."

Lady Larenby appeared puzzled but made a deprecating gesture. "The season has scarcely started. I'm sure you will meet as many people as you could wish, or more, very soon. I hope you and your cousin will attend a small evening party I'm giving next week to introduce Amelia?"

"Oh, we should be pleased. It is excessively good of you. I am a complete stranger." She stopped in confusion.

Lady Larenby smiled graciously. "My son spoke highly of you, I hope we may not remain strangers."

At this further inexplicable remark, Elisabeth gave it up. "Your son?" she asked.

Once more, the viscountess looked startled. She glanced fleetingly at her daughter, but found no help there. "Yes, my son Derek," she added. As Elisabeth continued to gaze at her uncomprehendingly, she went on, "Derek Wincannon, my son. He told us that he had met you. Did that graceless creature not tell you we would call? He reminded me often enough, I promise you."

Elisabeth's brow cleared, and she laughed. "Oh, dear," she replied. "I'd completely forgotten my encounter with Mr. Wincannon. And he certainly did *not* tell me he was a viscount," she finished severely.

"Well, he isn't as yet, you know," said Lady Larenby, her eyes dancing. "He is only a Right Honorable. My husband is Viscount Larenby."

"How scatterbrained you must think me!" Elisabeth said, shaking her head. "I couldn't understand who you were, and I was desperately trying to gather clues from your conversation." Her expression invited them to share her laugh at herself, and both ladies smiled.

"I should have written a note," replied Lady Larenby. "But I assure you that my heedless son gave us to understand you were expecting us. He will hear of this." She also shook her head.

"And I thought it a mere polite nothing when he said his mother would call on me." Elisabeth met the viscountess's twinkling eyes, and they shared a moment of helpless resignation at the unfathomable ways of men.

Just then, Belinda came into the drawing room.

She had changed into a dress of crisp white muslin trimmed with knots of blue ribbon, and a blue riband was threaded through her curls, which had been, like Elisabeth's, recently cut and dressed by Ketchem. Elisabeth introduced her, and she sat down next to Miss Wincannon. The conversation faltered for a moment, then Amelia complimented Belinda on her gown and asked where she'd had it made. When Belinda replied that she had made it herself, Amelia was suitably impressed, and the two young girls embarked on an extended discussion of the latest modes.

The viscountess smiled at them benignly. "They look to be of an age," she said, turning to Elisabeth. "Amelia is just eighteen, and she's chiefly interested in her dresses at this period in her life."

"Belinda is the same," smiled Elisabeth.

"She is a lovely girl." And indeed the pair sitting across from them made a striking picture. Amelia's dark, but brilliant coloring set off Belinda's paleness to a nicety and vice versa. They were a study in contrasts. Lady Larenby lifted an eyebrow. "I remember when I was Amelia's age my best friend was a blond." She smiled and cocked her head as Elisabeth laughed appreciatively. "You said your cousin was to come out. Will you not be making your bow to society as well this year?"

"Oh, I shall accompany Belinda, but I am past the age for a come-out, I fear."

The viscountess's eyes twinkled. "Indeed? I took you for a girl in her twenties. How easily one may be mistaken about these things."

"Well, it is not my age precisely. I've lived on my

own these five years, you see, supporting myself as a teacher at Bath. And my feelings and behavior are now very far removed from those of a girl just coming out. I should not be 'right.' Belinda is the one to make a success in that line."

"I predict you will both take the *ton* by storm," replied the viscountess. There was a short pause, then she continued hesitantly. "You have not concluded, I hope, that because of your experience as a teacher you can serve as Belinda's only chaperone? Forgive me, but it would not do. You are really not of an age to live alone in London."

"So I have been told," answered Elisabeth wryly. "And you may be easy on that head. Besides Belinda's brother and his very large dog, we are chaperoned by Cousin Lavinia. Oh dear, I've forgotten to ask her to come to the drawing room."

Lady Larenby laughed at her patent dismay. "Cousin Lavinia?" she echoed encouragingly.

Elisabeth looked toward the door. "I really should go fetch her. She is one of my mother's family, Lavinia Ottley. She is much older than I."

This disjointed explanation appeared to interest her guest. "Was your mother Elisabeth Ottley? I didn't know. We came out in the same season, years ago."

"Really? Yes, she was my mother; she died when I was very young. Did you know her well?"

"Alas, no. Though I believe we did meet once or twice, we never became friends. And after her marriage…" She stopped, looking embarrassed.

Elisabeth nodded. "Her family cast her off, and she went to live in the country."

"There were many who thought them very wrong to treat her so."

The girl shrugged. "It matters little now." She shifted in her seat. "I really should find Cousin Lavinia," she repeated. But she made no move; she felt a little nervous of introducing her odd relative to her visitors.

To her relief, Lady Larenby rose. "I'm afraid we must be going now. We shall hope to meet her soon. Do bring her to call." With some difficulty, she pulled Amelia away from an intense discussion of the relative merits of braid trim and ribbons, and the two took their leave, promising to send round a card of invitation for the evening party.

Just after they left, Cousin Lavinia bustled into the room. Immediately, Elisabeth felt guilty, but it appeared that Lavinia had only just returned from a walk. She held a small piece of notepaper in her hand. "Well, you will never guess," she fluttered. "I have just received this note from my distinctive friend Judith." She waved the paper about. "We were in school together, you know, oh, many years ago now, and then she went off to make a grand marriage. A very grand marriage, my dear. Of course, Judith was an exceptionable girl. So lovely, with those great dark eyes, and very intelligent, though not in the least 'blue,' I assure you. Her father was rich as Midas. Not that she wouldn't have married well otherwise, but her portion was very large."

"She's written to you?" put in Elisabeth, seeking to stem this flow of information.

"Oh, yes. We corresponded faithfully for several

years, you know, but then gradually, we got out of the habit. It's sad how often that happens, isn't it? One's very closest friends drift away, and soon one knows no more about them than any stranger." She appeared to sink into melancholy reflection at this observation.

Elisabeth prompted her. "But she has written you once again."

Lavinia started. "Oh. Yes. Yes, indeed. I thought of her straightaway when I saw you'd come up against a cult-de-sock in London. I hoped she might introduce us to her acquaintances, you know, and here she's written that she means to call. Isn't it wonderful?"

"Splendid," replied Elisabeth. "You shouldn't have troubled, Cousin Lavinia."

"Oh my, no trouble at all. It will be so magnetic to see Judith again. I'm sure you will like her. And anything I can do, you know, anything at all, to repay your kindness to me, why, I should be the most ungracious creature in nature if I didn't leap to do it. And such a simple pleasant thing as this. You know, Elisabeth…" But they were not to hear what Elisabeth knew, for at that moment Ames entered the drawing room.

"The Duchess of Sherbourne," he announced impressively, ushering a diminutive gray-haired woman into the room.

Elisabeth and Belinda stared incredulously, first at Ames, then at the visitor, and their mouths dropped slightly open. But Cousin Lavinia bustled forward joyously. "Judith!" she cried. "How gratuitous. We were just speaking of you."

It took the two younger women a moment to recover from their astonishment. By the time they'd done so, they'd been introduced to the duchess, and she was sitting on the sofa beside Lavinia chatting happily of their school days together. Elisabeth watched them with a mixture of amazement and mirth as she berated herself for her snobbish underestimation of her cousin.

At a pause in their conversation, the duchess remarked, "So, Lavinia, you're bringing out your young cousins this season?"

"Yes," responded Lavinia complacently. "I should think they will 'take.'"

"Oh, no question of that. They're lovely. I'll get you vouchers for Almack's from Sally Jersey, if you like. And I'll send my son round." She chuckled. "He's something of a slowtop, but he is a duke, after all." She looked Elisabeth and Belinda over more carefully; Elisabeth struggled not to laugh as she endured this scrutiny. "Yes," she continued finally, "they'll do. Shall I give a ball for them, Lavinia?"

"Oh, Your Grace!" murmured Belinda, dazzled.

The duchess gave a bark of laughter. "I shall," she decided. "I never had a daughter. I'll take them under my wing."

"Very kind of you, Judith," replied Lavinia. "I hoped you might just give them a push, you know. Introduce them to some of the indispensable people."

"You mustn't put yourself to any trouble," interjected Elisabeth. She felt she must put a damper on these plans before she was engulfed by the powerful personality of the duchess.

This lady looked at her with greater interest. "So you're old Elham's niece," she said. "You don't much resemble him. Which is fortunate," she added dryly. "The man was a clutch-fisted croaker from the time he was twenty. *And* no beauty." She directed a sharp glance at Elisabeth. "So you don't want me meddling in your affairs, eh?"

Elisabeth felt herself blushing, and she heard a choking gasp from Belinda. "Oh, I didn't say…I never meant," she began, but the duchess interrupted.

"I have a very good idea what you meant. You haven't learned to guard your tone of voice." Her expression softened, and she smiled winningly. "And I can understand why you might object to my some-what toplofty offer. But I know the *ton* and London pretty well after thirty years, and my position is con-siderable." Her eyes twinkled. "You may ask anyone. It would be a coup for you to make your debut under my sponsorship." She looked wickedly at Elisabeth. "And I understand you know no one else."

Elisabeth was beginning to like the duchess, but she couldn't let this opportunity pass. "Actually," she answered, brushing a bit of fluff from her skirt with studied unconcern, "I have a small acquaintance. The Viscountess Larenby and her daughter have just this moment taken their leave. She was kind enough to call as soon as she returned to town." She heard another stifled gasp from Belinda, but Elisabeth looked steadily at the duchess, sternly ordering her twitching lips not to betray her.

"A hit," cried the duchess, "a palpable hit. I am quite set down. But this only makes me the more determined to sponsor you, my child. I declare you're a wit." The laugh died, and her expression became benevolently serious. "I shan't try to run you, Elisabeth. I hope I may call you Elisabeth? But I promise I can help, and I should like to, both for Lavinia's sake and your own." Her eyes lit again. "If you knew how abominably bored I've been these past two years," she added, "you could not be so disobliging as to deny me a little amusement."

Elisabeth bowed her head. "That would be shockingly rude of me," she replied.

"Good. It's settled then. I shall plan my ball." The duchess's wicked smile reappeared. "Now where can you have met the Wincannons, I wonder?" she mused.

Elisabeth smiled. "They are our neighbors in the country," she replied smoothly. "Their land adjoins Willowmere." Her gaze met the duchess's innocently.

"I daresay," responded the older woman. She gazed at Elisabeth speculatively for a moment, then turned back to Lavinia. "And now, I must go, my friend. I'm sorry to hurry off, but I'm promised to my sister for tea."

"Oh, dear," answered Lavinia. "I hoped you would stay to take tea with us. Is it Alice or Arabella?" she added, evidently in reference to the sister.

"Arabella," was the reply. "Alice has lived in Northumberland these fifteen years, Lavinia."

When Lavinia had agreed that she remembered this, they said their farewells, and the duchess departed. It was indeed nearly teatime, and Ames brought in the tray just as Tony strolled into the drawing room. He'd been out all day and was full of news. Not only had he found a stout chain for Growser, he'd fallen in with some fellow canine-fanciers at the shop where he purchased it. They'd exchanged views on the various breeds of hunting dog and the best means of training them, and Tony was completely engrossed in a scheme for educating Growser in the intricacies of the chase.

Belinda soon grew impatient with this recital. "What can it signify?" she snapped finally. "He will never be more than a mongrel, after all. I don't see that it matters whether he is trained. But, oh, Tony, you will never guess what has happened to us today."

Tony's lip curled. "You bought a new ribbon, I suppose. Or found some rubbishy novel at the circulating library."

Belinda's chin went up. "No such thing. We met a duchess." She awaited his reaction; when he said nothing, she added, "And a viscountess."

Tony shrugged, unimpressed. "Well, I met a man who runs prizefights," he replied. "And you may be sure I had liefer go to one than meet some starched-up duchess."

Belinda sniffed. "You are such a fool, Tony. I can't think how I came to have such a brother. Don't you see that this could be the making of us in London society?"

Her brother shrugged again. "I don't care. I'm not certain I mean to go about in society as yet. Frankly, I find it a dead bore."

With an angry shake of her head, Belinda turned away. Tony grinned at Elisabeth. "I shall take Growser to the park tomorrow," he told her. "There are several things I wish to try. Elkins says one may teach a dog to keep the scent with beefsteak. Do you think I might borrow some from the kitchen, Cousin Elisabeth?"

Elisabeth laughed. "No. Under no circumstances

can you *borrow* it. But you may tell Cook I said you could have a bit, if there is any to spare. Don't tease her to death, mind."

"Oh, no," answered Tony gratefully, showing signs of wishing to descend to the kitchens immediately.

"Such a splendid notion," put in Lavinia, "educating your dog. My father abrocated education for every member of the household, you know. He felt it to be absolutely vital. I remember I had a cat when I was small. A beautiful tortoiseshell. So affectionate. Well, my father would have it that she was lazy, though she was nothing of the kind, I assure you. But he held that she must be trained as a mouser. Well, at first, he was at a loss. I mean, how does one teach a cat, after all? Such indivertible animals, are they not? But at last, he hit upon a scheme. He procured two field mice, you see, and cunning little things they were, too, so tiny, and he put them..."

Elisabeth gradually ceased to attend to her cousin's chatter. She let out a deep sigh, leaned back on the sofa, and sipped her tea meditatively. Her final problem appeared to be solved in a manner far beyond her modest expectations. She now had two exalted acquaintances in London, one of whom threatened to overwhelm her with kind attentions, and the process of entering society seemed assured. Why then did she feel so breathlessly unsettled? She shook her head. Perhaps because it had all happened so fast, she thought. Events had begun to have a momentum of their own, and the independence her inheritance was to have brought her seemed to have vanished in a single day.

# *Seven*

THE FOLLOWING MORNING, AS ELISABETH SAT IN THE library puzzling over columns of figures, Ames entered the room. "Pardon me for disturbing you, Miss Elisabeth," he said. "I know you left orders that you were not at home to visitors, but a gentleman has called who appears to be very anxious to see you. I told him you were not receiving, but he insisted upon being announced. It is…"

Elisabeth, at the end of a long addition, had lost count once already and had had to start from the beginning, so she hardly looked up as she interrupted Ames. "Show him in, then. It is probably the draper Mr. Tilling is sending round. But tell him I am very busy and have little time today."

"But miss, it is not…"

"Never mind, Ames, just send him in," said Elisabeth impatiently.

"But, Miss Elisabeth…"

"Oh, piffle. I have lost it." Elisabeth glanced up, annoyed. "I shall have to start it over again. Please, Ames, just do as I ask."

Ames's expression stiffened. "Yes, miss," he said.

Well into the column of figures for the third time, Elisabeth heard someone enter the room. "Sit down," she said distractedly. "I shan't be a moment."

But it was several minutes before she cried, "Aha!" and looked up triumphantly from the account book to find Derek Wincannon sitting in the armchair opposite her desk and watching her with bland amusement. "You!" she exclaimed. "I thought it was the draper."

He laughed. "So your butler told me. I persuaded him to let me in quietly. My mother raked me down so pitilessly that I wished to apologize to you at the first opportunity."

Elisabeth smiled. "Well, it was too bad of you to sit there and say nothing. You might have announced yourself."

"On the contrary," he replied. "It was much more amusing to observe your struggles with your accounts."

"Unfeeling man. I've been going over and over them all morning, and though I believe I have mastered them at last, the process was extremely unpleasant. I was never fond of arithmetic, but until today, I thought I understood it, at least. Is it possible that I have spent five hundred pounds for wallpaper, do you think?"

Mr. Wincannon laughed more heartily. "I've found that anything is possible in one's accounts. Many of my friends have given up looking at them altogether."

Elisabeth sighed, gazing at the columns of numbers again. "I can certainly understand why. I wonder if perhaps I preferred being poor." She looked up at him with an enchanting, mischievous smile. "I suppose not, all in all."

"I must say I agree," he answered, returning her smile. "But I called this morning to apologize. You must allow me to do so."

"For sending your mother and sister to me? It was only what you said you would do, after all. Indeed, I am the one who should apologize. It was my fault for stupidly forgetting the incident."

His answering smile was a little wry. "I should have told my mother to send a note, of course. I hoped you might allow me to make amends for my misdeeds by taking you driving in the park this morning. And now that I see how you have spent the first part of your day, I insist upon it. A drive will clear out your head."

Elisabeth looked at him. His town dress was as elegant as his riding clothes had been the day they met in the country, but his shirt points barely reached his chin, and there was nothing of the dandy in the single fob chastely hanging on his waistcoat front. The intricate folds of his neckcloth would have sent any young sprig of fashion into agonies of jealousy, yet he wore his modish outfit with ease and no sign of vanity. Elisabeth's first impression of him was confirmed.

As she hesitated, he spoke again. "If you refuse, I shall have to believe that you're angry with me for thrusting my family upon you. Am I not to be forgiven?"

Elisabeth laughed. "How ridiculous you are. All right, then. But I must fetch my hat."

In a few minutes, Elisabeth was sitting beside him in his high-perch phaeton, a groom hanging on behind.

"Your team is beautiful," she said as they turned the corner at the end of her street. "I have never seen bays so perfectly matched."

"Thank you. I bred them myself at Charendon. I'm quite proud of their form."

"Oh, you're a sportsman. My cousin Tony will be eager to meet you."

He smiled down at her. "My mother says that you have two cousins living with you. Tony must be the one with the large dog, I collect?"

"Yes. But your mother should have said three cousins. She didn't meet Cousin Lavinia."

"You seem well supplied."

"I am indeed," replied Elisabeth feelingly. "And they have turned out to be much more than I bargained for, I promise you. Only yesterday, I discovered that my cousin Lavinia boasts an old friend who is a duchess. I was never more surprised in my life." She caught herself. "Oh, dear, my tongue is beginning to run away with me again. What is it about you that makes me talk nonsense?"

"Do you call it nonsense?"

"I do indeed. I still blush to recall the excessively foolish things I told you when we first met. How idiotish you must have thought me."

"On the contrary. I thought you one of that exceedingly rare breed, a sensible woman. I have no patience with milk-and-water misses; they're not worth speaking to, though they litter our drawing rooms today."

A gurgle of laughter escaped Elisabeth. "Litter? What an expression."

"There. That is exactly what I mean. Now, let us have no more apologies. Which duchess?"

Elisabeth eyed him narrowly, half inclined to take exception to his high-handed manners, but the humor of the situation overcame her. "The Duchess of Sherbourne," she answered. "A charming lady, but a bit overpowering."

He nodded. "So I have heard. I don't know her well." They had by now reached the park and turned down an avenue within it. Elisabeth fell silent as she gazed at the crowds and was surprised to hear her own name called.

Mr. Wincannon pulled up near the edge of the roadway, and Elisabeth saw that Belinda and Amelia Wincannon were walking toward them.

"Oh, Cousin Elisabeth," said Belinda, "Amelia has asked if I may return with her to luncheon. You do not object, do you?"

"Not at all," replied Elisabeth.

"I shall have her sent home in the carriage," Amelia assured her, and Elisabeth nodded again.

"The girls appear to have struck up a friendship," Derek said to Elisabeth, as they continued their drive.

"Yes, I'm pleased to see it. Belinda needs a friend who shares her interests."

"Is Belinda then as much of a widgeon as my sister Amelia?"

"What a shocking thing to say about your own sister."

He shrugged. "I find bores difficult to tolerate. It's one of my besetting sins, I admit. And my sister is one of the most boring girls I've ever had the misfortune to meet. Talk of milk-and-water misses! Indeed, I am always hard put to explain it. The rest of my family is quite needle-witted."

"You include yourself, I suppose?"

"Well, of course. What a silly question."

"I beg your pardon," answered Elisabeth rather haughtily.

"Now, don't fly up into the boughs. If your cousin is not a widgeon, I apologize most sincerely."

"It's not that. I mean, of course she isn't. Belinda is not precisely needle-witted perhaps, but..."

He laughed. "Admit that you hate being bored as much as I."

Elisabeth sat back in the seat and crossed her arms. "I don't know that I shall admit anything to you. Has no one ever told you that you have very odd manners? I quake to think what outrageous thing you might say of me if you were to become bored. And to complete strangers, too."

"No fear of that. I cannot conceive finding you the least boring."

A little nonplussed by this unexpected compliment, Elisabeth glanced at her companion. "It's no use trying to turn me up sweet now," she told him. "You've shown too much of your true self. I shall be on my guard."

Wincannon only smiled.

After half an hour, they turned back. As he helped her down from the phaeton, Derek said, "I shall see you at my mother's evening party on Friday, I hope?"

"Oh, yes. Belinda is wildly excited. It is our first outing in London."

He bowed. "I shall look forward to it."

Was it possible, Elisabeth wondered as she went into the house, that she had acquired an admirer? Mr. Wincannon had been very attentive, and something in his manner had suggested that he found her attractive. As she thought it over, Elisabeth realized that the possibility unsettled her. After so many years of considering herself on the shelf, she hardly knew how to include the idea of an admirer in her life. In her bedroom, removing her hat, she frowned at herself in the mirror. "Don't be ridiculous," she told her reflection severely. "One ride in the park doesn't mean the man is smitten. You're acting like a green girl." She shook her head to banish the thought and went downstairs to luncheon.

Later that day, as Elisabeth and Belinda sat in the drawing room discussing what Belinda was to wear to the Wincannons' party the following evening, Ames stepped in and handed Elisabeth two calling cards. "The gentlemen are waiting in the library," he said.

Elisabeth looked down at the cards. She thought ruefully of her desperate wish of a week past that they had some friends in London. It seemed to have been granted with a vengeance. "The Duke of Sherbourne," she read, "and Lord James Darnell."

Belinda had risen from her seat and was looking over her shoulder at the cards. "The duchess *has* sent her son," she said wonderingly. "How splendid."

Elisabeth turned back to Ames. "Ask the gentlemen to come up," she said resignedly.

The duke was a small man. His hair and eyes were brown, his skin dull, and his dress, though fashionable, nondescript. In fact, thought Elisabeth to herself with guilty amusement, he was just the sort of man that one would never take for a duke.

His companion, Lord James Darnell, was more

striking—tall and very fair, with hair about the color of Belinda's and blue eyes. His slenderness gave him a very elegant appearance, which was accentuated by a touch of the dandy in his dress.

"Good afternoon," said Elisabeth. "I am Elisabeth Elham, and this is my cousin, Belinda Brinmore. Please sit down."

"Thank you," replied the duke with an embarrassed cough. "Must apologize for calling without a proper introduction. M'mother sent me over, you know. Tried to tell her it wasn't the thing to call on females one has never met, but she wouldn't listen." He paused, his flush deepening. "I don't mean to say I'm not very pleased to call. But you don't know me, you know. No wish to push in. That is, m'mother insisted, you know." He stopped miserably.

Elisabeth, who had a very good idea of what he had been through with the duchess, took pity on him and smiled. "Indeed, it was excessively kind of you to call," she said. "Please come in and sit down."

The duke bowed awkwardly, and Elisabeth's pity increased. She imagined that this poor young man was dominated by his formidable mother.

The duke started toward the sofa where she sat, but Lord Darnell slipped ahead of him. "I shall sit here," he said. "Go on over there, John." And he sat down beside Elisabeth, leaving the duke to join Belinda on the other sofa. When they were settled, Lord James turned to Elisabeth. "I have got it right, haven't I? You are the heiress?"

"I beg your pardon?" she answered.

"I have it on the best authority that one of you is a

great heiress. And since you are Miss Elham, I believe it must be you. Are you not an heiress?"

"I believe I am," said Elisabeth. The corners of her mouth twitched. "Though it is such a recent occurrence I haven't become quite used to it. Do you talk only to heiresses?"

"When addressing ladies, I make every effort to do so," he replied mock-seriously. "My mother is terrified that I will fall in love with a girl with no money and we shall be ruined." He produced a highly engaging smile. "I am a fortune hunter, you know. I daresay you won't agree to marry me on such short acquaintance?"

"I will not," said Elisabeth, her laughter escaping her. "Do you offer for every heiress the moment you meet her?"

"Only if she is exceedingly pretty," responded Lord James solemnly. "For the plain ones, I have to screw up my courage."

"And do you tell them all that you're a fortune hunter?" continued Elisabeth, much amused. "Doesn't it discourage them?"

Lord Darnell made an airy gesture. "Very rarely. My honesty charms them out of their disapproval. Don't you find it so?" He gazed at her hopefully.

"Perhaps. But it doesn't persuade me to marry you."

He shrugged, grinning. "Yes, that has been the chief obstacle to my progress so far. Most girls find me appealing, but none can be induced to marry. But it does no good to hide the fact that I must marry money, I promise you. I've tried, but someone always informs the young lady; and then she feels I've deceived her." He shook his head.

Elisabeth laughed again. "And why, pray, must you marry money? You don't look to be starving. Or even particularly indigent."

He seemed offended. "Well, you can't suppose I'd enter a lady's drawing room dressed in rags. And in any case, I come from a very fine old family; I mustn't disgrace my ancestors." He grinned once more. "Even if they were all so dashed improvident as to leave me without a groat and the estates in the hands of the bankers."

"I see," said Elisabeth. "That was too bad of them."

"Wasn't it?" he said agreeably. "But I mean to put everything right by snagging a rich wife."

"A laudable ambition," Elisabeth remarked. "I'm sorry I must disappoint you."

"Oh, I haven't given up. I shall make a determined effort."

"Now you've put me on my guard."

He laughed. "It shall be a contest between us. I'd wager a hundred pounds on my chances if I could find anyone to take the odds." He grinned. "Or lend me the blunt."

"You are a gambler, Lord Darnell?"

"Lord, yes. It's in the blood. M'grandfather once lost five thousand pounds on a duck he backed to outrun a parson's goose. And my father spent so much time at the tables that they called him 'Black Jack Darnell.'"

"Quite scandalous."

"I suppose so. But dashed romantic, don't you think?"

Elisabeth laughed and shook her head. "I must speak to my other guest," was her only reply. She turned to the duke. He was talking to Belinda with every appearance of enjoyment.

"There are fireworks, you know," he was saying. "And lanterns hung in the trees, making it look quite exquisite. The ham is excessively good, too." He noticed that Elisabeth was also listening to him. "I have been telling your cousin about the delights of Vauxhall," he said to her. "I am trying to persuade her to join a party I'm getting up to go there next Tuesday week."

"I swear he had no such idea until he saw your cousin," murmured Lord Darnell, almost inaudibly.

"It sounds heavenly, doesn't it, Cousin Elisabeth?" put in Belinda. "Do say we will go." She looked at Elisabeth eagerly, an imperative command in her eyes.

Elisabeth smiled. "Certainly, if you would like to, we can." Belinda clapped her hands.

"You won't be so shabby as to leave me out, I hope, John," said Lord Darnell, and he was assured that he was also invited.

At that moment, Cousin Lavinia hurried into the room. "I beg pardon," she said breathlessly. "But I have only just this minute discovered we had callers. And Judith's son among them." The duke rose politely, and Lavinia rushed over to him. "How do you do. I am so pleased to meet you. I am a relict of your mother's, you know."

The duke looked rather confused, but murmured a polite greeting.

"Oh, yes, Judith and I were friends even before she met your father, when you weren't even a conception."

Elisabeth heard a choking sound from the gentleman

beside her. "Come and sit down, Cousin Lavinia. I sent Ames to fetch you when our callers arrived, but he couldn't find you."

"I was writing a note in the breakfast room. He didn't think to look there, I suppose. Indeed, I almost never sit in the breakfast room. But the sun was coming in so prettily this morning that I thought I would just write my letters there, you know, after Betty cleared up. And I became so engrossed in telling Mrs. Simpson, one of my fellow lodgers, you know, or former fellow lodgers I should say, about meeting Judith again that I quite lost track of the time." She turned back to the duke. "You are the image of your mother, I declaim. I should have known you for Judith's son anywhere."

"Th-thank you," responded the duke, obviously at a loss.

Elisabeth intervened once more. "The duke has very kindly invited us to join his party at Vauxhall Gardens in a few days," she told Lavinia.

"Oh, we shall be delighted," responded that lady brightly.

"You honor me by accepting," said the duke rather ponderously. His unease under Lavinia's barrage of chatter was clear, and now he looked toward Darnell. "I think we had better go now. James?"

"Oh, yes." Lord Darnell was looking highly amused. "I shall look forward to seeing you soon then, ladies." Elisabeth rose to escort them to the stairs, and as they went out, Lord Darnell murmured in her ear, "Wherever did you find your delightful dragon?" Elisabeth frowned and shook her head warningly, but he only laughed.

Belinda and Lavinia discussed the duke for some time; both, it seemed, had been struck by his impeccable manners and air. Elisabeth admitted to herself that she found his friend infinitely more amusing and interesting. Of first proposals of marriage, she thought to herself, hers must certainly rank among the most original.

# Eight

AT NINE THE FOLLOWING EVENING, ALL ELISABETH'S cousins stood before her in the drawing room, ready to set out for the Wincannons' evening party. Elisabeth surveyed them with some pride as they waited for the carriage to be brought round. Great changes had been wrought in the past few weeks. Anthony's tall rangy frame was clothed in a dark blue coat from Weston which fitted him admirably and complemented his fair coloring. His pantaloons were fawn-colored and also fitted him well. If his shirt points were a trifle crumpled and his waistcoat a bit too arresting for Elisabeth's taste, she knew better than to mention it. And in any case, he'd done very well for a young gentleman thrown on his own resources in the matter of dress.

Belinda looked dazzling in a gown of the palest possible blue muslin. The delicacy of the color and the simple style she'd created set off her beauty to perfection. Her blond hair was dressed in ringlets about her face, and she carried a filmy wrap. The overall impression was of pastel fragility; Elisabeth thought, a bit guiltily, that she looked exactly like a Dresden shepherdess Miss Creedy had kept in her drawing room. Cousin Lavinia wore one of her new dresses, a lavender crepe, and she had produced a stunning cameo brooch and a pair of silver bracelets from her jewel box. She looked very well and extremely pleased with herself.

When Ames came in to tell them the carriage was ready, Elisabeth glanced quickly at her own reflection in the drawing room mirror. She had chosen a peach-colored crepe which complemented her honey-toned hair and warm complexion. Its tiny puffed sleeves showed her arms to advantage, and she'd had Ketchem do her hair in a knot on top of her head once again. She wore a string of pearls as her only jewelry. All in all, she thought to herself as they descended the stairs, a rather fine-looking group.

An elegant crowd already filled the Wincannons' drawing room when they arrived. Belinda joined Amelia and a circle of her young friends, and after a moment Tony followed her. Elisabeth saw that they were being introduced, then turned to find the viscountess approaching. She greeted her warmly and presented Lavinia.

"I see Belinda and the young man I assume must be her brother have taken care of themselves," said Lady Larenby. "Come, I want to introduce you to some of my guests."

The two cousins followed her across the room, and the viscountess began presenting them to a number of ladies who sat there. Elisabeth soon realized that her hostess was seeing to it that she met all the mothers who were bringing daughters out this season. She smiled to herself; they would certainly receive as many invitations as they could wish after this. She was then presented to the Viscount Larenby and was left to chat with him. The viscount was a tall dark man, like his son, though somewhat more slender. His hair was touched with gray here and there, and his eyes were more green than blue, but otherwise he much resembled Derek. He smiled at Elisabeth admiringly and with what she thought was curiosity. "So you are to be our new neighbor at Willowmere?" he said. "We must congratulate ourselves on gaining such a fair addition."

"I perceive you are a flatterer, sir," laughed Elisabeth.

"Not I. I leave that to the young men." He looked at her. "Like my son," he added.

Elisabeth felt her cheeks grow slightly hot. "Your son doesn't seem a man who pays compliments," she answered.

"Well, no," he agreed amiably, "he never has been. Quite the contrary, in fact. But there's no saying when he might change."

Elisabeth could think of no reply, and in a moment, the viscount turned the conversation into easier channels. "You're having work done on Willowmere, I understand?" he asked her.

Elisabeth nodded. "Though I fear it will be some time before I can officially take up residence."

"I can readily believe it. Your uncle neglected the place shockingly. I spoke to him about it once. But I made no impression, except to anger him."

"Did you know him, then?" asked Elisabeth

interestedly. "You're the first person I've met who was actually acquainted with him. Except my father, of course, and he rarely spoke of his family."

The viscount smiled. "I knew him to bow to in the street," he answered. "But Anthony Elham did not encourage any of his fellow men to know him. He was an odd creature."

"So I have heard. But I wish I'd met him in spite of that."

"You might feel differently if you'd been unceremoniously put out of his house. Yes, and had a pitcher of milk hurled after you."

Amusement lit Elisabeth's violet eyes, and they sparkled irresistibly. She raised her eyebrows in a question.

"Yes, that happened to me," continued Lord Larenby. "I admit it was the second time I called. He evidently did not approve of me on the occasion of my first visit." His eyes twinkled. "I'd told him that if he didn't do something about Willowmere a neighborhood committee would take him to law. But nothing ever came of it."

Elisabeth laughed aloud. "Oh, how I wish I might have seen it."

At that moment, a voice behind her said, "If you set yourself to charm all the pretty girls, Father, we younger men may as well give over. We'll never be able to cut you out."

Elisabeth turned to greet Derek Wincannon, who smiled down at her warmly. He met his father's eyes with an echo of the twinkle in them.

"What do you say?" continued Derek. "Will you

not retire from the field and give the next generation a chance?"

The viscount laughed. "Indeed. I know that none of you young here-and-there-ians are up to my weight." He turned back to Elisabeth. "I'm delighted to have met you, Miss Elham. I hope we can talk again later in the evening." He bowed slightly and walked away.

Elisabeth looked up at Derek Wincannon. "I was quite enjoying my conversation with your father," she told him.

"I could see that," he said. "But I couldn't allow him to monopolize you. I'm too selfish."

"London is certainly a very odd sort of place," Elisabeth replied. "People begin detailing their faults on the slightest pretext."

Her companion laughed. "What makes you say that?"

"Why, you have already told me that you are selfish and intolerant of bores," she answered. "And without my showing the slightest inclination to accuse you of such things, I think. And only yesterday I met a young man who confessed to being a fortune hunter before I had talked to him five minutes."

He frowned. "Who might that have been?"

"Lord James Darnell," she replied.

"Ah. Well, it is true, the Darnells are all to pieces. But I didn't know James went about proclaiming it."

"Oh, indeed. He first made sure that I was truly an heiress, then he promptly made me an offer."

Mr. Wincannon appeared to be torn between amusement and outrage. "He did not?"

"Oh, yes," Elisabeth assured him airily. "He told me that he often does so."

"What a ramshackle young coxcomb he must be."

"Is he not a friend of yours?"

"No," he replied, surprised. "I hardly know him. Did he say so?"

"Oh, no, it was my own notion. You see, Lord Darnell is one of the least boring men I have ever met. I thought you must have sought him out here now."

"Perhaps I should," responded Derek with a frown. "You seem quite taken with him."

"I found him outrageously amusing. He is certainly most unlike his friend the Duke of Sherbourne. Can it be true, do you think, that his father lost five thousand pounds betting on a duck?"

Her companion gave a crack of laughter. "What, the old duke? Absolutely not. He was as much of a slowtop as John."

"No, no. Lord Darnell's father. Or was it his grandfather? I've forgotten."

"It might have been either. All the Darnells are gamesters. Did James tell you of it?"

She nodded. "He said they called his father, I'm certain it was his father this time, 'Black Jack.'"

"I can see you're quite fascinated by Lord Darnell," he answered dryly. 'I should advise you to take care. He would game away your fortune in a year."

"What a shabby thing to say! I was merely repeating some amusing stories, and you take me up quite ruthlessly. I see how it is now. You may say what you please to me, even call my cousin a ninny if you like. But when I respond in kind, you fly up into the boughs. How unfair."

He was looking down at her appreciatively. "Does it seem so to you? I must apologize, then. The two things do not appear at all the same to me."

"I think I should go and see how Belinda and Tony are getting on," was Elisabeth's only reply.

His eyes twinkled. "I'm not to be forgiven all at once, I see. Very well. I'll take you to them." He offered his arm. "Young Tony has done rather well for himself thus far. Shall I put his name up for my club, do you think?"

Forgetting that she was supposed to be angry, Elisabeth stopped and turned to him. "Oh, could you do so?" she asked eagerly. "I've been rather worried about Tony. I don't know what is the best way for him to go on, and he has no one else to give him a hint. If you would befriend him, why then…" She remembered her annoyance suddenly. "But I daresay you would find that excessively boring."

Mr. Wincannon's eyes continued to register amusement. "I might," he conceded, "though he seems a bright enough lad. I'll keep an eye out to see that he doesn't come a cropper, if you like."

They'd nearly reached the group including Tony, and Elisabeth had only time to say "thank you." But her anger had disappeared, and she felt quite kindly disposed toward her companion.

Mr. Wincannon excused himself from joining the younger group, and Elisabeth could soon see why. Belinda and Anthony eagerly introduced her to a number of very young persons of both sexes, and made every effort to include her in their conversation. But the talk was exceedingly dull, limited to the parties they had attended, horses, and juvenile flirtation. Elisabeth was soon looking about for some means of escape. She saw Cousin Lavinia talking to a gentleman across the room, and she excused herself to join them, though no one appeared to take the least notice.

Lavinia received her excitedly. "Only fancy, Elisabeth," she said. "Mr. Jarrett was a friend of my brother William. Is that not astringent? They were in the same regiment. Though Mr. Jarrett was not at Salamanca. I thought, you know, that he might tell me…but of course no one can blame him for selling out. If only William had done so, indeed, he might be here with us tonight. He never did care for parties, but I daresay he might have changed a great deal as he grew older." She caught Elisabeth's eye. "Oh, Mr. Jarrett, this is my cousin, Elisabeth Elham. Mr. George Jarrett, my dear."

Elisabeth inclined her head. Mr. Jarrett appeared to be between thirty and forty years of age. Though not more than an inch taller than Elisabeth, he was stocky, and powerful arms and shoulders showed beneath his coat. His complexion was vivid, apparently burned by the sun rather than naturally ruddy, and his hair sandy red. His upper lip boasted a small neat mustache, unusual in a time when clean-shaven faces were the rule, and his eyes, looking out from under thick sandy brows, were sharp but peculiarly colorless, of a gray so pale as to be almost white. They stood out boldly against his skin. His dress was quiet, not at all shabby but with no pretensions to elegance or fashion. His face showed deep lines about the mouth and around the eyes, reflecting, Elisabeth imagined, past hardship and an ironic temper.

He suffered Elisabeth's examination with no change of expression. Indeed, it seemed to her that he allowed her time to weigh him before speaking. Then he said, "How do you do. I've just been telling your cousin that William and I were at Oxford together and did later join the same regiment. I left the army soon after, however, to pursue my fortunes abroad, and was thus luckier than he."

"Indeed?" replied Elisabeth. "I'm sorry to say I never met my cousin William."

Lavinia nodded. "Yes. It is very sad. William was younger than I, of course, and he was still at school when I made my few visits to Elisabeth's family. Then her mother died and William went into the army, so there was no further opportunity. I told him of you, Elisabeth, several times. But you know what boys are, I daresay he wouldn't have reminisced. And then, well…well, I simply lost touch. I should not have done so."

Smiling slightly, Elisabeth looked up and met a twinkle in the eyes of Mr. Jarrett. In spite of their paleness, she noticed, they compelled one's attention.

"I should have come more often," continued Lavinia. "I knew it even then. But Father began to be ill, you know, and there was no one else to look after him. Nursing an invalid takes so much of one's time. But I blame myself still. I could have visited you, and I should have."

With just a shade of difficulty, Elisabeth disengaged

her gaze from Mr. Jarrett's. "Well, it wasn't entirely your fault, Cousin Lavinia," she said. "My father hardly encouraged visitors after my mother's death."

"Yes, dear, I know," responded Lavinia, "but that doesn't really excuse me."

Elisabeth thought it best to abandon this subject. "You've been living abroad, Mr. Jarrett?" she asked, looking briefly into his face once again, then turning her eyes to the floor.

"Yes, chiefly in the West Indies, though I also spent some months in New Orleans."

"The West Indies," echoed Elisabeth. "I've heard that it is very beautiful there."

He shrugged. "There is beauty, right enough," he replied, in a curious, almost grim tone. "But there is also much that is not beautiful. It's an uncivilized part of the world, Miss Elham, whatever the planters may pretend."

He said this with no hint of boastfulness. Elisabeth was frankly intrigued. "And did you, that is, were you a planter yourself?" she asked.

"I?" He smiled at her, his teeth very white against his sunburned skin. "Oh, yes, I tried my hand at raising sugar cane. I tried many professions."

"Sugar cane?" put in Lavinia eagerly. "I have read of it. It seems quite mysterious to me. I can never get, you see, how it *looks*. It is the silliest thing, but I always visualize fields full of peppermint candy sticks." Her companions laughed. "So foolish of me," she murmured.

"I fear the reality is not nearly so romantic," Jarrett told her. "The plants are tall and thin indeed, but they are green and not particularly appealing. They're chiefly good for making rum."

"Oh, rum," answered Lavinia wisely, "such a nasty drink, I believe."

Elisabeth and Jarrett shared a smile. "Have you returned to England recently?" she asked him.

He nodded. "A matter of weeks. I feel very much a stranger here yet."

"It must be very different." Elisabeth's eyes held a faraway look. She was imagining to herself the difference.

"Yes," he said rather curtly, "it is."

His stern expression quickened Elisabeth's interest and made her wish to explore this subject, but Lavinia had other ideas. "Mr. Jarrett, you simply must tell me all you know of my brother," she said. "I saw so little of him after he left home, and I'm interested in all the details, you know."

Mr. Jarrett bowed. "I should be delighted. But unfortunately, I'm forced to leave rather early this evening, as I'm engaged to a party of friends. Perhaps you will allow me to call one day this week?" His eyes turned toward Elisabeth as he said this.

"Oh, certainly," fluttered Lavinia. "No question. A friend of William's. We shall have so much to discuss."

Mr. Jarrett seemed not quite satisfied. "If Miss Elham agrees," he put in smoothly.

Elisabeth inclined her head.

"Thank you," he continued. "I shall look forward to it. And now I must take my leave." He bowed formally.

They said goodbye, and Mr. Jarrett turned and walked away. Elisabeth noticed that he didn't stop to bid his host and hostess good night, even though the viscountess was walking toward them, but went directly out of the drawing room. She shrugged, but later she mentioned him to Lady Larenby.

"Jarrett," repeated the other, frowning and putting her finger to her lips. "I can't recall…wait, I believe Maria Coatsworth mentioned his name to me. She's old Lady Brandon's companion, you know. Such a poor cowed creature; I always feel so sorry for her. She asked if she might invite an acquaintance of hers; I'm sure the name is the same. She said he was recently back from the tropics and knew no one in London. And so he has turned out to be a friend of your family as well?" She looked about the room.

"He has gone," said Elisabeth. "He said he had another appointment."

The viscountess smiled. "Well, this is hardly likely to endear him to me. A hostess never appreciates a guest who rushes off to another party. But how strange that I didn't meet him at all. I'll make a point of doing so another time, so that I may scold him."

"Yes," said Elisabeth. "I thought it strange that he did not bid you good night."

"Well, perhaps he's shy," suggested Lady Larenby. "He knew no one here. I'm sure he felt somewhat uncomfortable."

Just then a group of guests came up to say good night to their hostess, and Elisabeth excused herself. She went to gather her party, for it was getting late. Lavinia was agreeable, but Elisabeth had some trouble pulling Belinda and Tony away from their new friends. They insisted that it was terribly early to leave, but when Elisabeth pointed out that more than half the guests had done so, they reluctantly consented.

When Elisabeth reached her bedroom later that night, she sat down in the armchair wearily. She had never realized how very exhausting a life of leisure could be. She'd rarely been so tired when she was earning her own living.

# Nine

INVITATIONS DID BEGIN TO COME IN AFTER THEIR introduction at Lady Larenby's house, and soon Elisabeth felt as if she saw her younger cousins only when they all went out together for the evening. Tony was kept constantly busy by his new friends, and he was seldom to be found about the house. Belinda's activities were less mysterious, but she too was often occupied. Even Cousin Lavinia seemed to have more to do than Elisabeth; she was always hurrying off on one errand or another.

Thus, when Mr. Jarrett called the week after the Wincannons' evening party, Elisabeth was the only member of the family in the drawing room to receive him. She was sitting in an armchair by the window, a volume of Scott open before her, when Ames ushered him in. "How do you do," she said. "How sorry Cousin Lavinia will be to find that she's missed you."

"She is out?" asked Mr. Jarrett.

"Yes. She's gone in search of rose pink embroidery cotton, but she may return at any moment. Sit down, won't you?"

When they were seated opposite one another in front of the fireplace, Mr. Jarrett said, "I must apologize for my departure after we were introduced last Friday."

"You needn't tell me," replied Elisabeth playfully. "But Lady Larenby was quite out of charity with you. She plans to scold you roundly when she meets you at last." He'd begun to look a little alarmed, and she smiled. "No need to worry," she added. "She's very charming. You simply wounded the hostess in her by hurrying off to another engagement."

Mr. Jarrett's frown didn't lift. "I suppose I have been rag-mannered again. Only now have I realized that I never introduced myself to her or her husband." He ran a hand through his sandy hair and sighed. "Having been out of England for nearly twenty years, I'm unused to polite society. Will Lady Larenby forgive me, do you think?"

"Oh, of course," answered Elisabeth. "I was only teasing you a little." He looked up, and once again, the power of his gaze surprised her. What was it about the man, she wondered, that held one's attention so. She blinked. "Tell me about the West Indies, Mr. Jarrett," she said. "I've always longed to see such places, but I've never had the opportunity to travel. Where did you live?"

He made a deprecating gesture. "I was settled in Martinique for a while, then moved to Jamaica. There is little to tell, I fear."

Elisabeth smiled. "I cannot believe it. Even the names are beautiful. Martinique. Now I grew up near a village called Sterington-on-Marsh. You cannot tell me that such vast differences in the names of places do not spring from widely divergent ways of living."

Jarrett returned her smile. "I would never say that, no."

"Well, then. There must be a great deal to tell of a place called Martinique. It is a French name, is it not?"

He nodded. "The island is French, and most of the inhabitants, except the blacks, of course."

Elisabeth's eyes widened a bit. "I...I hadn't thought. Were there, do you mean, slaves?"

The lines around Jarrett's mouth deepened. "Yes, Miss Elham, I do. So you see, I was right to say that everything is not beautiful in the Indies."

"Yes." Elisabeth stared across the room for a moment, then said slowly, "I knew, of course, that such practices were common elsewhere. But somehow, my knowledge was...was of an abstract nature. How can they let it go on?"

Mr. Jarrett seemed impatient. "If you travel in Russia, Miss Elham, you will see slaves. Indeed, if you were to look into some of the manufacturing plants in this country, or better yet into some of the slums not more than a mile from this house, you would see them also, though they don't bear the name. Men in the Indies are no better or worse than their counterparts elsewhere. It is part of human nature to enslave."

This harsh indictment left Elisabeth speechless for a moment. Finally, she said, "You're very cynical, Mr. Jarrett. For my part, I prefer to believe that mankind is more compassionate."

Mr. Jarrett smiled at her. "And I hope you will never have reason to think otherwise," he said. "I must again beg your pardon. You can see, no doubt, how unhappy I was in the Indies. I didn't like it, and I was not a success there. As soon as I was able, I returned. It is hot and provincial, and the work is bitterly hard, even if one is not a slave. As I must have by now made you aware, there is no society to speak of; thus, I have lost whatever manners I once possessed. I think you would find traveling much less exciting than you seem to imagine. Let us talk of something else."

Elisabeth was taken aback by this abrupt command, but she was less offended than interested. This man was an original. "Very well," she answered. "But I must say, you're a great disappointment to me. I understood that travelers were uniformly eager to tell about the countries they visited. You've quite discredited that impression." She saw that he was frowning and hurried on. "Tell me instead about my cousin William, then. We're a very odd family, you know. We've all kept very much to ourselves, so that I'm ridiculously ignorant about my relations. Was cousin William like his sister?"

Mr. Jarrett smiled. "Not very like. There was some physical resemblance, I believe, though I never met Miss Ottley as a girl. William was extremely level-headed and sensible, and very intelligent. He was one of the finest officers in our regiment."

"Ah. It's doubly sad, then, that he was killed."

Mr. Jarrett nodded soberly. "When I got the news in Martinique, I was stunned. He was one of the best friends I ever had, indeed, one of the only friends I had left in England," he added more quietly.

"Lavinia told me he died very bravely," put in Elisabeth sympathetically.

"Yes. He led his men in a suicidal charge which turned the tide of battle in his area, though it did not, of course, turn defeat to victory. That has never reconciled me to his death, however. I've never understood why anyone imagined that it would do so." He looked up and smiled. "But he was a good man and a jolly one; you may be proud to claim him as part of your family."

"Indeed, I am," answered Elisabeth. A silence fell, as she cast about in her mind for a subject that would cause this oddly interesting man to reveal more of himself. But he spoke first.

"You are also new to London, I understand?" he said. "Your cousin mentioned that you've recently taken up residence in town?"

Elisabeth nodded. "During the past few months."

"Your cousin was full of your kindness to her," he replied. He looked full into her eyes and smiled. The whiteness of his teeth and their evenness was again striking against his tanned skin.

Elisabeth looked down. "I've been very fortunate," she told him. "It's easy to be kind in such circumstances, is it not?" She felt a little flustered by his bluntness of speech and steady gaze.

"It is," he agreed. "That is a truth not many discover. I see you are an intelligent woman, Miss Elham."

Elisabeth smiled ironically. "Why, thank you, sir."

He returned her smile, a hint of self-mockery dancing in his eyes. "And a reader." He picked up the volume of Scott she'd laid aside. "Ah, this is the fellow who's all the rage nowadays. I haven't yet tried him. Shall I?"

"Certainly," answered Elisabeth. "You won't care for Scott, but he'll provide you with subject matter for drawing room conversation." Her eyes twinkled.

He gave a crack of laughter. "Something I want badly, I suppose you mean." He leafed through the book. "But why do you say I shan't like it?"

"Oh, it is very romantic. Not at all your sort of thing."

He raised his eyebrows, his smile widening. "You think not?"

"Oh, no. A man who can talk as you do of the Indies, and who won't even relate his adventures there, can have no interest in Scott's imaginary pirates and brigands. You'll find it stupid and silly, I predict."

Mr. Jarrett laughed again as he put the book back on the table. "You are severe. I see that I must guard myself. I'm not to be allowed any airs, it seems."

"Was it only airs?" asked Elisabeth, cocking her head at him. "How disappointing."

Jarrett threw up a hand. "Peace, Miss Elham. I cry mercy. You must not make a game of a poor provincial, home at last."

Elisabeth sobered immediately. "Indeed, I didn't mean to do so. I hope I haven't offended you."

"Of course not. I don't think you could."

Before Elisabeth could reply to a remark she took to be a compliment, Lavinia came into the drawing room, all aflutter to find Mr. Jarrett there. The conversation turned back to her brother once more, and she told a number of anecdotes involving William, turning to their visitor for corroboration in each case. He obligingly gave it, but after a few minutes, he rose to take his leave. In spite of Lavinia's protests, he insisted on going.

"Well, if that is not exceedingly fractious," continued Lavinia when they were alone once more. "If I had but known, I certainly wouldn't have gone out this morning. I might have picked up the things I needed another time, you know; and in any case I couldn't match my yarn. Can you credit it, Elisabeth? They've discontinued making the shade I need. How vexatious that Mr. Jarrett couldn't stay for luncheon. It is so seldom that one meets anyone acquainted with the family. Of course, Uncle Elham was a sort of recluse, and so was your own father, Elisabeth. Not of course, that he was at all like your uncle. Tony, now, has turned out quite differently, fortunately."

Her flow of talk continued, but Elisabeth answered somewhat absently. She couldn't put their oddly arresting caller out of her mind.

❧

The next event of importance on their schedule was the visit to Vauxhall Gardens in the party of the Duke of Sherbourne. All of them were to attend, and Belinda was wildly excited. When their host's carriage came to fetch them, it was seen to contain his mother also, and sitting across, next to Lord James Darnell, was a younger woman. The duchess introduced her as Jane Taunton, a young friend. As Elisabeth sat down in the chaise, she said, "I've brought Jane along to meet you, Elisabeth. You'll be great friends, I'll be bound." The two women looked at each other. Jane appeared a little older than Elisabeth; she wasn't at all pretty, being over tall and very thin with pale hair, freckled skin, and washed-out brown eyes. Her expression was not encouraging.

The duchess laughed. "Yes, I daresay you will eye one another like strange cats for quite a while. And now you're angry because I've forced you upon one another. At any rate, Jane is. But I know what I'm about." She leaned back in the corner of the carriage, chuckling.

By this time, Belinda had settled herself, and they started out. There was little conversation as they drove, and soon the duke was escorting the ladies to the box he'd reserved for the evening and seating them at the table. Elisabeth was placed at the duke's right hand next to Lord Darnell. Belinda was across from her, on the duke's other side, then Tony, Lavinia, and the duchess at the bottom of the board. Jane Taunton was on the other side of Lord Darnell.

It immediately became apparent that the duke meant to devote his attention to Belinda. Tony began to look bored almost as soon as he sat down; Elisabeth hoped, a bit ruefully, that he would last the evening. Lavinia and the duchess became engrossed in a discussion of the latest *on dits*, occasionally trying to pull Jane into it, so Elisabeth perforce turned to Lord Darnell.

"What is it?" he asked when he saw the expression on her face. "It's exceedingly selfish not to share a joke."

Elisabeth's smile broadened. "Is it, indeed? But it wasn't a joke I was thinking of."

"What a bouncer!" he replied. "I think it a very good joke to see poor Tony sitting between your cousins. He looks blue-deviled."

She laughed. "You're quite right. That's what made me smile."

"A man who lives by his wits must be clever. By the by, would you care to meet my mother?"

"Your mother?" echoed Elisabeth. "Why, ah, of course. I should be delighted."

"No, you wouldn't. But she wants to see you. I told her about you, you know."

Elisabeth's eyes twinkled. "You told her you'd unearthed a new heiress?"

"That's the ticket," he agreed breezily. He leaned back in his chair and threw an arm across its back, smiling winningly. "Told her I'd found a gem of the first water. But I should refuse her invitation, if I were you."

"What idiotic things you say," she laughed. "Why?"

"My mother's a regular Leaky Liz. I came across a word once when I was at school that describes her perfectly. 'Lachrymose.' Have you heard it? There never was a woman cried as much as my mother."

Elisabeth was torn between laughter and shock. "What a ramshackle son you must be."

"On the contrary," he responded indignantly. "I'm a model son. Do I not make every effort to get her a rich daughter-in-law? But she's given up on the Darnells, she tells me. I believe my father was a disappointment to her. As she must have been to him," he added meditatively. "They did not deal together particularly well."

Elisabeth shook her head. "You are incorrigible. What am I to think if you insist on talking so?"

"Why, you are to think me charming," he answered with innocent surprise. "What else? And very open and honest. And altogether the sort of person with whom you would choose to spend your life." He grinned.

"And pass my fortune to?" she added.

"Of course. You know, really, I'd enjoy it more than anyone else I can think of. Because I know what it is to want money, you see, and to work to get it. And how to live well, that is extremely important."

"Since I believe you've just described talking to me as work," replied Elisabeth humorously, "I don't feel the slightest inclination to part with a penny."

Lord Darnell gave a shout of laughter. "Oh, you're worth my steel," he said. "Have you any notion how many heiresses are utter dunces?"

"I have some idea," she answered, her lips twitching. "I was a teacher of several."

"It's wonderful indeed to find a girl who is both needle-witted and rich." Lord Darnell tried to look very serious. "You know, I think perhaps I could really fall in love with you."

"If you think I will believe such a remark coming from you," replied Elisabeth, "you must think me a dunce, after all."

He grinned. "I deserved that, but I almost believe I'm serious. We shall see. Meanwhile, what do you think of Vauxhall? That seems a safe subject. Have you been here before?"

"No," said Elisabeth, looking around at the lantern-lit trees and the elegant crowd. "It's lovely. I like it very much."

"We might go for a stroll along the paths," he suggested. "Some of the avenues are quite interesting." His innocent look was hilarious.

"Certainly," replied Elisabeth, relishing the surprise on his face. "Miss Taunton, Lord Darnell has suggested a walk about the grounds. Will you come?" Her eyes danced as she turned back to the young man, and he made the gesture of a fencer acknowledging a hit.

Miss Taunton agreed without visible enthusiasm, and the three of them started off. At first, Lord Darnell kept up his stream of outrageous chatter, with Elisabeth responding occasionally and Jane Taunton silent. But the young man could not allow any female to ignore him for long, and he soon addressed the unattending girl. "You don't seem to approve of my conversation, Miss Taunton," he said. "Perhaps you wish to talk of something else?"

"I cannot imagine we have any interests in common," answered Miss Taunton in a voice devoid of any interest or any hint of flirtation.

"What a setdown!" Lord Darnell struck his forehead. "I'm put in my place. You have cut me to the quick, Miss Taunton." She said nothing, only looked at him skeptically. "You don't care for that?"

"If it were true," she said, "I should apologize, certainly. But I don't believe it."

"Whew! Suddenly I feel a cold draft. Why do I begin to sense that you don't like me?"

"Oh, I don't dislike you," replied Jane Taunton equably. "I merely think you a scatterbrained fribble who isn't worth my time." She gave him a thin smile. "And you would have to admit, if truthful, that you think me an unattractive female with neither the wit nor the money to interest you. I dislike hypocritical chitchat."

Elisabeth smiled delightedly, and Lord Darnell gaped. "Good God," he said. "What is a man to answer to that?"

"I congratulate you," said Elisabeth to the other girl. "I never thought to see him silenced."

Jane shrugged.

"Ah, you're going to combine against me, I see," said the young man. "It always happens when one makes the mistake of going about with more than one female. I'm overmatched, I protest. Let us go back to the box."

Laughing, Elisabeth agreed, and they turned back. When they reached the table, they found Belinda and the duke still deep in conversation, but the duchess had shifted her attention to Tony and was firing a series of questions at him. Tony looked less bored, but very harried. Elisabeth changed her seat, placing herself next to Jane. She was intrigued by this outspoken girl. It's strange, she thought to herself, but all the people I've liked so far in London are out of the common way—she glanced over at the duchess—one could almost say eccentric.

"We should try to get better acquainted," she said to Miss Taunton. "The duchess thinks we'd like each other, it seems."

The other girl looked at her hesitantly. "Yes, it is odd. It's not like her to take one to meet people."

Elisabeth smiled at her. "Well, I must say that I agree with her so far. You're quite the most interesting girl I have met in London."

Jane's expression softened. "I am not sure that's a true compliment. Girls in London tend to be horridly insipid." Her eyes moved involuntarily in Belinda's direction.

Elisabeth suppressed a smile. "Do you find it so? How do you avoid them?"

"I don't go out," said the other girl rather defensively. "It's generally a waste of time, and I have tasks to occupy me."

"What?" asked Elisabeth.

The other looked at her doubtfully, but Elisabeth's expression showed real interest. "I'm most interested in literature," she said. "I do a great deal of reading and some writing." She smiled deprecatingly. "Didn't the duchess tell you? I'm a hack journalist, and she's the closest thing to a patron I've yet acquired. She takes an interest in me because she knows my mother."

"A writer!" exclaimed Elisabeth. "I've never before met a writer. What do you write?"

Jane's eyes dropped. "Articles for the ladies' magazines. On the relative virtues of Denmark Lotion and crushed strawberries for removing freckles, for example, a subject which ought to be of the highest interest to me, of course."

Her tone was so bitter that Elisabeth blinked. "But if you don't like it," she asked reasonably, "why do you continue?"

Jane seemed to recall herself. "I'm sorry. My struggles can be of no interest to you."

"On the contrary, I'm extremely interested."

Seeing from her expression that this was true, Jane flushed slightly; her pale complexion made the color seem even brighter. "I support myself thus," she said, "so that I may do my real work." Her voice dropped to a whisper. "I write poetry, you see."

Realizing that she was sensitive on this score, Elisabeth went carefully. "I think that is splendid, admirable, in fact. Have I seen any of your poems, I wonder?"

"Oh, they're not published," said Jane sadly. "No one wants them. They care only for rubbishy articles on feminine fashions."

Elisabeth looked sympathetic. "That will change, I'm sure. But perhaps I've seen one of your pieces in the journals, at least?"

"I never use my real name there." Now that she saw she was not to be mocked, Miss Taunton was more communicative. "You might have seen something of mine in the last *Ladies Home Companion*; a stupid thing, but mine own, on French twill trimming."

Elisabeth shook her head. "I must look for it; I believe Belinda has a copy."

"No doubt," replied Jane, shrugging. "It's pure rubbish." She paused, then smiled with genuine good humor for the first time. "As are all my articles. I do them for the money, little as it is, and to become known in literary circles, so that I can someday be recognized as a real writer. One must start somewhere."

"I'm very impressed and perhaps a bit envious. I

should like to be able to write. Will you show me some of your poetry?"

Miss Taunton looked down. "I…that is, we might look over a little. I'm not sure you would enjoy it."

"I am sure I would," said Elisabeth.

Just then, the duchess turned toward the girls and claimed their attention. She'd finished with Tony, leaving that young man looking rather hunted, and now said, "There, didn't I tell you you'd like each other? And was I not right?"

"You were," answered Elisabeth. "I might have known that any friend of yours would be fascinating."

The duchess chuckled. "How? After meeting my son." She shook her head. "Well, at least he seems ready to settle at last. I have great hopes for my grandchildren." She turned back to the girls. "I've observed that intelligence is often inherited by the third generation even when it deserts the second."

Jane laughed, and Elisabeth shook her head.

"Well, and so you are to be friends," continued the older woman. "It will do you both good. Elisabeth will have someone sensible to talk to, and Jane will be drawn out of the horrid little garret she inhabits. You'll both learn something, I daresay."

"Hardly a garret, Your Grace," put in Jane. "You will give Miss Elham quite a distorted impression of me."

"Ha. I wager she can draw her own conclusions without my help. And does, too." The duchess turned to Elisabeth. "And so, when shall I give my ball for you, Elisabeth?"

"That must be up to you."

"Nonsense. Choose the day. What about in three weeks' time?"

Elisabeth smiled. "That is agreeable," she said.

"Good." She looked at Jane. "I daresay you will refuse to come, as usual?"

The girl nodded.

"What your mother must think," sighed the duchess. "Girls nowadays. It wouldn't have been allowed in my time."

"My family feels as you do," said Jane, "but I am not a child, after all. I must be allowed some freedom."

The duchess snorted. "Not a child? Why, of course you are. Do you call six-and-twenty grown up? Your father, were he still alive, would have fetched you home without delay and set you to samplers once again."

"Yes, he would," replied Jane stiffly. "You cannot oppose my independence more than he did."

Seeing that she'd offended the girl, the duchess softened. "Well, it's none of my affair, I suppose. I simply believe you'd be happier at home with your mother than living in some out-of-the-world rooms and writing all the day long."

"You are wrong," said Jane decisively.

The duchess nodded. "I daresay. I don't understand young people these days. Now, in my day…well, well, enough of that. Let us talk scandal or some other innocuous thing. There, at least, we can agree."

Jane's countenance relaxed, and Elisabeth smiled. Soon, the duchess was regaling them with a most improper anecdote about the Prince Regent, and she kept up a flow of such talk until it grew late and they began to think of leaving.

# *Ten*

Elisabeth went out early the next day to call on her banker. She had a pleasant conference with this distinguished gentleman and had started home when a noise in the street ahead attracted her attention. She leaned out the carriage window to see what was the matter. Several vehicles were stopped, obstructed by a group of men standing in the middle of the street, shouting. They paid no heed to the objections of the drivers; indeed, they didn't seem to hear them at all. Three of the men had their backs to Elisabeth, but the other two faced her, and she stared at them curiously, for their appearance was unusual. Both were dark-skinned, very tall and strong-looking. They wore loose shirts and trousers of white cloth fastened by belts of black leather. Though they contributed little to the argument in progress, their presence attracted most attention.

Suddenly, one of the more conventionally dressed gentlemen began to shout very clearly. "You'll not get away with this," he cried. "Perhaps you don't believe the law will touch you, but some means will be found.

I swear it." There was more unintelligible conversation, then this man shouted again. "You blackguard! You care nothing that her heart was broken. The money is not the half of it." One of the other men murmured something that seemed to fan the speaker's rage. He clenched his fists and swung wildly, but the others restrained him gently. After further inaudible talk, they took their still raging companion over to the side of the street and remonstrated with him quietly; the fifth man started off along the opposite pavement away from them.

The carriages were able to move once more, and when Elisabeth's vehicle passed the solitary man walking down the sidewalk, she turned curiously to look at him, wondering idly whose heart he was supposed to have broken so cruelly. To her astonishment, she recognized him. It was Mr. Jarrett. He was strolling casually now, his hands in his pockets. Elisabeth watched him, amazed, until he was lost in the crowd behind the chaise. Then she leaned back in her seat. Whatever had that been about, she wondered? It seemed that Mr. Jarrett had a more interesting past than he had let on.

When she reached home again, she found that Mr. Wincannon had called and was being entertained by Belinda and Lavinia in the drawing room. Upstairs, she removed her hat and tidied her hair, then started down to join them, smiling wickedly at the thought of him in that company.

Entering the room, she found her amusement justified, and her smile broadened. Mr. Wincannon did indeed look exceedingly bored as he listened to

Lavinia's description of their expedition to Vauxhall. He rose with alacrity when he saw Elisabeth and greeted her with what she could only call relief. Her eyes were dancing as she returned his salute and inquired about his health, causing him to shrug and say, "Yes, I'm quite well." They all sat down, and the conversation faltered for a moment. Then Mr. Wincannon ventured, "You've been trying out your new carriage, I'm told. How did the team do? Tony chose very well for you, I must say."

"He did indeed," answered Elisabeth warmly. "They are beautiful steppers and good-tempered into the bargain. I'm very pleased with them."

"I considered buying them myself, when Barton put them on the market," said Derek. "But I have several young colts coming along now in my own stables, so I decided not to bid."

"It is fortunate for us you didn't. You might have run the price up quite beyond our touch."

Mr. Wincannon laughed. "Oh, no," he replied. There was a short pause, then he added, "I came by today to see if you would care to go for a drive. However, since you've just come in, I imagine you not. Perhaps another time?"

Elisabeth inclined her head. "I should like that."

He nodded briskly. "I shall take my leave, then. I have kept Miss Ottley and Miss Brinmore too long already waiting for you to come in." He rose.

Elisabeth went down with him, and they stood for a moment in the hall.

"Thank God you came in," he said. "I should have done something rash otherwise."

"What?" asked Elisabeth. "I could see you were bored. What is your method in such cases?"

He shook his head at her. "Not something you would care to see in your drawing room, I assure you. I shan't call again when you're not at home."

"Actually, I was about to leave. That would have been my only revenge."

"Very tame," mocked Elisabeth.

"Alas. My bark belies my bite. I'm really the meekest of men." His eyes twinkled.

"Indeed," she replied in the same spirit, "I'm glad to know it." Her smile faded. "But as it happens, I wished to speak to you. I'm glad you didn't go."

He looked at her inquiringly. "Is anything amiss?"

"No, at least, I hope not. It's just that we see nothing of Tony these days. Or only rarely see him, I should say. I've been a bit worried. He almost never says where he's been or with whom. I know I can't keep him in leading strings, but you were kind enough to say that you would watch over him, and so I thought…" She stopped and looked up at him.

"Watch over him," repeated Derek with distaste. "He would object if he heard you say that. And I didn't promise to do it, either. I said I'd keep an eye out." He went on before she could reply, raising a hand to forestall her. "And I have done so. Somehow I felt you'd hold me to it." He smiled to take the sting out of this remark. "You needn't worry. Tony is indulging in some of the usual amusements of a young man thrown on the town, but he's done nothing beyond the line. I should imagine he's completely happy."

"Oh, yes," replied Elisabeth. "He seems so. But I

was thinking the other night…that is, I am afraid he has been to a…a gaming house."

Mr. Wincannon laughed. "I imagine he's been to several by this time." Elisabeth's shocked expression appeared to amuse him. "My dear Miss Elham, all young men of fashion in London go at one time or another to Watier's or one of the other reputable gambling houses. That doesn't mean they become addicted to gaming. These are not hells where a green youth is fleeced, you know."

"I know nothing about it," she answered a little impatiently. "Is it also accepted practice for a young gentleman to drink too much and attempt to…to 'mill someone down' at a boxing parlor and stay out half the night doing heaven knows what?"

Her companion nodded. "Young Tony is simply trying his wings. You have nothing to be concerned about." Seeing that she didn't look particularly reassured, he continued, "I'll tell you if he gives you cause for worry. Will that satisfy you?"

Elisabeth brightened. "Oh, it would make me feel immeasurably better to know that you are overseeing him. I know I'm taking monstrous advantage of your kindness. But I have no one else to consult, you see." She hesitated for a moment. "And somehow, I feel that you're exactly the sort of man…that is, I believe that you can be trusted to…" She foundered to a stop. "I do thank you for taking the trouble to help me."

"It's a pleasure," he said. His eyes were dancing, but his smile was warm. "I can think of few things I'd rather do."

Elisabeth almost thought he meant to take her hand.

She moved toward the stairs a bit nervously. "Thank you," she said again.

He bowed slightly. "I shall call again to take you driving. I hope to be more fortunate in finding you in. Goodbye."

"Goodbye," answered Elisabeth. He went out the door, but she stood motionless on the first stair for some time, her expression unsettled. There was a slight frown showing about her eyes, but a smile played across the corners of her mouth. Finally, she shook her head slightly and turned to go back to the drawing room.

The next morning, Elisabeth set out to call on Jane Taunton. Warned that Jane lived "quite out of the world" in lodgings in Kensington, Elisabeth was prepared to find herself in an unfashionable neighborhood, but looking around Jane's two cramped and shabby rooms, she was a little shocked. Clearly, Jane had not yet succeeded in making her own way as a writer.

The parlor was set up as a study, with tall bookshelves covering most of the walls. They were crammed with books, piles of which overflowed onto the worn carpet. Two long windows looked out onto some straggling flower beds, and Jane sat at a large but tidy desk in front of one of them. She wore an old gown of pale green, which did not become her, and a pair of gold-rimmed spectacles. These she removed when Elisabeth came in, rising to greet her with a mixture of gladness and unease. She indicated an armchair near the desk, and Elisabeth sat down facing her.

"How comfortable this is," said Elisabeth kindly. "I wish I had made myself such a room." She surveyed the amber curtains, noticing a large gray cat on the windowsill, who returned her scrutiny from under lowered lids. "I haven't nearly so many books, of course." She smiled. "You look very much at home here."

"I am," answered Jane. "You needn't praise it overmuch. I know it isn't smart or conventional, but it's worth living so to maintain my freedom." She looked around. "I am most often happy here."

"I'm certain you are," replied Elisabeth, trying to show that she meant it. Jane's tone had been both defensive and a bit embarrassed. She looked over the books nearest her on the shelves. "Pope, Dryden, Shakespeare. You have an enviable collection. But don't you read the modern poets?"

"Oh, yes," said Jane. "They are there." She pointed to another shelf.

"Ah. Cowper, Scott, even Byron. Yes, I see. Which is your favorite?"

Jane smiled. "Actually, I'm much taken with two other modern poets. I was rereading this when you came in. Do you know it?" She held up a slim leather-bound volume.

Elisabeth read the title on the spine. "*Lyrical Ballads.* No, I haven't heard of it. Is it very new?"

"It's been out more than fifteen years. Relatively new, I suppose." Her tone became didactic. "Mr. Wordsworth and Mr. Coleridge are trying to do something quite fresh. They wish to bring poetry closer to the common man's experience and also infuse a sort of mystery into it."

Elisabeth frowned. "That seems a contradiction to me. Pardon me, I know nothing about it, of course."

"No," responded Jane eagerly. "You've hit upon a very important point. It is very difficult to do. But there is a sort of mystery, I think, that has nothing to do with the intellect. To put it into words, that's the thing." She clenched a fist and looked off through the window.

"Do these two succeed?" asked Elisabeth.

"What? Oh, it's hard to say. Some of the poems I like very much, but others are failures, I think." She paused and smiled again. "You mustn't allow me to run on about my particular hobbyhorse."

"You weren't. And I'm very interested. I was a teacher of literature for several years, you know."

"I didn't." Jane looked interested. "I've thought of teaching myself."

Elisabeth made a wry face. "You wouldn't like it. The students are rarely interested in literature. In fact, most see it as a form of punishment from which they will be released only upon achieving a certain age."

Jane laughed. "A lowering reflection. I was always fascinated by what I read."

"You must have been a model pupil."

"Oh, no, you should talk with my old governess. She thought me quite hopeless. I was incapable of learning geography or arithmetic, and I only endured languages because they allowed me to read more works of fiction. She finally gave up in despair."

Elisabeth laughed. "I was nearly the same, though I doubt my dedication to my studies was so strong." She looked up at the shelves again. "Are you fond of Byron? I have read only a little myself. Miss Creedy, the mistress of the school where I was, didn't approve of him, so it was difficult to keep a copy about."

"I'm not really," said the other girl, "though I know it's an unfashionable attitude. I find him affected." She shrugged. "But perhaps I'm too much influenced by his absurd antics about town. I'm not a good judge of living writers, I fear. It may be that I envy them too much to see their value."

"Oh, dear," replied Elisabeth, "I suppose then you wouldn't like to hear about a Byronic hero I've discovered among my acquaintance."

Jane raised her eyebrows and laughed. "Another? I'd have thought that one Lord Byron was enough for any society."

Elisabeth frowned. "Well, actually, Mr. Jarrett isn't much like Lord Byron. His manners are a bit abrupt, but I can't see him sitting down to vinegar and potatoes for dinner, as Lord Byron is said to do. But he appears to have a mysterious past, full of unnamed crimes."

Jane leaned back in her chair. "Jarrett," she repeated meditatively. "The name is not familiar."

Elisabeth described the incident she'd witnessed the day before. "So you see," she finished, "he's haunted by a broken heart."

"It does indeed fit," agreed Jane. "A spotted past, an irate pursuer, a stoic exterior, the romantic West Indies. It might be out of *The Corsair*. Have you seen this Mr. Jarrett since you observed this?"

Elisabeth shook her head. "He's only a distant acquaintance. I've talked to him just once, really."

"We must find out more about him," said Jane.

"Do you think so? It was my first wish, I admit."

"Oh, there's no question. One cannot leave such a

mystery unsolved. I shall make some inquiries. I have certain rather unconventional friends, shall we say."

"He is not much known in London, however," put in Elisabeth.

"Nonetheless." Jane smiled mischievously.

"Ah. Well, I wouldn't want to cause him any trouble."

"I'm not a gudgeon. I will be most circumspect. It will remain our conspiracy." Jane smiled.

Elisabeth returned her smile. "I admit I'm curious." She glanced at the clock on the mantel. "Oh, I must go. I promised Belinda I'd help her with some sewing this afternoon. She's making a gown for the duchess's ball, and she's nearly frantic over it."

"Ah," replied Jane, rising. "You may see me there, after all. The duchess is very insistent. She refuses to give up the idea that I may yet marry and cease to worry my mother by living in such a scandalous way."

Elisabeth smiled. "I'll be glad to see you."

"Well, since there will be someone sensible to talk to, I may give in." Elisabeth started toward the door. "Wait a moment," continued Jane. She walked over to one of the farther shelves and pulled out three slender volumes. "Here's something you might like," she said, holding them out to Elisabeth. "You seem to be fond of the modern writers, and this is scarcely two years old."

Elisabeth took it. "*Pride and Prejudice*," she read. "What is it? A volume of essays?"

"It's a novel. And a most unusual one, at that. It reminds me much more of *Rasselas* than of the silly works popular today. Try it and tell me what you think. By the by, the heroines are namesakes of ours."

"I shall," replied Elisabeth, tucking it under her arm. "Thank you."

Jane escorted her to the stairs. "I am glad you came," she said. "I see very few people. By choice, you understand. But you're welcome to call again. I enjoyed our talk." She smiled wryly. "Something I seldom say, I should tell you."

"Thank you. I enjoyed it also. I will certainly come again soon." She paused in the doorway. "Oh, dear, you were to show me some of your poetry; I quite forgot to ask."

Jane flushed. "It's not terribly good, you know."

"Indeed I do not. I'm eager to read it. But it must wait until another time now. I'm sorry."

# *Eleven*

ELISABETH BEGAN HER NEW BOOK IMMEDIATELY AND found it delightful. But continual interruptions soon made her wonder if she'd ever finish. Three mornings after her visit to Jane Taunton, she was sitting in the drawing room with a volume open before her. She expected no one and had settled down confidently when Ames entered the room and handed her a card.

"Lady Darnell," Elisabeth read. "Oh, dear. Lachrymose."

"I beg your pardon, miss?"

"What? Oh, never mind, Ames." She frowned at the card. "I suppose I must see her."

When Lady Darnell came in, Elisabeth surveyed her with some surprise. She didn't know exactly what she'd expected, but it wasn't this slender, willowy lady dressed in fluttering draperies. "How do you do," she said. "It's kind of you to call. Please come and sit down."

Lady Darnell opened her very pale blue eyes even wider and gathered her diaphanous shawl closely about her shoulders. "Oh, you are very beautiful," she cried. "James told me so, but I longed to see for myself."

A bit nonplussed, Elisabeth smiled. "Thank you. But I'm afraid he exaggerated if he said that. Do sit down, won't you?"

Lady Darnell made no move to do so. Rather, she put one beringed hand to her forehead, neatly avoiding any disarrangement of the blond curls clustered there. "You *are* beautiful," she said, with a hint of petulance in her voice. "I won't have you criticizing yourself."

Elisabeth's eyes began to twinkle.

"Oh, how happy I am to meet you at last," said her guest as she sank down on the sofa. "James talks of nothing else. He is utterly *bouleversé*, you know."

"Ah," said Elisabeth. "Would you care for a cup of tea?"

"Oh, no. I never take anything at this time of the morning. My health is rather delicate, you see, and I must take great care."

"I'm sorry," replied Elisabeth.

"Yes," answered her guest airily. "It's a great trial to me. It comes from my mother; she was excessively sickly. I daresay she hardly enjoyed four well days a month after my youngest sister was born." Lady Darnell seemed to take a certain satisfaction in this fact.

"How…how unfortunate." Elisabeth cleared her throat. "We all enjoyed our outing to Vauxhall Gardens with your son last week. I am sorry my cousin Lavinia is away from home. I know she'd like to meet you."

Lady Darnell murmured a polite rejoinder. "This is a lovely room," she continued. "Have you refurnished it lately?"

"When I moved into the house, yes. My uncle left a great deal to be done."

"A great deal," echoed her visitor absently. "Those curtains are very fine velvet. I daresay they were frightfully expensive."

"Why, yes, I believe they were." Elisabeth might have been offended had she not been so amused by her companion's expression. Greed, envy, and acquisitiveness were about equally mixed with desperate hope on her face.

Lady Darnell seemed to recall herself. "I'm so fond of blue," she said.

"A lovely color," agreed Elisabeth. A short silence fell, during which it seemed to Elisabeth that her guest was totting up the value of every object in the drawing room.

"I hope you will come to dinner," said Lady Darnell at last, with great difficulty tearing her eyes from the Chinese vase on the mantel. "I should so like you to meet my daughters."

"You're very kind. You have more than one daughter, then?"

Lady Darnell gave a high laugh. "Oh, lud, yes. I have three daughters. Is it not diverting? Though everyone says we look more like sisters."

"I'm sure you do," answered Elisabeth obediently. "When you came in, I could hardly believe you were of an age to be Lord Darnell's mother." She consoled herself with the fact that this statement was absolutely true.

Lady Darnell preened a bit. "Oh, you are too kind. I must reconcile myself to advancing age now that James is old enough to set up his own household." Here she gave Elisabeth a sharp glance. "And my second daughter is ready to come out."

Elisabeth was finding this conversation difficult. "One of your daughters is out, then?" she asked. "What is her name? Perhaps I've met her."

"Aurelia is my oldest. She has been eighteen these six months, but she is only just out. She has not gone about much as yet." Privately, Elisabeth wondered whether they lacked the money to bring her out properly. "Then Portia is seventeen. She is only too eager to leave the schoolroom also. And Augusta is fifteen, though anyone would take her for a year older, as I tell her."

"What, uh, splendid names you've given them."

Lady Darnell looked pleased. "Are they not? I prefer the old Roman names. They have such a solid sound."

"Umm," replied Elisabeth. "Well, I shall hope to meet them one day."

"Perhaps you can come to dinner on Thursday next?"

"I'll have to ask my cousins if they're free," said the girl, looking for a way to avoid this invitation.

Lady Darnell pouted. "Oh, I'd so hoped you would come alone, just a quiet family party, you know. Are you already engaged for Thursday evening?"

"No," said Elisabeth. "That is, I am not precisely certain…"

"Wonderful," interrupted Lord Darnell's mother. "You may bring your maid with you, of course, and I'm sure James will be happy to escort you home. We shall expect you at seven."

"But, I…" began Elisabeth.

"No need to worry, my dear," continued Lady Darnell airily. "It will be quite informal. And now I must go. I promised Aurelia I would go shopping with her today. She is utterly dependent on my judgment in matters of dress, you see." Lady Darnell rose with these words and drifted toward the door. Elisabeth could see no way of evading her invitation, short of outright rudeness, so she accepted the inevitable with as much grace as she could muster.

Elisabeth returned to her book, but her enjoyment of it was broken. She spent some minutes going over the conversation just past, trying to determine how she could have managed it better, but no amount of thinking gave her the answer. Lady Darnell had been an irresistible force. Still, Elisabeth was annoyed with herself. "Stupid," she said aloud. "You certainly made a mull of that."

"What have you made a mull of?" asked an amused voice from the doorway behind her, and Elisabeth turned quickly to see Derek Wincannon standing there.

"I told Ames I would come straight up, since I'm a few minutes late, and I thought you might have given me up." He raised his eyebrows at Elisabeth's uncomprehending expression. "We had fixed today to go driving, had we not?"

"Oh, dear, I'd completely forgotten. How bird-witted I am today."

Mr. Wincannon smiled wryly. Though he'd never spent much time with young ladies of the *ton*, the few such engagements he'd made had been treated with flattering enthusiasm. He was not accustomed to having his attentions ignored or his appointments forgotten. This was part of his fascination with Elisabeth, he did not doubt. Her unconscious originality, which made her unlike any woman he had met hitherto, compelled his interest and dispelled his customary boredom. But these welcome sensations were accompanied by a good deal of unease and chagrin. Had she any interest in him except as a preceptor for young Tony? His smile twisted further. "You are not a flatterer, are you, Miss Elham?" he said.

"I beg pardon?"

"Nothing. Are you occupied then? Shall we have to put off our expedition once again?"

"Oh, no, I should like to go. If you will only sit down a moment while I get my hat."

On their drive, she told him about her new book, excusing her forgetfulness by extolling its virtues, and he expressed interest. "One seldom finds a really good new novel," he said. "I must try this one, if you recommend it so highly."

"Oh, I'm not sure you would care for it," faltered Elisabeth. "Gentlemen wouldn't be interested in it, I think."

"Is it so improper?" replied her companion, his eyes twinkling.

"Of course it is not improper!" She laughed. "But it is, well, not precisely a romance, but a story of young ladies. You may try it, certainly, but don't blame me if you're disappointed."

"I promise," he said. "And I protest I am very fond of young ladies."

Elisabeth laughed again. "Read it and welcome, then. I may never finish it myself, and you can tell me how it comes out."

"Is it slow going?"

"Oh, no, but I'm constantly interrupted. I never have time to read any more."

"Is this aimed at me?" asked Mr. Wincannon. "Perhaps I should turn the horses immediately and leave you to your book?"

Elisabeth looked sheepish. "Not at all. I must apologize. I had a…a rather annoying caller this morning, and I'm punishing you. Inexcusable."

"You've removed a great weight from my mind," said Derek, smiling down at her. "Who was this visitor who awakened your wrath?"

"Lady Darnell, Lord James's mother. I'm not angry with her, really. I was berating myself when you came in. I couldn't manage to avoid a dinner invitation she pressed on me, and I was annoyed at my ineptitude. She's so eager for me to marry her son it's ridiculous. She actually asked me whether my drawing room curtains were very dear." As Mr. Wincannon gave a shout of laughter, Elisabeth hung her head. "Oh, dear, I shouldn't have said that. But she's such an odd creature, she quite put me out."

"I have never met the lady," he said. "How is she odd?"

"I shall say no more," replied Elisabeth. "You must already think me a spiteful gossip. Let us simply say that I wish I'd avoided her invitation."

"Why not cry off?" he suggested.

"I'd do so immediately if I weren't convinced it would leave me open to even more unpleasant recriminations. The lady has already told me that I am not to criticize myself in her presence."

"You're giving me a strong desire to meet Lady

Darnell," said Derek. "Do you suppose she would ask me to dinner also?"

"She has three daughters on her hands, two of them out. You'd be welcomed with strewn roses."

He laughed again. "You are the most interesting girl in London."

Elisabeth blushed and hastened to say, "You haven't met Jane Taunton, I imagine, if you can say that honestly."

His eyes dancing, Mr. Wincannon shook his head. "I don't believe I have."

"Ah. Well, she's much more interesting than I. It was she who gave me the book." She paused as a thought occurred to her; her eyes lit. "I shall introduce you." She paused again and turned to him with a look of irrepressible mischief. "In fact, I believe I shall give an evening party and introduce all my odd friends to one another."

He smiled down at her. "Have you so many odd friends?" he asked. "I confess to some apprehension. And do you include me among them?"

"All of my friends are odd," she replied. "I don't count mere acquaintances. But all the really interesting people I've met in London are a bit eccentric. Don't you find it so?"

"I must refuse to answer lest I compromise myself. But let me entreat you to invite my father to your party. He would be enchanted."

"Is he fond of odd people?"

"Immensely."

"I shall, then. You don't think I really mean to do it?"

"I'm only afraid you will," he answered. At that moment, they heard someone calling to them. Mr. Wincannon slowed his team to allow several carriages to pass, and Lord James Darnell rode from behind them on a showy bay hack.

"Hello," he cried. "Well met indeed. I was going in search of you this afternoon, Miss Elham." He nodded a greeting to Wincannon, who returned it.

"In search of me?" asked Elisabeth.

"To apologize," replied Lord Darnell. "Did my mother lay it on too thick this morning? I expect she extolled my virtues the whole time she was with you."

Elisabeth shook her head. "I can't recall any mention of your virtues," she said. "Perhaps you should remind your mother of them. I did discover that you have three sisters, however. You never told me that."

"Of course, I didn't. Do you take me for a flat? It's just like Mother to put me out that way."

"She asked me to dinner to meet them," added Elisabeth.

Lord Darnell struck his forehead. "Trust m'mother. The worst possible move."

Elisabeth laughed outright. "Is this a way to talk of your sisters?"

"Wait until you've met them, then I will answer you." Seeing Elisabeth's questioning look, he went on, "Oh, I don't say they aren't good enough girls, especially Augusta, but Mother has trained them to think only of catching rich husbands. Makes them prodigious boring."

"Ah," said Elisabeth. "I see what you mean. A

person who thought only of making a great match might become tiresome." Her eyes sparkled.

"A facer," cried Lord Darnell. "You are a paragon of wit, Miss Elham."

Mr. Wincannon said, "I do not like to keep my horses standing so long." His voice sounded rather flat.

"Of course," answered Elisabeth. "I'm sorry. Goodbye, Lord Darnell. I shall see you on Thursday, I expect."

"You may count on it," replied that gentleman, bowing slightly in his saddle.

The phaeton moved forward slowly. Derek said nothing for some time, and Elisabeth eyed him speculatively. He looked annoyed. "I'm sorry we kept you waiting," she put in finally.

"It is of no consequence. I wouldn't wish to spoil your enjoyment."

Her lips turned up a bit. "You're very kind," she said.

"I admit," he continued after a pause, "that I find rattles like Darnell rather a bore. His conversation seems pointless."

"Ah," was Elisabeth's only reply to this.

"However, you may do as you please, I suppose."

"Thank you," she said. "There is your sister. And Belinda with her." She waved.

"I shall not stop to talk to *them*," he replied.

"No, I think we need not do so. I should be getting back in any case."

Mr. Wincannon turned his horses without comment, and they started home again.

As Elisabeth walked in the door, Ames stopped her. "I beg your pardon, Miss Elisabeth," he said, "but a gentleman has called. He's in the library. I told him you were out, but he insisted on waiting." Ames's usually impassive face showed distaste briefly. "He said, miss, that it was a matter of life and death."

"Really?" answered Elisabeth. "I expect I had better see him then. He didn't say what it was about?"

"No, miss. I inquired about members of the family, fearing that Mr. Tony might have overturned his curricle, but he said it didn't concern any such thing." He hesitated, then lowered his voice. "I think that he may be a foreigner of some kind."

"Ah. Well, you may tell him that I shall be with him directly."

A short time later, Elisabeth entered the library, to find herself confronted by a total stranger. The man was small and very dark, with black hair and snapping black eyes. His coat and pantaloons were well cut but not in the first stare of fashion, and the design of his waistcoat was a trifle florid. When he replied to Elisabeth's cool greeting, his voice showed a very slight accent. Elisabeth could not identify it. "Will you sit down?" she asked, seating herself behind the desk.

"Thank you," he replied, taking the chair in front of it. "I know you're surprised to find me here. You do not know me. I thank you for seeing me." Elisabeth inclined her head, still puzzled, and the stranger went on. "I've come because I fear you may be in danger. I wish to speak to you about George Jarrett."

"Mr. Jarrett?" echoed Elisabeth wonderingly.

"Yes, he is a friend of yours, I believe?"

Elisabeth shrugged slightly. "I have met him."

The small man became excited. "He is a fiend," he said. "I am come here to warn you." Elisabeth raised her eyebrows, and this appeared to rouse the man further. "You must stay away from him," he cried, waving his arms.

As he gestured, something caught Elisabeth's attention. She realized suddenly that this was the man she'd seen arguing with Mr. Jarrett in the street. "You," she said.

He cocked his head. "Your pardon?"

"Nothing, nothing," said Elisabeth, recovering from her surprise. "You have the advantage of me. You seem to know me, but I have no idea who you are."

Her cool tone seemed to calm him a little. "I am sorry. When I think of that man, I am enraged, you see. My name would mean nothing to you. I come from Martinique. You have heard of it?" As Elisabeth nodded, he went on, "I am a Creole. You do not know what that means, perhaps?" Elisabeth shook her head, and his eyes lighted fiercely. "It means my honor is more to me than life. When I saw that Jarrett comes here, I could not let you go blindly to destruction, knowing what I know. I must tell you to satisfy my honor."

"Ah," said Elisabeth. She didn't particularly like this excitable gentleman who refused to tell her his name, but her curiosity was roused. "But so far you have told me nothing."

He bowed his head. "That is true. It is a difficult matter. It involves the person who was dearest to me in all the world, you see, my sister. And I will not spread her folly through the world. Though she had no fault in it, I cannot tell her story to a stranger."

Elisabeth frowned. "I'm not sure I see why you've come here in that case," she said.

"To warn you," he responded quickly. "To tell you not to trust this man of no honor and no scruples. He is not a man to be allowed near ladies."

"But if you give me no reasons for what you say, Mr....how then can I accept your warning?" asked Elisabeth a little impatiently.

"Bah, you English! Always you must have the reasons and the laws. You will not move without them." His accent became more pronounced as he said this, and the man appeared to be struggling with himself. "I...I cannot tell you all," he said finally. "It would be cruel to Desirée's memory. But I will say that this Jarrett drove my sister, the sweetest, loveliest girl on Martinique, to her grave. If you allow him to approach you, he will ruin you. He is a fiend."

Elisabeth rose. "I assure you that I hardly know Mr. Jarrett. He is the most distant of acquaintances. I think you've come on an unnecessary errand." She held up a hand as he started to speak. "It was kind of you, I suppose, to attempt to warn me of someone you distrust, but now that you've done so, we can have no more to say, I think." She rang for Ames.

The man sighed. "You have not listened to me. Perhaps I have made a mistake coming here." His shoulders sagged, and he looked defeated for a moment. "Perhaps it was a mistake to come to England." Ames entered the room as he spoke and eyed him with distinct disapproval.

Elisabeth said only, "Our guest is just leaving, Ames."

The man executed a sweeping bow, turned, and strode out of the room.

Elisabeth sat down again, a frown wrinkling her brow. She was irresistibly reminded of Lord Byron once again. "I seem to have stumbled into a melodrama," she said aloud to herself.

# Twelve

THE DAY OF THE DUCHESS OF SHERBOURNE'S BALL arrived at last. Belinda was as excited as they'd ever seen her. She'd been out driving with the duke several times and attended a theater party of his arrangement as well as the Vauxhall expedition. Elisabeth was beginning to think that she expected an offer and was becoming more and more convinced that she was right.

Belinda, Lavinia, and Elisabeth gathered in the drawing room at eight, attired for the ball. Tony was not yet in evidence. All three looked splendid in their new gowns. Lavinia wore amber crepe trimmed with ruched ribbon of the same hue and carried a fan of white ostrich feathers which pleased her greatly. Belinda had outdone herself. Her dress was of white satin with a net of floating silver gauze over the whole, from the tiny puffed sleeves to the ruffled demitrain at the back. She had found silver ribbon to tie at the high waist and thread through her blond curls, and Elisabeth told her honestly that she looked angelic.

Elisabeth had chosen to wear a gown made up from a length Belinda had found for her. The color, somewhere between blue and violet, exactly matched her eyes. The cut was very simple, round-necked and short-sleeved, with a deep wide ruffle about the hem. They'd trimmed it with bands of deeper blue velvet, at the waist, above the ruffle, and in narrow strips around the neckline and sleeves. Elisabeth carried a bouquet of iris, violets, and white rosebuds, procured with much difficulty and expense, and Belinda pronounced her complete to a shade.

They stood about the drawing room, restlessly adjusting a ribbon or a flounce, for quite half an hour, and still there was no sign of Tony. "Where can he be?" repeated Belinda petulantly at ten-minute intervals. "It is excessively unkind of him to keep us waiting. I've told him that the duchess asked us to arrive in good time."

"Oh, I do hope the dear boy has not met with an accident," replied Lavinia to Belinda's fifth repetition of this complaint. "He drives that curricle in such a deleterious fashion."

"It's more likely he's forgotten the ball entirely," answered Elisabeth dryly. "He drives to an inch."

Belinda turned from the mirror. "Let's go without him," she said to the two older women. "He has no consideration for us. I don't see why we should wait for him." She gazed at them defiantly.

Elisabeth sighed. "I suppose we must," she replied. "We shan't arrive before nine, as it is, and we did promise the duchess to come early." Belinda's face cleared as Elisabeth went to ring for Ames.

They arrived to find the duchess awaiting them. She immediately hurried them to the head of the stairs, hardly giving them time to greet her son, and sent Lavinia off into the ballroom with the duke, saying, "I'm the chaperone tonight, my friend. You may toddle off." Then she turned to the young ladies. "You stand here, Elisabeth, and Belinda, you stand just beside her. I shall introduce Elisabeth first, of course; she is oldest. You both look fine as a fivepence. I'm pleased with you."

Elisabeth's eyes twinkled. "Thank you, ma'am," she said meekly, dropping a slight curtsy.

The duchess's lips curved in response, but she shook her finger at Elisabeth. "You, miss, must be on your best behavior tonight. You're going to meet a great many very stuffy people, and I don't want to see any of your impertinence." She smiled. "If you do as I say, you will be a huge success, I promise."

Elisabeth laughed. "Such a promise must command my obedience."

"I hope so," answered the duchess. Just then, the first guests were announced, and soon the only conversation possible was greetings and polite responses to countless introductions. The duchess had gathered the cream of the *ton* in her house this night, and even Elisabeth felt a little awe at the brilliant crowd. She met three of the powerful patronesses of Almack's, including the haughty Princess Lieven. As the duchess had predicted, her friend Lady Jersey readily promised them vouchers. The Wincannons were present, as were Lady Darnell and her son, and many others whose names Elisabeth strove to remember. It was nearly an hour before the duchess released them to the ballroom.

The duke immediately solicited Belinda for the first dance, and Lord James Darnell was not slow to ask Elisabeth. As the music struck up, Elisabeth felt an unfamiliar excitement rise in her. She might be four and twenty years of age, but this was her very first ball, and she experienced the sensations any young girl with a new gown, an admiring partner, and a fresh perspective might have felt. She threw back her head, looking into Lord James's eyes, and laughed.

"What is it?" he asked.

Elisabeth shook her head. "Just high spirits." Her smile became mischievous. "Your mother must be very pleased with you for dancing with me."

"I refuse to talk any more about my family. Isn't it enough that you'll meet them all this week at dinner? How am I to captivate you if we talk constantly of my relatives?"

"But I'm fascinated," replied Elisabeth. "Your family is quite out of the ordinary. Tell me again about the duck race."

"Absolutely not," he said firmly. "I don't want you getting the idea that the Darnells are all dashed loose screws. You're looking bang up to the knocker tonight. Where did you get your posy? Did Wincannon send it to you?"

Elisabeth raised her eyebrows. "Why, no. I bought it myself, and at great expense, I may add."

Lord Darnell grimaced. "That's telling me. I meant to send a bouquet, but the truth is, it slipped my mind. I was sitting at the Daffy Club last evening, thinking I must get flowers, and then someone said something to me and it went clean out of my head."

"I'm beginning to get a clear notion why you haven't yet captured an heiress," replied Elisabeth with some amusement. "They usually require these little attentions, you know."

"Lord, yes," he sighed. "But I was persuaded that you would understand." He gave her a winning smile. "I wouldn't have found such a bang-up posy in any case."

She laughed again.

The rest of the set passed agreeably, and the duchess introduced her to eligible partners for the next three as well. But when the orchestra struck up a waltz, Elisabeth could not participate, not being officially approved by one of the patronesses of Almack's. As she walked around the edge of the ballroom, she encountered Jane Taunton for the first time that evening and greeted her warmly. "I didn't think to see you here, after all," she told the other girl. "You arrived late?"

Jane nodded. "As late as I could manage without arousing the duchess's wrath. A ball is what I dislike more than anything."

"Do you?" asked Elisabeth a bit wistfully. "This is my first, and I must admit that I'm enjoying it excessively."

"Of course you are. So should I if I had partners clamoring for my hand at every dance. But it is very unpleasant to have only partners forced to ask one by the hostess."

"Well, most of the young men here are more interested in my fortune than in me," said Elisabeth.

"Perhaps a few," agreed Jane. "But not so many as you think."

"Oh, I must tell you what happened. I nearly forgot," exclaimed Elisabeth. "I had a very unusual visitor." And she told Jane about her mysterious caller and his warning.

"That is strange," said Jane when she'd finished. "He wouldn't tell you his name?" Elisabeth shook her head, and Jane looked thoughtful. "Very strange," she repeated meditatively.

"I'm even more determined to find out about Mr. Jarrett," said Elisabeth. "He seems quite gentlemanly, you know, not like the sort of person my caller described."

"Perhaps he was exaggerating. If his sister was hurt, he would naturally be vehement in blaming the man involved."

At this moment, Belinda and the duke came to join them, and further talk of Mr. Jarrett was impossible. Belinda seemed very excited, and after a while it became clear that she wished to speak to Elisabeth privately. Jane excused herself and left the three alone.

"Oh, Cousin Elisabeth," blurted Belinda as soon as she'd gone, "John has asked me to marry him. I hope you will approve."

Elisabeth must have looked rather surprised, because the duke spoke quickly. "I know it is rather early in our acquaintance, but I'm certain of my feelings, I assure you. We needn't announce it just yet, if you do not care for it, but…"

Elisabeth held up a hand. For some reason, she felt rather old suddenly. "You have no need for my permission," she said. "Belinda isn't my ward. I wish you every happiness."

The duke beamed, and Belinda sighed ecstatically.

"Let us go to my mother," said the young man. "She'll be very pleased."

Elisabeth smiled as she watched them approach the duchess. She wondered if her reaction would be unalloyed happiness. As she mused, someone behind her remarked, "Sherbourne appears smitten by your cousin."

Elisabeth turned. Derek Wincannon was smiling down at her. "Yes. If you will keep it in confidence, I'll tell you that they are just engaged."

His eyes twinkled. "And if I will not?"

She laughed. "Then you are ungentlemanly, sir. But I daresay it will be talked of everywhere after this evening. Belinda will tell your sister or another of her bosom friends, and that will be the end of it."

He nodded. "Well, I wish them happy. They are both nodcocks, so I daresay they will be."

Elisabeth raised her eyebrows. "Do you associate happiness in marriage with stupidity?" she asked.

"I do not," he replied. "But I'm glad you have at last admitted that your cousin is a silly little gudgeon."

"I did not," began Elisabeth.

He laughed. "No, no, you can't retract it now. I came over to ask you to dance. Will you do me the honor?"

She looked up at him ruefully for a moment, then inclined her head, and they started out onto the floor. "Tell me," said Elisabeth as they joined the set, "have you seen anything of Tony today?"

Mr. Wincannon gazed down at her with an odd expression. "Tony. Somehow it always comes down to that. Do you know, Miss Elham, that many young ladies would consider it an honor to be asked to dance by me? I don't wish to sound like a coxcomb, but it's quite true. I very rarely dance." As Elisabeth stared up at him in surprise, he went on, "Exactly. You are an excellent antidote for vanity. To answer your question, no, I haven't seen your young scamp of a cousin today, and I cannot say I'm sorry for it. I wish I could rid myself of the notion that you talk to me chiefly because I foolishly promised to look out for him."

Elisabeth was considerably embarrassed by this speech. "But I…of course, I…I am very sensible of the honor…" she stammered.

He shook his head. "You needn't try to turn me up sweet now," he said, smiling slightly. "I see how it is. Is Tony missing, then?"

"I expect he has only forgotten the ball. He went out this afternoon and didn't return for it. I daresay he's at home now, wondering where we've all gotten to."

Her partner looked thoughtful. "I would say you're right. A boy of his age is not much interested in balls and evening parties, you know."

"I'm learning," responded Elisabeth wryly. "The interests of young men are extremely peculiar. I believe he spent the greater part of an evening last week watching two roosters tear each another apart. Ugh."

"A cockfight? Yes, young Tony is enjoying his freedom. But he'll come out all right."

Elisabeth was relieved to hear him say so.

When the music ended, Derek escorted Elisabeth back to the edge of the dance floor. "May I get you some lemonade or orgeat?" he asked her.

"Thank you. I should like some lemonade. Oh, there is your father. I must speak to him."

He bowed. "I shall join you there in a moment."

The viscount welcomed her cordially. "I've just been told," he said, "that your cousin has captured one of the greatest matrimonial prizes in London within a month of her come-out."

Elisabeth smiled. "Has it begun to be talked of already? And Belinda swore me to secrecy."

"Did she indeed?" said Lord Larenby. "Amelia told me as if it were public knowledge."

"No, no. I was only funning. I see no reason why we shouldn't announce it. I'm very happy for them. I think they will suit."

He nodded. "I hope you will wait a while before following her example. If all the young ladies marry so soon out of the schoolroom, we old men will have no one to flirt with."

Elisabeth laughed. "I have no ambitions of that kind. You may rest easy."

The viscount looked at her a bit sharply, she thought, but he said only, "Will you risk dancing with an old man?"

"I should be delighted," said Elisabeth. "Where is he?"

The viscount offered his arm. "Your kindness matches your beauty." Just then, his son returned with a glass of lemonade for Elisabeth. As they walked away from him, the viscount grinned and said, "You may drink that yourself, Derek. Miss Elham and I are going to dance." His son looked down at the glass in disgust.

The viscount, Elisabeth found, was an accomplished and elegant dancer. "Has your son told you of the party I am planning?" she asked him. "He said you would like it above all things."

"No," answered Lord Larenby interestedly. "What is it to be?"

"I'm going to invite all the odd people I've met in London to an evening party and introduce them to one another," said Elisabeth. "I expect it to be excessively diverting."

He laughed. "It sounds rather like one of Prinny's fetes. But who are these odd people you've met?"

"Well," replied Elisabeth, smiling, "there is a fortune hunter and his family. He calls his mother Lachrymose, but she is really quite willowy. Then, there is a Byronic hero and his pursuer." She frowned. "Though I don't know the latter's name, so I suppose it will be difficult to invite him."

Her partner was laughing.

"And there is also a wonderful literary young lady, whom I truly like. And your son."

The viscount continued to smile, but his eyebrows lifted. "A fortune hunter, a blackguard, a bluestocking, and my son. That will be interesting. I hope you will invite me as well."

"That is what he said you would say."

"Dare I ask why you include Derek in this menagerie?"

Elisabeth's smile faded slightly. "I'm only joking you, you know. Most of them are quite nice and highly respectable. I included Mr. Wincannon merely because he's so outspoken. He has fallen into the habit of telling me all his faults before I accuse him. I thought it just a trifle…not odd, of course, but…" She trailed off in confusion.

"Does he indeed?" said the viscount meditatively. "I wonder what can be his object with that? Or if he has one?" Since Elisabeth had no idea, she remained silent. Her companion stared into space for several moments, then recalled himself. "I beg pardon," he said. "It's just that Derek hasn't seemed quite himself lately. I've been wondering why."

"I...I'm not sure what you mean."

"Nor am I, actually." He looked over her head into the crowd, then he glanced down with a smile. "Are you enjoying your first ball in London?"

"Oh, very much," she replied. "It's my very first ball anywhere, you see. I feel quite like a seventeen-year-old."

Before Elisabeth knew it, it had begun to grow late. Guests were bidding their hostess farewell, and the ballroom was emptying. With some regret, Elisabeth's family also took their leave.

When they reached the house, Elisabeth went first to Ames. "Has Tony come in?" she asked him.

The tall butler shook his head. "His valet has heard nothing, and we have received no note or letter," he answered.

Elisabeth frowned. "I daresay he has forgotten to tell us he meant to be out late."

"Yes, miss." Ames's expression was highly disapproving.

Elisabeth thought for a moment, then sighed. "I don't see that we can do anything now," she said finally. "I have no idea where Tony may be." She turned and started slowly up the stairs.

Elisabeth found Ketchem waiting in her bedroom. She'd given up telling her that she needn't wait up. "I've torn my hem just a trifle, I'm afraid."

Ketchem looked down at it. "Yes, miss."

Elisabeth made ready for bed in silence. She was thinking about Tony and that she must make certain he told them where he was going in future so that they needn't worry like this.

Ketchem had been observing her expression, and as she brushed out her hair, she said, "Has Mr. Tony come in yet, miss?" When Elisabeth shook her head, Ketchem nodded; her expression seemed to say "I told you so," though Elisabeth couldn't imagine why. "At least he's taken that animal with him," the maid said.

Elisabeth looked up in surprise. "He's taken Growser?"

"Yes, miss. And very glad everyone is belowstairs, I may say. That animal is a menace. Just yesterday, he chewed up the housemaid's…"

"Never mind, Ketchem," said Elisabeth absently, not even noticing how the dresser bridled. "I cannot think what Tony was about," she continued to herself. "Oh, I wish I knew where he was."

## Thirteen

Elisabeth rose at dawn the next morning, after a restless night, and walked down the hallway to Tony's door. After getting no response to a soft tap, she opened it and found that what she feared was true. Tony had not been in his bedroom that night. Elisabeth looked around, but she could see nothing out of the ordinary. The room looked neat and completely undisturbed.

Sleep was out of the question. Elisabeth returned to her bedchamber, sat down at the dressing table, and tried to calm down. Tony had become so independent lately, she told herself, that it was very likely he had simply forgotten to tell anyone that he wouldn't be home. Perhaps he was staying with some friend. She bit a fingernail. Why had he taken the dog, she wondered. Where could he be that such a large energetic animal would be welcome? She made a wry face. Surely no house in London. She tried to recall what he'd said when she saw him yesterday; they'd met at breakfast, and she'd teased him about the florid pattern of a new waistcoat he was wearing. Elisabeth frowned. They had said nothing of consequence, as far as she could remember. She looked at her reflection. "The really frustrating thing," she told her image, "is that I can do nothing whatsoever for hours yet. No one will be up."

The intervening hours were indeed hard. Elisabeth washed and dressed. She paced about her room. She went down to the library and paced there for a longer time. Several times she sat down at her desk and stared at a blank sheet of paper, pen in hand. Finally, she wrote a note to Derek Wincannon, asking him to call as soon as possible. It was the only thing she could think of to do. She then went in to breakfast and tried to reassure Cousin Lavinia, whose concern over Tony was only partly overshadowed by Belinda's great news.

Derek arrived soon after, and Elisabeth breathed a sigh of relief. Now, at least, something would be done. She held out her hand. "It was kind of you to come so quickly. Tony has not turned up, and I'm beginning to worry about him. You will say I'm being foolish. Indeed, that may be why I've called on you, so that you will say so. I'm in need of reassurance."

But Mr. Wincannon was frowning. "He didn't return all night?" Elisabeth shook her head, and his frown deepened. "Graceless young pup," he murmured.

"Do you think something has happened to him?" asked Elisabeth anxiously.

"What?" He looked up sharply. "I beg your pardon. I do not. But I think he has been very thoughtless indeed not to tell you where he's gone."

"You…you think he may be visiting friends, then, or… You do not believe he is in any kind of trouble?"

"No more trouble than any youngster thrown on

the town for the first time may get into," he replied. "But I did think he was more sensible than to worry you."

"But where do you think he is?"

Wincannon shrugged. "He may have dipped a bit too deep and stayed at one of his cronies' rooms to sleep it off. That is what I think most likely. He has not, ah, expressed any interest in females? You will pardon me for asking."

Elisabeth smiled ironically and shook her head. "Oh, no. It can't be that. He took Growser with him."

"The dog?" asked her companion. And as Elisabeth nodded, he frowned again. "That is odd. And he left no word with anyone?" She shook her head. Derek looked thoughtful. After a while, he said, "May I speak with his valet? Privately."

Elisabeth cocked her head. "Do you think he will tell you something he would not say to me?"

He shrugged. "Perhaps. At least he may be able to give me some idea of Tony's usual haunts."

The valet was duly fetched, and Mr. Wincannon was closeted with him for some time. Elisabeth, not wishing to be idle, questioned Belinda about Tony's friends and collected a list of his closest companions. She managed to do this without alarming Belinda too much, though she had to admit that he hadn't yet returned. Belinda thought it typical of her brother that he hadn't informed them, and she maintained that he must be staying with Mr. Penswreath.

When she returned to the library, Elisabeth found Derek thoughtful. He glanced up as she entered. "I got very little information," he said.

"I've found out who his best friends are," she replied. She mentioned them.

He nodded. "Well, I suppose we have enough to go on with. I'll look for him. But I must tell you that I shall give him a rare dressing down if I do find him."

"I hope so," answered Elisabeth. "I plan to do that myself."

He smiled down at her. "I should like to see that. May I?"

"Certainly. If you bring him back, you may help me beat him."

"So motivated, I cannot fail," he said lightly, as he made ready to go. "I shall keep you informed of my progress."

"Thank you." Elisabeth held out her hand and smiled. "It is so kind of you to do this. It must be excessively annoying. I don't know how to thank you." He looked at her with an unreadable expression for a moment, then bowed over her hand and went out. After he'd gone, Elisabeth felt an immense relief, as if her problem had been lifted from her shoulders. She also felt a bit shaky, but she put this down to worry. "How I shall scold him!" she said aloud to herself.

The afternoon was interminable. Elisabeth could find no task that held her attention. When Ames came in to tell her that Mr. Jarrett was below, her first impulse was to refuse to see him, but then she decided that the time might pass more quickly if she had someone to talk to.

They exchanged greetings and a few commonplaces about the weather. As they talked, Elisabeth recalled the scene in the street and the peculiar warning she'd received. She eyed Jarrett with renewed interest. Their conversation faltered.

Mr. Jarrett watched her narrowly for a moment, then said, "I don't mean to pry. There is nothing I dislike more than thrusting myself into others' affairs unasked. But I would be of help if I could."

"Help?"

"Pardon me. You seemed worried about something." He looked at her. "You may tell me to sheer off, you know. I won't take offense." The concern in his eyes appeared genuine.

"There's really nothing wrong. It's just that my care-for-nobody young cousin forgot to inform us of his plans, and I have been a little worried about where he may be."

Mr. Jarrett frowned. "He's missing?"

"Oh, no," answered Elisabeth quickly. She already regretted having said so much. It would not do to have the story of Tony's disappearance spread. "I expect him to turn up at any moment. It is of no consequence."

The man looked at her closely again. "Of course," he agreed. "But would you like…that is, if you should care for it, I might poke about in town to see whether I can get word of him." He said this diffidently, as if he did not wish to push himself forward.

"That's very good of you," she said, rather more warmly than before. "But a friend is already doing that. I expect he'll return with Tony very soon."

"Who?" asked Jarrett sharply.

Elisabeth raised her eyebrows. "A good friend of the family," she replied coolly. "You may be easy."

Mr. Jarrett bowed his head, acknowledging her

rebuke. "I'm glad," he said. There was a short silence, and then he spoke again. "I hope you aren't offended. I offered my help sincerely, as I think you know. Finding myself back in England with neither family nor close friends has been somewhat difficult. I refine too much, perhaps, on the little kindnesses you and your family have extended. I have no right to consider you anything more than acquaintances."

This rather melancholy speech and Jarrett's downcast look roused Elisabeth's pity. "We don't know each other well," she agreed, "but that may come with time."

Jarrett brightened. "I hope so indeed. I have been much alone of late years. But when I met your cousin, and spoke to her about William and the past, her kindness made it seem as if I could start afresh here at home." He stopped and shook his head. "How maudlin I sound. Please forgive me. I'm a brute to be going on in this way when you have your own worries to occupy you."

Elisabeth had been rather moved by his confession. "Not at all. If I do have worries, you divert my mind. I'm certain you will soon feel quite at home in England and make many new friends."

He leaned forward eagerly. "If I could believe that…" he began. Then he paused, took a breath, and rose from the sofa, walking over to throw an arm along the mantelpiece. His striking eyes focused on Elisabeth. "Miss Elham," he said, "you have seen that I'm reluctant to talk of my life abroad. I can tell you that there is much about it I regret and much I would change if I could. One gets wisdom with age, they say, and I hope

I have done so. I really wish to make a fresh start." He seemed to wait for an answer, but Elisabeth had nothing to say to this. "You must think me strange, to be saying this to you," he continued, "but something in your face tells me I can trust you absolutely."

"It is good of you to say so," responded Elisabeth. In spite of herself, she was a little amused at Jarrett's dramatizing.

He saw this immediately. "Ah, you think I'm putting on airs once again." He smiled ruefully. "Well, who can say, perhaps I am. But I'm sincere in my wish to be your friend, Miss Elham, and to help you in any way at any time."

"Thank you. I shall remember it."

He seemed satisfied with this. "Good. And now perhaps I should go."

Elisabeth rose. "Please believe that I am very sensible of your kindness, Mr. Jarrett." She held out her hand.

He took it and held it for a moment. "It's nothing. You do not know. Remembering William, I…well, it makes no matter. I have no right to say anything further as yet, but I would do you any service in my power, Miss Elham. In the short time since we met, I have…" He stopped, hesitated, then raised her hand to his lips. "I must say no more. Goodbye." He didn't wait for an answer, but strode out of the room immediately.

Left alone, Elisabeth looked first at her hand, then toward the door, then out the front window. Jarrett was just leaving the house and turning down the street. She drew a deep breath. "Well," she said aloud, "this is a fine development. Whatever am I to do with him?"

Just then, she heard a carriage pulling up outside, and all thoughts of Jarrett were driven from her head. She reached the landing in time to see Derek Wincannon entering the hall. When he glanced up, she gave him an anxious look, but he merely shook his head slightly as he started up the stairs. Elisabeth returned to the drawing room to wait for him. She sat down and folded her hands tightly together.

When he walked in, she said, "You haven't found him. Oh, I'm beginning to be truly worried. Tony wouldn't go away for so long without telling me."

Wincannon sat down beside her. "You must not upset yourself or jump to conclusions," he answered. But he looked grave.

Elisabeth sighed. "Have you no news at all?"

"I have some word," he said, "though I'm not sure it does us any good. It appears that Tony made the acquaintance of an animal trainer recently and has been very enthusiastic about the possibility of training his dog." He smiled slightly. "I understand the animal is not thoroughly domesticated."

"You are a master of understatement."

He laughed. "In any case, Tony had talked of taking Growser out for a training session, and since he has taken the dog, I hazard a guess that's where he is."

"It would be just like him. And I suppose that horrid dog has run off after rabbits or some such thing, and Tony has become so involved in searching for him that he hasn't thought we might be worrying." She felt a great relief.

"Perhaps," answered Derek, but he looked a little doubtful.

Elisabeth didn't notice. "So we need only find this trainer's home, and we shall find Tony. Or word of him, at least," she amended.

"That's the odd thing," said Mr. Wincannon. "I can't seem to find out anything about the man. None of Tony's friends knows his name or direction. In fact, they haven't even seen him. I don't understand it."

"What are you saying?" asked Elisabeth.

"I'm not saying anything other than that I cannot find the man," he replied. "Don't excite yourself unnecessarily. None of Tony's friends was much interested in his dog. It's probably reasonable that they wouldn't meet this trainer. However, I must say it is a bit unusual. I have some superficial knowledge of the set the fellow should have frequented, and no one there can tell me anything. He may be new to London, of course. Or any number of other things. But I think I shall hunt a bit more seriously now."

Elisabeth wrung her hands. "I keep imagining Tony lying in a ditch somewhere…"

"Good God," exclaimed Derek. "You've allowed your imagination to carry you far beyond the limits of what is probable. The very worst I expect—mind you, the worst—is that Tony has fallen in with a ruffian who hopes to get money out of him. And even that I consider very far-fetched."

"I…I see," said Elisabeth shakily. "You must pardon me. I don't mean to be a ninny, but I have never been party to a kidnapping before, you see. It's very odd. Life in London appears to be much more like fiction than I was ever allowed to believe. I think I must begin to read some lurid novels. Then I should know just how to go on in this situation. Shall I receive a ransom note, do you think?"

"No, I do not," replied Mr. Wincannon sharply. "But you may receive a scolding if you persist in this folly. We have no reason to believe that Tony has been kidnapped. I hope you will not spread such a story about."

This brought Elisabeth back to earth. "Of course I won't," she said indignantly. "Do you think me idiotic?"

"I was becoming uncertain," he said with a smile. "You had begun to act very like a delicate female—these die-away airs."

"Oh," declared Elisabeth. "That is unfair. I have been worrying all afternoon."

His smile faded. "I know," he said. "And I wish you will stop. It does no good and may do you harm. I'll find him. You may be easy."

"That is easily said. But I feel very responsible for my cousins, you know."

He nodded. "Yes. But fidgeting yourself into the vapors won't help. Do you have an engagement this evening?"

Elisabeth looked surprised at this abrupt change of subject. "Yes," she replied. "But I shall cancel it, of course."

"That is what I feared you would say. I think it very unwise."

"But I cannot..."

"No good will come of sitting and worrying. I think you should go out. I shall call tomorrow morning with news."

"But if you should hear something tonight…"

"You may be sure I will let you know it. It is much better for you to be occupied, however."

Elisabeth looked up at him ruefully. "But I don't wish to go," she answered plaintively. "I would be so pleased to cry off."

Derek smiled. "What is it?"

"Lady Darnell's dinner party. Won't you give me leave to miss it?"

He smiled again, but shook his head. "Go, by all means. It will keep your mind off Tony. I daresay it will be a very amusing evening."

Elisabeth made a face. "You wouldn't say so if you were invited." She held up a hand as he started to speak. "All right. I get nearly frantic waiting here. I shall go."

"Good," he said. "And I shall find Tony. Never fear."

Some hours later, when her carriage set her down at the door of the Darnells' townhouse, Elisabeth nearly changed her mind and returned home. The amusement this dinner would provide would not equal the discomfort it was sure to inspire, and she really didn't wish to go in. But the door was being opened; the butler was bowing. Elisabeth shook out the ruffles of her primrose gown and walked resolutely up the steps and into the hall.

The whole family awaited her in the drawing room. Lord Darnell stood with a smile as she entered, and his mother held out a languid hand from a recumbent position on the sofa. "So pleased you could come, my dear," she said. The three girls sat together on a sofa opposite their mother, and when Elisabeth was introduced to them, she had some trouble keeping her countenance. Not only had their mother dressed them all alike in pink muslin dresses trimmed with deeper pink ribbons, but she'd obviously warned them to be extremely deferential to this rich potential sister-in-law. All the girls rose and curtsied when presented. The eldest, Aurelia, looked quite overawed. Her sister Portia looked sly, and the youngest, Augusta, appeared slightly rebellious. Lady Darnell watched complacently as each girl expressed her pleasure at meeting Elisabeth.

Introductions over, Elisabeth was made to take the armchair that Lord Darnell had vacated. "The most comfortable chair in the room," his mother insisted, as he pulled up another from across the room.

Elisabeth surveyed the family group. All were blond and had some of the slender elegance she'd first noticed in Lord Darnell. The sisters' identical costumes seemed to emphasize their differences. The eldest closely resembled her mother, with very pale blond hair and delicate features. She was also the most slender, and Elisabeth had no trouble picturing Aurelia in twenty years; she would become Lady Darnell.

Portia and Augusta were less ethereal. The middle sister had yellow-blond hair; her eyes were not the pale blue of the rest of the family's, but rather a clear hazel. She looked at their guest with avid speculation so clear in her glance that Elisabeth nearly laughed. There was a smile in her eyes, in fact, when she turned them toward Augusta, and she found that this young lady was gazing openly back at her. Their glances met, and seeing only frank curiosity, Elisabeth did smile. The younger girl seemed surprised at first, then smiled tentatively in return. Her blond hair was tinged with red, and she had some tendency to freckles. She seemed uneasy about the evening, and Elisabeth thought that she would like her better than the others.

During this time, Lady Darnell had kept up a constant chatter about commonplace things, but when her eyes sharpened suddenly, Elisabeth got the feeling that the preliminaries were over. "Do you know what I heard when I stopped in at Hookham's this morning, my dear?" Lady Darnell asked, then answered her own question, "Emily Cowper told me, in the strictest confidence, of course, that your cousin had become engaged to the Duke of Sherbourne. Is it indeed so?"

Elisabeth smiled. "Yes," she replied. She couldn't bring herself to be angry with such frank cupidity, but she didn't feel inclined to provide them with more gossip, either.

"A duke," murmured Aurelia, "and so very rich."

Portia nodded. "A splendid match," she added. "How old is your cousin? She's just out, is she not?"

Elisabeth nodded. "She is eighteen."

The two girls twittered excitedly. "The same as Aurelia. Only think."

Lord Darnell had been unusually quiet up to this point, but now he addressed Elisabeth with the air of a man hard pressed. "I told you Sherbourne liked her. Remember?"

"I do," answered Elisabeth. "You were very right."

"I should think they will suit admirably." Elisabeth nodded. She'd never heard him utter such commonplaces.

Portia sighed. "He must have twenty thousand a

year." This remark did not meet with her mother's approval, and Portia received a sharp look. "Shall we go in to dinner?" said Lady Darnell.

At dinner, the conversation turned to Aurelia's come-out, and Elisabeth soon realized that she'd been asked to dinner not only as a possible daughter-in-law, but also in the hope that she'd help Aurelia into society. Her mother, it appeared, was too frail to go about with her. Elisabeth found this assertion incredible and concluded that Lady Darnell hoped both to save herself expense and to put her daughter in the path of eligible gentlemen by pushing her on Elisabeth. She was well acquainted with the size of Elisabeth's fortune and her generosity to her cousins. She seemed, in fact, well pleased by the news of Belinda's engagement, despite the consequent removal of a highly eligible bachelor from the ranks. She professed to believe that Elisabeth would now be quite lonely and in need of other female companionship.

Aurelia appeared only too eager to fall in with this plan, and Elisabeth felt sorry for the girl. It was so obviously her only chance to get out, for her mother was not likely to exert herself for anyone, Elisabeth saw, even her own family.

Though Lord Darnell tried several times during the meal to steer the talk into new channels, he was forestalled each time by his mother. Elisabeth was astonished, in fact, to see how differently this young man behaved at home. He seemed cowed by his mother's personality, and his usual amusing chatter disappeared, a strong disappointment since Elisabeth had counted upon him to make the evening bearable.

As it was, by the time coffee was brought to the drawing room, Elisabeth was very tired of the Darnells and very bored. Lady Darnell was not amusing for more than ten minutes, and the girls seemed interested in nothing but clothes and finding husbands. She'd been longing to leave for quite an hour before she dared broach the subject. And even then, she was forced to stay half an hour more. Finally, unable to bear it, she pleaded fatigue and a headache and escaped. She wouldn't allow Lord Darnell to escort her home, but he took her down to her carriage, and as he handed her in, he looked at her gravely. "You were very kind to come," he said: "And now it is over. Thank you."

"Why, I...I had a pleasant evening," faltered Elisabeth.

His old smile appeared. "Gammon," he said. "I know you didn't. But you are very good to say it. And it is kind of you to let Aurelia come see you, too. She never gets out, you know, and...well, I thank you for that, as well."

"Oh, but I...it will be..."

He grinned again. "I know just what you mean. But let us say no more about it." He shut the carriage door then, and gave her coachman the signal to start. He waved once as they pulled away, then turned and went back into the house. Elisabeth was left feeling surprised and somewhat touched by this new Lord Darnell. She wouldn't have thought him capable of such delicacy.

# *Fourteen*

ELISABETH FELT SLIGHTLY BETTER WHEN SHE ROSE THE next morning to see sunshine pouring through her window. "Today, we'll find him," she told herself briskly. "I know it." She washed and dressed and went downstairs with spirits much refreshed. She was about to begin her breakfast when she heard a commotion in the hall below. Someone was shouting, and she heard something fall. "Tony," she cried, and jumped up. She ran to the stairs and looked down. There was Growser capering about the hall, eluding every attempt by Ames and a footman to restrain him. "Tony," called Elisabeth again as she hurried down the stairs.

When she reached the hall, Growser greeted her affectionately. Elisabeth noticed then that he was very dirty, his coat matted, and there was what looked like a long cut on his side beneath the shaggy hair. She pushed him away gently but firmly with a "Have you been lost, beast?" and turned to Ames. "Where is Tony?" she asked him eagerly.

Ames looked grave. "I don't know, miss," he said. "I had just opened the front door to the postman this morning when the animal came in. I searched the streets carefully, but saw no sign of anyone with him."

Elisabeth's eyes widened. She bent to examine Growser more closely. The mark on his side was indeed a cut, and though it was not deep, it was a nasty scratch that extended all along his length. His long hair was matted with mud. She took hold of his head and gazed into his eyes, but his lolling tongue and responsive bark expressed only his joy at being home once again. "Yes," said Elisabeth. "I know you would tell me if you could." She straightened. "Someone must care for Growser. He needs a bath, and that cut must be dressed. He's probably hungry, as well." She looked at Ames.

"I daresay, miss," answered the butler. "I've never known him to refuse food."

The young footman spoke diffidently. "I could take him, Miss Elisabeth. M'father keeps dogs. I'm used to 'em."

"Oh, would you? I should be very grateful." As he led Growser toward the back premises, Elisabeth started into the library. "I shall need someone to carry a note for me, Ames," she said over her shoulder.

When she'd dispatched a hurried letter to Derek Wincannon, Elisabeth walked slowly back to the breakfast room. Her buoyant mood of the early morning was destroyed; she was now convinced that something terrible had befallen Tony. For some reason, she couldn't help blaming herself, though she knew this was nonsense.

Lavinia was in the room when she entered, scribbling on a sheet of paper at the small writing desk in the corner. When she saw Elisabeth, she said, "Good morning, my dear. Is there any news today?"

Elisabeth took a breath. "I don't wish to put you in a quake. But this morning, Growser came back without Tony."

Lavinia sat up straighter. "What? The dog came alone?"

"Yes. And he was all scratched and dirty." Elisabeth braced herself for the hysteria she was certain would follow this announcement.

But Lavinia surprised her. "What do you propose to do?" she asked quietly. Her resolute expression was quite new to Elisabeth.

"I've notified Mr. Wincannon. He's been looking for Tony, you know. He was not at all worried, but now…"

Lavinia nodded. "He seems a very culpable man," she replied sagely. "What shall I do?"

Elisabeth stared at her in astonishment. It appeared there was more to Cousin Lavinia than she'd imagined. "I…I do not…you might take care of Belinda for me. I've been so taken up with this…"

Lavinia was nodding. "Of course," she said. "I shall tell her what has happened. I am sure she will feel a little agitated, but we shall get along. Is there nothing else?"

Elisabeth shook her head. "I…I can think of nothing."

"Very well," answered her cousin sturdily. "But if you do, you must tell me straightaway." She rose. "I will go up to Belinda now." And she left the room.

Elisabeth remained standing by the door for a few

moments, marveling. Her cousin had exhibited a strength she hadn't known she possessed. Indeed, her quiet composure had comforted Elisabeth a great deal; she didn't feel quite so alone with her problems now.

When she explained the occurrences of the morning to Derek, he frowned and fired a series of questions at her. Then, he walked over to the fireplace and rested his arm on the mantel, staring into the fire with a look of concentration.

"What do you think?" said Elisabeth, when she could stand his silence no longer.

"I'm afraid there's been an accident or something of the sort. I admit I was beginning to conclude that yesterday, but this seems to confirm it. I've found no sign of him."

"What shall we do?" Elisabeth asked quietly. "Shall I call in a constable?"

He inclined his head. "You may, of course, if you wish it. But I think you would gain little beyond making this affair public. I suggest rather that I continue to search, with help."

"What kind of help?" she replied eagerly. "Oh, how I wish there was something I could do."

He smiled at her sympathetically. "I know. But unfortunately neither of us knows very much about such things. I shall go to my father, my man of business, and my groom."

Elisabeth was taken aback. "Your groom?"

"Yes. Wills joined my household several years ago from parts unknown. He has since exhibited a remarkable familiarity with some of the less savory elements of London society. I think he may be able to help us track down this trainer. Indeed, I thought of asking him ere this, but I didn't wish to start gossip about Tony's disappearance."

Elisabeth nodded. "I suppose there's no stopping that now."

"On the contrary. You must put it about that he has gone to the country on a visit."

Elisabeth brightened. "I shall say he has gone down to look over Willowmere for me. To oversee the work, you know."

"Excellent," he replied. "The only hard thing left is to keep you from worrying yourself into a decline."

"I don't think it will come to that," she said. "But it is hard not to worry."

"I know." He looked at her for a moment. "The best thing to do is keep up your social engagements," he said. "It will keep your mind busy. Was your dinner party last night enjoyable?"

Elisabeth made a wry face. "No," she answered, and she gave him a short description of the evening.

"All in pink," he laughed. "I must meet these young ladies."

"Oh, you will. Make no mistake. I'm sure you're high on their list of eligible husbands." She stopped abruptly. "Oh, what an old cattish thing to say."

"But true."

"Yes. However, I should be more charitable. They cannot help it, after all."

He raised his eyebrows. "I find that hard to credit."

"It's their upbringing," she replied. "But that is of no consequence. You must be on your way, I know,"

He smiled ruefully. "Yes. Tony." She nodded, and he

took his leave, commanding her again not to worry. Elisabeth only shrugged. But she had little opportunity to worry, for less than ten minutes later, Ames came in to announce, "Miss Taunton is below."

Elisabeth stood immediately. "Jane?" she said. "Oh, send her up." A few moments later, Jane walked into the room, and Elisabeth went forward, holding out her hands. "How good to see you," she said. "You are just the person to divert me."

Jane smiled. "Thank you," she replied. "What has put you in the dumps?"

Elisabeth hesitated. She wasn't sure she should tell anyone else of Tony's disappearance. But as she looked at the other girl's homely sympathetic face, she brushed such considerations aside. She was in need of a friend. "We have had some rather distressing occurrences lately," she began, and she told Jane the whole.

The other girl appeared shocked. "The dog returned alone," she repeated, frowning. "What can that mean?"

"That's what I keep asking myself," answered Elisabeth. "I fear it means that Tony is hurt, or worse. I cannot stop seeing him, lying somewhere in a ditch, his leg broken and in a fever, or..." She rose and began to pace about. "And I can do nothing! This is what maddens me."

Jane nodded soberly. "That is always the worst element of a crisis—waiting. But surely someone is searching for him?"

"Oh, yes." Elisabeth told the other girl about Derek Wincannon's help. "But I hear so seldom how it's going. I feel so useless."

Her friend nodded once more. "Yet the affair is in good hands. The Wincannons are very capable men. However, I understand exactly what you feel. It's difficult sometimes, being a woman. We must always wait when we would wish to act."

Elisabeth sat down on the sofa again and clasped her hands tightly, "If only we had some notion of where he'd gone," she said. "I can think of nothing but Tony, yet there is nothing to think of. Oh, I wish we might get some news."

"I am sure you'll be informed as soon as anything is known. You mustn't allow this to overset you."

Elisabeth smiled ruefully. "You sound just like Mr. Wincannon now. You all insist that I must not upset myself. But how am I to help it? None of you tell me that."

"Well, perhaps I can take your mind off the problem for a few minutes," replied Jane. "I called today to give you some other news, in fact. I've found out something about our Byronic character."

In spite of herself, Elisabeth was interested. "Indeed? What?"

Jane settled herself more comfortably on the sofa. "I told you that I would make inquiries among my friends. Well, one of them had been to the Indies in recent years and had heard a bit about this man Jarrett. It seems that he went to the islands years ago in hopes of making his fortune as a planter in Martinique. But after putting all his money into the venture, he found that he had no talent for managing a plantation. He lost nearly all he had and was on the verge of ruin when he married a very wealthy and very young girl of a French family."

"The sister!" exclaimed Elisabeth.

Jane nodded. "It sounds right, doesn't it? Unfortunately, my friend knew little more. Soon after the marriage, Jarrett sold his holdings on Martinique and took his bride to Jamaica. There was some talk that her family wasn't pleased about the move. But that is all I have found out as yet. I didn't wish to attract too much attention to our researches, you know."

"Of course," said Elisabeth. "And then his wife died."

Jane shrugged. "So it would seem, from the reports of Mr. Jarrett's pursuer. And clearly he has got her money."

Elisabeth raised her eyebrows.

"Well, he had none of his own left," continued the other girl. "And he appears to have an income now. Where can it have come from, if not his wife?"

"I suppose you're right."

"It seems certain," agreed Jane. "And if he was left her money, her brother is probably angry about it."

"But he said that Mr. Jarrett had ruined her."

Jane shrugged. "People say outrageous things when money is involved. I've seen it in my own family. A great-aunt of mine left her fortune to charity, and the outcry was enormous. You should have heard the things my cousins said to one another." She looked thoughtful. "And living on the edge of poverty is not particularly amusing. It's hard to see money slip away. One can imagine going to some lengths to keep it."

"Then you don't think Jarrett did anything wrong?"

"Oh, I didn't say so. I meant only that it is silly to believe everything said by a man who may have lost out on a fortune. He may be painting his rival blacker than he is."

"I'm sure that must be so. Mr. Jarrett seems a gentleman. When he called here recently, he was very kind and understanding. Villainy is something for novels, not real life. Indeed, I'm a little uneasy about your inquiries. Is it fair to snoop about as we have been doing?"

Jane smiled. "Now you're being naive, I think. What harm can it do? And I should say simply that we don't know the man's character or his past sufficiently to say what he is."

"You're right, I suppose."

Jane smiled. "It will hurt no one to continue our researches, Elisabeth. You cannot wish to abandon such a fascinating character just as we are discovering things at last?"

Elisabeth shrugged. "If you wish it. But it seems we shall find no romance after all. Only a family squabbling over money."

The other girl laughed. "Much too realistic. We'll have to rely on poetry to supply our adventures, I suppose. They refuse to intrude on our ordered lives."

Elisabeth's smile faded. "If only they did," she replied, her thoughts turning back to Tony.

Seeing her expression, Jane said quickly, "Did you like the book I lent you?"

Elisabeth looked up again. "Oh, yes. I forgot to tell you. It's delightful."

"I have another, if you like."

"I should like it above all things. I don't know when I have enjoyed a book so much. But I haven't yet finished. I've had so little time."

Ames entered the drawing room. "A note has been delivered, Miss Elisabeth," he said. "It is from Mr. Wincannon, and I thought you would wish to have it immediately."

Elisabeth jumped up and took the paper from his hand. "Oh, yes," she said. She tore it open quickly and scanned the contents. Looking up again, she sighed. "He says nothing of import. He believes he may have found the trainer Tony was seen with. There will be no answer, Ames." The butler bowed and left the room. "He says I shouldn't worry," continued Elisabeth wryly.

"It sounds as if he is making progress."

Elisabeth shrugged. "Perhaps. But we have no assurance that this trainer knows anything of Tony. We simply know nothing." She crumpled the paper in her hand.

"Soon you will hear. I'm sure of it."

Elisabeth turned back to her with a wan smile. "Thank you. I hope you are right."

Jane fidgeted. "I'm afraid I must go," she said. "But I hate to leave you so distraught."

Elisabeth shook her head. "I'm perfectly all right. I can't help worrying, but I'll be fine. I promise you." She added, to herself, the wish that she could be as sure of Tony's well-being.

# Fifteen

As the time passed with no news, Elisabeth carried through on the social engagements she'd made, but she was always distracted; and many of her acquaintances commented on this. Only with the Wincannons and Jane Taunton was she free to discuss her fears, but even with them, she was often silent. Derek had succeeded in tracing the animal trainer, but the man first disavowed all knowledge of Tony's whereabouts and then disappeared.

This highly suspicious action suggested that he had known something of Tony, after all, which made their unavailing efforts to find him again all the more frustrating. Elisabeth enlisted Mr. Tilling in the search, and he joined Wincannon's man of business in investigating all possibilities. The viscount, too, made inquiries. But none of these men had any more success than Derek and his groom could boast, and at the end of the week, there was still no news.

Elisabeth rose the following morning with a sense of despair. She'd done everything she could think of, even calling in the Bow Street runners to search for her cousin. But nothing had worked, and she was beginning to believe that nothing would. She became more and more convinced that Tony was lost to them. Her uncharacteristic fatalism arose from her helplessness in this case. She was forced to leave everything to others, and this galled her.

Belinda and Lavinia were already breakfasting when she went downstairs. There was little talk during the meal, since even Belinda had been subdued by their loss now. Elisabeth said nothing at all as she mechanically ate and stared out at the clouded sky. When Ames entered with a note, Elisabeth took it automatically. There had been so many notes in the last several days, and none had held good news. But her cousins looked at her expectantly, so she tore open the envelope and unfolded the sheet within.

The script was extremely shaky, so that at first she didn't recognize it. It was only when her eyes strayed to the signature that Elisabeth realized that the note was from Tony. "I'm all right," it read. "Took a ball in the shoulder but better now. Do not worry. Tony." With a cry, Elisabeth thrust the paper at Lavinia and ran out of the room, calling for Ames as she went. The butler came into the hall as she reached the bottom of the stairs.

"That note. Who brought it?" asked Elisabeth quickly. "Is he here still?"

Ames was surprised. "Why no, miss. It was left by a carter who stopped at the door for a moment. Not used to such a neighborhood, I would say."

Elisabeth was already pulling the front door open and looking eagerly into the street. "We must find him." She searched in both directions, but the pavement was empty. Running down the steps, she extended the range of her vision, but there was no sign of a cart. She turned to Ames, who had followed her out looking perplexed. "That note was from Tony," she told him. "But he doesn't say where he is. He's been wounded."

The butler appeared chagrined. "If I had only known…" he began.

"Would you know the man again?"

Ames frowned. "I paid no special heed to him, miss. I'm not sure I would." He shook his head. "Had I known," he repeated.

They walked back into the hall, finding Belinda and Lavinia awaiting them there. Elisabeth shook her head at their questioning glances. "At least we know now that he's all right," she said. "We may be easy on that score."

"How like Tony to forget to tell us where he is," said Belinda. "He is always so thoughtless."

"He was wounded, Belinda," answered Elisabeth sharply. "I daresay he was not thinking clearly. His writing shows that he was weak. Oh, I must get to him."

Lavinia agreed. "Let us tell our friends who have helped us. Perhaps Mr. Wincannon or Mr. Jarrett can find the man who brought the note."

"Mr. Jarrett?" asked Elisabeth.

"Why, yes," replied her cousin. "He's been such a comfort to me. He always believed we should hear some good news before long. He supported my spirits amazingly."

"That was kind. But I think we need not ask his help

in this. Mr. Wincannon can do all that is necessary. And we wish to keep the truth as quiet as possible."

"Oh, yes, I would never violate your confidence. Should I not have talked to Mr. Jarrett? He gave me to understand that you had told him the whole. Why, he inquired about Tony before I even mentioned the matter. He was excessively worried about us all, Elisabeth. Such a truly considerable man. But I didn't mean to do anything against your wishes, as I hope you know. I would never do so. Oh dear."

"It's quite all right, cousin," responded Elisabeth. "Do not upset yourself. I did tell Mr. Jarrett of our loss, and he was exceedingly kind about it, as you say. I am glad he's been a comfort to you."

Lavinia brightened. "Well, he has, you know. You have been so very busy and so worried that I didn't like to come to you with my silly fancies, but Mr. Jarrett has been so kind. I don't know how I would have gotten on without him."

Elisabeth felt a twinge of guilt for neglecting her cousin and a good deal of gratitude toward Jarrett, who had evidently spared her this task. She knew, with some shame, that Lavinia's chatter might have driven her half mad during this period, despite the older woman's good intentions and staunch support. She turned away. "I will write the Wincannons," she said.

Derek Wincannon called very soon after he received Elisabeth's note. He examined Tony's letter with frowning concentration, but when he looked up from it, he had little to say. "You're sure it is Tony's hand?" he asked Elisabeth. The two were standing once more before the library fire.

Elisabeth nodded. "It is shaky, and I admit I didn't recognize it at first. But I have looked very carefully since, and I am sure it is his."

Wincannon nodded also. "Well, then we know he's safe." He put the note on the desk and turned back to Elisabeth. "I must say I consider it unlikely that we'll find him before he communicates with you again. There is no clue here. He might be anywhere."

Elisabeth agreed soberly. "I only wish I might go to him," she added. Derek smiled, but said nothing. Elisabeth suddenly noticed that he looked very tired. She held out her hand. "You have been so kind to us through this time," she said. "You have quite worn yourself down, I believe. I don't know how to thank you."

He took her hand and looked directly into her eyes. He started to speak, hesitated, then said, "It has been my pleasure to assist you." His tone was very serious, and Elisabeth felt a little uncomfortable. She drew back her hand gently.

"You must go home now and rest," she went on. "Knowing Tony is safe, we can all relax."

After a moment, Derek nodded. "I shall continue my inquiries, however, so that we can bring him home where he belongs."

Elisabeth's restlessness did not diminish as the days went on. There was nothing she could do. Others would find Tony, or he would write to send for them. No task she began diverted her mind, however, from thoughts of him. Finally, late one afternoon, she gave up and readied herself for a walk. She might at least use this nervous energy, she thought. She stared out the window of her bedchamber. Perhaps the brisk wind she could see tossing the trees would scour her mind of fancies.

She was pulling on her gloves in the hall when she heard noises from the back garden. Growser was tied up there, she saw, and he didn't look happy about it. He was howling, in fact, though one of the footmen was trying to attract his attention to a large bowl of scraps set on the lawn. Elisabeth hurried down the back stairs and into the garden. "Growser," she said as she reached them, "I am sorry. I'd nearly forgotten you. Do you miss Tony also?" The young footman started and turned, rising to his feet. Elisabeth recognized him as the one who had bathed Growser and smiled. Thus encouraged, he said, "He is frettin', miss. He won't eat or pay me any heed."

Elisabeth looked down at the dog sympathetically. "And he hates being tied. I shall take him on my walk. He needs exercise."

"Oh, yes, miss," agreed the footman. "I was about to ask leave to take him out myself."

"Does he have a lead somewhere? I can't let him run free, though I would like to."

"I'll get it for you."

Within minutes Elisabeth and Growser were making their way down the street toward the park. Elisabeth thought she might be able to let him run a bit there. Growser was extremely excited. He jumped about her skirts and strained at his lead. She was actually as grateful as he for the company, for she had used Growser as an excuse to keep Ketchem from accompanying her. The maid's dislike of the dog had overcome her rigid sense of propriety, much to Elisabeth's amusement.

They entered the park at the southwest corner and began to walk along its length. It was relatively empty at this time of day. Most fashionable strollers had returned home for tea or to change for dinner. Growser investigated every bush and bench along the way. When they had nearly crossed the park, Elisabeth decided she could risk freeing the dog. There was no one about, and she thought he must run toward home, since all of the park lay in that direction. She unfastened the lead from his neck, saying, "There, now you can have a good run," and stood back.

Growser stood perfectly still for a moment, then gave a joyous bark and raced for a clump of trees that stood a little off the path. Elisabeth smiled and began to stroll back the way they had come. She went slowly, wishing to prolong this quiet interlude. Growser ran back and forth between her and the fascinations of the park. His energy, expressed in prodigious leaps and bounds, gave her some idea of how restless he'd been.

They were about halfway home when the dog's behavior suddenly altered. Elisabeth had paused for a moment near a gate at the side of the park, and Growser came running up to her to see what was the matter. But as he reached her, he stopped abruptly and raised his head. He stared out the gate and down the street that led away from it, whined softly, and stepped stiff-legged to the pavement. "No, Growser," Elisabeth commanded. "We're going this way." She made as if to walk down the path.

Growser ignored her, continuing to whine, and

looked about in a manner that irresistibly suggested uncertainty. Elisabeth frowned and walked through the gate to where he stood. "Come along now," she said. "I've been kind enough to take you out, but now we must go home. They'll be looking for us." Growser looked up at her and whined more loudly. He ran out into the street, stopped, looked back at her, then went on to the opposite side. "Growser," responded Elisabeth sharply. "This is not the time for games. I shan't take you walking again. Come here." Her tone was commanding, and the dog started toward her. But halfway across the street he stopped again, looked back down the adjoining avenue, and half turned. "Growser!" called Elisabeth.

He turned once more, and Elisabeth would have sworn that he looked pleadingly at her. She frowned, puzzled by this uncharacteristic behavior, and walked out into the street toward him holding out her hand. "What is it?" she asked. "Do you scent something here in the city? All the rabbits are in the park." Growser jumped and capered excitedly, ran to the opposite side of the street, then stopped and looked back at her. Elisabeth frowned again, paused, then followed.

They repeated this performance several times, proceeding some way along the street leading away from the park. Elisabeth was by now convinced that Growser was trying to show her something, and it looked remarkably like a path through town. When they reached a road going north and Growser showed every sign of turning along it and starting out of London. All at once, Elisabeth felt certain the dog was leading her to Tony. The walk in the park had reminded him of his adventure, and he had perhaps caught some lingering scent or seen something which set him going. She called him sharply, and when he ran back to her for a moment, she seized his collar and attached the lead again. It was late, and there was no time to pursue this trail today. Tomorrow, they would follow it and find Tony.

Exultant, Elisabeth hurried homeward, urging a reluctant Growser with her. She must write Derek at once, she thought, and organize a party to ride behind Growser. But at this point, she paused. She would almost certainly not be allowed to join such a party, she realized. Wincannon would protest that it might prove too taxing; her family would agree, and she would again be left to wait while others searched. Elisabeth's chin lifted, and a glint came into her eyes. She had had enough of waiting, she thought, and of running to Derek Wincannon for help like a lost child. Tony had said that he was safe; there was no longer any danger, if indeed there had ever been. She would follow Growser herself.

When she reached home, Elisabeth handed Growser over to the footman and went directly up to her room to change for dinner, saying nothing about her discovery. She retired early, saying she had letters to write.

In her room, Elisabeth did sit down at the writing desk, but she wrote a note to her own family, explaining her idea and what she planned to do. She would leave it on the mantelpiece, she thought, to keep them from worrying. That done, she pulled a small leather case from her wardrobe and put a few necessary items in it— some clean linen, a hairbrush, and some tooth powder.

She allowed Ketchem to make her ready for bed, and then dismissed her, saying that she hoped to sleep rather late in the morning. Ketchem looked disapproving, but said nothing. When she was alone again, Elisabeth took out her new blue velvet riding habit and looked at it disapprovingly. It was too fine for the sort of travel she was planning. Putting it back, she pushed aside several of her other new gowns and reached far into the closet for her old habit she had sometimes used in Bath to ride with her pupils. It looked just the thing. She dragged it out and surveyed its drab brown folds; no one would take her for a rich Londoner in this, she thought. She hung it on the front of the wardrobe and shut the door. She was ready.

# *Sixteen*

ELISABETH WOKE WITH A START AND SAT UP QUICKLY. She hadn't thought she would sleep, but here was light showing through a gap in the curtains at her window. She jumped out of bed, afraid she'd missed her chance to leave the house, but when she pulled the curtains back, she saw that it was only just dawn. She could hear no noises in the house below. She dressed quickly in her old riding habit and picked up her case. If she could just get away without attracting anyone's attention, she thought, they could do nothing. She went softly down to the hall and stood listening a moment. Still, no sounds. She crept to the kitchen, and seeing no one about, added a bit of bread and cheese to the things in her case.

Gently, Elisabeth unlocked the door into the back garden and went out, pulling it closed behind her. Growser was lying with his head on his paws, but he jumped up as soon as he saw her and strained at the chain clipped to his collar. He barked once before Elisabeth could reach him, but when she put her hand on his head and begged him to be quiet he complied, rather surprising her. She loosed him quickly and entwined her fingers in his collar. Together, they traversed the garden and came to the stables.

It was here that Elisabeth was most afraid of discovery. The grooms were often up very early, she knew, and it would take her a little time to get her horse saddled herself. She paused in the stableyard, listening again. She heard nothing but the movements of the horses in their stalls. They advanced to the stable door, and Elisabeth peered around it. She could see no one in the building. She pulled Growser into the room and shut the door. With some difficulty, she got her saddle down from its high hook and saddled her mare.

Checking the stableyard once more, Elisabeth directed her small party out. She mounted at the block and urged her horse to the yard gate. This was the time when she might be caught. They reached the exit; Elisabeth leaned down and opened the gate, and they were out. Growser capered about excitedly. Kicking her horse's flanks, she got them all under way.

Growser was eager. He led them in a lope past the park and on to the north road. There were almost no pedestrians about at this early hour, and most vehicles were heavy delivery carts. Some of their drivers looked curiously at Elisabeth, but no one offered to accost her. They traveled rapidly at first, and very soon, they were nearing the outskirts of town. Buildings gradually gave way to open fields and farms, and Elisabeth relaxed somewhat.

They had ridden for about an hour and were well out of town when Growser stopped for the first time. He looked about him for a minute, then sat down by the side of the road and began to scratch his ear. Elisabeth pulled up and watched him. When he finished scratching but still showed no signs of moving on, she said, "Growser, you wretched dog, what are you doing? You aren't giving up now, certainly?"

Growser cocked an ear and gazed up at her, his tongue lolling out amiably. He stretched out on the grass at the verge of the road and panted.

"Are you just tired, perhaps?" continued Elisabeth without much hope. She leaned back in the saddle and sighed. "How bird-witted I shall seem," she said to herself, "arriving home from my adventure with nothing to show." Two carriages passed as time went on; the driver of one looked at Elisabeth very insolently, she thought. At last, she addressed Growser again, feeling at once very annoyed and very silly. "All right, you tiresome animal, either go on or turn and go home. I shan't wait here any longer."

To her astonishment, Growser rose and began to trot along the road once more. She paused a moment, wondering at the wisdom of following him further, then shrugged and rode forward. "I may as well go on to the end now," she murmured. "I can't appear any more foolish than I shall if I go home now."

Moving more slowly, they traveled a good distance; then, Growser stopped again. But before Elisabeth could scold him, he turned and headed down a small lane that intersected the main road. Elisabeth's spirits rose; perhaps the dog did know where he was going after all. This road was tortuous and very long. The sun began to be hot on Elisabeth's head. Ten o'clock came and passed. Elisabeth munched some of her bread and cheese guiltily, scolding herself for forgetting to bring anything for Growser. They'd been riding for nearly four hours, and she was tiring. Too, the lane was narrow and unkempt—the hedges nearly meeting in the middle in some places—and she was forced to bend and duck repeatedly. The exertion tired her even more, and the state of the lane made her a bit uneasy. What could be at the end of such a thoroughfare?

Her question was answered soon after. They came out of the lane into another highway, and Growser turned unerringly to the right. Elisabeth pulled a stray twig from her hair, shrugged, and followed. This road was well-kept and well-traveled, though it was not one of the main London roads. They passed several prosperous-looking farms and were greeted pleasantly by passersby. Elisabeth relaxed again.

By noon, however, she was tired out. She pulled up and called to Growser to stop. "I must rest a moment," she told him. "I am too stiff and cramped to go on." The dog halted with seeming reluctance, and when Elisabeth started to dismount, he jumped up at her, barking. His insistent leaps prevented her from climbing down; she was afraid he would cause her to fall. "Growser," she commanded, "stand away, sit down." But the dog showed no signs of obeying. Elisabeth sat back in her saddle, sighing. "This is not at all what I expected," she said aloud. "Apparently, an adventure is nothing more than a tired back, a headache, and a good deal of annoyance." Growser had moved away a little, and again she tried to get down. The dog hurried back and jumped at her once more.

She put a hand to her aching forehead. For a moment,

all was quiet. "Very well," she said looking up, "let us go on, then. But I tell you now, Growser, if we do not find Tony at the end of this journey, you'll have to find a new home." She kicked her horse, and they started forward.

Half an hour passed, and they began to follow a high stone wall which ran along the right side of the road. Even mounted, Elisabeth couldn't see over it, and the top appeared to be spiked and strewn with broken glass. However, ivy also grew thickly across it, and the mortar between the stones was crumbling in places, rather defeating its ferocious purpose. It was a very long wall. Elisabeth stood in her stirrups and tried to see the end, but it curved out of sight far ahead. However, there was a large gate further on; she looked at Growser hopefully.

But the dog stopped almost immediately, a good distance from this opening. He turned to the wall at a place where it had begun to collapse and had been propped up with wooden beams inside. The top third of its height was gone here, and the remainder was more a pile of stones than a wall. This section extended for at least six feet, leaving a sizable gap. Growser looked at the opening, whined, peered over his shoulder at Elisabeth, and then, just as she was about to call him, jumped up and clambered over the wall, disappearing into the park beyond. "Growser!" called Elisabeth sharply. "Come back here." She waited; there was no response. She pounded on her leg with a gloved fist. "Growser," she shouted again. The dog did not return. Elisabeth looked at the wall, then at her horse, and finally at the empty road before her.

"Splendid," she said to herself. "Whatever am I to do now?"

Ten minutes later, after a hurried survey of the area, she hadn't yet answered this question to her own satisfaction. The only way for her to follow Growser was either to try to climb over the wall in her cumbersome habit or to ride boldly up to the gate and inquire for her cousin. Neither seemed attractive to her at the moment. She was, in fact, wishing she had remained quietly at home while Derek Wincannon and his groom followed Growser across the countryside.

Providence did not intervene, and at last, she straightened her shoulders and started for the gate. Having ridden all this way, she had to carry through. When, or if, the gatekeeper disavowed all knowledge of Tony, she would turn and go home, leaving Growser to fend for himself as he had left her.

Elisabeth rode smartly up to the gate and looked about her. The intricate wrought-iron panels stood open, and she could see some rust here and there. The lodge was a little distance up the avenue, nearly hidden behind a dense screen of currant bushes and weeds. Like the drive, it was not well kept up; clearly, the park grounds had not enjoyed the attentions of a gardener for some years. "It looks rather like Willowmere," said Elisabeth meditatively, "though not quite so dilapidated." She rode over to the lodge and rapped on the door with her riding crop, steeling herself for an encounter with the gatekeeper.

There was no answer to her knock, nor to the second or the third. Elisabeth was forced to conclude

that no one was home. She leaned down and hesitantly peered through the dirty window of the house.
At first, she could see nothing, but when she had
rubbed a clean spot on the glass, she realized that the
room beyond was empty. The house was disused.
"Well, that is anticlimactic," she said, speaking aloud
to herself again. "I wonder if Growser has led me to
an abandoned estate. Perhaps he has only run off after
a rabbit." She guided her horse back to the middle
of the avenue and sat still for a moment, then, with a
shrug, she started up the drive.

It led her on a winding progress of at least a mile,
through a heavily wooded park much overgrown
with underbrush. The afternoon sun was disappearing
under thick clouds, and it was dark under the trees;
Elisabeth increased her pace a bit. Finally, she saw
a house ahead, and the lights visible in some of the
windows reassured her. "At least it isn't abandoned,"
she said, and urged her mare on. The drive curved
about in front of the house and continued on behind.
There was no block to be seen, so Elisabeth slid from
her horse near the door. The stiffness of her muscles
was even more obvious as she walked up to it.

She hesitated only a minute before knocking; she
was, after all, committed now. This time, her first
attempt brought an immediate answer. A young housemaid opened the door and looked at her with some
astonishment. "Good evening," said Elisabeth, with all
the assurance she could muster. "I am here to see my
cousin, Anthony Brinmore." She was rather pleased
with this statement. It expressed so much more confidence than she felt.

"Mr. Brinmore?" replied the maid. "Oh, yes, miss. Please to come in."

"Y-you mean, he *is* here?" Elisabeth's surprise overcame her poise.

The maid blinked. She looked at Elisabeth warily.

"I wasn't certain I'd found the house," added Elisabeth hastily, trying to recover her original tone. She stepped into the hall. "Will you tell him, please, that his cousin Elisabeth has arrived? And can someone see to my horse?"

The housemaid nodded silently and shut the door. She indicated that Elisabeth should enter a room off the front hall, and when she had seen her do so, disappeared.

Elisabeth walked into a small saloon papered and hung in dark green satin. There was no fire and no candles had been lighted, though the afternoon sun hardly penetrated through the heavily draped eastern windows, and the room was a little dark. But she sank down gratefully on the sofa in front of the fireplace, wearily rubbing the muscles of her neck and shoulders. She sat thus for at least ten minutes, surveying the old-fashioned furniture and murky pictures that dotted the walls. She was becoming impatient when she heard a noise from the doorway and turned to find a very odd-looking gentleman confronting her.

In her surprise, Elisabeth said nothing at first, and the man was also silent. It was not so much his appearance that was unusual. He was a slight person of medium height and about sixty years of age, she thought. But his dress was such as must catch the eye and amaze. He looked like an historical portrait. His full-skirted coat was of satin and liberally embroidered.

There were cascades of lace at his wrists and throat, and he wore knee britches and white silk stockings ornamented with clocks. His shoes had three-inch red heels and ornate buckles that seemed to Elisabeth to be made of diamonds. She was still blinking at this vision when he pulled an enameled snuffbox from his coat pocket, flipped it open with one thumb, and said, "Good evening."

"G-good, evening," replied Elisabeth. "I…I am sorry to arrive at an inconvenient hour, but Tony gave us very little idea of how far he might be from London."

The man raised his eyebrows. "Indeed. I am told you are Mr. Brinmore's cousin, Elisabeth, ah, Brinmore?"

"Elisabeth Elham, sir." She was beginning to resent his tone. "And I am told that my cousin is here? May I see him, please?"

"In a moment. Young Tony arrived here in rather odd circumstances, you see. I remain somewhat puzzled. Shall we sit down?" He motioned her back to the sofa and sat down beside her.

Elisabeth sat very straight and lifted her chin. "What do you mean, odd circumstances?" she asked. "And why can I not see Tony? Is he worse?"

"Worse?" answered her companion, looking at her closely.

Elisabeth was too tired for such sparring. "I believe you heard me. My cousin said in his note to me that he had been wounded but was recovering. I wish to see him immediately."

The man held up a hand. "I understand your anxiety," he replied. "But you must understand that Tony has been in some sort of danger, and I don't wish to see him harmed in my house. I must be sure you are indeed his cousin." His brown eyes remained hard. "Why do you arrive alone and without warning?" he continued, surveying her critically.

Elisabeth leaned back on the sofa with an angry sigh. "Because I'm a fool," she said. "As is Tony. He neglected to give us his direction, and I followed his wretched dog here." At the gentleman's uncomprehending look, she explained the events of the last few days to him. By the time she'd finished, he was looking less forbidding.

He smiled slightly. "I must say, had I not become somewhat acquainted with Tony in the last several days, I would dismiss your story as nonsense. But having done so, it sounds remarkably likely. You and your cousin have much in common."

"I sincerely hope not," answered Elisabeth fervently.

This time, the man's smile was warm. "Come," he went on, "I will take you to Tony." He rose and waited for her.

Elisabeth had nearly forgotten his strange costume as they talked, but now she was made aware of it again. Why, she wondered, did he dress in this outmoded way? No one had worn such clothes for thirty years, at least.

As they started up the stairs in the hall, the man spoke again. "I should introduce myself. You must think me abominably rude. I am Lucius Aldgate, and this is my house, Steen. Belatedly, I make you welcome."

Elisabeth smiled. "Thank you," she said, "that is reassuring. But I could not think anyone rude who took such care of Tony as I fancy you have. I'm very eager to hear what happened."

Mr. Aldgate nodded. "We must give your cousin his part in the telling, however. He would never forgive me else."

They had by now reached the second floor, and her host turned into a bedchamber on the left. A fire was burning there, and it looked very cozy. In a huge four-poster bed against the far wall lay Tony, his face a little white. His shoulder was bound up, and the nightshirt he wore was uncharacteristically ornate, but otherwise he appeared all right. He looked up when they entered. "Cousin Elisabeth," he cried. "I hoped you would come."

Elisabeth walked over to the bed and embraced him gently. Then, she stepped back. "Did you indeed?" she asked, smiling. "I might have come sooner had you put your direction in the note, you graceless scamp."

Tony's eyes widened. "Did I not? I can't precisely recollect what I did say, but I must have told you where I was and how kind Mr. Aldgate had been."

Elisabeth shook her head, her eyes twinkling. "You did not."

"Tony was burnt to the socket when we found him," put in their host. "I was amazed he could write at all."

At this, Elisabeth's expression sobered. "And where was he found?" she asked. "There is a great deal I want to know about what has happened." She looked at both of them with raised eyebrows.

"Will you begin, Tony?" said Aldgate.

Nodding, the boy said, "Yes, I suppose I must. I

believe now that it began when I met an animal trainer in London who promised he could teach Growser all manner of things."

"Growser!" interrupted Elisabeth suddenly. "Has someone found him?"

Tony looked surprised; he shook his head sorrowfully. "No," he said. "He's been gone for days now. Mr. Aldgate's servants have searched everywhere."

"No, no. He came with me. He must be here somewhere."

"What!" Tony sat up suddenly, then winced and sank back on the pillows. "What are you talking about?" he went on more quietly.

Elisabeth told the story of her journey once more. Tony was delighted and full of admiration for his dog. "I knew he was a prime 'un," he said as she finished. "What other animal could have led you here in such a way? We must find him."

"He must be somewhere in the park," said Elisabeth, looking to Mr. Aldgate. "He jumped over the wall where it is broken down."

Aldgate went to the bellpull and summoned his valet. "We'll find him directly."

Elisabeth sat down in a chair beside the bed. Her fatigue was catching up with her. "Now," she said, "you may continue with your story."

Tony nodded. "Well, as I said, the trainer, Gibbs, convinced me that he could teach Growser to hunt. I see now that he never meant to do any such thing, but he did teach him to sit on command." Tony looked at them defensively, but Elisabeth only nodded, smiling slightly. "At any rate," the boy continued, "we had some talks about it and finally agreed to meet at the house of a friend of Gibbs's outside the city. He said he needed a large space for proper training. I went out there one afternoon, expecting to return early, but when I arrived Gibbs and his friend offered me a glass of ale to cut the dust of the journey. I drank it, and the next thing I knew I was in a dark room, trussed up like a chicken, and feeling sick and dizzy."

"They drugged you!" exclaimed Elisabeth.

Tony nodded, and Mr. Aldgate said, "It seems so indeed."

"This is outrageous. They must be caught and punished. To think we had that trainer in our hands and let him slip away."

"Did you?" said Tony interestedly. "You were on my trail, then?"

"We and all our friends have been searching for you for days," replied Elisabeth. "What did you think we would do?"

"I knew you'd try to find me," answered Tony seriously. "Indeed, that was my first thought when I awoke in the darkness, and it kept up my hopes throughout the whole adventure."

"Did you see your captors?" asked Elisabeth eagerly.

Tony shook his head. "Never. A maid brought me food and helped me eat, but she was always very frightened and obviously knew nothing of their plans. She would hardly talk to me and told me nothing of them, though I asked at every opportunity."

"So we still don't know why they kidnapped you," said Elisabeth slowly, tapping the bedside table with one finger and staring meditatively across the room.

"Ransom?" suggested Mr. Aldgate.

She turned to him. "Perhaps. But I received no such request; I heard nothing, in fact."

"Revenge?" added Aldgate more tentatively. "For some imagined wrong?"

Elisabeth shrugged and looked to Tony, torn between amusement and concern.

Tony snorted derisively. "A fellow would have to have quite an imagination to think I'd wronged him. I haven't quarreled with anyone in London."

Elisabeth shrugged again. "So it remains a mystery. But tell me how you came here, Tony. Did Mr. Aldgate rescue you?"

Tony looked outraged. "Of course he didn't. I escaped." He paused dramatically, waiting for Elisabeth's reaction.

"Did you indeed?" she said appreciatively. "How did you manage it?"

Her cousin's eyes sparkled. "Well, they kept me in an upstairs room, you know. But after a few days, they had the ropes removed. Didn't think I could go anywhere." He looked scornful. "So, I watched the yard below my window and learned the household's schedule while I worked loose one of the bars." He paused. "They were very old. Why do you suppose bars were put on upstairs windows?" Neither of his listeners appeared ready to answer this question, so he continued. "I could see Growser; they had him tied in the yard. And very unhappy he was about it. He howled the day long. Finally, I got one bar free, and that night, I skinned out and jumped for it. Twisted my ankle a bit, but not so that I couldn't walk. I untied

Growser, and we legged it for the road, but they had a man on watch at the gate. I didn't expect that, hadn't seen him before. He's the one who shot me. But we kept running, and I stumbled onto Mr. Aldgate's land where he found me the next day and kindly took me in. Growser had gone. Back to London, I guess." Tony looked very proud at this idea.

Elisabeth turned to Mr. Aldgate, frowning. "The house where he was kept must be very close then," she said.

"Oh, yes," replied her host. "I believe we've found the house. It only remains for Tony to confirm it when he can get about again. But it's quite deserted, of course. They left when Tony escaped."

"But we can inquire..." began Elisabeth.

Mr. Aldgate inclined his head. "I have done so. The house was rented two months ago to a Mr. Smith from Bristol."

"Oh." She looked down. "There is no possibility of tracing them, I suppose."

"I fear not."

"Perhaps Growser could find them," put in Tony. "He found me, after all."

Elisabeth smiled at him. Mr. Aldgate rose. "I'll inquire about Growser," he said. "I hope he is found. And I'll have a chamber prepared for you, Miss Elham. You will stay with us, I hope?" Elisabeth nodded. "And perhaps you would like to dine here with your cousin? I will give the orders." He nodded to them and went out.

Left alone with her cousin for the first time, Elisabeth turned to him. "I'm truly glad to have found you again, you know, Tony," she said. "Thank God you're all right."

"Thank Mr. Aldgate, rather," answered Tony irreverently. "I don't mind telling you I was run off my legs when he came upon me. He's been truly good to me."

Elisabeth nodded. "I'm grateful to him indeed. Why does he wear such strange clothing? Do you know?"

Tony frowned for a moment, then his brow cleared. "You know I've become so used to them, I forgot how odd they must look to you. But I don't know why he wears them. Likes 'em, I suppose." The topic didn't seem to interest him much. "I wonder if they've found Growser yet."

"If they've searched near the kitchens," replied Elisabeth drily, "I wager they have."

Tony laughed. "I daresay you're right. It's good to see you, Cousin Elisabeth. I've had no one to laugh with for ages."

There was a light tap on the door, and a middle-aged woman entered. "Hello, miss," she said, curtsying slightly. "I am Mrs. Deal, the housekeeper. I'll show you to your chamber when you're ready."

Elisabeth rose. "Oh, thank you. I should love to wash and get tidy again. Tony, I'll see you later."

"Mind you hurry," was her cousin's only reply. "I'm devilish hungry."

# Seventeen

THEY SAT DOWN TO DINNER ABOUT AN HOUR LATER. The two cousins asked Mr. Aldgate to join them, and though he was at first reluctant, their sincere wish to have him present won him over. A table was arranged next to Tony's bed, and Elisabeth soon understood that this had become the customary arrangement since Tony's arrival at the house.

When the servants had brought coffee and retired and she had duly praised the food, Elisabeth turned to Mr. Aldgate. "I'd like to hear your part in Tony's story," she said. "I don't yet know how you found him."

"Ah." Mr. Aldgate sat back in his chair. "I really had little part in the adventure, I fear. I'd taken my gun out just before dawn in hopes of getting some birds. I walked down through the park rather sleepily at first, not trying too hard to find a target, and when I reached the wall, I turned along it. As I passed the broken place you noticed, I heard a low moaning and stopped. When it came again, I began to search, and soon, I found Tony lying in some underbrush, very well hidden. He showed a great deal of sense in crawling there, wounded as he was." He nodded at Tony, who beamed. "But he'd taken a chill during the night and was nearly delirious, so I covered him with my coat and got help as fast as possible. We brought him in and sent for the doctor." He looked up at Elisabeth. "And that is my entire participation in the story."

"I'm so grateful to you," said Elisabeth. "You saved Tony's life."

"He did," continued Tony. "And he's said nothing about the trouble he's taken, searching for Growser and investigating my kidnapping. He's been nearly run off his legs waiting on me."

Mr. Aldgate made a deprecatory gesture. "Nonsense. This has been the most exciting thing to happen at Steen in thirty years. It is I who should be grateful."

Tony snorted, but the older man went on quite seriously. "It's true. I've shut myself up here too long. It was very good for me to be shaken up a bit." His eyes twinkled. "In fact, I found I quite liked it. Perhaps I shall come up to London once again and call on you when you return."

"Do," cried Tony.

And, "Of course, you must," said Elisabeth at the same time.

Mr. Aldgate smiled at them warmly. "You're very good," he added. "But of course, I shan't. You have no wish to be saddled with an old eccentric."

"That is not true," said Elisabeth.

"Of course it isn't," insisted Tony. "You can come home with me when I'm fit and stay as long as you like."

Mr. Aldgate looked over their heads into space.

"London," he said meditatively. "I haven't seen her for more than thirty years." He looked down again and smiled at them before either could speak. "Well, well, it's not yet time to think of travel. Tony will require rest and quiet for some time."

Diverted, Elisabeth turned to look at her cousin. "Yes. You are still very white, Tony. Perhaps you should sleep now."

"At seven o'clock?" replied Tony, aghast. "I'm not the least sleepy. And in any case, I can't sleep until I find out that Growser is safely back."

Elisabeth looked at their host, but he shook his head. "He was not yet found when I last checked," he said. "I'll ask again." He rose, and before Elisabeth could protest, he was out of the room.

"What a kind man he is," she exclaimed.

Tony nodded. "But he never gets Holy Ned about it. That's what I like."

Elisabeth laughed. "I see. Well, you were exceedingly fortunate to fall into his park. I hope you feel it." Tony vowed that he did, and Elisabeth's expression sobered. "Perhaps he wears clothes like those he had when last in London," she added meditatively. "I wonder why, though?"

"Are you still fidgeting over that?" asked her cousin. "What does it matter?"

"It doesn't *matter*," answered Elisabeth. "I'm curious; that's all. Aren't you at all interested in the question?"

"No," replied Tony promptly. "He might wear rags for all me. I shan't like him one whit the less." He shrugged. "What can have become of Growser? Do you think he went back to London again?"

Elisabeth frowned. "It seems unlikely. He appeared to know just where he was going. I thought he would come directly to you."

"Perhaps he went back to where I fell and hid," suggested the boy.

Elisabeth rose. "That is a sound idea," she said. "I must tell Mr. Aldgate to have them look there." But as she was preparing to leave the room, their host entered.

"They've found him," said Mr. Aldgate. "He was searching the park for you, it appears. He is in the kitchen, devouring a large bowl of scraps. I thought you would wish him fed first of all."

"Oh, yes," said Tony. "Then can I see him?"

Mr. Aldgate nodded and smiled, as did Elisabeth. She rose. "I should write to my family in London and tell them I'm all right, else they may think I've also been kidnapped," she said. "And I'm so tired from the long ride today, I believe I'll retire early. Now that Growser is found, and all is well, I will say good night."

"Of course," answered Aldgate, bowing slightly as she turned to go.

"Don't forget to give your direction," called Tony.

Elisabeth turned back, wrinkled her nose at him, then threw up her hands helplessly. She left Tony laughing heartily and went to the chamber she had been given.

She didn't wake until nearly noon the next day, and when she first moved, she felt all the effects of her unusually long ride. Her legs and back were stiff and sore, and she was still tired, despite her long sleep. She rose slowly and rang for hot water, moving gingerly to sit before the fire. Soon, two maids entered, one carrying a large can of steaming water, and the other bearing a tray on which sat a pot of tea, a plate of buttered toast, and a large dish of marmalade. They curtsied briefly, and the second girl said, "Mrs. Deal thought you might be hungry, miss, it being so late."

"Thank you," answered Elisabeth. "That was very kind of her."

"Shall I help you dress, miss?" asked the other girl. She had set the hot water down on the washstand.

"No, thank you. I'll manage. And I believe I'll have some tea first. I suppose there hasn't been time for my clothes to arrive from town?"

Both girls shook their heads. "But your message went off first thing," volunteered one. "They should be along any time."

Elisabeth dismissed them, sitting down before the fire once again and pouring herself a cup of tea. She was just spreading a slice of toast thickly with marmalade when she heard horses approaching the house. Thinking her clothes had come, she went to the window, which overlooked the drive in front of the house. A curricle was sweeping up at a very rapid pace, and as it came closer, she recognized Derek Wincannon on the box.

He was driving so fast that she feared he wouldn't be able to stop, but right in front of the door, he pulled up his team sharply. He paused, surveying the house, and saw Elisabeth leaning from her second-floor window.

"You are here," he said, very loudly and harshly. "I couldn't believe you had been so bird-witted."

Elisabeth blinked. "What do you mean?"

"To ride off alone, following that ridiculous dog.

You might have had a fall or been kidnapped yourself or met God knows what kinds of ruffians on the road. I thought you had a little intelligence, a little judgment. But you've proved me utterly mistaken."

"I found Tony," snapped Elisabeth, thoroughly angered by his tone, "which is more than you could manage to do, even assisted by half of London."

Derek's hold on the reins tightened alarmingly. His horses sidled and tossed their heads. "Indeed. No doubt that is why you declined to take me into your confidence when you discovered something at last. My ineptitude."

"No," said Elisabeth quickly, feeling guilty for her last remark. "It was just that I had done nothing. I had been so helpless. I…I wanted to…"

"You wanted to hold us all up as fools, and you did. Smartly. I salute your enviable sagacity." He lifted his whip in a bitterly mocking gesture.

"Oh, that's not fair," she cried, "I…" At that moment, the front door opened, and Mr. Aldgate appeared in the drive. He greeted Derek, and following his gaze, saw Elisabeth in the window. He bowed to her gravely. "This young man is here in response to your message?" he asked.

"Yes, yes," replied Elisabeth distractedly. "This is Mr. Derek Wincannon. Mr. Lucius Aldgate, the owner of this house, who has been so kind to Tony." She trailed off in some confusion, suddenly becoming aware that she was leaning out the window in her nightdress, curls all about her face in disarray.

The gentlemen greeted one another. "I've brought Miss Elham's things," said Derek curtly.

Mr. Aldgate nodded. "I'll have someone fetch them. Won't you step down and come in?"

But Wincannon shook his head. "No. I must hold my horses." He pulled a valise from behind his seat and handed it down to Aldgate.

"Surely you will stay a moment," put in Elisabeth from above. She had partly withdrawn from the window; only her head showed. She'd been about to retire entirely when she heard Derek's pronouncement.

"I have pressing business," replied Wincannon. Mr. Aldgate looked from one of the young people to the other and said nothing.

"But Tony will wish to see you," continued Elisabeth urgently.

"I cannot see why he should." And with one piercing glance up at her, Derek turned his curricle and drove back the way he had come.

"Well," said Elisabeth, gazing after him with wide eyes.

Mr. Aldgate also followed the carriage with his eyes for a moment, then he glanced up at Elisabeth, shook his head, and walked back into the house carrying her valise.

Elisabeth spent several days at Steen. She wished to see for herself that Tony was mending. When she left at the end of the week, in her own carriage this time with Lavinia and Belinda, who had driven out to spend the day with Tony, she was satisfied that he would be able to return home soon. On the drive, she thought again of Derek Wincannon and the abrupt way he'd left her. Why had he come at all, if only to be so rude? She felt angry when she remembered his harsh reproaches, but mostly she wished that he'd stayed for a little while and allowed her to explain herself. She found that it mattered very much to her that he understand.

There had been no further word from him, and Lavinia and Belinda hadn't seen him. As they rode back to town, they talked of other friends, particularly those who'd asked for her or sent messages to Tony. They had put it about that Tony had been hurt while supervising some construction at Willowmere.

Belinda now thought of little but wedding clothes. She'd decided to be married in London at the end of the season, and all of her attention was taken up by preparations for that event. Lavinia entered into her enthusiasm unreservedly.

The sun was just setting when their carriage pulled up before the house, and Elisabeth jumped down gratefully. Ketchem stood by the open front door, arms crossed, glowering, but Elisabeth was happy to see even her and greeted her affectionately. Ketchem sniffed, but her expression softened; and she took charge of the luggage with no more than a muttered complaint.

Elisabeth strode into the hall and smiled at Ames, who was hovering there. "Well, I'm home," she told him unnecessarily. "And none the worse for my adventure."

"Yes, Miss Elham," he replied, continuing to look worried. "And very glad we all are. But I'm afraid there's a gentleman waiting to see you, miss. He insisted upon coming in, though I told him you were out of town. 'She's coming soon, isn't she?' he said. 'I want to welcome her back.' Very abrupt, he was."

"Is it Mr. Wincannon?" asked Elisabeth quickly.

"No, miss. It's Mr. Jarrett."

Elisabeth frowned. "Mr. Jarrett?" she repeated. "What can he want? Where is he, in the drawing room?" At Ames's nod, she started up the stairs. "I'll just say hello, but I'm not in the mood for callers."

Mr. Jarrett was standing with his back to the drawing room fire, his hands behind him, looking contemplative. When Elisabeth entered the room, he smiled and came forward eagerly. "Hello," he said. "I called to welcome you back to London. It has missed you sorely. I couldn't resist being the first to tell you so, since I believe I am one of the ones who felt it most."

Elisabeth greeted him rather coolly and sat down on the sofa. He joined her and sat for a moment watching her face. "Are you angry with me?" he asked finally. "I couldn't keep away. I wanted so much to see you and to tell you how glad I am that your cousin is found and safe."

The girl softened a little. "That is kind of you. I am only a little tired; I just this moment arrived home, you know."

He hit his knee with a loose fist. "And I have been rude to insist upon seeing you now. I beg pardon." He sighed, frowning. "When will I learn to keep the bounds? I have never thought myself a stupid man, but I admit that the conventions of polite society seem to escape me with a startling regularity." He smiled at her. "Let us admit that life abroad has ruined me and be done with it. I continue to let my feelings be my guide, and I continue to come a cropper."

Elisabeth returned his smile, her eyes held by his for a long moment. "It is of no consequence," she replied.

Jarrett shook his head. "You say so because you are the soul of politeness. Well, I can only promise to do better." He shrugged. "I shall try, at any rate." There was a short pause. "And so your cousin is found," he continued. "I congratulate you most sincerely."

"Thank you. I am very grateful for it."

"I know how you have been worrying."

Elisabeth inclined her head. "Yes, it is good to have it over. We only hope now to avoid talk about the whole horrid incident."

"Of course, I shall say nothing. Have you found out who was responsible?" Elisabeth looked up, startled, and he added, "Your cousin told me that it was definitely a kidnapping. I was never more shocked. And how I wished I'd been of some help to you. You have no idea how helpless I felt, watching friends in trouble and unable to do anything."

Elisabeth had been a little uneasy about Mr. Jarrett's knowledge of their trouble, but this sentiment, so much like her own feeling during the incident, reassured her and struck a responsive chord. She smiled up at him warmly. "You were a great help. Indeed, I must thank you. My cousin has told me what comfort you gave her through this time."

He brushed this aside. "It was nothing. Anyone might have done the same."

"No, indeed, I do not allow that to be true at all. Very few people would make such a sustained effort. We are all grateful."

He shrugged. "It was not to elicit your gratitude that I spoke; let us talk no more about it. When does Tony come home?"

"Soon, I hope. I'm not precisely certain."

"Is he badly hurt?"

Elisabeth shook her head. She didn't wish to go into the details of Tony's injury even with this kind friend. To her relief, he didn't inquire further.

"Well, if I can be of any assistance—taking messages to him or escorting him home—you have only to say so. I hope you will."

"Thank you. You are a good friend."

Jarrett looked at her seriously, then reached over and took her hand. "I should like to be a better one," he said. "I've done so little, when I would do anything."

Elisabeth gazed into his pale eyes and was transfixed for a moment; his tone was very unsettling. She took a breath and gently pulled her hand away. "I...you are very kind. But all is well now, you know. There's no need for you to be concerned."

He continued to look at her intensely for a short space, then he nodded. "Of course. And that is a matter for much rejoicing." He rose. "But you will be wishing me at the devil for keeping you when you want to rest. I came only to welcome you back, after all."

Elisabeth rose also. "And I thank you."

They walked toward the door together. "I hope I will see you again soon," said Jarrett when they reached the head of the stairs.

"Well, I'm not precisely certain of our schedule right now. But we shall meet soon."

He bowed slightly and started to go. But before he had descended two steps, he turned back to her. "I hope you aren't offended," he said. "My feelings sometimes carry me further than I mean."

Elisabeth looked down. "I am not offended," she answered.

Seeming satisfied, he nodded quickly and continued down the stairs.

When he was gone, Elisabeth returned to the drawing room and sat there by herself for a time. She breathed a sigh, partly of fatigue, partly of relief. What is there about that man, she wondered? He disturbs me. She sat back, shaking her head.

She rubbed her temples wearily. She had hoped that Derek Wincannon would call to welcome her home, and instead it had been Jarrett. When would she find an opportunity to explain to Derek? There had been no word from him since the confrontation at Steen, and this seemed strange to her after their almost daily contact in the previous weeks. Evidently, he was still angry with her.

Cousin Lavinia entered the room. "Belinda has gone upstairs to rest," she said. "You should do the same. We'll probably have callers this evening to welcome you back."

Elisabeth nodded. "I'll go in a moment. Mr. Jarrett was just here for that very purpose."

Her cousin nodded. "I met him on the stairs. He's been to see me several times in your absence. I begin to think he's dangling after you, Elisabeth. It's rather worrisome. I'm not just sure what I should do, you see. I've been cogitating, and I simply do not know."

Elisabeth smiled slightly. "I can manage for myself, cousin. You needn't get yourself into a pucker."

Lavinia looked shocked. "Oh, dear me, of course you can, my dear. Such a composed young woman as you are, I would not dream of…no, my dear, it isn't that. But I have begun to suspect that Mr. Jarrett was never a close friend of William's, and it has worried me a vast deal. What am I to do?"

Elisabeth sat up straighter. "What do you mean?" she asked.

Lavinia looked at her. For the first time, Elisabeth noticed that she had dark circles under her eyes. "He always tries to avoid talking about William. I had seen that. But sometimes I insist. He thinks I don't notice the discredences. In fact, he thinks me a fool." Lavinia looked down at her hands, folded in her lap. Her usual cheerful air seemed to have deserted her, Elisabeth saw with concern. "Many people do," she continued without looking up. "But I am not, you know." She raised her head with a simple dignity and met Elisabeth's eyes squarely. "And I can tell when someone is hedging about a subject I know very well."

Elisabeth reached out and took both her cousin's hands. She was at a loss for the proper words, and so was forced to be content with, "Of course you can. No one with any sense ever thought you a fool. But you look burnt to the socket, Cousin Lavinia. You are the one who must rest. I have been putting too much work on you lately." Elisabeth felt remorseful as she gazed into her cousin's tired eyes.

"Nonsense," replied Lavinia more brightly. "I want to be of help. That's why I tell you not to be taken in by Mr. Jarrett. I believe he claimed acquaintance with William just to incinurate himself into our family."

Elisabeth nodded. "I'll remember. And now, you are going up to your bedchamber for a good nap before dinner." Lavinia protested, but finally let Elisabeth propel her to the stairs. She went slowly up to her room, making the younger girl feel even sadder at the weariness in her gait. Elisabeth resolved to do something particularly nice for her cousin.

With a sigh, Elisabeth let her head droop on the sofa pillow. There was so much to plan. She must make arrangements for getting Tony home and for the wedding. Gradually, her head sank lower and her eyelids dropped. In a few minutes, she was asleep on the drawing room sofa, curled up at the end, looking completely comfortable.

# Eighteen

THE EVENING SEEMED VERY SHORT TO ELISABETH. As Lavinia had foretold, they did have several callers. The duke and his mother were the first to arrive, just after dinner. He'd been making a habit of this whenever Belinda was at home, and tonight his mother accompanied him. The duchess immediately seated herself next to Elisabeth.

"Well, and so you are back," she said when she had arranged her skirts. "You have had quite an adventure. Tell me all the details."

Smiling, Elisabeth said, "Surely you have heard them ere this?"

The duchess shrugged. "Of course I know all about it. Belinda tells John everything, and we are one family now, after all. But I'm never sure she has gotten it right, you know. I wish to hear it from you."

Elisabeth's smile broadened a little. "Well, you've heard of my ride with Growser, I know, and that I found Tony."

"Yes, yes. Come, girl, you can certainly tell a better story than that."

Elisabeth laughed. "I shall tell you about Mr. Aldgate, then."

The duchess seemed astonished. "Aldgate? No, it couldn't be."

It was Elisabeth's turn to show surprise. "Do you know him? Mr. Lucius Aldgate? He lives at a house called Steen."

The duchess's eyes widened. "Did you know him, Judith?" asked cousin Lavinia. "Fancy that. I should have told you his name."

"Lucius Aldgate," repeated the duchess in a strangled voice. "I thought him dead these twenty years." She shook her head as if to clear it, made as if to rise, and fell heavily back onto the sofa in a dead faint.

"Judith!" cried Lavinia, jumping up and rushing to her friend's side.

Elisabeth also rose. "Your Grace!" she exclaimed. She took the duchess's hand and began to chafe her wrist. "Water," she called imperatively, and the duke hurried out of the room.

There were some minutes of confusion as people ran in and out and offered various remedies to the stricken woman. Soon, she regained consciousness, and though she seemed to have suffered no ill effects, Elisabeth and the duke insisted that she lie still on the sofa.

"The vapors," she said in strong accents of disgust as she complied, "and at my age. Disgraceful."

Now that the duchess appeared to be all right, Elisabeth's curiosity awakened. "What happened?" she asked. "What upset you so?"

But her guest was not in the mood for revelations.

"Never mind, young lady. An old woman may faint as she pleases, I suppose."

Elisabeth directed a puzzled glance at her son, but he shrugged helplessly, obviously as mystified by this development as she.

The duchess heaved herself up a little higher on the sofa pillows and made an obvious effort to change the subject. "You must tell me what you think of these wedding plans," she said to Elisabeth. "Lavinia and I have discussed everything with Belinda, but I have not heard your opinion." The engaged pair, hearing this subject broached, returned to their private dialogue. The duchess smiled. "I believe Belinda wants to dazzle the *ton* and properly cap the season with the festivities. It is to be the final week, you know."

Though her curiosity remained strong, Elisabeth allowed herself to be diverted. "Yes," she nodded. "I think you are right. She means it to be dazzling."

The duchess leaned back, smiling slightly. "Well, that is permissible, I suppose. My mother felt the same; she sent me off with a flourish."

"You had a large wedding?" replied Elisabeth encouragingly.

"Mammoth. Do you remember, Lavinia?" The duchess's eyes grew faraway as Lavinia enthusiastically affirmed that she did.

"I imagine that everyone dressed in satin coats and knee britches then. Mr. Aldgate still wears them. Isn't that odd?" Elisabeth couldn't resist one more try to find out what had upset the duchess.

The older woman's eyes regained their customary sharpness. "Indeed," she replied dryly. "It was the fashion of the time." She sat up straight again. "I believe I am fully recovered, but perhaps I should return home early to rest. John." Her son rose and gave her his arm; a footman was hurriedly sent to summon her carriage.

"Well," said Elisabeth when they were gone, "that was certainly curious. I wonder what made her faint?"

"Oh, I hope she's not ill," added Lavinia.

"She's no longer young," Belinda put in from the doorway. "I suppose some weakness must be expected."

Elisabeth shook her head. "It was something else, I think, but what?" She had no chance to speculate further, for the duke reentered the room then, followed by Lord James Darnell and Ames with the tea tray.

The new caller came directly to Elisabeth's side and took the seat vacated by the duchess. "Thank heaven you are back," he said. "Town has been utterly flat without you. I cannot count the dull parties where I longed for your presence."

"Good evening, Lord Darnell," replied Elisabeth with a smile. "How is your mother?"

The young man looked at her suspiciously, but Elisabeth's expression was bland as she bent to make the tea. "She's well," he answered. "You missed Lady Sefton's rout party, you know. And the balloon ascension in Hyde Park. That was fascinating."

"And how do your sisters do?" asked Elisabeth, handing Lavinia her cup.

Lord Darnell paused before answering; a twinkle started in his eyes. "They are also well. Longing to see you again. They were quite thrown into raptures over you, you know, particularly Aurelia."

Elisabeth choked with laughter as she gave him

his tea, shaking the cup and nearly spilling it over his knee. "Really?" she said when she could speak. "I am flattered."

Lord Darnell took a sip of tea. "Of course you are," he agreed with his engaging crooked smile. Elisabeth found, somewhat to her surprise, that she was truly glad to see him again.

"And I am trying desperately to amuse you," he continued, "so that you will realize how you missed me off in the country. What made you rusticate in the middle of the season?"

Elisabeth's merriment faded a little. She remembered that she hadn't told Lord Darnell about Tony's disappearance. "Ah, well," she answered lightly, "there is a great deal of construction going on at my country house, you know." This was not a lie, she told herself guiltily.

Her companion nodded. "I'm certain it will be the showplace of its neighborhood. I should like to see it." He looked at Elisabeth suggestively, his blue eyes wide.

She laughed. "Were you not taught that it is improper to dangle after invitations?" she asked him teasingly.

"On the contrary, I was taught that it was vital. How else is one to be invited?"

"Oh, how can you be so outrageous?"

Lord Darnell looked solemn. "It *is* a rare talent," he said. "Many have remarked on it with envy. It appears one must be born to it. I have not succeeded in teaching anyone how to do it properly."

Elisabeth laughed again, shaking her head helplessly. Darnell smiled at her once more. "Admit it," he cried. "You have missed me. Who in the country amused you so?"

She raised her eyebrows. "My cousin is quite amusing," she replied.

"Tony?" Lord James looked incredulous. "Oh, he is well enough, but just a boy."

"Young but promising," laughed Elisabeth, "and his dog is a continuous source of surprises."

Darnell seemed both pained and astonished. "Are you comparing me to a dog now?" He fell back onto the sofa in mock prostration. "Tipped me a settler once again."

Just then, Jane Taunton came into the room, followed soon after by Lord Larenby and his wife and daughter, and their group assumed the dimensions of a small party. Elisabeth was kept busy serving tea and greeting them. But there was no sign of Derek Wincannon, and his family made no mention of him.

When Elisabeth told Jane something of her adventure, she was frankly envious. "Why did you not take me along?" she asked. "It is just what I have needed, some real excitement. I'm getting a bit tired of sitting in my two little rooms day after day. And what a story I could make of it!"

Elisabeth smiled. "I am sure you could. But I found that adventures make much better reading than doing. I spent much of my time feeling anxious and acquiring a host of sore muscles."

Jane looked at her ruefully. "Now you sound just like everyone who has done exciting things. But I'm not taken in. You do it just to discourage me, I know, and keep me from poaching on your ground."

Elisabeth shook her head. "I promise you it isn't so," she replied. "I give you leave to take on any adventure that comes to me in future. You are welcome."

"I may hold you to that," said the other girl in an oddly intense tone. Elisabeth glanced at her with amusement and some surprise, but at that moment they were joined by Lord Larenby, and she could not ask Jane about it.

"It is good to see you back," said the viscount as he joined them. "And even better to know that everything has turned out well. I congratulate you on your success in finding your cousin."

Elisabeth looked at him a bit uncertainly. Perhaps he, like his son, was angry with her? But his green eyes showed nothing but friendliness, and she smiled in return. "I was lucky," she said. "Who would have thought that Growser could lead me to Tony?"

"Not I," replied Lord Larenby. "None of us, in fact, but you."

Elisabeth shrugged. "But I didn't *think* of it, either. It was thrust upon me."

He laughed. "Well, whatever the case, it was well done"—he held up his teacup in a salute—"though we were very worried about you at first."

"When you disappeared," agreed Jane, "your cousin thought you were kidnapped also, I think."

Elisabeth looked down. "It was heedless of me, I know. But I did leave a note."

The viscount laughed once more. "Yes. It was that which frightened everyone and sent your cousin searching for help. But I think you did very well. When does Tony come home?"

"I'm not sure. Soon, I hope."

They were joined by Lady Larenby, and the talk turned to other matters. Elisabeth looked about the room. Amelia Wincannon was talking with Belinda and the duke, and Lord Darnell was amusing Cousin Lavinia with some anecdote. He caught her eye as she watched and beckoned her over to them. She hesitated, glanced at the chatting group around her, then went across. "I've just been telling Miss Ottley about the balloon," said Lord Darnell as she came up.

"Then you must tell me, too," replied Elisabeth promptly. "I've never seen one."

"Ah, they are amazing constructions. This one was easily fifty feet in height, and as it filled up with hot air, it grew to be as much around as well."

"Did you watch the whole process?" asked Elisabeth with some surprise. "I wouldn't have thought it would interest you."

"Yes, I know," replied Darnell, looking directly into her eyes with a mocking gleam. "You think me a worthless fribble without two thoughts to rub together." He held up a hand as Elisabeth started to protest. "No, no, I know it's true. But you have mistaken me. It's coins I have none of; I'm oversupplied with thoughts."

Elisabeth laughed, shaking her head at him.

"How high did the balloon go?" put in Lavinia.

"It rose well above the treetops and floated out across the city," he answered. "It was a splendid sight, like a great flower drifting over the rooftops. The balloon was red, you know."

"Lovely," said Elisabeth. She gazed at him with respect. "I wish I had been there."

"That's what I told you," he answered. "You missed a real treat."

"It's too bad," added Lavinia. "Belinda and I were to go, but at the last moment, she decided to stop in Bond Street instead. I must tell her how it was." And Lavinia trotted over to the corner where the young people sat talking.

Lord Darnell smiled at Elisabeth. "Your cousin has a kind heart," he said, surprisingly.

The girl agreed. "I realize it more and more."

Jane came up then. "I must take my leave," she said to Elisabeth. "I have work to do this evening."

Elisabeth held out her hand. "Then you must go, I know. Let us meet soon for a real talk."

Jane nodded and said goodbye. The Wincannons soon followed, and finally, Lord Darnell also went on his way, after making an appointment with Elisabeth to go driving the next day. Only the duke remained.

"I hope your mother is fully recovered," Elisabeth said to him.

He looked up from the fire, frowning, and nodded. "She seemed all right when I took her to the carriage, else I should have accompanied her home. She insisted I should stay. But I admit it worries me; I can't remember that she has ever done such a thing before. In fact, I've always thought of her as invulnerable." He smiled a little to show that he knew this was silly.

"We were talking of the man who rescued Tony," continued Elisabeth. "Mr. Lucius Aldgate. Have you heard the name?" She remained curious about this point.

The duke thought for a moment, then shook his head. "I don't believe so. I have no memory of it."

He frowned again. "You think this had something to do with Mother's attack?"

"I don't know," replied Elisabeth.

"It's quite mysterious," added Lavinia.

"I cannot understand it," the duke replied after a moment's thought. "It seems to make no sense at all."

"It's silly," said Belinda, appearing bored with the subject. "I don't believe it has anything to do with the duchess's fainting. She only felt ill."

"Perhaps," answered Elisabeth.

A silence fell. They all looked into the fire. After a while, the duke rose to go.

"I'll see you out," Belinda said, and the young couple went out of the drawing room.

When they were gone, Lavinia shook her head. "I've known Judith thirty years, and I've never seen her act so. There is some mystery. I am concurrent."

"But what can it be?"

Lavinia frowned and shook her head. "I have no idea."

Later, in her bedroom, Elisabeth considered the problem again, pacing back and forth in front of the fire. But soon the thought of Derek Wincannon displaced it. He couldn't be so angry that he meant to drop her acquaintance, she thought, frowning. That would make no sense. But the longer he stayed away, the more she wished to have the opportunity to speak to him and explain herself. Surely, he would understand, and all would be as before.

She sat down again and leaned back in the armchair. And how had things been before, she asked herself? What exactly was her relationship with this man who preoccupied her now? As she considered, a small smile grew on Elisabeth's face and her cheeks flushed a becoming pink. She sat thus a moment, then shook her head and rose. She climbed into bed and picked up a book. For a moment, it lay open in her lap and she stared across the room. Perhaps Derek would be in the park tomorrow, and she would have the chance to speak to him, she thought.

# Nineteen

LORD DARNELL ARRIVED IN GOOD TIME AND IN GOOD spirits the next day, blond and handsome in a coat of light blue superfine and dove-colored pantaloons. His waistcoat was a marvel of varying shades of blue. He handed Elisabeth into his curricle with a flourish, and soon they were driving through the crisp morning air at a spanking pace, Elisabeth was carrying a new parasol that had arrived from the maker during her absence from town, and she felt very modish as she raised it.

"What a lovely day," she said as they started. "The air is so clear."

"And you are looking even more beautiful than usual," Lord James replied gaily. "How do you manage it?"

Elisabeth shook her head at him. "How can I convince you that I don't like fulsome compliments?" she replied. "My looks will never be more than passable." She smiled at him, her violet eyes sparkling. "Though I must admit that I think my new parasol dazzling." She spun it above them, making the light flicker through the ivory silk and delicate frame.

Lord Darnell grimaced. "And when shall I succeed in convincing *you* that you are quite stupid on the subject of your appearance? Indeed, it's hard to credit in such an otherwise intelligent creature."

Elisabeth shrugged impatiently. "Tell me what's been happening in town while I was away. I wish to hear all the gossip."

"All?" asked Lord Darnell, a wicked twinkle springing into his eyes.

Elisabeth laughed. "Well, perhaps not quite all. I don't care for *on dits*."

"Ah. Then there is little to tell," he answered, shaking his head in mock disappointment. "There have been several engagements, and Prinny has sold some of his horses. The Queen was ill, but she is now better. Things are much as usual. I'd much rather talk about you."

"What about me?" asked the girl.

"Everything!" he replied, throwing out a hand. "I wish to know everything about you."

"What a hackneyed phrase," said Elisabeth pleasantly. "And quite impossible, too."

Lord Darnell goggled at her as they turned into the park. Then, he laughed. "You are dashed difficult to make love to, you know."

"Exactly," she replied. "So do let us talk about something interesting."

Her companion's expression was rueful, but he laughed again. "I don't know how to talk to you. Nothing I say seems quite right."

Elisabeth turned to him, surprised. "Nonsense," she told him. "You are a wonderfully amusing conversationalist."

"Am I? Amusing?" He urged the horses onto the crowded avenue that extended down the length of the park. "Well, that's something, at least."

Their dialogue was interrupted by the greetings of several acquaintances, and thus Elisabeth found it easy to change the subject. "I am thinking of giving an evening party," she said.

"Really?"

"Yes. Partly for Belinda, to celebrate her engagement. I should have done it ere this. And partly to gather my friends together and return their hospitality."

"Shall I be asked?" responded Lord Darnell hopefully.

"Do you think I would speak of it to you if I weren't planning to invite you?" Elisabeth laughed at him. "How rude you must think me."

"Oh, no," he answered, "but you might do so for a reason. To punish me perhaps."

Elisabeth frowned. "Punish you? For what?" He shrugged, and Elisabeth continued to watch him in puzzlement. "You are strange today," she said finally. "Is something wrong?"

Lord Darnell didn't look at her; he stared out over the horses' heads into the park. He shook his head, then spoke quickly. "Will you go out of town after the season? Or have you had enough of the country for a while?"

There was a short pause. Elisabeth gazed at him speculatively. At last, she said, "I believe we will go down to Willowmere. I haven't really thought, as yet. We will have Belinda's wedding, you know, before that. It is to end the season; had you heard?"

Lord Darnell nodded, keeping his eyes on the avenue before them.

"That will be a great deal of work. When it's over, I daresay we'll all welcome a rest in the country. Will you go to Brighton?"

He smiled crookedly. "Perhaps. My mother will wish to; she always does. I'm not certain whether I shall go."

Elisabeth was only half attending. She'd seen Derek Wincannon riding down the other side of the avenue, and she was wondering whether he would speak to her or ride past without noticing them.

"Have you been to Brighton?" Lord Darnell went on.

"What?" Elisabeth turned back to him. "I beg pardon?"

Her companion looked out over the people around them. He did not seem to find what he sought. "I merely inquired whether you've seen Brighton?"

"Oh, no." Derek was now closer; in a moment, he would be opposite them. He hadn't seen them, she thought, or he gave no sign if he had.

"You might think of staying there a few weeks in the summer," said Lord Darnell. "It can be amusing. But, of course, one must engage lodgings well in advance. My mother could probably help you if you wish it. She knows all the houses."

"Ah," replied Elisabeth vaguely. Wincannon was opposite; he seemed preoccupied. Elisabeth thought of calling to him, but she found she couldn't. A flash of shyness or embarrassment prevented it, to her surprise and chagrin.

"I can ask her about it, if you like," said Lord James.

"Umm." Derek was passing. He wouldn't speak. Elisabeth was bitterly disappointed. She looked down at her hand, clenched in her lap; she'd so wished to talk with him. Absurdly, she felt like crying.

"Shall I, then?" Lord Darnell sounded a bit impatient.

"Shall you what?" replied Elisabeth, turning to look at him.

"Ask my mother."

Elisabeth stared at him. She had lost the thread of the conversation. "To my party?" she said finally. "Oh, I'll send her a card, certainly, and your sisters. I won't forget them."

Lord Darnell breathed an annoyed sigh. "You haven't heard a word I said. What's the matter?"

Elisabeth felt sadly flustered. As she opened her mouth to make some reply, a voice spoke from behind them, and she froze.

"Good morning," said Derek Wincannon. "I beg your pardon. I didn't see you at first. I nearly passed right by." He came up beside the curricle and bowed slightly from the saddle. His coat was dark blue, accenting the color of his eyes, and the white of his neckcloth stood out against his dark skin.

Lord Darnell greeted him tersely, and Elisabeth murmured an indeterminate salute.

"I hope you had a pleasant stay in the country?" he continued.

Elisabeth raised her eyes. His unexpected appearance had caused her heart to beat very fast, and she felt a little breathless. "Yes," she said, "thank you."

There was a short silence. Elisabeth cast about

desperately for something to say, but her mind was blank.

Lord Darnell wasn't helpful, and Wincannon, too, appeared to be at something of a loss.

"A fine day," said Derek at last.

Darnell flicked a speck of dust from his coat sleeve.

"Oh, yes," replied Elisabeth. "I was just remarking on it." She didn't quite dare meet his gaze. What is the matter with me, she asked herself sternly? I wished to speak; I must do so. But something, perhaps the presence of Lord Darnell, kept her silent, and soon Wincannon bowed again.

"You won't wish to keep your horses standing," he said. "I'll take my leave."

Lord Darnell immediately urged the horses onward, and Elisabeth had not even time to say goodbye before they had left Derek behind, watching them from atop his mount, unmoving.

They rode on a while in silence. Elisabeth took several deep breaths. Then, her companion spoke. "I take it, then, that you don't wish to go to Brighton."

Elisabeth turned to look at him. The muscles around his mouth seemed tight, and he looked almost angry. "No," she replied. "I don't believe I do. I need to see what has been done at Willowmere." She watched his face, perplexed at his manner.

"You have just done that," he answered. "Surely your agent can supervise repairs."

"He could, no doubt. But I wish to see for myself."

Lord Darnell pulled rather sharply on the reins, turning the carriage into a cross lane. "I daresay you do. It's your way. You always do just as you please."

Elisabeth made no answer to this remark, and in a moment, he spoke again.

"I'm sorry. I didn't mean that as it sounded. It's just that knowing you will leave in a few weeks, and I shan't see you until next season, has upset me. There is something I wish to speak to you about."

"Lord Darnell," began Elisabeth.

"Yes, it is rather important, I think," he went on quickly.

"I wish you wouldn't…"

"I know it," he interrupted, speaking sharply and rather loudly. "But it can't be helped."

Elisabeth looked steadily at him for a moment, but his eyes did not waver. "Very well," she said finally, sighing a little.

"You might have expected it, I think," said her companion.

"I hoped I had discouraged you," she replied.

A muscle jerked in his cheek, and he kept his face forward. "You went a good way toward it. But I feel I must make you understand." Elisabeth said nothing, and he continued in a tight voice. "When we first met, I informed you that I am a fortune hunter of the worst stripe."

"Please," began Elisabeth, but he cut her off with a gesture.

"It is true," he insisted. "It has always been true. And I don't deny it. But nonetheless, Elisabeth, I love you."

The strain so evident on his face kept her silent for a moment. She couldn't think what to reply. Lord Darnell had never spoken to her so seriously, and she was afraid of wounding him. "I…I am very sensible of…" she began, but he interrupted.

"Wait. Say nothing yet. I wish to explain everything to you. I know you will refuse me, but I want you to understand." He gave her a speaking look, and Elisabeth nodded. "I made a push to meet you as soon as I heard of your existence," he went on. "Naturally. I do so with all heiresses." The smile he directed at her was twisted. "And I exerted myself to captivate you. It seemed an ideal match. You were young, beautiful, intelligent, *and* rich. I had never met such a woman."

"Lord Darnell," put in Elisabeth. "Please…"

But he shook his head emphatically. "You must let me say this." He looked at her again, and she bowed her head. "Soon, I found you were quite unlike any other girl. You never took me seriously; you teased me and laughed at me when I tried to attach you. But also, you laughed *with* me, as no one else ever had. I began to prefer your company to any other. In short, instead of dazzling you, I was dazzled. When you left town last week, I suddenly realized how I have come to depend on seeing you." His voice faltered a bit, and he paused. Elisabeth wished to interrupt, to stop him, but before she could form the words, he went on. "I love you, Elisabeth," he said. "I wish with all my heart to marry you and devote myself to your happiness."

"I…I don't know what…"

"Wait." He looked into her eyes, his gaze more compelling than she had ever seen it. "I admit to you that I am all to pieces. But the fault is not entirely mine, and I could mend my ways. There is the title, and my mother would welcome you." His mouth twisted. "Not a recommendation, perhaps, but I would do anything for you. I would…"

"Stop," said Elisabeth in a positive tone. "I cannot let you go on." He was silent, looking at her with such a sorrowful expression that she could hardly bear it. "Oh, Lord Darnell, I don't wish to hurt you. I think of you as my friend, but…"

"But you are not in love with me," he finished. She could think of no kind answer, and they rode on in silence for some moments.

"I knew it, of course," he went on after a while. "You did let me see it. And in any case, I never believed such good fortune could befall me. My luck has never been so good." Again, silence fell. Elisabeth looked down and tried to find words to lighten the atmosphere.

The pause lengthened. They reached the park gate, and Lord Darnell guided the horses out into the street once more. "It doesn't signify," he said then. "I'm still glad I told you of my feelings. I couldn't stand the thought that you might consider me only a fortune hunter, even now." He looked at her. "You do believe me?"

"Of course," answered Elisabeth quickly. And she did. The sincerity of his emotion had been unmistakable.

He nodded. "That's good, then; that's something." He seemed to swallow, and then he went on lightly. "I continue to hang out for a rich wife, of course. You will tell me if you come across a likely candidate?"

She tried to return some equally flippant answer, but the words stuck in her throat. She had to content herself with nodding. Then she looked away, out over the busy streets around them. They said nothing more until they reached her house.

When Lord Darnell helped her down from his curricle, she held his hand a moment longer than necessary. "I am truly sorry," she told him. "I wish things might be otherwise."

He squeezed her hand gratefully and nodded. "As do I," he replied feelingly. She smiled a little. "That's better. We can remain friends, can we not?"

Elisabeth nodded. "Of course. I should miss you sadly."

He, too, smiled slightly. He brought her hand to his lips and kissed it, then released her and bowed. She turned to the door, and he climbed back into the curricle. Elisabeth stood in the doorway and watched him drive away.

She went straight up to her bedchamber without seeing any of her family, wanting a little time to herself. The depth of her reaction to Lord Darnell's proposal surprised her a bit. It hadn't been unexpected, but the sincerity of his feelings was. She'd set him down as an agreeable rattle, without profound emotions of any kind, and she had been proved wrong. The realization that he really did care for her, and the necessity of refusing him, combined to make her feel very low. Added to this was her disappointment over her encounter with Derek Wincannon. This latter emotion, she found, was at least as strong as her regret over hurting Lord Darnell, and she suddenly realized that her feelings for Mr. Wincannon were far deeper. Wincannon's early concern for her welfare in London, and, more important, his recent help, which had brought them into close contact over a period of time, had affected her strongly. And his absence over the past few days had completed the process, she saw. Clearly, he was much more important to her than she had known.

Elisabeth felt her cheeks growing hot, and she put her hands to them. I'm in love with him, she said to herself. She stared into the mirror at the flushed figure reflected there; she looked very young and foolish. She lowered her hands. "This is folly," she told her reflection severely. "You are well past the age for such romantic fancies. And he knows it as well as you. I refuse to allow you to indulge yourself this way." The figure in the mirror smiled foolishly in response.

But after a moment, she shook herself. Mooning about would accomplish nothing. It was imperative that she see Derek and explain her behavior so that things could return to normal between them. But how to manage it?

Finally, after trying and rejecting various schemes, she chose the simplest. She went to her writing desk and wrote a note asking him to call. Leaving it in the hall to be delivered, she took a deep breath. The matter was out of her hands now.

# Twenty

DEREK REPLIED TO HER NOTE THE NEXT MORNING, saying that he would call in the afternoon with pleasure. His response seemed a bit cool to Elisabeth, and she wondered whether she'd been right to ask him to come. The decision that had seemed so logical now appeared foolish.

Resolving to put the matter from her mind for a while, she set out to call on Jane Taunton. She found her in her study, as usual, and settled into the rust-colored armchair with a pleased sigh. "It's good to be in this room once more," she told her friend.

"I wonder whether you'd say so if you spent as much time here as I do," Jane replied, looking around her.

"Do you tire of it?" Elisabeth was a bit surprised. "But then, you can always go out."

"Of course," said Jane wryly. "Come, you must tell me how things are with you."

Elisabeth smiled. "Well, now that Tony is safe, the only terrifying task left me is Belinda's wedding. Then the season will end, and we can go to the country."

"Belinda is very lucky," said Jane.

Elisabeth stared at her.

"Because you have been so kind to her," added the other girl quickly. "She's certainly been given all the advantages without much being asked in return."

Frowning, Elisabeth looked at her friend. She didn't sound like herself. In fact, she sounded quite petulant and bitter. She needed some rest, Elisabeth thought, and a chance to get away from her two little rooms. Perhaps she could help with that. She started to speak, but Jane, noticing her expression, forestalled her.

"Will the wedding be so terrifying?" she asked with a strained smile.

Elisabeth shrugged. "The ceremony itself will be nothing. It's the planning, the wedding clothes, the breakfast, and so on and so on—the details, in short—which daunt me. I'm even now preparing to send out cards for an evening party in honor of the engaged couple. And that should have been done weeks ago. I wish it were all over and we were on our way to Willowmere. And talking of Willowmere, I hope to prevail upon you to come with us. The house should be ready for guests, and I should like you to be the first."

Jane seemed a bit surprised, but she accepted the invitation. "That would be very agreeable. I spent last summer in London, and it was uncomfortable. I had thought of visiting my mother this year, since I haven't been home in some time, but she says she feels rather too ill for guests right now." Jane's expression was bleak.

Elisabeth saw that she wasn't telling the whole story and pitied her sincerely. "That settles it," she said. "You must come. There will be no party, you understand, only Tony, Cousin Lavinia, and me."

"It sounds delightful."

"Good." Elisabeth sat back. "Now you must tell me, how does your work go?"

The other girl sighed and looked down. "My work." She laughed rather harshly. "I wonder that anyone, including myself, can call it that."

"What's the matter?"

Jane shook her head. "I spend all my time scribbling these ludicrous articles," she gestured toward a pile of papers on the desk in front of her, "to earn my bread. It's a rare moment indeed when I can turn to poetry." Her mouth twisted, and she turned away. "It's just not fair."

"It isn't indeed," responded Elisabeth sympathetically. "Could I...perhaps I could be of help?"

Jane glanced at her sharply, hesitated, then shook her head once more. "Thank you for the offer, but I don't think so. It's no good my borrowing money or living off my friends. I might just as well, or better, stay with my mother." She smiled. "And in any case, your generous invitation will give me a free time to work."

Elisabeth nodded eagerly. "Yes. All you like." Surely this free time would restore Jane; and perhaps after it, Elisabeth could be of more help.

"One piece of news I'd forgotten," Jane went on. "I met your Byronic hero while you were out of town."

"Mr. Jarrett? You mustn't call him that."

Jane laughed. "All right. You're determined not to allow my imagination to run wild, I see."

Elisabeth smiled back a bit uneasily. "What did you think?"

"He has interesting ideas. He was present at a musical evening given by Lady Brandon, which the duchess dragged me to. It seems that Lady Brandon's companion, a little mouselike woman, is a friend of Jarrett's. We talked for quite some time."

"And what was your opinion of him?"

"I fear he was not up to my expectations," laughed Jane. "After all the hair-raising stories, I looked for a combination of the corsair and a slave trader, but he seemed quite an ordinary gentleman. A bit abrupt, perhaps."

Elisabeth laughed. "Poor Jane. Did you really hope to meet an adventurer in a London drawing room?"

"You cannot know how much. And at first, I had great hopes. There is something about Jarrett, I can't say just what, that brings a word like 'adventurer' to mind when one meets him. But as we talked, the impression faded. He seemed annoyingly conventional, pleasant, an interesting talker, with striking eyes, I do admit. However, there was nothing of the murderer about him."

"Murderer!" exclaimed Elisabeth. "I should hope not indeed. What makes you say that?"

Jane looked surprised. "Didn't I tell you? I thought I had. One of my friends uncovered some further rumors about Mr. Jarrett. There was talk when his wife died."

"What sort of talk?"

The other girl shrugged. "The story spread that he'd killed his wife for her money. I suppose it may have been her family who said so, considering what we know about the brother. My friend warned me that it was no more than idle rumor; there was no proof whatsoever. Still, I hoped to see some indication, a fiendish gleam in his eyes, perhaps, and there was nothing."

Elisabeth's eyes twinkled. "It wanted only that. Now he is the complete Byronic hero, isn't he?"

Jane laughed. "I suppose he is, in our imaginations, at least. But he's hardly so romantic a person."

"Oh, sometimes he seems rather brooding. He ought to be darker, however."

Jane laughed again. "I'm sure he would be if he knew you wished it."

"I? What have I to do with it?"

"Oh, he's quite taken with you, you know."

Elisabeth frowned. "Did he tell you so?"

Jane looked down at the book lying on her desk. "No," she replied slowly, "not precisely. But he talked of you a great deal and asked several questions. I guessed it from his manner."

"Well, I hope you are mistaken," said Elisabeth. "I have had enough of that sort of thing lately."

"What do you mean?"

Elisabeth hesitated. "I shouldn't have said that. Well, I know you will say nothing about it. Lord Darnell offered for me yesterday. I refused him, of course, but it is so very hard to treat a friend so."

Jane bowed her head. "I shan't mention it."

"I know you won't. Indeed, I am glad now that I told you. I wished to talk with someone. You can't think how low I felt at being obliged to refuse him."

Jane raised her eyebrows and turned away slightly. "No, I suppose I can't. No one has ever offered for me."

Elisabeth looked at her a little impatiently. "And Lord Darnell would never have made me an offer had I not been rich."

Jane shrugged, and after a few moments, she rose. "I am afraid I must excuse myself now," she said. "I have promised an article for this afternoon, and I haven't yet begun it."

Elisabeth rose with some relief. Jane really was becoming hard to talk to lately. She hoped that a rest in the country would help.

Her two cousins had once again been out shopping during the morning, and Elisabeth was treated to an exhaustive account of what they'd bought. She could muster little interest until Lavinia mentioned the duchess.

"Is she all right?" Elisabeth asked her.

Lavinia nodded. "I went to inquire early this morning. Judith seems fully reconstituted. But it is strange...." She trailed off, her tone puzzled.

"What?" asked Elisabeth.

Her cousin looked up, a frown wrinkling her brow. "She refuses to discuss her fainting spell or Mr. Aldgate or anything about them. It isn't like her; she usually talks to me quite freely."

"You didn't know Mr. Aldgate also?"

"Oh, no. When Judith left school, she came directly to London, you know. I went home." Lavinia paused, still perplexed. "We wrote a great many letters, and she told me of the people she met after she came out. I can't remember them all after such a time, but Mr.

Aldgate's name doesn't seem familiar." She continued to look concerned. "I don't know. I've never seen Judith act so. I cannot completely expurgate it from my mind."

Belinda rose impatiently. "I don't see that it is at all important," she said and left the room.

Elisabeth watched her older cousin for a moment, then reached out to press her hand. "I don't think you need to be really worried," she said. "I'm sure it's something logical and trivial. We'll laugh when we find out."

Lavinia smiled weakly up at her. "Yes, of course you're right. I mustn't fall into the dismals over such a small thing."

After luncheon, Elisabeth settled herself in the drawing room to write cards of invitation for her evening party and await Derek Wincannon's call.

She wrote dutifully at first, working through Belinda's list and beginning on the one she'd compiled of her own friends, but as the time Derek had set grew closer, Elisabeth began to feel nervous and spent more time looking out the window or staring unseeing at the drawing room wall than writing. After she had caught herself several times, she shook her head angrily. This is ridiculous, she thought. I am acting like a mooncalf again. Resolutely, she turned back to the pile of invitations and finished them.

It was not long afterward that she heard the bell and Ames ushered in Derek. Elisabeth rose and held out her hand. He took it briefly and bowed.

For a moment, Elisabeth feared she couldn't speak. Once more, her heart was beating rapidly and her mind was in a turmoil. With a strong effort, she controlled herself and gestured toward the sofa.

As she sat down, she said, "I'm glad you were able to come. I've been wanting to speak to you about our last meeting." Her voice sounded remarkably even, she thought.

Derek looked both relieved and a bit uncomfortable. "Indeed," he replied. "I was pleased to receive your note. I've wanted to speak to you as well."

Having established this, neither appeared to have anything further to say. A silence fell and lengthened.

Finally, Elisabeth took a deep breath. "I wished to explain…" she began.

But at the same instant, Wincannon said, "I must apologize…"

Both broke off, laughing awkwardly. "Pardon me," he said.

Elisabeth shook her head. "This is foolish. I merely wished to tell you why I went off so precipitously and alone to find Tony. I didn't mean to make you angry or exclude you."

He held up a hand. "Whatever your reasons, I had no right to speak to you as I did. I have very much wished to apologize to you since, but I didn't know whether you would see me."

Elisabeth looked blank. "But of course I would. You can't think I would have refused even to talk with you."

"I've never spoken so to any lady," answered Derek. "I feared I had offended you irretrievably. I'd been so worried, you see, and I allowed my emotions too much license."

"You were right to rebuke me. It was foolish to ride off alone on such an errand. It turned out well, but not through any efforts of mine. I was lucky."

"That does not excuse me," he answered.

Elisabeth smiled slightly at his serious tone. "Well, now that we have rated ourselves soundly, do you think that we might forgive each other and cry friends again?"

He looked at her, surprised, then smiled. "I suppose I have been coming it rather strong."

Elisabeth nodded, suppressing a laugh.

Derek did laugh. "Very well. Let us forget the whole matter."

"Good. And the next time I set off on my own to have an adventure…" She broke off, laughing, at Derek's quick change of expression. "I'm only bamming you. No need to look so thundery."

"I'm not sure I can promise to ignore your 'adventures,' as you call them. I'd worry about you." This last was said very seriously, and Elisabeth's pulse quickened once again.

"You needn't," she said a bit unevenly. "I'll leave the adventuring to others from now on."

There was another short silence. Elisabeth took a breath. "So," she continued, "that is settled, and we are friends again. You can't think how relieved I am. And now I can give you this." She rose and went to the writing desk, returning with an envelope addressed to Derek.

"What is it?" he said as he took it.

"An invitation to my evening party for Belinda and the duke. I sent the others, but I thought I would either give you yours myself or throw it away, depending on how you behaved today." Her eyes were twinkling once more.

"I'm fortunate to have passed muster, I see."

"You don't know how fortunate," she responded with a laugh. "This is to be the occasion for inviting all my odd friends, you know. Your father was much taken with the idea, by the by, just as you said he would be."

"You're asking all these eccentrics to meet your cousin and her fiancé?"

"Oh, no. I've invited a great many of their friends as well. And I haven't met so many eccentrics as that. I'll keep them apart in a corner and introduce them only to my special friends."

"I hope you number me among them then. I shan't be able to resist the spectacle."

"You shall meet them all, to be sure. But I suppose it will present a strange appearance. Perhaps I'll have to scatter them about the room."

"To leaven the group, as it were," suggested her companion.

"Exactly," agreed Elisabeth. "How well you understand. Of course, it may be difficult to hide Mr. Aldgate."

"Aldgate?"

"Yes, you met him. He's the man who rescued Tony. He's to escort him home late next week, and I shall beg him to stay with us for a while and attend the party."

"And what is his particular eccentricity?" asked Derek. "Is he hunting-mad perhaps? Or has he invented some new method of estate management? It's difficult to see how a country squire could achieve sufficient oddness for this party."

Elisabeth stared. "But you spoke to him for quite five minutes. You must have noticed."

Derek shook his head. "I remember talking with someone, that's all. Does he have a lisp?"

"No, no," she cried, half amused and half exasperated. "You are singularly unobservant. He dresses in the style of thirty years ago."

"What, powdered wigs and satin coats? Is that all?"

"Well, the Duchess of Sherbourne falls into a dead faint at the mention of his name," added Elisabeth.

"I beg your pardon?"

Elisabeth recounted the history of the duchess's attack to him, after warning him to keep silent about it. "So you see," she finished, "there is some mystery there."

"Indeed." He smiled at her warmly. "And if anyone can discover what it is, you can."

Elisabeth colored slightly. "Do you think me a tiresome meddler, then?"

"Not at all. Merely a very determined and curious woman. I shouldn't like to try keeping something from you that you wished to know."

"Well, I hope I never pry. I certainly don't mean to plague the duchess if it is clear that she doesn't wish the matter known."

At this moment, Lavinia entered the drawing room in search of some wafers, and their private conversation came to an end. Derek politely stayed a little longer, but soon he rose to take his leave. Elisabeth went with him to the hall, holding out her hand as he stood ready to depart. "I am so glad we've put things right," she told him. "It is a great relief to me."

He bowed his head. "Perhaps you will go driving with me next week to seal the bargain?"

"I should be delighted," she answered.

# Twenty-one

ELISABETH WAS COMPLETELY OCCUPIED FOR SEVERAL days after that. Tony returned home with Mr. Aldgate, who insisted upon opening his own townhouse rather than staying with them. At luncheon the day they arrived, Elisabeth couldn't resist saying, "We found last week that one of our friends claims acquaintance with you."

"Really?" replied Aldgate. "Who might that be?" He didn't seem astonished.

"The Duchess of Sherbourne," answered Elisabeth.

Lavinia was watching Mr. Aldgate anxiously. "Judith Chetwood," she added. "She was, I mean. Before she married, you know."

"Ah," responded Mr. Aldgate.

There was a short pause. Elisabeth watched her guest, but she could find no clue in his expression. "You did know her, then?" she asked finally, determined not to be put off so easily.

Aldgate looked at her and smiled a bit. "Judith Chetwood I knew, yes. I was in town the year she made her come-out."

Lavinia frowned, but said nothing. Elisabeth tried to be encouraging. "Really? How interesting. You'll meet her again at my evening party next week, you know. I hope you still mean to come?"

"Indeed. I look forward to it."

"It will be nice to see an old friend again," the girl suggested.

Mr. Aldgate merely bowed silently. Before Elisabeth could press him, Tony interrupted. "You should have seen Growser in the country, Cousin Elisabeth. He went nearly wild. He even sniffed out a fox one day and chased it across the property line into the next stand of timber. I think he'll make an excellent hunting dog. I shall try him when we go down to Willowmere."

Elisabeth was smiling. "What sorts of game did he bring you?"

"Oh, well, as to that, he never actually brought in anything." Tony was airily unconcerned. "But he has the instinct, you see. The fine points can be taught him."

Elisabeth laughed. "I daresay. But I believe Mrs. Lewis keeps chickens. You must see that he is trained not to molest them."

"Oh, he wouldn't," exclaimed Tony, indignant at this slur on his pet. "He's not so rag-mannered. And besides, chickens!" His expression showed contempt.

"You've asked nothing about my wedding, Tony," Belinda interrupted. "It is rather more important than your horrid dog, I should think. You are to give me away, you know."

Tony looked aghast. "What! I shall do no such thing. Fancy me making a cake of myself marching up the aisle with you."

"But you must." Belinda's eyes widened. "Who will do it if you don't?"

"I don't care a farthing. I shan't do it."

Belinda's eyes filled with tears. "But Tony…" she began.

Elisabeth intervened hastily. "I'm sure we can come to some agreement. We'll talk of it another time. Has everyone finished? Shall we return to the drawing room?" She rose, as did Mr. Aldgate, and they managed to quell the rising quarrel. When they got back to the drawing room, Aldgate took his leave, promising to call again after he had gotten settled.

Belinda was engaged to go walking with Amelia Wincannon, and Lavinia was off on her never-ending errands, so Elisabeth and Tony were left alone. She looked at him, smiling. "You will do, I think," she said. "You seem almost wholly recovered. Are you tired?"

Tony shook his head. "At first, I was tired all the time, but I hardly notice it now." He raised his eyes challengingly. "Will I have to be in Belinda's wedding?"

"Well, if you really don't wish it, I suppose we might make other arrangements. But Belinda particularly wants you, and you are the man of the family, of course."

This gave him pause. "Oh. But there is my uncle; he would do much better than I."

Elisabeth nodded. "We could ask him. The family will be down for the wedding. But as I said, Belinda hopes to have you beside her."

Tony looked mulish. "I don't see why. I'll probably make a mull of it."

Elisabeth smiled. "I'm sure you won't. And we'll have instructions in what to do, you know."

"What, are you to be in it too?"

She nodded. "I'm to stand up with Belinda as a…a sort of bridesmaid."

Tony gave a shout of laughter. "Very well. If you are to be there, I'll undertake to endure it. What fools we'll look."

"Good. That is settled."

She was about to go on when Ames came into the room. "Mr. Jarrett is below," he said in response to Elisabeth's inquiring look.

"Mr. Jarrett?" echoed Elisabeth. "Oh dear, he chooses such awkward times to call. Tell him that I am occupied and cannot see him now, Ames." The butler bowed and went out, and the girl continued. "I wish to talk more about your kidnapping, Tony, while we are private together. Did you see the house Mr. Aldgate thought to be the one where you were held?"

"Yes. And he was right. But there was nothing left to help us. They were too careful."

Elisabeth frowned. "You must keep thinking over the incident. Perhaps you can remember something that would lead us to the kidnappers."

Tony shook his head. "So I hoped. But I've gone over and over it a thousand times. There is only the maid. I daresay I could recognize her, but they've gotten her well away by now, I wager."

"Yes." Elisabeth struck her knee with a closed fist. "It galls me. They go free after what they did to you, and we have no recourse."

Tony agreed.

Elisabeth rose from the sofa and turned, feeling the need to pace about the room. But as she stood, she saw Mr. Jarrett standing in the drawing room doorway, his hat in hand. "Mr. Jarrett!" she exclaimed involuntarily.

The man bowed. "Excuse me," he said. "I overbore your butler inexcusably. I wished urgently to speak to you. But I see I have chosen a bad moment." Jarrett spoke very abruptly; he seemed agitated about something.

Elisabeth raised her eyebrows, annoyed at this intrusion. "You might have realized that when I refused myself," she said coolly.

"Indeed, I should have. But I am... I was..." He paused a moment and put a hand to his forehead.

Jarrett looked up. "If I might come tomorrow?" He looked at Elisabeth.

"M'cousin is engaged tomorrow," said Tony belligerently.

"Tony," said Elisabeth. She looked at Jarrett apologetically. "I've been much involved in planning an evening party, you know. You received the card?"

"Yes, yes, I did, I believe. But I..."

"Well, then, you can see my cousin there, can't you?" put in Tony.

"Tony, please," said the girl, "you are being rude." Tony looked unrepentant.

Jarrett didn't seem to notice Tony's remarks at all; he continued to gaze intently at Elisabeth. "I must talk to you," he said. "It is vitally important."

His tone unsettled her. She dropped her eyes in the face of his piercing stare. "I'm sorry," she continued. "I have no time before the party; it takes place in a very few days, you know, and there is much still to be done. But we will have a good conversation that evening, I promise you."

Jarrett didn't relax. "It's difficult to be private at a party. I need to see you alone."

At this, Tony again took exception. "I believe you heard the lady say she was busy," he said.

The scene was becoming too much for Elisabeth. "Later next week, perhaps," she put in hurriedly. "Or...or...oh, I do not know precisely, but I assure you we'll find some opportunity to talk."

Mr. Jarrett opened his mouth to speak, thought better of it, then started again. But before he could say anything, Elisabeth walked toward the bell pull. Jarrett frowned, made a quick gesture, then bowed and strode out of the room.

Tony followed. "I'll just see that he really leaves this time," he said over his shoulder, making little effort to lower his voice.

Elisabeth sat down again, and Tony returned a moment later. "He's gone," he said. "I don't like that fellow. A queer customer. I saw Ames as I was coming back up. Jarrett didn't push past him at all. Ames said he showed him out. Must've waited outside, then come back in once Ames had left the hall. Dashed havey-cavey way of visiting."

"He is a strange man," agreed Elisabeth. "But he has lived in the Indies for many years. Perhaps their conventions are different."

"Did he, by Jove? Well, I doubt if sneaking into people's houses is fashionable even there. I don't like him, I tell you."

Elisabeth shook her head. "No, I begin to think I don't either."

The next morning, Elisabeth drove into the City to see her banker one last time before leaving town. It was not a lengthy visit. In less than half an hour, she returned to the street. She had started to climb into her carriage when she heard someone call her name. Turning, she confronted a small dark man hurrying along the pavement in her direction. "Miss Elham," he repeated. "I wish to speak to you, please."

For a moment, Elisabeth looked blank. Then she recognized the Creole gentleman who had called on her some time ago. She hesitated.

The man came to a breathless stop before her. "You must excuse me," he panted, "but seeing you there across the street, I wanted to speak. I apologize again for my presumption." His face was bright red from exertion, but he seemed happier than when Elisabeth had seen him last. "I'm leaving England now," he went on. "I go back to Martinique on Wednesday, to the warmth, thank God. It was like an omen, seeing you; I wished to tell you."

Elisabeth bowed her head slightly. "I hope you have a good voyage."

He laughed, showing a nervous excitement. "I will," he replied. "I will. I have just been to the banker for the last meeting." He laughed again, and Elisabeth eyed him uneasily.

"I was just returning home..." she began.

"Yes, yes," he said. "I will not keep you. I only wished to say that you need not consider Jarrett any longer."

"I beg your pardon."

The man rubbed his hands together gleefully. "I have succeeded. I couldn't get the law to help me publish his guilt, but I have recovered some of my sister's wealth, at least. The monster who had her life shall not enjoy her money. He will be ruined, Miss Elham. He will have to leave London. That is what I wished to say. There is no need to regard him now."

"I see," answered Elisabeth. She felt a little sorry for Jarrett suddenly. This man's enjoyment of his plight was so intense.

The Creole seemed to notice this. "You think me hard-hearted, perhaps? But then you didn't know my sister, mademoiselle. You would think differently then."

"Perhaps so," acknowledged the girl. "Now, if you will excuse me."

He stood back. "Of course. I do not mean to keep you. Goodbye. I felicitate you on your escape from Jarrett."

"My escape?" Elisabeth turned back to him curiously.

The man looked surprised. "He pursues you. You do not yield. You are right."

She frowned and started off. Looking back, she saw the West Indian disappearing down the street in the opposite direction. "Who would have thought I would see him again," she murmured to herself.

She was thoughtful all the way home, and the subject recurred to her off and on through the afternoon. She longed to tell Jane about this development and see what she made of it. If Mr. Jarrett had indeed married for money, he must be bitterly disappointed now.

# Twenty-two

SEVERAL DAYS LATER, ELISABETH STOOD AT THE HEAD of her hall staircase watching the first of her guests walk toward her. She'd received a flattering number of acceptances to a party coming in the hectic last weeks of the season, and the drawing room would be very full. She knew she looked dashing in a robe of sea-green satin with an overdress of paler green gauze; she wore a set of emeralds which had been part of her uncle's estate, and Ketchem had dressed her hair in a mass of honey-colored curls.

Beside her stood Lavinia, beaming in a gown of gray lace, and Belinda and the duke, who had joined them for dinner. Tony had hastily excused himself from greeting their guests; he waited in the drawing room.

Belinda was radiant in a gown of palest pink trimmed with lace. She received a great many compliments from her friends and their families as the arrivals filed by, and she was looking very happy.

The Wincannons arrived early, and Derek smiled at Elisabeth and took her hand in a way that made her eyes sparkle. Mr. Jarrett also came in betimes; he made some effort to speak to her at once, but other guests waited behind him on the stairs, and he was forced to move on. Jane Taunton came late, looking rather reluctant, and, nearly the last to arrive, Lady Darnell and all of her daughters swept up the stairs, followed by an uncomfortable Lord Darnell. His mother took Elisabeth's hand dramatically. "Dear Miss Elham," she exclaimed.

It was indeed a squeeze, Elisabeth thought somewhat later, as she looked around at the chattering groups that filled the drawing room. There had been no sign as yet of Mr. Aldgate or the duchess, but everyone else she had particularly wanted to see was present. Belinda and the duke were the center of the largest and noisiest knot of people. Elisabeth made her way to them with some difficulty and said quietly to the duke, "Your mother has not come. I hope she is not ill again?"

He seemed surprised. "Oh, no. She means to be here, of course. She was talking of what she would wear when I saw her last. Perhaps she's been delayed, but I'm sure she'll come soon."

Elisabeth nodded. "I'm sure you're right." She moved away, greeting her guests once again as she passed through the crowd.

She headed toward the corner of the room, where she saw the Viscountess Larenby talking with some of the other matrons. Elisabeth had seen little of her in the past few weeks, and she wanted to make a point of talking to her this evening. But as she crossed the room, someone caught her arm. Turning in surprise, she found herself facing Mr. Jarrett. She pulled her arm free gently, but firmly, and said, "Good evening."

Jarrett was dressed very correctly in a dark brown coat and buff pantaloons. But as Elisabeth surveyed him, she felt that, in spite of his dress, something about him was not suited to a London drawing room.

"I'm glad you could come this evening," she said. "You'll find some interesting people to talk with, I think. Come, I'll introduce you to…"

But Jarrett interrupted. "There's no one else I wish to talk to. I came only to see you." His tone was intense, and Elisabeth was put off at once. He glanced about the room. "Is there not somewhere we might sit down out of this infernal crush?"

Elisabeth raised her eyebrows. "Is that a way to speak of my social triumph?" she asked. "You will put me out."

Jarrett made an impatient gesture. "You cannot really care for such fripperies. I have something important to discuss."

Elisabeth's eyes began to glitter, a clear warning to anyone who knew her well. "Of course, my party cannot be as important as your wishes. But at this moment, I'm rather engaged in being its hostess."

He took her arm again. "Please. Elisabeth." And yet again his eyes met hers with an unsettling intensity.

But she was now thoroughly angry. She pulled away. "I'm sorry. I must see to my guests." And she walked away before he could reply.

When she approached the viscountess, that lady had just left the group she'd been chatting with. Elisabeth's expression was such that the older woman said, "Heavens, what is the matter?"

Elisabeth shook her head. "Mr. Jarrett annoys me

so sometimes. He seems unaware of anything but himself."

"He's the man you were just talking to? I haven't met him."

Elisabeth made a wry face. "I'm not sure you should. He can be very abrasive. I was just thinking to myself that he's not really a creature of the drawing room at all."

The viscountess raised her eyebrows and smiled quizzically. "Would you wish any man to be such a creature? For my part, I prefer less smoothness and more character."

"I suppose I do also," Elisabeth replied slowly. "But not quite in Mr. Jarrett's style."

Lady Larenby smiled again. "I'll make an opportunity to meet this Jarrett just to see what you mean. You've piqued my curiosity."

Elisabeth was about to reply, when a sudden silence in the room made her turn around instead. Everyone was gazing toward the doorway. Some seemed amused, some shocked, and others simply looked blank. Following their glances, Elisabeth saw Mr. Aldgate. He was dressed tonight in satin and lace of varying shades of lavender, deep purple, and silver. She, too, paused for a moment, her breath taken away by the opulence of this vision, then she hurried forward to greet him.

Mr. Aldgate was scanning the crowd. He seemed amused by their reaction. But when Elisabeth reached him, he took her hand apologetically. "I'm sorry," he said before she could speak. "I had a particular reason for wishing to wear this costume. But I appear to be creating a minor sensation. You'll be congratulated on unearthing such an oddity."

"I hope no one dares to say such a thing to me," responded Elisabeth indignantly. "No one in the room looks so magnificent." She wanted very much to ask what his particular reason was, but something in his manner stopped her.

Aldgate was looking around the room. "They do look rather drab, don't they? I must say I find modern dress a bore. That man Brummell did a great deal of harm." He turned and looked down at her, smiling. "I'm frightfully out of touch. You must point out the notables to me. I suppose that is the young duke standing with your cousin?"

Elisabeth nodded. "His mother is late, but she promised to come," she added. Her companion's expression showed nothing. She began to name other guests, particularly picking out her friends, who could be counted on to receive Mr. Aldgate cordially. When she was nearly done, Ames entered behind them and announced, "The Duchess of Sherbourne."

Mr. Aldgate and Elisabeth turned at the same time. The duchess was standing in the doorway looking at them. She was wearing a splendid dress of red brocade, cut in the latest mode, with a turban of the same cloth. But Elisabeth thought her skin looked rather pale against the bright color. For a moment, no one moved. Then, the duchess put out a hand as if seeking support, and the other two hurried forward.

Elisabeth took both her hands. "Good evening, ma'am," she said. "I'm glad to see you. I hope you weren't delayed by anything of consequence."

But the duchess didn't appear to hear her; she was looking fixedly at Mr. Aldgate. "Hello, Judith," said the latter. "It's been a long time since we met, but you are as beautiful as ever."

Elisabeth's eyes widened slightly, but she said nothing.

The duchess seemed to have trouble speaking; she opened her mouth, shut it again, then finally got out, "Lucius." Her eyes never left him; their expression was unreadable.

A short silence fell, during which Elisabeth's curiosity mounted steadily. But she didn't dare break it.

At last, Mr. Aldgate spoke again, holding out his hand to the duchess. "Well, Judith, you had more to say to me the last time we met. Shall we find a chair and talk over the past a bit?"

The duchess said nothing, but she allowed him to take her arm and lead her to a sofa at the side of the room. Elisabeth was left standing alone in the doorway. Her eyes followed their progress bemusedly.

"What a scene that was," exclaimed a voice behind her, "quite worthy of the stage." Lord Darnell had come up when the others walked away.

"Was it not?" answered Elisabeth, turning to him. "But I have found out nothing. It is too vexing."

He grinned. "If I didn't know better, I'd swear you arranged the whole. It was prodigious dramatic. The *ton* will talk of it for days."

"So long?" replied Elisabeth, laughing. "I have scored a coup indeed."

Darnell was watching Aldgate and the duchess. "They must have been sweethearts," he mused.

Elisabeth looked up at him, surprised. "Mr. Aldgate?"

she said. "Nonsense." But as she followed his eyes to the couple on the sofa, her expression became speculative. "Do you really think so?"

He merely made a small gesture toward the sofa.

"It does look like it. How funny. Why will they say nothing about it?"

Lord Darnell smiled. "Obviously, there's some mystery there. Unrequited love, perhaps?" She looked up quickly, stricken by the implication of this phrase, but he waved aside her concern. "Don't look so frightened. I shan't retreat from the world. In fact, I've discovered a new heiress."

Elisabeth's answering smile was a little uncertain. "Have you? That's marvelous."

"You needn't worry about me. I always come up right. Like a cat, my mother says. You aren't the first girl to refuse me, you know." But his gaiety sounded a little false, and they both heard it. He shook his head. "I shouldn't have come, I see. I thought myself completely recovered, but I realize now that I'm not."

"Is there not something I can do for you? I could lend you some money perhaps or…"

Lord Darnell's mouth twisted. "It needed only that," he said. "Don't let my mother hear you say such a thing." In answer to Elisabeth's distressed look, he continued, "No, no, of course you can't lend me money. I never repay loans. I'm quite all right, or shall be shortly. But if you will excuse me now." He bowed to her quickly and strode out of the room.

Elisabeth turned back toward the crowd. She suddenly wanted very much to talk to Derek Wincannon, and she scanned the groups of guests for him. Belinda and the duke remained near the center of the room talking to a circle of young people, including Tony. Jane Taunton was in the far corner, chatting with Mr. Jarrett and Lavinia. Mr. Aldgate and the duchess had drifted over to talk to the Wincannons, Elisabeth saw, but Derek was not there. Finally, she found him, farther down the same side of the room on which she stood. He was alone, and he was looking at her fixedly.

Feeling nothing but relief, Elisabeth started toward him. He greeted her gravely, surveying her flushed face with some reserve. Elisabeth was dismayed to realize that she had nothing specific to say to him, and they stood awkwardly together for a moment. Finally, she blurted, "Did you remember Mr. Aldgate after all?"

"Aldgate? Oh. No, I had no recollection of meeting him. I can't imagine how I can have forgotten such a striking figure."

Elisabeth smiled. "You were too angry to observe properly, I would say. You concentrated on raking me down."

Derek smiled back at her, and it seemed to Elisabeth that the atmosphere between them lightened. "Shall I apologize again?" he asked.

"No, no. But I can't let you entirely forget your transgressions."

But Wincannon did not laugh. "Has Lord Darnell gone so early?" he inquired. "It isn't like him."

"Yes, that is, I believe so," faltered Elisabeth. "He did not say, or…yes." This sounded foolish in her own ears.

Derek was watching her closely. "Darnell is a very engaging fellow. I've heard him held up as a model for young men aspiring to fashion. He's very popular with the feminine half of society."

With a sudden suspicion, Elisabeth looked up at him. "Is he?" she replied lightly. "That's not surprising. He is very amusing. He was telling me only now about his search for a suitable heiress."

Her companion glanced at her sharply. "Indeed?"

Elisabeth nodded. "Yes. Do you know of anyone? I should so like to see him creditably settled. I like him."

A smile awoke in Derek's eyes, though his expression remained bland. "I'll have to think," he answered. "It's not a subject I have considered."

"No, and why should you? You are very rich, I think. But it is not so easy for others to get on, you know."

Now he laughed. "I begin to realize."

They exchanged a warm smile, and Elisabeth took a deep breath. She started to ask him what he thought of the duchess's behavior when they were joined by Portia Darnell, very eager to meet Derek. Elisabeth introduced her, and from then on, there was little opportunity for the older members of the trio to speak.

Portia gazed up at Derek with wide green eyes. "My brother has told me so much of you," she breathed. "He admires you excessively, you know."

"Does he?" replied Derek dryly. "How odd that I have never seen any signs of it."

"Oh, he wouldn't say so to you. But men sometimes tell their sisters things."

"Do they?"

Portia nodded. "And I believe it is so important. I think a woman's chief duty is to listen. Do you not agree?"

Derek cocked a mocking eyebrow at Elisabeth. "No, not at all."

Portia was all interest. "Pray, what do you choose, then?" She gazed at Wincannon breathlessly.

Elisabeth was finding this exchange annoying and more than a little stupid. "I should say that a woman's chief duty is to do what's right," she put in sharply, "as is a man's." Her eyes snapped alarmingly.

Derek seemed amused. "Indeed?"

"What do *you* think, Mr. Wincannon?" asked Portia again.

"I decline to enter the lists. It's too dangerous a question for me." He smiled at Elisabeth.

"Coward," she murmured.

He bowed his head very slightly, but Portia said, "Oh, no, how can you say so? I think Mr. Wincannon is the wisest man I ever met."

Elisabeth's look was quelling, but before she could reply, Derek said, "Ah, I think I see your mother beckoning you, Miss Darnell."

Portia looked annoyed. "Mother?" she echoed, turning to look across the room. "Oh, I do not think…"

"Yes, indeed." Derek said, "I saw her unmistakably."

"Oh." The girl shifted uneasily. "I suppose I must see what she wants."

"I think you should," he said.

Shrugging her shoulders, Portia walked away.

"What a silly girl," exclaimed Elisabeth when she was gone. "I'm sorry I invited her."

"She's very young," responded Wincannon with a twinkle in his eye. "I daresay she'll improve."

"I doubt it. What insufferable twaddle! The wisest man she ever met indeed."

"Am I not the wisest man you ever met, Miss Elham?" asked Derek teasingly.

Elisabeth flushed. "No, you are not."

"Alas."

"Well, if that is the sort of talk you wish to hear," began Elisabeth indignantly.

But he stopped her. "It is not," he said positively, "not at all." He looked directly into her eyes, a distinct message in his own.

Elisabeth's flush deepened.

At that moment, Lavinia came up to them. "I am sorry to interlope, Elisabeth," she said, "but I need to speak to you."

Elisabeth could not decide whether she was irritated or relieved as she excused herself to go with Lavinia. But Derek was very satisfied with their conversation. As he watched her walk away, a smile played about his lips. He'd learned what he wished to know, he thought.

When the two cousins were alone, Lavinia said. "It's Judith. She is just not herself. I don't understand it at all. I wish you will come and speak to her."

Frowning a little, Elisabeth complied. She found the duchess sitting on a sofa on the other side of the room; she was alone.

Sitting beside her, Elisabeth said, "Are you having a pleasant evening, ma'am? I've scarcely seen you."

For a moment, it seemed the duchess hadn't heard her, but then she looked up and favored Elisabeth with an exceedingly sharp glance. "You don't fool me, young woman," she said. "Lavinia sent you to me to discover whether I'm all right." She sniffed. "As if one cannot sit alone for a moment."

Much heartened by this characteristic response, Elisabeth smiled. "Perhaps she did. She cares very much about you, you see."

The duchess's expression softened. "I know. And an evening party is not the place to sit and think. You're right. But I have a deal to think about; I've had a most unusual evening."

"Seeing an old friend again," prompted Elisabeth.

"Indeed." The older woman's eyes twinkled wickedly. "Don't think I don't know that you're consumed with curiosity about me and Lucius Aldgate. Nor are you the only one, of course. But I shan't tell you—not now, at any rate."

"I don't mean to pry into your private affairs," answered Elisabeth.

"Oh, no, no one ever means to pry, or to be caught spying about, I should say not." Seeing Elisabeth's expression, she said, "Oh, I don't refer to you, girl. Don't draw yourself up so." She smiled a little. "If I tell anyone besides my son, it shall be you, Elisabeth. You are the closest thing to Belinda's guardian, after all."

Puzzled, Elisabeth said nothing.

The duchess rose. "But not now. I have not got it all straight in my mind. I must speak to some of your guests." And with these cryptic remarks, she was gone.

During the rest of the evening Elisabeth had no further chance for private conversation with the duchess, or indeed with any of her friends. She sat for a few moments with Lady Darnell, who had settled herself gracefully on a sofa in the corner. Her youngest daughter she kept beside her, but Aurelia and Portia were sent ranging through the crowd. Elisabeth watched with nettled amusement a scene Lady Darnell enacted several times. One of her older daughters returned to her escorted by a young man. The careful mother evaluated him with one glance and with a flick of her eyelid let the girl know whether he was suitable or out of the question. Elisabeth saw three young men expertly disconnected from the Darnell girls after their test; they were gentlemen of moderate means. However, Portia finally captured a very wealthy man, and though he was five and forty and quite fat, he received every attention from the three women. Augusta, in her first venture out of the schoolroom, found little to do but stare.

As Elisabeth got up to see to some of her other guests, Lady Darnell seemed to recall something. "By the by, my dear," she said in her usual languishing accents, "wherever has James gone? You were speaking to him, weren't you? I haven't seen him for nearly an hour."

"He said something about taking his leave, I think," answered Elisabeth carefully. She had no wish to expose herself or Lord Darnell to his mother's penetrating questions. "Perhaps he had another engagement. There are so many evening parties these days; it wouldn't be wonderful if he had gone on to another."

"Nonsense," replied Lady Darnell very positively. "He would do no such thing. Have the two of you quarreled? James did not seem himself tonight. And last week, when I wished to send the girls to visit you, he positively forbade me."

"Of course not," said Elisabeth lightly. "Why should we?"

Lady Darnell did not appear convinced. She stared at Elisabeth. "You mustn't mind James, you know, when he gets into one of his moods. He can fly up into the boughs in a moment, but it is over as fast." Her voice was commanding. Elisabeth felt a bit uncomfortable, but she had no intention of revealing the truth to Lady Darnell. She nodded pleasantly and started away.

"Don't be angry," Lady Darnell called after her, and Elisabeth increased her pace.

The rest of the evening passed swiftly. It was not long before the first of the guests came to bid Elisabeth good night, and soon, few were left. Derek Wincannon was among the last to go, and he paused to chat with her for a moment. He complimented her on the success of her party.

Elisabeth smiled. "Thank you. I'm only glad it is over."

Raising his eyebrows, he returned her smile. "Why?"

"It's such work playing hostess. I much prefer attending other people's parties to giving my own, I find."

He laughed. "Well, now you can do so with a clear conscience. You have performed your part with grace."

Elisabeth sighed. "How can you say so? Belinda's wedding is only three weeks away. I have just begun my work."

"Ah. You are very busy these days, aren't you?"

Elisabeth nodded. "We all are. You can't know how I look forward to the day when it's all over and we leave for Willowmere."

He smiled again. "I can understand that feeling. I also look forward to going to the country. I prefer it."

"Do you? I'm not so sure. I enjoy town life too much."

"Ah, but you haven't spent time at Willowmere yet. I think you'll find the neighborhood very pleasant. We're pleased to see you added to it, at any rate."

Elisabeth colored very slightly. "You are very kind."

He looked into her eyes. "Not at all. It is the truth. I, for one, shall find the country doubly pleasant now." He emphasized the final word.

# Twenty-three

THE NEXT THREE WEEKS WERE A WHIRLWIND OF ACTIVITY. Elisabeth never remembered them later without a shudder. From the evening of her party to the day of the wedding, her life was an endless round of details and crises. When the day of the ceremony dawned bright and warm, she felt only a mixture of fatigue and relief.

By nine thirty, they were all ready and gathered in the drawing room together for the last time. Belinda looked resplendent in her gown of white satin with an overdress of Belgian lace, and her eyes sparkled excitedly. Tony was also looking well in a new coat of dark blue, his linen snowy and his boots polished to an extraordinary high gloss. Though his shoulder was still a little stiff, this hardly showed in the way he held it.

Elisabeth's blue-violet gown became her, and Lavinia was very dignified in dove gray silk. The flowers had just arrived, white roses for Belinda and violets for Elisabeth. As they stood there chatting a little nervously, Ames came in to announce the carriage.

Elisabeth looked at the others and smiled, "Well, shall we go, then?" she asked.

St. George's in Hanover Square was very busy when they arrived and went through a back entrance. Guests were pulling up to the front in carriages that jostled for position and a chance to add to the crowd filling the interior pews. Elisabeth herself took a deep breath; the occasion was rather impressive when it finally came.

Of the ceremony, she remembered only a sea of faces in the church and Belinda's radiant look as she walked up the aisle toward her. Elisabeth felt almost the proud mama at that moment, and the beginning of tears stung her eyes.

The wedding breakfast went smoothly, to Elisabeth's profound amazement. Lady Larenby complimented her on it when she paused to point out that the duchess had come to the wedding with Mr. Aldgate.

Elisabeth smiled. "I saw. I wonder how they met?"

The viscountess shook her head. "I am afraid I can't enlighten you. I admit I asked some of my mother's old friends, but no one knew anything of a Mr. Aldgate. It's quite a mystery."

"Yes," sighed Elisabeth.

"Speaking of mysteries," the older woman went on, "I finally met your Mr. Jarrett, you know. Maria Coatsworth introduced him at the play last week."

"He is hardly my Mr. Jarrett," responded Elisabeth. "Indeed, I'm not at all certain I like him. He called four times in the last two weeks, and Ames says he was very rude when I refused myself. What can the man have expected? I haven't had a moment free."

Her companion smiled. "Men often find it impossible to understand when a woman is busy with domestic tasks."

They were joined by Derek Wincannon, and soon after, his mother excused herself to speak to some of her friends. Derek looked down at Elisabeth and said, "I've seen very little of you lately. How are you?"

"Tired," replied Elisabeth feelingly. "I've been terribly busy."

He nodded. "I know. I haven't called because I thought you would have no time free. I begin to wish I'd coaxed you to take a drive, however. You've knocked yourself up with this wedding."

"Not quite," answered Elisabeth, smiling warmly in response to his concerned tone. "But I'll be very glad to forget it all and leave tomorrow. Your mother has promised me a picnic at Charendon."

"Has she indeed? I'll look forward to that, then, and not plague you now. I'm happy we'll be seeing one another in the country."

As it grew toward noon, the crowd began to thin, and Belinda and the duke made ready to depart. There was a flurry of preparations. The remaining guests followed the young couple to the door and saw them to their carriage. With much waving and calls of farewell, Belinda and her husband drove off, heading for Dover and the boat to France. They were to spend their honeymoon touring the Continent.

In half an hour, Elisabeth was left in the drawing room with her family and Jane Taunton. She sank down on the sofa and leaned back, sighing. "It's over. Thank heaven."

Jane agreed. "Mr. Jarrett was rather upset not to see you," she added abruptly.

Elisabeth turned to her in amazement. "Mr. Jarrett?" she echoed, her tone clearly questioning.

Jane appeared abashed. "I happened to see him. He mentioned to me that he couldn't get in to speak to you. He feared you were offended." Elisabeth began to look indignant, and Jane went on hurriedly. "I told him it was no such thing, of course."

Elisabeth was frowning. "Mr. Jarrett certainly discusses me very freely. As you know, I was simply too busy to see anyone."

"And so I told him," said Jane. She rose. "I must go. Until tomorrow, then."

"Yes." Elisabeth held out her hand. "We're going to have a splendid time, you know." Jane nodded and took her leave. When they were alone, Elisabeth said to Lavinia, "Imagine Mr. Jarrett speaking of me to my friends. I'm quite out of patience with the man."

"It's ill done of him," answered her cousin. "So contentious. I'm sorry I ever introduced you to him."

Elisabeth shrugged and smiled at her. "Well, it makes no matter. We'll be gone after tomorrow, and I daresay he may not even be in town next season."

Rather to Elisabeth's surprise, they got off early the next morning. The three ladies rode in her carriage with Tony mounted beside them, and Ketchem, Ames, and some of the other servants followed with the luggage in a post chaise. Growser had once more been relegated to an obliging carter, in spite of Tony's protests.

The short journey to Willowmere passed calmly. In a very few hours, Elisabeth was leaning out the carriage window eager to catch the first glimpse of the lane. From the moment she spied the tall stone gateposts, she knew that great changes had taken place. The weeds that had nearly obscured the posts had been cleared away, and the stones themselves had been cleaned. The surface of the lane had been smoothed and the great oaks cut back, and when they pulled up before the broad front door, the alteration was even more marked. Gone were weeds, brush, and untidy lawns. The gardens were neat and filled with early blooms. The grass was cut and rolled, and even the house itself looked brighter, perhaps because each windowpane now sparkled in the afternoon sun.

These sights galvanized Tony, who rode this way and that, exclaiming and drawing his cousins' attention to various details. Lavinia and Jane could have no real sense of the change, as they had never seen Willowmere, but both admired it sufficiently to assure Elisabeth that her pleasure was not misplaced. It really was transformed.

Inside, Elisabeth found more to marvel over. Everything had been thoroughly cleaned, and the covers were gone from the furniture. The beautiful old oak paneling in the hall gleamed richly in the afternoon light, and the fine parquet floor reflected back the glow. There were flowers everywhere, and the new rugs and hangings she'd chosen were in place. The house didn't seem the same one she had toured with such misgivings. "It's lovely," she exclaimed, as they started up the stairs. She turned to the Lewises, who'd come out to greet her. "You've done wonders."

They made an early night of it after their journey, the ladies seeking their chambers by ten, but everyone was up betimes the next morning, and all the talk at the breakfast table was of walks, rides, and exploring the gardens. Jane planned to sketch the various views the park commanded, and Tony was chafing to try out a new hunter he'd brought from London. Lavinia wished to go all over the house with Mrs. Lewis. Elisabeth walked in the gardens and breathed the scent of early roses that blew across the lawn.

A week passed full of such pursuits. Tony ran wild across the countryside, blissfully happy to ride the whole day long. He'd designed a training program for Growser which he now put into effect, though no change was evident in that exuberant animal. Jane began to accumulate a sheaf of watercolors and pronounced the country air very conducive to writing as well. Lavinia and Mrs. Lewis hit it off amazingly and were soon deeply involved in the mysteries of calves' foot jelly and the relative merits of blackberries and currants for jam.

As they sat in the drawing room after dinner one evening, Ames brought Elisabeth a note. When she tore it open, she found the promised invitation from Lady Larenby within. "How delightful," she exclaimed. "We are asked to a picnic. And there's to be a sort of festival."

"What do you mean?" put in Tony. "What sort?"

"Lady Larenby says that there is a tradition at Charendon of holding a celebration when the family arrives from town every year. All of their tenants and household will be there. Her sister and her family are also visiting, so there will be quite a party."

"Must we go?" asked Tony. "I thought we had left all that flummery in London."

Elisabeth smiled. "Alas. But we shall ride over, you know. And I daresay you might get a tour of the Charendon stables."

Tony brightened. "I hadn't thought of that. All right. Let's go."

Elisabeth laughed. "On Wednesday next, we shall." She looked at Jane. "Will you scold me? I promised you that we wouldn't fill our time with parties. But surely this is an exception? Will you come?"

Jane nodded. "Of course." She didn't smile, but Elisabeth didn't press her further. She'd done everything she could think of to make Jane comfortable, she thought. The girl might try harder to enjoy it.

When they arrived at Charendon the following Wednesday, they were cordially greeted by Viscount Larenby near the front door. "Don't dismount," he said. "I stationed myself here only to take you on to the festival field." He mounted, and soon they were all riding around the house.

Elisabeth rode beside the viscount. "Is it far?" she asked him. "We might have gone directly there and saved you waiting."

"Nonsense. It's no distance at all, and I wished to escort you. In fact, I cut out Derek for the privilege of seeing your face when you first glimpse the spectacle."

She smiled. "Is it very impressive?"

"It is, really. Last year, the vicar's son organized all my tenants for a medieval tournament. He's quite a scholar, you know, and he arrayed every farm worker and village maid in tunic and gown."

"I had no notion it was to be so elaborate," laughed Elisabeth. "What is the idea this year? Should we have come in costume?"

"No, no. It's all organized by the neighborhood. I have nothing to do with it and am always to be surprised with the program. I cannot tell you what they have gotten up this year. But since Daniel, the vicar's son, has gone off to Oxford, I fear you may be disappointed. Most likely, there will be no great show but only a bit of dancing and a picnic."

"It sounds delightful."

"I hope you'll enjoy it. Did you have a pleasant journey down from London?"

"Oh, yes, and my arrival was even more pleasant. You must come to see what they've done at Willowmere. It is utterly changed."

"So I have heard from my agent. I look forward to viewing the marvels he describes. You are the heroine of the neighborhood, you know, for the wonders you have wrought there and, more important, the work you have provided."

"I've done nothing, really. It's all Mr. Lewis."

"You commanded it all, however, as your uncle never did. I daresay you may find yourself cheered this afternoon." He smiled at her surprised look.

"Goodness, do you think so? That will be a new experience."

Music had begun to be audible, and now as they rounded a small copse, the site of the festival came into view. Two awnings had been set up in a large field, and they and the spaces around them were filled to overflowing with people. Some were dancing to the

tunes three country musicians provided. Others had
gathered in groups to talk and exchange news. On the
far side of the field, games were in progress. In one
of the tents, women bustled about a fire preparing tea
and picnic fare, and in the other, smaller shelter, Lady
Larenby and her daughter sat surrounded by a group
of guests.

The viscount directed Elisabeth to this area and
helped her dismount. All of them entered the tent to
greet the viscountess and be presented to her sister. A
quick look told Elisabeth that Derek Wincannon was
not present.

When they had said everything that was polite,
Elisabeth looked at the crowd. "Jane, do you care to
stroll and see what is here?" she asked.

Jane was agreeable, and the two women started out
across the grass, leaving Tony to talk to Amelia. They
went first toward the dancers and spent some minutes
watching them. "What energy," exclaimed Elisabeth
at the end of a particularly rousing country dance.
"And they are starting another immediately. I'm not
sure I could stand the pace."

Jane smiled, and after a moment, they moved on.
"Have you ever seen such a festival before?" continued Elisabeth. "I haven't, and I find it wonderful."

"I have, one or two," replied Jane, "near my family's place in Yorkshire."

"You are all so offhand about it. I wonder at you.
Would this not make a first-rate subject for your
writing?"

Jane looked about her, smiling slightly. "Pastoral
swains, and that sort of thing? No, I believe I'll continue

to leave that to imitators of Virgil and Walter Scott. I can't see the fascination myself."

Elisabeth shook her head and walked on.

A loud cheer was heard ahead of them, and they quickened their pace a bit. Reaching the area where games were being held, they moved through the crowd until they could see an open space around a huge old oak tree. A dart board had been nailed to it, and several competitors stood about nearby. Two were a little apart from the others preparing to throw, and as she turned to watch, Elisabeth started, for one of the men was Derek Wincannon.

He did not see her at first, but took his turn, placing all but one of his darts in the innermost circle of the target. There was scattered applause and some cheers as he threw the last. When he moved to allow his opponent room, he turned and saw the ladies standing at the edge of the crowd; he came up to them immediately. "How do you do," he said. "You have come at just the proper moment. Jack Crowley and I have eliminated the competition and are about to determine the winner. I must tell you that Jack and I have been arch rivals at darts for nearly twenty years; if he bests me today, however, he may take the championship, for it will be the third year running." Jack, the subject of this explanation, bowed to the ladies and turned back to the target with great concentration. "We must be silent while he throws," finished Derek.

There was complete silence around the tree. After another minute of studying the bull's-eye, Jack Crowley threw his five darts in quick succession. Each of them struck within the inner circle, almost on top of each other. As the last hit, a great cheer broke out among the spectators, and most of them rushed forward to congratulate him. Jack fought through the back-pounding and laughing to shake hands with Derek, who added his own congratulations, then set off with friends to celebrate his victory with a mug of ale. The three companions were suddenly left almost alone beside the oak.

Derek laughed down at the ladies, "Alas, you see me in defeat," he said. "Jack has gotten too good for me. I may have to give up our games, though I wonder if I shall be allowed to."

"Have you really played for twenty years?" asked Elisabeth.

"Yes, indeed. We began as lads and continued more or less even until lately. But he has outstripped me, I fear."

"And did you participate in the tournament last year as well?" asked Elisabeth, her eyes twinkling up at him.

"I did not, though it was a very near thing. I thank God young Daniel has gone off to school, and I need no longer resist his importunities to deck myself out in my ancestor's armor or lend the farm horses for jousts."

Elisabeth laughed. "Oh, how can you say so? I only wish I might have seen it. I daresay you would look splendid in armor."

An answering twinkle awoke in Derek's eyes. "That temptation was outweighed by the extreme discomfort armor entails. I frankly balked. Have you any notion of the weight of plate armor?"

"I have not." Their eyes met and held for a moment.

"It is beginning to be quite warm, isn't it?" put in Jane Taunton. "I believe I'll go back to the tent and sit in the shade."

Elisabeth turned a little guiltily. She had almost forgotten Jane. "Of course, let us go. The sun is getting hot."

"I'll escort you," said Derek.

"I'm perfectly capable of walking across the field alone," said Jane. "There's no need for you to accompany me."

"Nonsense," said Elisabeth, a little annoyed at her tone. And they started off together.

When they rejoined Lady Larenby, luncheon was about to be served. The servants brought around trays of cold meats, fruit, and bread and butter, and left pitchers of ale, wine, and lemonade on the table before going to join their friends outside the tent. Lady Larenby poured. "We wait on ourselves today," she told her guests, smiling at her cook, who was hastily placing one last large tray of cakes and sweets on the table before her.

When they'd finished, Derek leaned across to Elisabeth. "Would you care to look about a bit more?" he asked her. "You haven't seen everything, you know."

"I'd love it," replied the girl, rising.

Derek offered his arm, and they strolled out of the tent and across the grass. Most of the people were sitting in groups now, on blankets and cloths, and eating the picnic lunch. Many called greetings to Derek or nodded to him as they passed by. A few of the children had finished and returned to their games, and they watched a dart match between two small boys.

"Another rivalry in the making," said Derek, after he'd laughingly refused their pleas for a game or a lesson and judged the results of a hotly contested match.

Elisabeth returned his smile. "This is delightful," she said. "How lucky you are to have such a thing every year."

They moved on toward the dance area. Some of the younger people had returned, and the music was beginning again. They stood still to watch for a moment, then Derek suddenly took Elisabeth's hand. "Come," he said.

He pulled her into the country dance, whirling her about dizzily. Within a few moments, Elisabeth was breathless, but she turned and swooped with the others until the song ended. When it was over, she stepped back out of the crowd and put a hand to her chest. "Oh, my," she breathed.

Derek laughed down at her. "You aren't quitting so soon?"

"Indeed I am. I'm not so young as these dancers. They will wear me out."

"How careless of me. I should have seated you with the dowagers; I had forgotten your advanced age."

Elisabeth laughed. She'd caught her breath again now. "Not that. But I think I'll watch the dancing rather than join it."

Tony and Amelia came up then. Having seen her brother dancing, Amelia was eager to try as well. And they were soon followed by Lord and Lady Larenby, to keep up the tradition of one dance together. Elisabeth was pulled back into the set thus formed, and she danced with the viscount in the next. After that, despite importunities, she returned to the tent for a rest.

Lavinia and Jane were sitting there chatting desultorily. "Jane, you must go out," said Elisabeth. "Tony is searching for a partner, and I am worn out."

"No, thank you," said Jane.

"Are you not having a good time?" said Elisabeth. "Do go and dance."

"I'm perfectly all right. You know I simply prefer my own work to parties."

Elisabeth sat down with them for a while, but Jane seemed cool, and she herself was nettled at her friend's sulkiness. After a while, Tony called her out again, and she had her dance with him. The afternoon passed quickly. Elisabeth danced again with Derek and shared some lemonade he fetched for her. The sun was beginning to set before they sent for their horses and prepared to leave. As Elisabeth was gathering up her belongings in the tent, Derek approached her. "I hope you've enjoyed yourself," he said.

"Very much," she replied. "I don't remember when I've had such fun."

"I am glad." He looked down at her, started to take her hand, then changed his mind. "It's very hard to have any private conversation at an event such as this," he went on. "But I should very much like to talk about something rather important. Perhaps tomorrow?" The look in his eyes made Elisabeth's heart beat faster; she looked down.

"Certainly," she replied unevenly. "I am often at my accounts in the library at midmorning."

He nodded. "I will call about eleven then." He took her hand, quickly placed a light kiss on it, and turned away.

# Twenty-four

THE NEXT MORNING, ELISABETH WENT INTO THE library at ten and tried to settle down to her accounts, but repeatedly she found herself daydreaming instead, and finally she gave it up.

At half past, she heard a horse outside and then a ring at the front door. Smiling, she rose and went to the door of the library. He's early, she thought. But when she looked into the hall, she didn't see Derek Wincannon. Ames was talking to Mr. Jarrett.

As the butler said he would see whether she was in, she started to shrink back into the study, but Jarrett noticed her when she moved and came forward eagerly.

"Miss Elham," he said, holding out his hand. "I'm fortunate to find you in. I have ridden down from London expressly to see you."

Feeling trapped, Elisabeth sought to put him off. "Indeed. I fear I have an appointment in a very few minutes. If you had informed me of your visit…"

"I must speak to you," interrupted Jarrett. "Please."

His tone was imperative, and he more or less ushered Elisabeth back into the library as he spoke.

Reluctantly, she seated herself behind the desk once more and gestured toward a chair opposite. "I hope you'll be quick," she told him rather coolly. She indicated the papers before her.

"You haven't been eager to see me of late," responded Jarrett. "Indeed, quite the opposite. I hope I have done nothing to offend you?"

Elisabeth raised her eyebrows. "No, how should you? As you know, in London I was taken up with my cousin's wedding. I had no time for anything else."

He bowed his head slightly. "Of course. Nonetheless, it was a hardship, getting no sight of you for weeks."

Elisabeth smiled slightly. "Hardly weeks, Mr. Jarrett."

He returned her smile and made a deprecating gesture. "I suppose I exaggerate. You must know that it has become vital to me that I see you often. And not simply during morning calls."

Elisabeth did not care for the direction the conversation was taking. She put on what she hoped was a discouraging expression and said, "Indeed?"

"Yes. In fact, I have fallen deeply in love with you, Elisabeth. I want more than anything in the world to make you my wife." His eyes held hers.

The girl was only a little startled. She'd seen something of the sort coming. "You do me a great honor, Mr. Jarrett. I am fully sensible of it. But I fear I must refuse."

Jarrett's eyes narrowed. "Are you engaged to someone else?" he asked.

Elisabeth flushed a little as she shook her head. "But that has nothing to do with it. My feelings are such that…"

"That you do not love me," finished the man. "No need to wrap it in clean linen. It's plain enough." He paused, seeming to search for words. "You might learn to do so, you know. Marriage is not all romance and cooing. I would be a good husband to you."

Elisabeth rose. "We seem to have very different ideas about marriage, Mr. Jarrett. I think we need say no more."

He stood up also, but showed no signs of disappointment or of leaving. He simply frowned intently, shifting his grip on his hat. "My ideas are not unalterable," he said finally. "And I have told you that I love you. I'm willing to change; could you not try to also?"

Elisabeth was growing angry. She had answered him honestly, but he refused to heed her. "I think not," she replied coldly. "And now if you will excuse me."

Jarrett's frown deepened, and he made an impatient gesture. "You simply dismiss me, is that it? Do you think you can send me on my way like an importunate tradesman?"

"Not at all. But our discussion is concluded, I think."

"Do you indeed?" Jarrett's eyes hardened, and a queer expression played about his mouth. "You're very sure of yourself, aren't you?"

Elisabeth didn't deign to reply to this but started toward the door. Jarrett suddenly stepped in front of her and grasped her arm tightly. "It's Wincannon, isn't it? I thought as much. So you've set your heart on a title just like all the greedy little debs."

Trying to pull her arm free, Elisabeth stepped back. "How dare you?"

"Dare?" He laughed harshly. "You would be surprised what I would dare, depending on the stakes."

The girl managed to get free; her eyes flashed indignantly. "Such as my fortune?" she snapped.

The look Jarrett directed at her made her quail for a moment, then bland amusement descended over his features. He shrugged. "I never thought you stupid. I admit that your money means something to me. To whom would it not? You cannot blame me for prudence."

"I can and do." Elisabeth managed to get to the library door and held it open. "I must ask you not to call upon me again, sir," she said icily and gestured toward the hall.

Jarrett hesitated a moment; he seemed to be struggling with himself. A series of emotions showed in his face—rage, chagrin, hope. He made as if to speak, changed his mind, then bowed slightly and strode out of the room. Elisabeth saw that he was leaving before she shut the door. As she did so, she noticed Jane Taunton descending the stairs from the drawing room with her sketching equipment. I hope she doesn't meet Jarrett, she thought to herself. What an unpleasant man!

❧

She paced about the library for some minutes, trying to regain control of herself. She'd just taken a deep breath and sat down again, feeling more composed, when Ames knocked and entered the library. "The Duchess of Sherbourne has just arrived, Miss Elisabeth." Ames's tone indicated that he considered these unannounced arrivals highly unsatisfactory.

"The duchess?" echoed Elisabeth. "But what can she be doing here? She was to go to Brighton."

"I'm sure I couldn't say, miss," answered Ames.

Elisabeth rose and started out of the room. "Where is she? Of course I'll see her. You shouldn't have kept her waiting."

"She refused to leave her traveling carriage," responded Ames in freezing accents.

Elisabeth hurried out and stepped up to the window of the duchess's carriage. She was indeed still inside. "Good morning, ma'am," said Elisabeth. "This is a most pleasant surprise. Won't you come in?"

The duchess sat up straighter and shook her head decisively. "No. I've stopped for a moment only on my way north. I wish to talk to you before my courage fails me."

The girl frowned. "You aren't going to Brighton after all, then?"

The duchess made an impatient gesture. "No, of course I'm not going to Brighton. Do get into the carriage, Elisabeth, so that we may talk."

Surprised and puzzled, Elisabeth moved toward the open coach door. "If you like," she answered, "but would we not be more comfortable in the house?"

"I'm in a hurry. And I don't wish to be overheard."

Elisabeth saw now that some of the older woman's abruptness was the result of a nervousness wholly uncharacteristic of her. "Of course," she said soothingly. "But we might go into the garden, you know, away from the house, instead of sitting cramped in the carriage."

The duchess hesitated. "That would do, I suppose,"

she replied finally. "Yes, perhaps that's better." She moved quickly to step down.

"Good," said Elisabeth. "If you'd care to walk on a moment, I'll speak to Ames and then join you in the garden."

Frowning in puzzlement, Elisabeth turned back to the house. She found Ames in the hall. "I'm expecting Mr. Wincannon to call. Will you tell him please what has happened, and give him my apologies? Tell him that I'll try to get free as soon as possible."

"Yes, miss," replied the butler.

After a moment's searching, she found the duchess seated on a rustic bench next to a small clump of yew. She quickly sat down beside her. "There," she said, "we can talk privately here."

The duchess was looking at her gloves, which she held twisted together in her hands, but she raised her eyes when Elisabeth spoke. "I'll tell you frankly that this is rather difficult for me," she began. "I'm not in the habit of explaining myself to anyone, much less a young woman who might be my daughter. However, I believe it is only fair that someone in Belinda's family know the story, and I refuse to speak of it to anyone but you. I've decided not to tell my son."

"I...I'm very flattered," said Elisabeth.

"Well, you needn't be. I don't wish to tell you, either." The duchess smiled thinly. "But you're a sensible girl, and I do feel that I can trust you."

Not knowing how to reply, Elisabeth said, "Thank you."

The duchess looked at her gloves again, stared off across the flower bed opposite, then sat back on the bench and sighed. "Very well. There's no good way to begin. I must simply tell it.

"I was very young and silly when I first went to London. Your cousin Lavinia could tell you, if she would, how silly. I had a head full of romantic notions, combined with a great deal of stubbornness and arrogance. My family was wealthy, and I was very much indulged as a child. I expected to always be given whatever I wanted, and I brooked no interference from anyone." She looked over at Elisabeth. "I say this not to place the blame on anyone else or even excuse myself, but only so that you will better understand the situation."

Elisabeth nodded; these revelations coming from a woman so much older than herself effectively silenced her.

"Well, and so I was wild and imprudent," the duchess went on. "It was a time of some turmoil, the uprising in France and so on, and I behaved as I should not. I refused to listen to anyone's advice.

"What it comes down to is the usual tale. I met a young man and fell in love." The duchess sighed. "As you may have guessed, it was Mr. Aldgate. Lucius was in the army, a very dashing and completely penniless young soldier. I was *bouleversé*, as we used to say then." A faint smile lit the duchess's face. "Everyone spoke against it, of course, including Lucius himself, but I was too headstrong to listen. And he loved me; I controlled him by that." She looked across at Elisabeth. "We eloped, at my insistence. I was utterly imprudent. But I'm not entirely ashamed of that. I loved him very much." She put a hand to her head for a moment.

"What I am bitterly ashamed of is what followed." She rubbed her hand across her forehead several times. "In a space of a very few days, I found I couldn't live in genteel penury. Lucius had no money at all, and the little I'd been able to bring was soon gone. We stayed in mean inns going north to Gretna Green and were forced to give up our post chaise for the stage. I hated it!" This was spoken intensely, and the duchess hit her knee with a doubled fist. "I despise myself still, but I could not endure it. I left Lucius before we reached the border and fled back to my parents. I accepted the duke, who had been on the point of offering for me, and married him immediately. Lucius never reproached me or indeed communicated with me again. He attended my wedding clad in a magnificent suit of purple and silver. I knew it must have cost everything he had. But I never even spoke to him; I did nothing."

"Dear ma'am, you needn't tell me this," Elisabeth interrupted. "But please believe that I understand what you must have felt."

The older woman took a deep breath and appeared to recover herself. "I doubt it," she said in her usual dry tones. "In any case, this is only the preface of what I wish to tell you. John is Lucius's son."

In her surprise, Elisabeth gasped.

"Yes," the other went on. "You are a sensible young woman, as I observed, and not missish. I think I need say no more."

Wide-eyed, Elisabeth shook her head.

"I never told anyone, naturally. Any remorse or guilt was mine to bear. But this is why I was so affected when you mentioned Lucius to me. The past I had thought forever buried seemed to come to life again. I was afraid."

She seemed to wait for an answer, but Elisabeth could summon no words.

"But when I had talked with Lucius," she went on, "I saw that it was all right. He was the same noble character. He wished to do nothing that would embarrass me, but he said he could not resist seeing me again after all these years." A faint pink flush tinged the duchess's cheeks. "I told him the truth. It seemed to me a kind of penitence to put my secret in his hands; he will tell no one else." She looked into Elisabeth's eyes. "You will say I should have told you before the wedding, and you are right, but my nerve failed me, I admit. John is still my son, and I wished him to be happy. I did not dare."

She stopped, and Elisabeth struggled for the proper words.

"Are you angry?" asked the duchess finally.

"No, no, I'm not at all angry," replied the girl quickly. "I'm overcome with surprise, I think."

The older woman laughed a bit sourly. "Natural enough, I suppose. But is there anything you would wish done?"

"Done?" echoed Elisabeth rather stupidly.

"Indeed, that is what Lucius and I concluded. There is nothing to be done. John is my only child. He cuts no one out, save some very distant cousins who never thought to inherit the title. Things must remain as they are."

"I…of course," faltered Elisabeth, "it is hardly my affair. I cannot quite see, in fact, why you have told me."

"I'm not sure I know," answered the duchess meditatively, "except that I wished to be done with deceit, to start fresh, you see. But I couldn't face Belinda with this story, as I ought." She shrugged and rose. "I must go; I'm on my way north to meet Lucius. We are to be married on Thursday."

Elisabeth got quickly to her feet. "Indeed? That's wonderful."

"If a trifle late?" asked the duchess drily. "Frankly, I've ceased to care what anyone thinks, even myself." Her tone softened. "And I mean to do everything to make him happy now." She pulled on her gloves decisively. "There, now I've told you everything, and I can go." She began walking down the path before Elisabeth could reply.

The girl hurried after her, neither of them noticing a movement in the bushes behind the bench as they disappeared.

She watched the chaise drive off, then returned to the house, her mind whirling. Ames stopped her for a moment to say that Mr. Wincannon had waited for half an hour before going away again, promising to call the following day. Elisabeth was too occupied to do more than murmur an acknowledgment of this news as she entered the library again. She could not even care about having missed Derek at this moment.

# *Twenty-five*

ELISABETH ENTERED THE BREAKFAST ROOM RATHER after her usual time the next morning, due to a restless night full of uneasy dreams. To her surprise, she found Jane there. "Good morning," she said to her friend. "You're late today, too. I don't believe I've known you to breakfast after eight o'clock since we arrived."

When she turned to reply, Jane appeared a bit heavy-eyed. "Indeed, I didn't sleep very well," she answered.

Elisabeth sat down and rang for fresh tea. "Nor did I," she said, reaching for a muffin and beginning to butter it.

"I was thinking."

"It must be in the air, then, for I was doing the same. Were you composing a new poem or merely formulating an article castigating young women of today for their frivolity?"

"No, neither," said Jane. "I am... I have been concerned... I should very much like to have a private talk with you, Elisabeth."

The younger girl sobered immediately. "Why, of course. Is anything wrong? I hope nothing has happened to upset you."

Jane turned her head toward the window. "Not precisely. That is, I am a little upset. I wish to talk."

"Of course," responded Elisabeth after a pause. "What is it? How can I be of help to you?"

Jane turned back, moving rather nervously. "Oh, we can't talk here. Will you come walking with me this morning? I need to move about; I can't stay still." As if to demonstrate this, she got up and walked to the window.

Elisabeth hesitated. "I do have an appointment this morning," she began. "Could we perhaps go this afternoon instead?"

But Jane shook her head vehemently. She came back to the table and leaned across it toward Elisabeth. "No. Please, it must be now." Tension and anxiety were clear in her face.

"Very well," replied the other girl. "If it's so serious, then of course I can cancel my engagement. Did I understand that you wish to go immediately?"

"Yes. Please."

Elisabeth nodded. "If you will wait a moment while I write a note, then, and fetch a shawl. You had best do so, too; there is a little chill this morning."

Jane agreed. "But Elisabeth," she added, "please don't mention that you're walking with me when you change the appointment. I don't wish to be blamed, and it might be thought strange. I don't want anyone else to know of my worries."

Privately thinking her friend rather oversensitive,

Elisabeth went into the library to compose a note to Derek Wincannon. She found this a little difficult, since she was putting him off for the second time, but she finally asked him to call in the afternoon rather than the morning. She got a shawl from her room and descended to the hall where Jane awaited her. "Ready?" she said, smiling.

"Yes," answered Jane quickly, "but I have stupidly forgotten to bring my sketching things. Will you wait for me in the garden while I fetch them?"

"Do you need them today?" asked Elisabeth. "I thought you wanted to talk?"

"I want nothing to appear out of the ordinary," replied the other girl tensely. "Oh, Elisabeth, you don't know what has occurred. No one must find out." This last remark was so impassioned that Elisabeth frowned sympathetically.

"Indeed? Well, I will wait in the garden if you wish it."

"Please," begged Jane. "I will look for you by the stile."

Elisabeth walked down the path to the back garden. She waved to Mr. Lewis, who was crossing the stableyard some distance away, and greeted two of the gardener's boys who were digging in the rose beds. She took the path between high hedges of boxwood that led to the stile into the field beyond.

It was indeed a little cold; the sky was overcast and threatened rain later in the day. She waited only a few moments before Jane came hurrying up, carrying a leather case. "Do you think it will rain?" Elisabeth asked her. "I hope we're not in for a wetting."

"It will hold off," answered Jane, and she stepped onto the stile quickly.

Elisabeth followed her, and soon they were walking side by side along the footpath across the field. Jane set a brisk pace and remained silent.

After a while, Elisabeth grew puzzled. "What may I do to help you?" she asked the other girl at last. "Are you in some trouble, Jane?"

Without slackening her pace, Jane turned her head. "It's so hard to begin," she replied. "Forgive me. I know I'm acting strangely, but the exercise helps to calm me. Allow me a little time to gather my thoughts."

"Of course," said Elisabeth.

They walked. When they reached the end of the path and came into a lane, Jane turned left at the same brisk walk.

Thinking conversation might put her friend more at ease, Elisabeth said, "I've never walked this way before. I don't yet know the neighborhood at all well. Have you been down this lane?"

"Yes," responded Jane. "I've walked here several times."

They went on for a while in silence, Elisabeth becoming more and more puzzled. Finally, she could stand it no longer. "Jane," she began.

But the other girl interrupted her. "I know. I'm behaving very foolishly, and you're quite right to be annoyed. I must tell you what has happened."

"Shall we not stop and perhaps sit down somewhere?" Elisabeth looked about but saw only hedges and a few trees beyond them.

"No," answered Jane decisively. "It really helps me to walk. Please."

"Very well."

Jane frowned as if in concentration. "I received a letter yesterday," she began finally. "It held unsettling news; I have been worrying over it all night and morning."

"What was it?" asked Elisabeth sympathetically. "Your family?"

Jane shook her head. "No. A friend. A dear friend has been killed." She put a hand to her eyes as she walked on.

"Oh, my poor Jane. I'm so sorry."

Jane said nothing. She kept her hand before her face, and Elisabeth thought she cried a little.

They rounded a bend in the lane. There was a low building ahead of them near the intersection with the high road. Elisabeth held out a hand toward her friend. "What do you wish to do?" she asked. "Do you want to go to them? I can give you the carriage and come with you if you like. Or if you prefer to travel alone…"

Jane started to lower her hand from her eyes, took a false step in a deep rut of the lane, and fell headlong on the road surface, dropping her case and crying out sharply.

Elisabeth ran to her. "Jane," she cried, "are you hurt?"

To her relief, Jane sat up immediately. "No, no. How stupid of me. I wasn't watching where I stepped." She started to rise, but when she put weight on her left foot, she cried out again and clutched Elisabeth's arm. "Ahh. I seem to have twisted my ankle," she said through clenched teeth. "How foolish!"

Elisabeth put an arm around her for support. "Don't be silly. It wasn't your fault. But how shall we get you home again?" She looked about helplessly, seeing as she did so that the first few drops of rain were beginning to spatter the dust of the lane.

"That building is a small inn," answered Jane tightly. "It isn't elegant, but they will help us."

"How fortunate," sighed Elisabeth. "Can you walk there, or shall I fetch someone to carry you? Yes, that is best. Sit down here on this rock; I'll only be a moment."

"No, no, I can walk, with your help. It is only a step."

Slowly, Jane leaning heavily on Elisabeth and limping, they traversed the short distance to the inn.

They reached the door just as the rain began in earnest, and Elisabeth was very grateful to enter the close narrow hallway and ease Jane into a straight chair there. "How lucky we were that this inn was so near," she said. "Look, it's truly raining now, and I daresay it will keep up all afternoon."

Jane made no reply, and Elisabeth turned to peer down the corridor behind them. "I wonder where the innkeeper is?" she said. "There seems to be no one about." There were several doors along the hall, but all were closed. "Hello," called Elisabeth more loudly. "Is anyone here?"

"Who be that?" answered a deep voice from the recesses of the inn. And immediately afterward a large man appeared and came toward them. "Who's there?" he repeated.

"Hello," said Elisabeth. "Are you the innkeeper?"

"Mr. Crenshaw," said Jane.

"Ah, it's you is it? I never thought to see you in this rain, Miss Jane."

"Indeed, we were lucky to reach shelter before it began," replied Jane. "Is there a fire in the parlor? May we go in?"

"You know there is." He opened a door at the right and gestured them in. Elisabeth could see the gleam of firelight from inside the room.

She turned to their host. "Miss Taunton has twisted her ankle," she said to him. "We must help her to walk."

"You go ahead, Elisabeth," said Jane. "Mr. Crenshaw will give me his arm."

"Course I will."

Elisabeth looked from her friend to the burly innkeeper a bit doubtfully, then shrugged slightly and led the way into the parlor. It was rather dim, the only light coming from the fire and a small window.

It wasn't until she was quite close to him that she realized someone else was in the room. "Good day, Miss Elham," said George Jarrett. "Quite unpleasant weather, is it not?"

"Mr. Jarrett!" exclaimed Elisabeth. "What are you doing here?" She turned back toward the door, only to see it shut tight behind her.

She started quickly back, holding out a hand to grasp the doorknob. At the same time, she called, "Jane," sharply and with some distress in her voice. Was her friend all right? But before she could reach the door, it opened, and Jane strode into the room.

"Yes, Elisabeth," she said. "What is it?"

"Your…your ankle," stammered the other girl.

"Very well done, Jane," said Jarrett behind her. "I feared the rain would spoil everything."

"You underestimate me," answered Jane, smiling scornfully.

Elisabeth looked from one to the other, stunned. "What's going on?"

"To put no sugar coating on it," replied Jarrett, "you've been abducted, my dear Miss Elham."

"Don't be ridiculous," snapped Elisabeth. She turned. "Jane, what is this? Some sort of joke? I promise you I don't find it funny."

"I am afraid it's true," said Jane. She looked past Elisabeth to Jarrett. "I've done my part. I must return to the house."

"Jane! What are you doing?" Elisabeth's tone was both shocked and unbelieving. "You cannot make me believe you're involved in this preposterous scheme."

Jane shrugged. "I shan't try. But don't deceive yourself into thinking it preposterous, Elisabeth. I assure you it's well planned. You are taken. Mr. Crenshaw is in Jarrett's pay, and there is no one else here."

"I'll be looked for."

"True," continued Jane, "but you'll be long gone before that. And now I must go." She turned toward the door.

"Jane!" cried Elisabeth. "You won't leave me here?"

Jarrett spoke up then. "Indeed, I've thought it over, and I believe that perhaps you should stay. It might make things easier." He smiled. "And it would certainly prevent you from changing your mind about our little agreement. Crenshaw," he called.

But before the door could open completely, Jane

had reached into the pocket of her gown and pulled out a tiny pistol. Elisabeth watched astonished as she backed away to train it on both Jarrett and the entering Mr. Crenshaw. "You can't think me such a fool as to trust you, Mr. Jarrett," said Jane. "I'm disappointed in you."

Jarrett bowed deeply. "As I am not in you, Miss Taunton. You will, of course, do just as you please."

Jane smiled. "You don't wonder whether I can shoot?"

"I assume it."

Jane laughed. "And you are right. Good day, Mr. Jarrett. You will post the cheque to me in London. You know the consequences if I don't receive it."

Jarrett bowed again.

Jane turned. "Crenshaw, is the fly outside?"

"Yes, miss, just as you ordered." Crenshaw was looking from Jarrett to Jane with some puzzlement and eying the gun fearfully.

"Good." Jane backed toward the door.

Elisabeth moved abruptly. "Jane, take me with you. Do not do this thing." She started toward her friend, but one of Crenshaw's broad arms restrained her.

Jane paused, surveying her with hard eyes. "I'm honestly sorry for it, Elisabeth, for you have been generally kind to me. But it's necessary."

"Why?" cried Elisabeth.

"I must have my independence," replied Jane. "And for that, I must have money. A great deal of money. This was my chance to get it. I shall go abroad, perhaps to Italy." A faraway look came into her eyes. "I'll travel for some time, then settle abroad. I'll really write then." She recovered herself. "Goodbye, Elisabeth, I'm sorry."

"But Jane. I would have given you money, if you had asked," said Elisabeth. "Indeed, I will, if you take me with you."

Jane smiled tightly. "Everything is so easy for you, isn't it? But I prefer to do this for myself. I will take the money, not receive it with meek gratitude. I'm sick of meekness." And with this vehement statement, she backed out of the room, shut the door, and was gone.

Elisabeth heard quick footsteps, then the sound of a horse. She bowed her head a little, feeling terribly alone. She turned back to the fireplace, facing Mr. Jarrett. He smiled. "Well, Miss Elham," he said, "won't you sit down before the fire? You must be chilled. And we have a great deal to discuss."

# Twenty-six

THE CRACKLING FIRE MADE THE ONLY SOUND IN THE inn parlor as Elisabeth struggled with her anger. She was trembling with the effort to control herself, not to lash out or burst into tears.

"Shall I take the lady to the sofa?" asked Crenshaw after a few moments.

"No, no, Jud," replied Mr. Jarrett. "In fact, you may return to the hall. I am sure we'll have no problems. Watch the road; I'll call if I need you."

The burly man nodded and left the room, shutting the door behind him. Mr. Jarrett turned his gaze on Elisabeth once more. "Won't you sit down?" he asked. "You look quite done up."

"You cannot mean this," said Elisabeth. "You are not so foolhardy."

Jarrett shrugged. "I'm not foolhardy," he answered, "but I assure you I do mean it. I have no choice, you see. I must have money, and I must have it soon."

"But you can't think to ransom me. It's an insane plan. You'll be caught straightaway."

Jarrett appeared surprised. "Ransoming?" he echoed.

Then, he laughed. "Oh no, I have no plans to ransom you, none at all."

Elisabeth frowned. "But you said…you called it a kidnapping."

"It is, but not for ransom. That is nearly always clumsy. An abduction should have a more easily accomplished purpose."

"Indeed? You seem very conversant with the subject. What might this purpose be?" Elisabeth tried to put the scorn she felt into her voice.

Mr. Jarrett looked into the fire meditatively. "Motives can be various. In the case of your young cousin, for example, the purpose was actually quite harmless."

Elisabeth was struck speechless; she swallowed. "You!" she said at last. "You kidnapped Tony?"

He smiled. "Well, let us say I was behind it, at any rate. I didn't seize him myself, of course."

His careless manner shocked Elisabeth and made her more fearful. "But why? You sent no ransom note."

He gestured impatiently. "My purpose was otherwise, as I told you. Actually, I did it hoping to win your regard."

This statement left Elisabeth gasping. For a moment, she couldn't speak, then she stammered, "You kidnapped my cousin and held him prisoner in order to win my regard? You must be mad."

Jarrett laughed. "It's ironic, is it not? But I assure you I'm not mad. I planned, you see, to hold him for a short time, long enough to create anxiety, and then to gallantly rescue him and bring him to you. Your gratitude and admiration were to be the groundwork for a lasting passion. Clever, was it not?

Unfortunately, I rather underestimated the young man's resourcefulness."

Elisabeth said nothing, merely staring at him incredulously.

Jarrett held his hands to the fire and continued to smile at her over his shoulder. "You are struck dumb by the neatness of it, I see. I tell you the story to impress upon you my seriousness in this venture. I shall not give in."

The girl put a hand to the side of her throat. "What do you wish of me?"

"That is better. Sit down and be warm by the fire. We won't leave before dark, you know. You will be here some time."

Elisabeth hesitated, then walked to the sofa and sat down. It was indeed much warmer on this side of the room, and some of her trembling subsided with the chill. She looked at Jarrett coldly. "What will you do?" she asked.

He shrugged. "Having failed in all other schemes, I shall hold you until you consent to marry me. Jane informed me that Wincannon has become very particular in his attentions and that you appear to be encouraging him, for which you cannot be blamed, of course. But I couldn't allow it. Such a waste, to unite two such large fortunes."

Elisabeth made a gesture of loathing. "I'll never marry you."

"Ah well, we shall see. There are one or two points I will make on that subject later. But now, are you hungry? Do you require something? I must leave you for a moment. Can I have Crenshaw get you something?"

Elisabeth shook her head angrily and turned away.

"Not even a cup of tea?" When the girl made no response, Jarrett shrugged and left the room.

Elisabeth heard him say something to Crenshaw, confirming her guess that the burly man would be left to guard the door, and then his footsteps continued down the corridor and into the back of the inn. As soon as they died away, she got up quietly and hurried to the window at the front of the room. It was smudged with dust and very small, but she had some hopes of forcing her way through and escaping into the driving rain she could see outside. She unhooked the clasp and pushed with all her strength. It was meant to open outward, but the pane did not move an inch when she threw herself against it. Impatiently, she repeated her effort, but it was either fastened on the outside or stuck; she couldn't move it.

Finally, she gave up and returned to the sofa. She was trembling again. Holding her hands out to the flames, she thought furiously. It seemed to her impossible that Jarrett could force her to marry him; she knew that her consent was necessary, and she would never give it. But this fact in itself didn't better her situation. She must get away.

She was about to return to the window when she heard footsteps approaching along the hall outside. She rose quickly and faced the door.

Jarrett entered, rubbing his hands together and looking pleased with himself. "All is well," he said to her. "Our travel arrangements are complete."

"Where are you taking me?" asked Elisabeth.

"To London. I can get cheap rooms there." He smiled. "You see how it is with me. I'm all to pieces."

Elisabeth turned her back on him and faced the fire again. "You're wasting your time," she said. "This scheme will not succeed."

"Ah, yes, that is what we must discuss now. All would be so much easier if you would agree. Indeed, I should much prefer it. I'm not a cruel man, Elisabeth, merely a desperate one. I shan't be a bad husband. Can't you reconcile yourself to me?"

Elisabeth looked at him scornfully. "So that you may serve me as you did your first wife? No, thank you."

Jarrett looked at her sharply. "What are you talking about?"

"You killed her, didn't you? I never believed it till now. But I see you are without scruples. Her brother was right."

The surprise on Jarrett's face had been building until her last remark, then it cleared. "Did Étienne get to you as well? He was damnably thorough. I owe my present penniless state to him, in fact. But those accusations were false. My wife died of a fever." He stared out the window, his expression stony. "And if you think I wished her to die or had any hand in it, you are greatly mistaken." For a moment, he stood so, his hands clenched at his sides, his eyes hard, then he recovered control of himself with a visible effort and relaxed. "After all," he said, with an attempt at lightness, "one does not kill the goose that lays the golden egg."

His strong reaction to her words made Elisabeth pause a moment before replying, then she said,

"Nonetheless, you married her for money. You cannot deny that."

Jarrett shrugged. "Nor do I attempt to. I should as soon disavow any wisdom or cleverness in dealing with the world. What else should I marry for, having no income of my own? But having married, I did my best to make her happy. And I did so, except when her family got at her and upset her with attempts to separate us. They all hated me, especially Étienne. They hoped she would marry a man they'd chosen, a very rich man, of course. I was not an acceptable son-in-law."

Elisabeth remained silent, gazing at the fire.

Jarrett came nearer. "I swear you would never regret marrying me, Elisabeth. My regard for you is real. Everything shall be done just as you wish."

The girl flung up her head. "You dare to say this to me," she said contemptuously, "when you hold me here against my will? Don't expect to win my agreement by such means."

Jarrett sighed. "You really have decided to take Wincannon, haven't you? I feared it. He is a formidable rival, possessing so much I do not."

"Yes, indeed," snapped Elisabeth before she thought, "honesty and consideration, for example."

Jarrett surveyed her speculatively. "I see how it is. Very well, I shall have to use other means. I had hoped to avoid it."

"You may say what you will. It will make no difference."

"We shall see. I tell you, then, my terms. I'll hold you until you consent to marry me. We shall live

together, without chaperone, in London. Your repu-
tation will be ruined; you will be forced to marry if
you are ever to go about in society again."

Elisabeth's lip curled. "Do you think I care for that?
I can live very well without society. And you can't
watch me every minute; I'll escape."

"You speak of what you know nothing about,"
replied Jarrett. "Your friends will not see you; you
will be left utterly alone if you run away from me. For
understand that when I say you will be ruined, I mean
it." His face was hard with purpose. Elisabeth's eyes
widened slightly, but she made no answer. "I see you
understand me," he finished.

Elisabeth raised her chin. "If you treat me ill, that
will only strengthen my resolve never to marry you.
Your threats defeat your purpose. You must have my
consent, and you will never get it."

Jarrett bowed his head slightly and continued as if
she had not spoken. "And after a reasonable interval, if
your stubbornness persists, I'll be forced to reveal to the
world the true paternity of the Duke of Sherbourne."

Elisabeth's head jerked and her eyes narrowed
before she could control herself. Then, she sat back
on the sofa and cocked her head. "Whatever are you
talking about?" she replied.

Jarrett smiled. "Come, come, you are very good,
but your response was still unmistakable. And Jane
Taunton overheard all of your *tête-à-tête* with the
duchess yesterday. I will publish that information
unless you come around to my way of thinking. Those
are my terms."

Elisabeth sat still for some time, furiously thinking

over her alternatives. She couldn't allow the duchess's secret to be revealed, yet neither could she consent to marry George Jarrett. She put a hand to her forehead. "I must have time to think," she said.

Jarrett smiled like a man who has won his point. "Of course. You will have hours to think. It is only now noon; we leave for London at dusk." He turned away as he spoke. "I'll have Crenshaw bring you some tea." With that, he left the room again.

When he was gone, Elisabeth slumped a little in her seat. She was overwhelmed by Jane's treachery and at a loss as to what to do. She didn't even look up when Crenshaw entered the room. Only when he drew up a small table before her and put a tray on it did she notice him. As he started from the room, she spoke. "Mr. Crenshaw."

The man turned. "Yes, miss."

Elisabeth swallowed and plunged on quickly. "I must get away from here, back to my home. Has Jarrett offered you money? I will give you more. I'm very rich, you know."

Crenshaw looked startled for a moment, then chuckled. "Bless me. Of course you've got money. We wouldn't be here else." His expression sharpened. "Have ye got it here?"

Elisabeth shook her head. "But I can get it as soon as I'm home."

The man's face fell. "Ah, well, it was an unlikely chance," he muttered, and he started for the door.

"Will you help me?" asked Elisabeth urgently, puzzled by his behavior.

Crenshaw turned and raised his eyebrows as if

surprised. "Oh, I couldn't do that, miss. Mr. Jarrett and me, we've been together since the islands. Saved my life he did, and he's always took good care of me since, too. I couldn't sell him out." He turned toward the door again and left Elisabeth alone.

# *Twenty-seven*

WHEN JANE TAUNTON LEFT THE INN, SHE DROVE VERY rapidly back along the now muddy lane. The roof of the fly didn't provide much shelter from the rain, but she'd pulled a heavy hooded cloak from the leather case she carried, and was thus able to keep fairly dry. She drove past the place where the footpath from Willowmere intersected the lane, turning right onto a road about half a mile beyond it. This thoroughfare curved gradually back toward the estate, at its closest point coming within a hundred yards of the house. Here a small wicket gate led into the park, and here Jane pulled up.

Quickly she turned the vehicle around. Then, pulling her case from behind the seat, she climbed down, carefully holding her skirts up out of the mud. She slapped the horse's rump once, starting him moving; the docile beast was trained to return home when given his head. Jane watched until the fly was out of sight, then she turned and slipped through the gate and back to the house.

Once inside, she was able to reach her room without

encountering anyone. It was a quarter past eleven, and most of the staff was busy belowstairs. When she had put away her cloak and sketching case, she started downstairs. On the landing, she paused, hearing voices in the hall below.

"Yes, I had an appointment with Miss Elham," a man's voice was saying. Jane recognized Derek Wincannon.

"I'm sorry, sir," answered Ames. "I believe she sent someone with a note to Charendon. Perhaps that explains it."

"Ah. I drove out to see my land agent this morning; I wasn't at home to receive a note. Will Miss Elham be gone long?"

"I couldn't say, sir, not knowing where she has gone. I believe she may be out walking."

"In this rain?" exclaimed Derek.

"Yes, sir," answered Ames, his tone reflecting similar disapproval. "One of the undergardeners saw her go through the back garden."

"Alone?"

Ames hesitated, as if a bit offended by this intense questioning, but he unbent at the concerned look on Wincannon's face. "I believe so, sir."

Derek pulled his gloves through his hand uneasily. "She will be soaked; it is pouring rain out there now."

"I'm sure she must be sheltering somewhere until it passes," replied Ames. "Indeed, I haven't looked for her return for just that reason."

"Perhaps you're right." Derek paused, frowning. "Still, I think I'll drive about a bit on the nearby roads. I can take her up if she hasn't found a haven."

At this moment, Jane judged it best to continue her descent. She turned the corner from the landing and came into sight in the hall. "Good day," she said. "I thought it was your voice I heard, Mr. Wincannon. Did you not receive Elisabeth's note?"

Derek looked up quickly. "No," he answered. "I was out all morning. Do you know where she has gone?"

Jane raised her eyebrows very slightly. "Why, I believe she was bound for the house of one of the tenants who has requested some aid. I'm not certain. I offered to accompany her, but she said she wished to go alone." Jane hesitated for an artistic second. "I believe, I am not sure, but I believe Elisabeth may have gotten some bad news yesterday." She made a deprecating gesture. "I daresay I'm quite wrong, but she has been preoccupied. She appeared to want some time to think."

"Ah. Still," Derek said, "I wonder if I shouldn't go in search of her."

Jane frowned. "Is something wrong?" she asked, her tone very innocent.

Wincannon shrugged. "This rain," he said, "she may be caught in it."

"Oh, I doubt it. I am sure she is in a cottage nearby waiting for it to pass."

"There is no nearby cottage on the way she took," replied Derek. "In fact, it is altogether the wrong way to go to visit any of the estate's tenants. I wonder what she was thinking of?"

Jane shrugged. "Perhaps I misunderstood or she changed her mind. But I don't understand your anxiety. What do you fear has happened?"

Derek seemed a bit embarrassed. "I did not mean… I know you must be right. I wished only to save Miss Elham a wetting or a muddy walk."

Jane smiled slightly. "So kind," she murmured. "But I daresay she may find someone to bring her back if the rain keeps up."

"You're right," answered Wincannon. He began to pull on his gloves.

"But may I not offer you something in Elisabeth's absence? A cup of tea, perhaps, or a glass of wine?"

"No, thank you." Derek turned to Ames, who had retreated to the far end of the hall during their conversation. "You'll tell Miss Elham I called?"

"Yes, sir," replied Ames, coming forward again to open the door.

Derek nodded. "Good day," he said to Jane.

"Good day." She watched Derek move toward the door, a small smile lighting her face as he went out. Descending the last few stairs, she turned and entered the library.

# Twenty-eight

THE DAY PASSED VERY SLOWLY FOR ELISABETH IN THE cramped inn parlor. She had nothing to do, and soon boredom was added to her other preoccupations. Once, she opened the parlor door slightly and peered into the hall. Mr. Crenshaw was sitting there in the battered wooden straight chair. "Good afternoon, miss," he said when she looked out. "Was you wanting anything?"

"I...I should like another cup of tea," answered Elisabeth uncertainly.

"Yes indeed, miss. I'll get that for you as soon as Mr. Jarrett comes back."

"Has he gone?" inquired the girl eagerly.

"Bless me, no. He wouldn't leave you, never fear. He's just upstairs packing his gear."

"Oh," said Elisabeth, and she retreated to the sofa once more.

When her tea had come, and she had drunk it, and she had paced before the fire for some time, there was still nothing to do. Jarrett didn't approach her throughout the long afternoon, and this made her partly grateful and partly impatient. She didn't wish to see him, but she longed to do something about her situation, and as long as he was absent, she couldn't argue him out of his foolhardy plan.

She sat on the sofa, gazing blankly into the fire, and thought of the duchess. How was she to prevent her secret from being revealed if she didn't marry Jarrett? As she would never do, she thought fiercely to herself. Let him do his worst, she would never reward him with her fortune.

The rain finally stopped about four o'clock, but the sky remained overcast and dark. Elisabeth had tried the window several more times, once seeking to pry it open with a teaspoon. In any other circumstances, she would have laughed at herself for this ridiculous gesture, but she was in no mood for laughter now. At about four thirty, Jarrett entered the parlor once more. He had changed into traveling dress and was carrying a dark garment over his arm.

He nodded to her. "I think we can prepare to go," he said. "The day is so dark that we needn't wait for sunset. Here is a cloak; you'll need it. It's gotten even colder." He held out the wrap.

Elisabeth made no move to take it. She stood with her back to the fire and spoke quickly and urgently. "Mr. Jarrett. I've done a great deal of thinking as I sat here today. As you meant me to, perhaps. I cannot believe you really will do what you've threatened. But I've decided to offer you a ransom in spite of that." She stood very straight and tried to make her voice as resolute as possible. "I will arrange for an annuity to be paid to you. We can settle on certain guarantees that will assure you of payment. Your life will be comfortable, your need for money satisfied, but we needn't continue this ridiculous charade of kidnapping."

Jarrett had been listening with an admiring expression on his face. "You're not one to be intimidated, are you? Many females would have dissolved in a fit of hysterics by now, but you hold up marvelously."

Encouraged, Elisabeth continued. "We would also agree that you would not reveal the things you have discovered, of course, and that you would not remain in London."

Jarrett laughed. "No, no. Your scheme is unworkable. Don't you think I considered mere blackmail? I thought of the duchess immediately, of course. She can and would pay me a great deal more than you. But it will not do. I'm tired and soon will be past my youth. I've had enough. I want to settle down and cease worrying about the future. Neither of you would give me enough to do that, and in any case, blackmail is a very uncertain kind of income. Indeed, you don't really understand what you propose. Once you admit a blackmailer into your life, you're never free again. Who knows but what I might make new demands from, say, the new Viscountess Larenby, in future. A change of your state could alter my mind on the subject."

Elisabeth's cheeks reddened, and Jarrett nodded. "Yes. And I might go to the duchess, as well, to increase my take. You'd never be secure. Take my word; I know of what I speak." For a moment, his expression was black, then he smiled at Elisabeth once more. "No, I've considered well, and my plan is best.

We'll deal very well together, I promise you. Now, put this on, and let us go." His tone was commanding, and he held out the cloak once more. Elisabeth still hesitated, but he forced it into her hands with a curt, "Come along," and left the room again.

Elisabeth remained before the fire, her shoulders slumped. She was trapped, it seemed. But as she nearly gave in to the urge to burst into tears, she shook herself sharply. Nothing was lost as yet, she told herself. There might be many opportunities for escape before even this day was ended. Jarrett couldn't keep her still in an innyard, for example. She would cry out for help to the first person she saw. Elisabeth straightened and put on the cloak, her expression stony. They'd see who came out of this the loser.

Jarrett came back, startling Elisabeth so that she jumped. He took no notice, merely saying, "Come along."

They went down the hall to the door of the inn and the chaise waiting outside. The driver didn't look around as Elisabeth emerged. She surveyed him speculatively.

As if reading her mind, Jarrett said, "The driver is my man." He grasped Elisabeth's elbow firmly and urged her to climb into the vehicle.

The girl hesitated. More than anything in the world, she wished to keep out of that coach. Giving in to impulse, she jerked her arm out of Jarrett's grip and tried to run away down the muddy road. But before she had gone three yards, he was upon her, grasping her waist and forcing her back to the carriage.

"Come, come," he said with infuriating amusement. "You mustn't be foolish." Pulling open the door of the chaise, he pushed her up the steps and into it. In a moment, he climbed in beside her, gave the driver the order to start, and the vehicle was moving.

# Twenty-nine

AT FOUR, DEREK WINCANNON CALLED AGAIN AT Willowmere. "Has Miss Elham returned?" he asked Ames when he opened the door.

The old butler shook his head solemnly. "No, sir. And I admit that I'm beginning to worry. She's sent no word to us, and it's been hours. It's not like Miss Elham to go off without a word."

Derek nodded decisively. "Well, this time no one shall dissuade me from going in search of her. Who knows, she may have fallen and twisted an ankle or any such thing."

At that moment, Jane Taunton entered the hall from the library. She looked faintly surprised. "Why, Mr. Wincannon, are you back?" she asked. "I didn't think to see you again so soon."

"Miss Elham asked me to call at four," responded Derek shortly. "And I find she has not yet returned."

Jane nodded. "Yes, and I am beginning to think her rather naughty. She really ought to have sent word if she meant to stay with old Mrs. Whitlock so long. But you know how old women can be. I daresay Elisabeth is longing to get away but cannot break in on her flow of talk without being rude, which she never is, of course."

Wincannon listened to this rambling recital with a frown. "She went to Mrs. Whitlock's?"

Jane nodded. "I inquired after we spoke."

Derek turned to Ames. "Why didn't you tell me?"

Ames went rigid. "I was not informed of Miss Elisabeth's intention, sir."

"Oh, it was her maid told me," added Jane. "Elisabeth happened to mention it to her as she was dressing. Won't you step into the library for a moment, Mr. Wincannon? I'll order some tea. You may wait for Elisabeth if you like."

But Derek was still frowning. "I cannot understand why she went out through the back garden if she meant to visit Mrs. Whitlock," he said meditatively. "It is quite the opposite direction."

"She wanted a longer walk, I suppose," replied Jane. "Won't you come in and sit down?"

Derek looked incredulous. "Longer than three miles? It is quite that to the Whitlock cottage."

"I-Is it?" asked Jane a little uncomfortably. "Well, then, that silly girl of Elisabeth's must have misunderstood her, that's all." She looked down.

A strangled noise came from Ames's vicinity, though he said nothing. Derek still frowned. "I don't like it," he said finally. "I'll walk along the field path to make sure Elisabeth hasn't fallen and been hurt or perhaps lost her way."

Jane laughed. "Elisabeth?" she said incredulously. "It's not possible. She has pored over maps of this district."

Just then, Lavinia was seen descending the stairs from the upper floors. When she saw the group in the hall, she hurried forward. "Oh, good day, Mr. Wincannon. You cannot think how fallicious it is to see you. I've been so worried."

"Why is that?" asked Derek sharply.

"Elisabeth has gone out, no one knows where, and it has been four or five hours," said Lavinia. "She's never done such a thing before, only excepting the time she went careering across the country after Tony."

There was an arrested expression in Derek's eyes. He turned back to Jane. "Are you certain you've told me all you know?" he asked her.

"I don't know what you mean," she answered.

He looked at her with narrowed eyes. "I think perhaps you do," he said. He addressed the group. "I'm going out to look for Elisabeth." And he turned on his heel and strode out of the hall.

Ames held the door for him and followed him through onto the porch. He shut the door carefully behind him and said, "Pardon me, sir, but I would like one word with you before you go. I don't know what's going on, and it may not be my place to say this, but I'm worried about Miss Elisabeth, you understand."

"Yes. What is it?" asked Derek impatiently.

"Well, sir, I have to say that Miss Taunton is mistaken. I personally inquired of Miss Ketchem, that is Miss Elisabeth's dresser, and she had no knowledge of where her mistress had gone." He sniffed. "And to call Miss Ketchem a silly girl! Well, sir, that is outside of enough, if you'll pardon my saying so."

Derek's eyes narrowed. "Yes, I think there's more

here than meets the eye. I think Miss Taunton may be hiding something at your mistress's request. Please say nothing to anyone. I intend to get to the bottom of this."

"Yes, sir."

Wincannon left Ames standing on the porch and walked around the house and into the garden. He looked carefully at the now muddy path, but the rain had washed away any marks it might have shown. He went rapidly across the garden, climbed the stile, and set off into the field. As he went, he looked carefully along the sides of the path, occasionally pushing aside a clump of grass with his riding crop.

He reached the lane on the other side of the field very quickly. Once there, he stood for a moment, perplexed. He turned at first to the right, then stopped, hesitated, and reversed his direction. He traversed the lane more slowly, straying from side to side, examining the ditches and hedges, often shaking his head disgustedly.

When he came around the curve that brought the inn into view, Derek stopped. He appeared puzzled for a moment, then his brow cleared and he gestured sharply with one clenched fist. "Of course," he said aloud to himself. "I'd forgotten this old place." As he started to move forward again, a post chaise pulled up to the inn's front door and stopped. Derek also halted and watched as a man came out of the inn, had some conversation with the driver, then disappeared again. When he was gone, Derek started to walk quickly forward. He was halfway to the building when the man returned escorting a woman, and Wincannon halted again.

He watched as the woman started to climb into the coach, then resisted. As she struggled for a moment with her companion, her face was turned toward Derek, and he recognized Elisabeth. He broke into a dead run as the man forced her into the carriage and climbed in after her. The chaise began to move, and Derek put every bit of energy into overtaking it, but he failed, his grasping hand missing the tail of the carriage by three feet. It drove on, oblivious, and he was forced to give up. He stood in the center of the lane, his chest heaving, and called "Elisabeth!" once. But he was winded, and the word was hardly audible. He panted harshly for a few moments, then turned and ran back the way he'd come.

# Thirty

AS THE CHAISE TURNED INTO THE HIGH ROAD BEYOND the inn, Elisabeth leaned back in her seat, sighed wearily, and closed her eyes. This can't be real, she thought to herself. She'd already tried the door handle on her side of the carriage, but it was somehow secured from the outside, so her plan of jumping out if she became desperate enough was thwarted. There was nothing to do but await an opportunity to call for help.

"Sleep if you can," said Jarrett. "The ride may be a long one, and I fear rough and tiring. I regret the necessity of traveling in the darkness."

Elisabeth naturally opened her eyes at these words. "Do we go straight to London?" she asked.

Jarrett nodded. "Don't be afraid. The driver is very good; he will go slowly when he must. But I fear we'll arrive at an unreasonable hour." He smiled mockingly. "I wager no one will be about, even in the streets of London."

Elisabeth couldn't keep some of her disappointment from showing in her face, and Jarrett's smile broadened. "I'm not an amateur at this, you see," he added.

"Won't you agree to marry me, Elisabeth, and save us both a great deal of trouble?"

Elisabeth turned her head away disdainfully, but a sinking feeling began to invade her.

They drove slowly along the highway for some time. The sky remained overcast, and a rising mist further obscured the road. The driver had to be very careful to avoid ruts and patches of thick mud. As the evening was very cool, Jarrett closed and fastened the window on his side of the coach, further depressing Elisabeth's spirits. Her window had been closed and swathed in curtains when she entered the coach, and now this last opening was sealed. She could see nothing of the landscape they passed, and thus had no idea of where they were.

After a time, Jarrett said, "I shall try to sleep. I advise you to do the same. This journey promises to be tedious." He sat back, leaning his head on the squabs in the corner of the chaise and was soon asleep, or at least so it seemed to Elisabeth from the rhythms of his breathing.

She watched him and listened for what seemed to her quite half an hour. Finally, convinced that he was not feigning sleep, she leaned forward and cautiously reached toward the door handle next to him. She kept her eyes fixed on his face until her hand was just above the handle, then she looked down at it. In dismay, she saw that Jarrett's hand was curled around the lever, holding it fast. She raised her eyes, expecting to see him regarding her with a mocking smile, but to all appearances, he still slept. She reached forward again, hesitated, then very gently sought to disengage his hand from the door handle. As she pulled his fingers free, he stirred. And even as she sat back quickly, wide-eyed, he woke.

He shook himself, stretched, and said, "You would do much better to sleep than to sit there fretting. The time will pass much more rapidly." And resuming his former position, he returned to sleep himself.

Jarrett slept restlessly, and to Elisabeth's surprise and chagrin, she started to feel rather drowsy. The movement of the coach and the growing lateness of the hour were combining to urge her to follow the man's example. She jerked herself awake several times, but at last, it seemed sleep would overcome her. She nodded once again, leaned back into the corner of the chaise, and was just about to succumb when a sound banished all thought of sleep from her mind. A vehicle was coming up behind them!

Exerting a good deal of control, Elisabeth managed to avoid sitting bolt upright. She looked at Jarrett, saw that he was still sleeping peacefully, then gently leaned forward. She reached across him once again, but this time she concentrated on the catch of the carriage window, which he did not hold in his hand. Working very slowly and quietly, with many glances at his face, she managed to release it. She pulled the curtain out so that it would shelter him from any draft, then opened the window a crack at the top. Cautiously, she shifted herself to the opposite seat and put her eye to the small aperture thus provided. She could see the lamps of the vehicle behind them, but nothing else.

At that moment, the chaise lurched violently as the driver attempted to speed up and hit an unseen rut in the road. Elisabeth was thrown forward, and though she made a heroic effort to hold herself, her knees jostled Jarrett's. This, combined with the movement of the coach, awakened him immediately. He shook his head, saw Elisabeth across from him, and glanced quickly at the open window. "Here," he said roughly, "what are you up to now?"

When she said nothing, he heard the sounds of a carriage behind them. Instantly, his attention shifted to this potential source of danger. Grasping her arm and pulling her roughly back into her original seat, he turned and opened the window completely. "Who is that behind us?" he called to the driver.

"No telling, guv'nor," was the reply. "Can't see nothing but the glims. He's moving fast, I will say that, for this dark road. He'll find himself in the ditch if he ain't careful."

Jarrett peered back into the darkness. "When did they come up with us?" he said sharply.

"Only just now," answered the driver. "Turned in from a side road 'bout five mile back. Has a team from the sound of it."

The first piece of information appeared to reassure Jarrett, but at this last remark, he swore. "They'll overtake us, then," he muttered. "I should have bespoken a team." He looked up toward the driver again. "Go as fast as you can," he told him, "but if they wish to pass, let them by." He closed the window again and leaned back uneasily. "You see what it is to be poor," he said bitterly to Elisabeth. "I hired a pair instead of a team, trying to economize, and now I must fear every equipage on the road behind me."

Elisabeth said nothing, but a small hope began to grow in her mind. Surely she could make some opportunity to cry for help when this vehicle came up with them, she thought. If necessary, she would shout from within the closed carriage.

Time seemed to pass very slowly, but in reality, the following carriage came up with them quickly. It had a clear advantage in cattle, and the driver traveled with a speed that suggested he knew the road well. Jarrett peered out once again as it neared. "Damn fool," he murmured as he did so, "driving at this time of day in a curricle. Must be some town sprig out to show his mettle." This reflection seemed to comfort him, and he pushed the window nearly closed again and sat back.

Before long, the other vehicle was directly behind them. They drove thus for a while, and Jarrett began to mutter, "why does he not pass," just as the curricle pulled out to do so. Their own driver moved as far to the side of the road as possible in the dim light of the lamps, and the curricle pulled level with them.

Now, Elisabeth thought, was her only chance. The noise of the horses and wheels was loud, but if she shouted she might just be heard by these travelers. She took a deep breath and turned toward that side of the chaise. "Help," she cried, "help me, please."

Immediately, Jarrett was upon her, grasping her waist and putting a hand over her mouth. "That was very foolish," he said between his teeth. "I'd thought you cleverer."

Both of them listened intently to see whether her cry had been heard. It seemed not. The curricle pulled ahead of them gradually and continued along the road. Elisabeth had given up, and Jarrett's grip on her was easing when the sound of a carriage being stopped abruptly came from ahead. Their own vehicle began to slow, and Jarrett shouted, "What are you doing, you fool?"

"Can't help it," came back the muffled answer. "We'll hit 'em else."

Jarrett pushed Elisabeth roughly to the floor of the coach and flung open the window once again. He peered out fiercely. Their driver was hauling desperately on the reins, trying to avoid colliding with the curricle, which was now pulled up across the road ahead of them. They approached so rapidly that at first it seemed they would crash, but at the last moment, their driver managed to stop the plunging horses.

Elisabeth had scrambled back into her seat amid the jostling, and now she cried again, "Help, help me," as loudly as she could.

"Keep quiet," said Jarrett, aiming a blow at her, which she dodged. "Turn," he called up to the driver. "Back them and turn."

"I'll try, guv'nor," replied the man, and he began to urge the pair backward.

At that moment, a voice came out of the darkness ahead. "Stop," it said. "Get down and release Miss Elham immediately. I have three men with me. You are outnumbered."

"Derek," whispered Elisabeth. A wave of relief and joy spread through her.

Jarrett glanced at her sharply, then leaned further out the window. "Back them!" he insisted again.

"I'm tryin," said the driver. The horses had indeed begun to move back from the curricle, and the man now started to turn them, a slow, awkward process.

The curricle also started to move. "Give over," called Derek Wincannon, "you can't get away now."

In the dimness of the chaise, Jarrett bared his teeth. "Can we not?" he said to himself. He reached into the pocket on his side of the coach and brought out a large pistol. Before Elisabeth could do more than stare in horror, he had aimed and fired it at the other vehicle.

The sound of the shot galvanized her. "No," she cried, and threw herself upon Jarrett's arm. Cursing, he flung her back.

Elisabeth sought to catch hold of Jarrett's arm again, but this time he did strike her, dazing her for a moment.

He fired once more as the chaise concluded its turn, and then they were galloping back the way they had come, paying no heed to ruts, mud, or darkness.

The curricle followed. Jarrett was busy reloading his pistol, and Wincannon soon began to close the distance between them. But then, Jarrett leaned out the window and started to fire again, one shot hitting a lantern and forcing their pursuer to drop back a little. Elisabeth sought to impede him in any way she could, but he hung so far out the window, she could not reach the pistol.

The chaise careened wildly about, hitting deep ruts, and the two passengers were thrown one way and then the other. Jarrett hung on to the window frame grimly, most of his shots wild, but Elisabeth was less well anchored, and she fell to the floor several times.

The curricle neared them again as Jarrett was forced to pause and reload his gun. The bouncing of the chaise made this difficult, and it took him some time. Just as he finished, the vehicle gave an extraordinary lurch, throwing them both down, and then began to slow. "What are you doing, man?" shouted Jarrett, scrambling up.

There was no answer at first, only more lurching and a diminished speed. Then, the driver's voice drifted down to them, strained with his efforts. "One of the beasts stumbled. He's gone dead lame. We've shot our bolt, guv." The chaise came gradually to an unsteady stop, and Wincannon's curricle pulled up directly behind them.

Jarrett swore fiercely. He looked around him, then seized Elisabeth's arm, thrust open the carriage door, and pulled her out. Standing in the muddy road, he pulled her against him and held his pistol to her head. "Keep off," he called into the darkness behind, "keep off or I'll shoot her."

Derek Wincannon appeared before them out of the gloom. "Let her go, Jarrett," he said quietly. "Your game is over."

"Not yet, I think," answered Jarrett. "You dare not try to take me while I hold her thus. And don't think I won't carry through my threats. I have nothing to lose now, you see."

Derek ignored him. "Are you hurt, Elisabeth?" he asked.

"No," she responded carefully, very aware of the gun, "only shaken."

"You don't seem to understand," said Jarrett. "I'll

kill her unless you stand off and allow us to continue our journey in peace."

"It is you who don't understand," said Derek coldly. "It is over. Your chaise is surrounded by my men, and your driver is taken. You must give up,"

"Do you not believe I'll fire?"

"I don't believe you're such a fool, no."

Elisabeth's eyes widened a bit, but she said nothing.

A tense silence began and stretched long in Elisabeth's mind. The gun remained pressed to her temple. She could feel Jarrett's nervousness in the taut trembling of his muscles. Derek watched them, a grim look growing about his mouth. When Elisabeth thought she would scream with anxiety and fear, a sound broke the tension. A single horse, hard-ridden from the sound of it, was approaching from the open fields on the left.

All of them looked toward the sound, startled. "Every idiot in the countryside is out tonight," muttered Jarrett, and he tightened his grip on Elisabeth. The horse came on fast. As the hoofbeats came closer and closer the little group appeared transfixed by them, unable to move. Then, as Derek made a hasty gesture, the rider burst upon them from the darkness of the field.

"Stop, let them go," cried a very disheveled and nearly hysterical Jane Taunton from the horse's back. "I have a gun."

"Jane!" exclaimed Elisabeth.

There were several moments of confusion. Jane couldn't control her foam-flecked and overexcited mount, which plunged here and there about the road. Elisabeth saw a man materialize from the gloom beyond the chaise, catch the horse's bridle, and pull Jane down. As Elisabeth watched, she was knocked to the ground as Derek Wincannon threw himself upon Jarrett. In a moment, he had wrested his pistol from him and was holding it aimed at his heart.

His man brought Jane to stand next to Jarrett, handing Wincannon her tiny gun as he did so, and another man brought the driver to join them. Derek handed the large gun to this man and turned to help Elisabeth to her feet. "I'm sorry," he said. "I had to take the opportunity when it was offered."

"Of course," agreed Elisabeth warmly. "And very well done it was. I'm not hurt; I was merely catching my breath."

But Derek's arm did not leave her waist, and she didn't move away from him. He continued to look at her as he said, "Take them to the nearest town in the chaise, Tom. I'll drive the lady home in the curricle."

"Her, too?" asked Tom, gesturing doubtfully toward Jane Taunton.

Derek looked up, seeming surprised to see Jane there. "Ah. I'm not...just what are you doing here, Miss Taunton?"

Jane appeared very weary and bitterly disappointed. She glanced toward Elisabeth, but the other girl looked at the ground. Though she wouldn't betray her former friend, neither would she help her. "I...I came to..." began Jane.

"She came to further our scheme," put in Jarrett. "She helped me plan the whole."

Derek looked shocked. "Is that true?" he asked Jane. She seemed to hesitate a moment, then her chin large coach move slowly away, then Derek signaled his horses, and they started home.

There was a short silence. "There is a lap robe behind the seat if you are cold," said Derek after a while.

"Thank you," responded Elisabeth, looking around and reaching for it. "It is cold for the season, is it not?"

He laughed. "Can you talk of the weather after the day you've had? You are incredible, Elisabeth."

The girl reddened slightly. "It's easier to talk of commonplaces."

He slowed the horses to a walk. "Very true," he replied dryly. "However, we have put off a rather important subject for too long now. Don't you agree?"

Elisabeth looked down. "I'm not sure..." she began.

"You are," interrupted Derek.

She raised her eyes and gazed into his. The warmth and love she saw there dissolved all her hesitations. She smiled. "We have," she agreed.

He stopped the curricle beside the road. "When shall the wedding be?" he asked her.

"Are you not taking a great deal for granted, sir?" answered Elisabeth, still smiling up at him. "You haven't asked me if I will."

"I had hoped I knew the answer. But I ask formally, then, if you desire it. Elisabeth, will you be my wife?"

"Very good," she replied. "I think September."

Holding the reins in one hand, he embraced her with his free arm. "August," he suggested.

Elizabeth laughed. "Perhaps." And then she could say no more for quite some time.

# About the Author

Jane Ashford discovered Georgette Heyer in junior high school and was captivated by the glittering world and witty language of Regency England. That delight was part of what led her to study literature and travel widely in Britain and Europe. She has written historical and contemporary romances, and her books have been published in Sweden, Italy, England, Denmark, France, Russia, Latvia, the Czech Republic, Slovakia, and Spain, as well as the United States. Jane has been nominated for a Career Achievement Award by *RT Book Reviews*. Born in Ohio, she is now somewhat nomadic. Find her on the web at janeashford.com and on Facebook. If you're interested in receiving her monthly newsletter, you can subscribe at www.eepurl.com/cd-O7r.

went up defiantly. "Yes," she replied. "And you'll be making a mistake if you have us imprisoned."

Wincannon's eyes had hardened at her affirmative. "I think not."

Jane turned to Elisabeth. "We'll make the duchess's story known to the *ton*," she said coolly.

Elisabeth gripped Derek's arm. "I'd nearly forgotten," she whispered miserably.

"What is it?" Wincannon looked down at her with concern.

Very quietly, Elisabeth explained to him what the duchess had told her and Jane's eavesdropping. As Derek's frown grew, self-satisfied smiles spread across the faces of Jane and Jarrett. "So you see," finished Elisabeth in a whisper, "we cannot let them talk to anyone. We must let them go."

"I doubt that many would credit their tale, coming from the prisons," answered Derek. Elisabeth pulled at his sleeve. "But since it upsets you, we must make it impossible for them to spread it about."

The smile faded from their captives' faces. Jarrett especially whitened. "What will you do?" he asked.

Derek smiled. "Not have you shot out of hand, if that's what you're thinking. You may threaten such things, but I don't promise what I will not perform." He surveyed the two. "No, I shall do justice only. Do you know the penalty for what you've done?"

Jane looked blank, but Jarrett said, "Transportation," with a grim shake of his head.

Derek nodded. "And oddly enough, it happens that a ship leaves the London docks tomorrow for the Pacific islands. I know this because two of my tenants are to be on it; they wished to try their fortunes in Australia, and I outfitted them. Tom here and his friends will escort you there and put you in their care. They'll see that you make the *entire* voyage safely." He turned to Elisabeth. "It's a journey of three months out and as much back. I don't think they'll have the will, or the means, to return. And it will be kinder done in this way; they'll arrive as settlers, not convicts."

Elisabeth looked distressed. "Jane," she said, "if only you would promise me, on your life and honor, not to speak of the duchess. I don't wish to send you on such a voyage."

Jane looked tempted. "You can't trust her," said Jarrett.

She looked at him venomously, shrugged, and shook her head. "Why not Australia?" she replied. "It can be no worse than London, after all, and I shall see the world, at least."

Elisabeth bowed her head, and Derek gave his men an unobtrusive signal. As he led Elisabeth back to his curricle, the three kidnappers were put into the chaise. Derek handed her up, then returned to his men for a moment. When he came back, he said, "They will go slowly with the lame horse to a nearby village where they can get a fresh pair. They are trustworthy."

"I suppose Jane will tell them about the duchess," answered Elisabeth uncertainly.

"They will say nothing," replied Derek as he climbed up beside her and took the reins. He pulled out of the way, so that the chaise could be turned and headed south. The two of them sat still to watch the